BY THE SAME AUTHOR:

Abyssinia on the Eve
Abyssinian Stop Press (ed.)
Palestine at the Crossroads
The Riddle of Arabia
German Psychological Warfare (ed.)
Axis Grand Strategy (ed.)
Behind Closed Doors (with Admiral Ellis M. Zacharias)
War of Wits
Burn After Reading
Strictly from Hungary
The Japanese: Introduction to Xenology
Tora, Tora!
Patton
The Last Days of Patton

LADISLAS FARAGO

Author of *PATTON*

The true story of the U.S. Navy's "phantom" fleet
battling U-Boats during World War II

THE TENTH FLEET

A DRUM BOOK
1986

THE TENTH FLEET

ISBN: 0-931933-37-4

Originally published by Ivan Obolensky, Inc.

Cover design by Joe Curcio

Drum Books are published by
Richardson & Steirman
246 Fifth Avenue
New York, N.Y.   10001

PRINTED IN CANADA

To Admiral F. S. Low
and the Men and Women
of the Tenth Fleet
this Book is Respectfully Dedicated

AUTHOR'S NOTE

This book does not presume to be a history of the Battle of the Atlantic. It is rather the story of a little known phase of the *American* effort in that furtive and epic campaign.

Aside from the fact that I myself was close to that phase and cherish the fondest memories of my life of my modest share in that venture, I was attracted to the subject by a significant aspect of this remarkable contribution to our eventual victory in the U-boat war. It was the fusion of brain and brawn in an unprecedented approach to the conduct of the war at sea.

Wars are usually viewed as violent conflicts in which armies, navies and air forces move by some occult pre-arrangement. In most appraisals and stories, the din of war outdrowns the imperceptible and silent work of the brains that manage them.

However, beyond their magnificent metallic spectacle, wars are *human* efforts, and never in the history of war was the human equation given a greater direct role to play in a difficult battle than in the Tenth Fleet of the United States Navy. Admiral King's inspired idea and Admiral Low's brilliant management thus established a new pattern in war and the success of the Tenth Fleet proved that it works.

I believe this book, although it deals with the events of a past war, has a certain topical significance in that it demonstrates how brainpower can be harnessed for victory.

LADISLAS FARAGO

*. . . this war of groping and drowning, of ambuscade
and strategem, of science and seamanship . . .*

WINSTON S. CHURCHILL

PROLOGUE

~~~~~~

> *Ye gentlemen of England
> That live at home at ease,
> Ah! little do you think upon
> The dangers of the seas.*
> Old English Song

At 1:15 P.M. on December 20, 1941, while Christmas shoppers filled the streets of San Francisco, an enemy submarine came within twenty miles of the California coast where it torpedoed and sank the tanker *Emidio*, two-hundred miles north of San Francisco.

Today a hostile submarine in that same location, firing a modern missile, could destroy, not a single tanker, but San Francisco itself. And before it had unloaded its entire armament of intermediate-range ballistic missiles, it could also "take out" Los Angeles, Denver, and El Paso, Texas.

On January 11, 1942, the German submarine *U-123* came within 160 miles of Nova Scotia to torpedo and sink the tanker *Cyclops*. An enemy submarine in that same spot today could destroy Boston, New York, Philadelphia, Washington, Chicago—and Duluth.

And the American nuclear submarine *George Washington*, firing Polaris missiles from her hideout in the depth of the Arctic Ocean, can spray havoc upon the U.S.S.R. from Leningrad and Moscow all the way to Vladivostok.

Thus has the face of war changed.

The Japanese torpedo that sank the *Emidio* had a speed of fifty knots, a range of 10,000 yards, and an explosive load of about six-hundred pounds. Today's submarines can launch missiles with a speed of 15,000 miles per hour, a range of up to 1,500 miles. They have thermo-nuclear warheads whose destructive power is the equivalent of 500,000 tons of T.N.T.

The sub does not even have to be nuclear powered. It needs only to be capable of launching nuclear missiles.

Thus has the power of the submarine changed.

It is no military secret on either side of the Iron Curtain that the Soviet Union is the foremost underseas-power of the world. It has up to 500 operational submarines of which some 280 are believed to be capable of reaching the United States. It has an unknown number of intermediate-range ballistic missiles. On October 14, 1957, Premier Nikita S. Khrushchev boasted: "I shall not be revealing any secrets if I tell you that we now have all the rockets we need."

The threat inherent in these statistics is clearly recognized. "We must be able to detect and kill *Polaris*-type submarines which might be deployed against us to launch a surprise attack," said Admiral George W. Anderson, USN, Chief of Naval Operations, adding the ominous postscript: "We see no major breakthrough on the horizon for antisubmarine warfare, no panacea to solve our problems. Detecting and destroying underwater ships remains a very, very difficult problem. The characteristics of salt water are such that our detection measures—the best in the world today—are only just so effective, just so reliable. We must rely on the combination of all these measures, on the skill and perseverance of our personnel. ASW is a long, tiring, unglamorous business, and it's difficult; but it is a vital part of our national defense."

Admiral Anderson made this statement in the spring of 1962; yet he could merely echo the findings of a Congressional committee whose Underseas Warfare Advisory Panel reported in the summer of 1958:

"The Soviets could mount a devastating nuclear warhead attack from the sea against the United States early in the 1960's. Our existing defensive system could not stop such a missile attack. No weapons system now in existence, even on an experimental basis, offers an adequate defense against non-snorkeling submarines which run quiet and deep." Almost four years of steady search and hard work did not bring a decisive improvement in this situation.

Thus it is no exaggeration to say that the submarine of today, armed with nuclear missiles, is a decisive weapon in war.

It makes obsolescent the big bombers of the strategic air force, even those which are but gleams in its generals' eyes. It makes superfluous the string of air bases scattered across North America and around the perimeter of the Soviet Union. It makes vulnerable even the hardened missile sites where the great rockets lie ready, pointed toward the enemy.

For the submarine—lying hidden under the warm waters of the Caribbean or the chill ice of the Arctic—now can strike anywhere, any time. It cannot be intercepted and shot down as it approaches through the perilous air. It cannot easily be sought out, hunted down, and killed. It cannot be, like a stationary base or a missile site, the constant, firm, and virtually helpless target of missiles which sit aimed, ready, and able to destroy it.

This is the hard face of today's war. Upon how we handle this weapon, upon our ability to use it effectively and to prevent the enemy from doing so, will depend the outcome of war.

The purpose of this book is to examine the past experience in submarine warfare, to show what worked and what did not—to see what we can learn from experience that can be of use to us in the present and the future.

The most successful antisubmarine operation *per se* was an almost totally unpublicized effort of World War II. It was conducted by a part of the U.S. Navy of which few people have ever heard.

It was called the Tenth Fleet.

Although it was called a "fleet", it had no ships whatever. It had no armament. But it had the greatest weapon of all—the human brain. Superimposing brainpower on sea power and air power, the Tenth Fleet—in comradely association with its British counterparts—became instrumental in winning an astounding total victory over an armada of German submarines.

The Tenth Fleet—through its organizational and operational experience in World War II—thus provides a pattern of defense: the premise on which this country's defenses should be developed today. The German U-boat arm, superb in technical equipment and human skill, supplies the pattern of the offensive.

The past, however, is not just a bucket of ashes. The whole cycle impenitently revolves, said Robinson Jeffers in his ode to practical people, and all the past is future.

From its traditional position of neglect in American strategic thinking, the submarine now moves both triumphantly and ominously to the forefront of all military considerations.

But only a bigot or a fool would advocate a single weapon for victory—either sea power or air power alone, either the nuclear bomb or some futuristic device still hatching in the brains of today's war-conditioned scientists.

Napoleon III lost a war because he relied almost exclusively on the "decisive" power of the *mitrailleuse*. History shows that Hitler lost his war when his dominant weapon, the *Luftwaffe*, failed to gain control of the air.

Even so, it is the contention of this book that the mighty new submarine should be made the backbone of this country's defense in an entirely new nuclear navy boldly adapted to the realities of war.

Beyond that, it is the conclusion of this book that the inherent power of this new weapon-system makes war itself hopelessly and irrevocably obsolete.

In this lies our ultimate promise of survival.

For man is certainly stark mad. To paraphrase Montaigne, he cannot make a worm, yet he is trying to make lightning.

TABLE OF CONTENTS

... you can liken seapower to the human hand where with the greatest delicacy, sensitivity, and perception it can be used to solve the combination of the lock on a safe, or the skilled hand of the surgeon who, with the greatest delicacy, can excise the cancerous growth from the human body, or again it can be clenched in a fist representing the brute force philosophy of an all-out nuclear exchange.

REAR ADMIRAL J. S. McCAIN, JR.
on Capitol Hill, April 12, 1962

☆

Part One

THE LONG AND CRUEL BATTLE

*The tide was now set and running strongly
against all Allied shipping. . . . It was like
a dark stain spreading all over the huge sea:
the area of safety diminished, the poisoned
water, in which no ship could count on
safety from hour to hour, seemed swiftly to
infect a wider and wider circle. . . .*

NICHOLAS MONSARRAT,
The Cruel Sea

CHAPTER I

"Verdammter Atlantik"

Kill! . . . Kill! . . . Kill!

Around Yuletide in 1944, when there was no peace on earth and only qualified good will to men, this sanguine injunction flashed on and off, like a colored bulb on a Christmas tree, in the perennially agitated mind of Vice Admiral Jonas Howard Ingram, USN, new commander in chief of the Atlantic Fleet.

It was sparked by a flood of secret signals Ingram was getting from New York, sent by Vice Admiral Herbert Fairfax Leary, USN, commander of the Eastern Sea Frontier. They warned in no uncertain terms that, according to intelligence piling up at Sea Frontier headquarters on Church Street in downtown Manhattan, the East Coast, which Ingram was duty-bound to protect, seemed to be slated for a novel kind of "cataclysmic" attack.

Leary's warnings gained qualified corroboration in a set of "advisories" Ingram was receiving from another good source. They came from Rear Admiral Francis Stuart Low, USN, chief of staff of a mysterious outfit called the "Tenth Fleet"—a fleet, at that, though it did not have a single ship it could call its own. And yet this phantom fleet—operating from a few frugally-furnished offices on the third deck of the old ramshackle Navy Department building on Constitution Avenue in Washington, D.C.—was the real master of American destiny in the Atlantic battle. The Atlantic Fleet leaned heavily on Low's wisdom and savvy in all matters of the Atlantic, and depended on his "fleet's" uncanny knowledge of the enemy in that ocean.

This time the habitually conservative Low was careful to point out that the "cataclysm" Admiral Leary expected momentarily might not turn out to be so cataclysmic. But he, too, warned that something enigmatically wicked was developing in the Atlantic. Ingram plunged into feverish activity.

He had just been upped to CINCLANT from his long and rewarding command of the Fourth Fleet in the South Atlantic, where his flag had flown flamboyantly and characteristically from a luxurious big Mississippi River houseboat called the *Big Pebble*. Now he presided over a vast and complex organization whose mission, honor, and privilege was to hunt down and destroy Hitler's U-boats. The ingenuity and daring, as well as the professional skill of the U-boat arm appeared to be inexhaustible. To those familiar attributes was now added a measure of desperation which could, Ingram thought, lure the Germans into adventurous gambles.

Kill! . . . Kill! . . . Kill!

The ominous signals kept coming; behind them was one of the most bizarre episodes of World War II at sea. It was a mixture of drama and melodrama, of prudence and bravado, of brilliant planning and hackneyed cloak-and-dagger. Chief protagonists of the thriller were American admirals and German spies. Its cast included the hopped-up crews of a flotilla of German submarines, and the officers and men of an American armada waiting for them in ambush.

If this was a game, the stake was extremely high. It was the Middle Atlantic seaboard of the United States. For several months at the end of the war, American cities like New York and Boston lived in the shadow of an obscure menace. The war was clearly drawing to its inexorable end; yet in its last convulsive throes, it seemed, it threatened the United States with a major blow.

It may be quite proper, I submit, to begin this narrative with the full and hitherto untold story of that hectic episode, not merely because it was the picturesque and exciting climax of a "long and brutal battle," but because it has special pertinence today. That nebulous threat of yesterday has become a real and present menace in our own uncertain days. It is the basic pattern of what could be called instant aggression.

It is the new form of the sneak-attack, designed by its planners to force a nation to its knees with a series of quick devastating strategic blows. Alternatively, it is the hidden weapon of deterrence and retaliation—the absolute weapon, indeed, that might prevent the cataclysmic sneak-attack from ever being mounted.

The strange chain of events began in the summer of 1944. August was a fine Allied month in the Atlantic, and an exceptionally painful one for the Germans. They still had hundreds of awesome U-boats, but their vaunted submarine force had become woefully disorganized by the Allied invasion of Europe. And though they still held their formidable U-boat bases in France, they found they could not make use of them because their umbilical cords had been cut.

The U-boats had to be withdrawn from their French coastal outposts and that by itself had a stifling effect on their camapign. Two years before, in the summer of 1942, the Germans could keep a monthly average of about a hundred U-boats on *Feindfahrt*, but now they could send only fifty into the Atlantic. While in August, 1942, they lost only nine boats out of eighty-six on war crusies, now only sixteen of the fifty managed to return to their new bases in Norway and the Baltic. This represented a frightening loss of almost 65 per cent, and no military organization as finely honed as the U-boat arm could long endure such savage punishment.

Spy Overboard

Among the U-boats destroyed during that fateful August was the *U-1229* of Korvetten-Kapitaen Armin Zinke. She was one of the newer subs equipped with the snorkel, the ingenious underwater breathing device that enabled the U-boats to stay submerged for longer periods of time and escape the predatory surveillance of Allied aircraft. And she also had something else aboard just as novel and unusual—a real-life Nazi spy consigned to the United States.

The official German roster of U-boat casualties lists the *U-1229* as *Totalverlust* (total loss), sunk on August 20, 1944, northeast of Newfoundland, *ohne Ueberlebende* (without survivors). In actual fact, the destruction of *U-1229* yielded quite a human haul—forty-two survivors—but there was a good reason for the Germans to have been misinformed. The *U-1229* was a sort of phantom boat shrouded in deliberate and elaborate mystery, first by the Germans who sent her on her super-secret mission, and then by the Americans who managed to intercept and sink her.

U-1229 left her berth at Trondheim, Norway, on July 26, with that extra passenger on board whose destination and purpose were presumably known only to Korvetten-Kapitaen Zinke. The passenger was a certain Oskar Mantel, a former bartender from Yorkville, a Manhattan district populated largely by men and women of German ancestry.

Trained somewhat perfunctorily in the various spy schools of Hamburg, Mantel was to be put ashore at Winter Harbor, Maine, on a secret mission important enough to be worth the risk of a new snorkel sub.

Unfortunately for Mantel, Commander Zinke was not the only one privy to his secret. By a mysterious chain of circumstances, his coming was also known on this side of the Atlantic. Thus it was not entirely accidental that the *U-1229* was spotted on the way to her pinpoint in Maine.

It was the complex electronic intelligence apparatus of Admiral Low's Tenth Fleet that, on August 13, first established the presence of a German submarine in an area which the escort carrier U.S.S. *Bogue* was assigned to patrol. The information was radioed to CINCLANT who was then kept appraised of the sub's progress as the high-frequency direction-finders—called Huffduffs—kept tab on her. The *Bogue*, which was sweeping westward to within a hundred miles of Cape Race, was ordered to turn southeast and sail in the direction of the Grand Bank of Newfoundland where the Tenth Fleet virtually pinpointed the sub.

It was a mighty force that now deployed to find the proverbial needle in the haystack, for the *Bogue*—a veteran of eleven kills to that date—carried nine Wildcat fighters and fourteen Avenger torpedo-bombers, and had four destroyer escorts as well as six Canadian frigates in her screen.

At exactly eleven o'clock on the morning of August 20, the U-boat was sighted by the pilot of an Avenger from the *Bogue*, Lieutenant (jg) A. X. Brokas by name. Young Brokas came upon the sub about three hundred miles south by east of Cape Race, as she was—despite her snorkel—cruising on the surface, trying to sneak at a leisurely pace into a line storm developing at the Grand Bank.

The Avenger attacked with everything it had and Brokas saw the U-boat, obviously hurt, vanish abruptly under the sea. But her skipper could take the battered boat only to snorkel depth. He desperately needed to breathe in order to get rid of chlorine gas escaping from battery cells which the accurate bombing of the Avenger had cracked.

In no time, the U-boat was under attack by five Avengers from the *Bogue*. By 1:10 P.M. she was so badly damaged that her skipper ordered all hands to abandon ship. It was not too soon. Only three minutes later, a 500-pounder from one of the Avengers delivered the *coup de grâce*. The U-boat kicked her stern high into the air, then plunged to her doom.

Among the survivors whom the *Bogue*'s destroyer escorts picked up was Oskar Mantel, the hapless Nazi spy. Holding on to $2,000 his employers had given him for the trip, Mantel turned out to be a bitter-end Nazi and a recalcitrant prisoner. Nevertheless, his interrogation by the FBI produced a major sensation. In a memo dated October 25, FBI Director John Edgar Hoover warned the Director of Naval Intelligence that, according to Mantel, the Germans were planning some sort of buzz-bomb attack against the United States from a special task force of missile-carrying U-boats. It appeared that Mantel's own mission, so rudely interrupted, was somehow connected with the plot.

The Director of Naval Intelligence sent the FBI's memo to Admiral Leary at Eastern Sea Frontier. It was the first straw in the wind. Others followed in rapid succession. A wayward piece of intelligence from the FBI described some loose talk of a seaman in a bar, a frequent source of useful information, about a projected buzz-bomb attack on New York from a task force of U-boats.

Without the information coaxed from Mantel, probably no special attention would have been paid to the bibulous bubblings of a simple sailor; but now the report was taken seriously and sent up to Admiral Leary in New York. Intelligence officers at the Eastern Sea Frontier were now inclined to accept this latest report at face value, but Leary directed that it be checked out with the Tenth Fleet. It was the natural thing to do. By then it was an axiom in all the naval units committed to the Atlantic that the opinion of the Tenth Fleet was the last word in everything concerning that ocean.

The Tenth Fleet

There never was anything like the Tenth Fleet in the U. S. Navy, nor for that matter in any navy of the world. Masterminded by an exceptional submariner, called "Frog" Low since his Naval Academy days, it was made up of some of the Navy's brainiest officers, both regulars and reservists; and even the handful of petty officers and yeomen attached to it were remarkable for their brilliance. The idea behind it all was to harness in a single, small and flexible, essentially intellectual unit the best of brainpower to aid the combat elements of conventional seapower in their physical struggle with the U-boats—to put teeth into the anti-U-boat campaign by fusing brain and brawn.

The Tenth Fleet was, in the truest sense of the phrase, a cloistered "think-factory" of chosen experts who played their anonymous part in the U-boat war around the clock, in the cold glare of incandescent lights, in front of huge maps and charts behind the closed doors of their plot room, in the bay of cackling teletypes. Their job was to analyze every aspect of the U-boat war from all angles, to supply split-second intelligence to CINCLANT, to recommend tactical maneuvers for offensive actions, to develop new hardware along abstruse scientific lines.

Intelligence was, of course, one of the key branches of the Tenth Fleet. It was handled by a tiny unit under Commander Kenneth Alward Knowles, USN, a studious and sophisticated intellectual who had been recalled from retirement for the job in which he had to wear two hats. Under one hat he headed the Atlantic Section of Combat Intelligence of COMINCH, while under the other he served as the seeing eye and hearing aid of the Tenth Fleet.

When Leary's teletyped query arrived in the Tenth Fleet, Low handed it to Knowles for analysis, and Knowles gave it to Lieutenant Commander John E. Parsons, USNR, his executive officer.

"What do you make of this, Number One?" he asked in his usual way of addressing Parsons, in the vernacular of the Royal Navy that somehow struck both men as salty and professional.

A young lawyer with a quizzical turn of mind, Parsons took the data under close scrutiny. He himself had had certain curious hints. Recent aerial photographs taken of U-boats at their Norwegian bases showed strange contraptions mounted on the decks of several submarines. British intelligence evaluated them as launching devices for buzz bombs.

Parsons subjected the photographs to minute examination. He concluded that those portentous contraptions, far from being missile launchers, were in reality ordinary wooden tracks the Germans used in the loading of torpedoes. But such were the occult exigencies of the U-boat campaign that nobody in his right mind could or would take an unequivocal stand against those prognostications. Knowles signalled a "very doubtful" to Leary in New York, the strongest negative the Tenth Fleet could afford without climbing out on a limb and cutting it off behind them.

The Mission of V-146

Then, just when it seemed that Knowles' "very doubtful" would place all further conjecture into sounder perspective, something happened again that revived the guessing game and deepened the apprehensions. Two German spies actually landed in the United States and brought with them obscure tidings of a pending buzz-bomb attack.

The date was November 27, less than a fortnight after Admiral Ingram had assumed his big new command; the place, just off Cape Cod. On that day, another big snorkel sub—the *U-1230* of Oberleutnant Hans Hilbig (sister-boat of the ill-fated *U-Zinke*)—raised land not far from

Race Point. She then turned northward and, sailing cautiously close to the alien coast, shaped a daring course for Mount Desert Rock, and then for Frenchman's Bay in Maine's Hancock County.

On the night of November 29, Hilbig eased his sub into the bay. The *U-1230* launched a rubber dinghy and debarked two men, rowing them boldly to Hancock Point on the mainland past a small U. S. naval base between Bar Harbor and Hulls Cove.

Judging by the funds they carried and the superior quality of their equipment, the men who now came ashore were definitely higher up than Mantel in the hierarchy of German espionage. One of them was a suave, glib, thirty-five-year-old pro, Erich Gimpel by name. For him, this was the culmination of a career in the Nazi secret service that had begun in Peru in 1935, when he was hired to entrap an American military attaché in Lima. Now he came to the States with neatly forged papers that presented him as Edward G. Green, although on the secret biography-card in his home office he was carried as one "Jakob Springer" and also more melodramatically as *V-Mann No. 146*, secret agent 146. Gimpel was his real name.

His companion, a weak-chinned, shifty-eyed, unattractive younger man, was a native-born American whose doctored credentials introduced him as Willie C. Caldwell. He was the son of an electrician from Old Black Point, Connecticut. A rabid pro-Nazi and Jew-baiter, Willie was recruited for the German secret service and smuggled to Berlin via Lisbon by a German consul in Boston. His real name stood engraved on the honor roll of local servicemen in his hometown of Old Black Point— "Apprentice Seaman William C. Colepough."

Although the Nazis had risked one of their best U-boats on the trip, had assigned to the mission one of their best spies and a rare American willing to work for them, and had given "Operation Elster" (as the mission was code-named by the Germans) all the earmarks of a major espionage enterprise, the venture had been prepared with amazing clumsiness. Gimpel had $60,000 on him, a huge sum which more than anything else indicated the importance of the mission. (He also had $100,000 worth of diamonds, presumably for a rainy day.) But the dollar bills he carried were crisp, brand-new banknotes, immaculately bundled like a payroll, with wrappers that had the words *Deutsche Reichsbank* (German Reichs Bank) printed conspicuously on them.

Gimpel and his sidekick landed in a snow storm, but they were unseasonably clad in flimsy raincoats and wore no hats. Their suitcases contained all the evidence needed to convict them on sight as Nazi spies—a couple of foreign automatic pistols, parts of a German radio transmitter with German markings, cameras and secret ink chemicals. So there they were, a couple of lonely strangers among strangers, in a blizzard in Maine, lugging their heavy suitcases in the fresh snow in their summer shoes along Route 37. It was inevitable for them to attract attention; they happened to bump into one Harvard Merrill Hodgkins, a clear-eyed, alert, sixteen-year-old lad. Young Hodgkins' Boy Scout training made him instantly suspicious. The lad let the men pass, then followed their footprints in the snow back to the water's edge—indubitable evidence that the strangers had come in from the sea.

Young Hodgkins notified the constable at Hancock and the FBI was promptly called. The spies were trailed to New York and quickly arrested. They talked freely, almost eagerly, about their mission—how Colepough had been picked for his special knowledge of the inlets and coves all along the New England coast to pave the way for other spies, and to guide furtive U-boats on their coastwise prowls. Then Gimpel opened up all the way and told the FBI about a task force made up of more Nazi agents and a flotilla of U-boats which was to follow them soon to the United States.

Gimpel said those U-boats were "being fitted out with a rocket-firing device for guided missiles, which would enable them to bomb the coast from positions well under the horizon." The detachment of agents was to carry out pinpointed sabotage acts, co-ordinated with the buzz-bombing, to intensify the damage, spread confusion and chaos, and deepen the panic the Germans expected to ensue.

Gimpel's intelligence about those sea-borne robot bombs did not seem to be just idle talk or a slick piece of terror propaganda. The development of rockets especially designed to be fired from U-boats was known to Commander Knowles in the Tenth Fleet. The idea had first popped into Admiral Karl Doenitz's fertile brain during a two-hour conference with Hitler in the Reichs Chancellery in Berlin on September 28, 1942. Hitler spoke hopefully of the strange new missiles a number of his faceless scientists were busy developing at Peenemuende in the Baltic, and Doenitz suggested that a special effort be made at once to develop rockets for his U-boats. Hitler was skeptical but promised he would send word to Peenemuende; and then, in due course, agents from inside the Third Reich began to report on them and prisoners from U-boats started hinting at them.

A few of the prisoners even claimed to know the name of the new rocket and that name by itself seemed to justify apprehension. It was called "RTG" for *Raketen Tauch-Geschoss*—rocket-propelled underwater missile.

Then an embarrassing development in the wake of the two spies' arrival gave the feared attack a high potential for success. After she had unloaded the agents, the *U-Hilbig* stayed on brazenly to prowl about Mount Desert Rock, only twenty to thirty miles off shore, in heavily-patrolled waters. Her presence there became definitely known on December 3, 1944, when she torpedoed a Canadian ship, the *Cornwallis*.

When the Tenth Fleet obtained fixes on the intruder and advised Jonas Ingram of the sub's approximate course, the admiral ordered an intensive search by two escort carrier groups. It was in vain. The *U-1230* slipped out of the tightening noose, then turned into a meteorological picket boat sending home weather reports which the Germans needed urgently in their planning of what was soon to explode as the Battle of the Bulge. She was shadowed steadily and fairly closely, the Tenth Fleet getting fixes on her whenever she broke radio silence to transmit those weather reports. But Hilbig managed to shake off his hunters. He actually succeeded in surviving the war.

Sortie into Headlines

In December, 1944, Knowles and his staff worked overtime to establish a pattern of German intentions and find whatever hard intelligence they could, either to confirm those fantastic claims or discount them once and for all. In the midst of their groping, reports pouring in from their net of high-frequency direction-finders introduced another element of mystery into the fast-developing thriller. The electronic sleuths from whom no U-boat could remain concealed the moment she used her wireless, now found that radio traffic had rapidly increased in the North Atlantic, from Rockall all the way to Greenland. This was taken as an indication that the Germans, after a long lull, had returned to their hunting grounds.

The evidence remained inconclusive, but the re-appearance of the U-boats added some weight to the frightening assumptions. Admiral Ingram in particular regarded the evidence as sufficiently convincing to burst into action in his own fashion.

Far from depressing him, the prospect of the sudden flair-up of the U-boat war positively invigorated Ingram. A compact, bulldog-faced, squirrel-eyed, flat-nosed old salt from landlocked Indiana, old Jonas was, next to "Bull" Halsey, the U. S. Navy's most colorful and aggressive flag officer. He was fondly remembered as a great football player in his Academy days and as the team's phenomenally successful coach.

A favorite of Admiral Ernest Joseph King, USN—who regarded him as part erratic genius and part court jester—and feeling smug in the protection of the Navy's big boss, Ingram would take things into his own enormous, cleaver-like hands whenever he thought Washington was too slow in giving him what he wanted. Early in 1942, he thus peremptorily promoted himself to vice admiral, when he found that Admiral Alfredo Suares Duarto of the Brazilian Navy, who outranked him at Recife, was cramping his free-wheeling style by insisting on seniority and prevented him from doing his best in the South Atlantic.

When he took over the Atlantic Fleet on November 15, 1944, the aggressive admiral was frankly fearful that his new assignment would be a mere sinecure, for the U-boat war was at a standstill and the European phase of the war appeared settled. An Allied victory seemed to be but a matter of time, delayed mostly by the weather that was foul on all fronts, causing General Eisenhower to quip that it was, indeed, Hitler's secret weapon. Gales whipped the Western Atlantic. In that November, only forty-one U-boats were at large in the whole ocean, the smallest number since 1941. Between September and Christmas, 1944, the forces of the United States could bag only five U-boats because so few of them were operating in their area—none, in fact, in the Caribbean and along the convoy routes of the Central Atlantic.

In view of the buzz-bomb possibility, Admiral Ingram decided to act on his own by dropping a bomb, not on any of the U-boats, but on the American public. So, on the morning of January 8, 1945, Ingram sailed into New York, bound for a date with Admiral Leary. His movements were concealed by the strict security arrangements of the war, and by a dismal winter sky so overcast that clouds obscured not only the top of the Empire State Building but even the antennae of the admiral's flagship. Leary was there to greet Ingram, and in his wake were reporters from the metropolitan newspapers and the press associations. They came eagerly to attend what public relations men of the Eastern Sea Frontier had promised would be an historic press conference.

As the reporters flocked into the wardroom, they found Ingram seated behind a long table, looking at them with squinted, quizzical eyes as if sizing them up one by one.

"Gentlemen," he said at last, "I have reason to assume that the Nazis are getting ready to launch a strategic attack on New York and Washington by robot bombs."

There was a unanimous gasp of amazement in the wardroom.

"You may recall," Ingram went on, "that on November 7 a joint Army-Navy statement warned explicitly that such robot attacks on the United States were entirely possible. I'm here to tell you that they are not only possible but probable as well, and that the East Coast is likely to be buzz-bombed within the next thirty or sixty days.

"The next alert you get is likely to be the McCoy," Ingram went on grimly, then added, "But we're ready for them! The thing to do is not to get excited about it. It might knock out a high building or two. It might create a fire hazard. It would certainly cause casulties in the limited area where it might hit. But it could not seriously affect the progress of the war."

Ingram paused to survey this hushed crowd in his wardroom, looking straight into the faces of the reporters. He was determined to make the warning stick by rubbing it in.

"It may be only ten or twelve buzz bombs," he said, "but they may come before we can stop them. They may hit before we know they're on the way. And the only way to stop a robot is at the source.

"We know," he added, "subs have been off the coast of Maine, but we're pretty sure none has been south of that lately. At any rate, I'm springing the cat from the bag to let the Huns know that we are ready for them."

Admiral Ingram's statement hit the United States from coast to coast. *The New York Times* headlined it: ROBOT BOMB ATTACKS HERE HELD PROBABLE BY ADMIRAL. Mayor Fiorello H. LaGuardia warned his New Yorkers: "We've got to hustle and provide our forces with everything they need so they can end the menace as soon as possible."

Colonel Edward C. O. Thomas, director of the New York State Office of Civilian Protection, added a grim note by announcing that there would be no blackout in the event of a robot attack.

"It would interfere," he said darkly, "with salvage and rescue."

The Snorkels Are Coming

Ingram stated that he expected the Nazi sneak attack to materialize within thirty or sixty days. Then, just when those sixty days were up, the Tenth Fleet became electrified again. This time it was a different pattern of intelligence that persuaded Commander Knowles that Grand Admiral Karl Doenitz *was* indeed assembling a task force of handpicked snorkel subs for that overdue "sneak attack."

After twenty months in the thick of it with a performance of dazzling brilliance as Chief of Staff and operating head of his shipless fleet, "Frog" Low had gone to sea. Now it became the responsibility of Rear Admiral Allan R. McCann, USN, himself a submarine specialist like "Froggy," to act upon inherited findings and conclusions—to have, so to speak, the courage of Low's convictions.

His job was made easy by the fact that he also inherited Low's seasoned staff, including Commander Knowles at the head of Intelligence. Knowles was not indulging in a guessing game when he, like a latter-day Paul Revere, told Ingram that the snorkels were coming. He was developing his new intelligence pattern from tidbits of information which, like random stones in a mosaic, he had been accumulating and collating for months.

It was almost uncanny. It sometimes seemed during those days that Knowles had his man at Sengwarden in East Friesland, inside the headquarters of the U-Boat Command, looking over the shoulders of Admiral Eberhard Godt, Doenitz's operations chief on the spot. At other times it appeared he was reading the encoded messages passing between Godt and his U-boats at sea. Then again it seemed that Knowles had access to the secret records of the U-Boat Command—their war diary, the logs, directives coming down from Doenitz at the Koralle and reports going up to him from Sengwarden.

Even today, nobody in the know—and Commander Knowles least of all—will shed much light on this remarkable penetration of the enemy's innermost secrets. At any rate, either by intuition or by other more sophisticated means, the austere and diligent Knowles was following the steady development of the long-expected threat, plotting it step by step like a cyclonic storm track. It was a superb feat, one of the outstanding intelligence achievements of the whole war.

Seven U-Boats Against the U. S.

In the end, Knowles had a comprehensive picture of the German design. He had a pretty good idea of the numbers and characteristics of the U-boats Doenitz had chosen to participate in what was destined to become his swan song in the Atlantic. He even knew some of its incidental details, such as the secret code name—"*Seewolf*"—by which Doenitz had referred to the impending operation. He had most, if not everything, Admiral Ingram needed to make his arrangements.

In March, the U-boats of *Seewolf* assembled inconspicuously at several Norwegian bases, their last refuge after their eviction from France. The attacking flotilla was to consist of seven "sea wolves," each of them recently refitted and equipped with the newest snorkel. They were the *U-518* under Oberleutnant Hans Offermann, the *U-546* with Kapitaenleutnant Paul Just in command, the *U-805* of Korvettenkapitaen Richard Bernardelli, the *U-858* of Kapitaenleutnant Thilo Bode, the *U-880* of Kapitaenleutnant Gerhard Schoetzau, the *U-881* of Oberleutnant Heinz Frischke, and the *U-1235* of Oberleutnant Franz Barsch.

It was the cream of the crop. Their orders called for staggered departure in March for assembly in two groups of three boats each, with *U-881* proceeding alone; for an approach march at snorkel depth; for extreme caution and radio silence while cruising towards the target area. They were expected to arrive off the American coast in mid-April and go into action under sealed orders.

Doenitz had absolute confidence in the quality of these battle-tested crews and these seasoned boats. They were Type VII boats, the standard 740-tonners which Doenitz had used in the Atlantic throughout the war, of which a total of 694 were built between 1936 and 1945. Their armament consisted of twelve torpedoes and the 20-mm. twin AA gun. They cruised at seventeen knots on the surface and eight knots submerged, and carried a crew of 44 officers and men. They had all the gadgets and improvements a well-equipped U-boat wore at this late stage of the war, including the snorkel—especially the snorkel.

In sheer numerical terms, this was a lopsided operation, almost ludicrously, painfully loaded against the U-boats: only seven little vessels aggregating about 5,000 tons, carrying a grand total of 84 torpedoes with an aggregate of but 50,400 pounds of explosives—a major offensive operation mounted by just 308 officers and men.

Yet in submarine warfare, bare figures are deceptive. A single such 740-ton Type VII—the *U-99* of Korvetten-Kapitaen Otto Kretschmer—disposed of more than 300,000 tons of Allied shipping; and three of Doenitz's early aces, Kretschmer, Guenther Prien, and Joachim Schepke, had sunk more than 800,000 tons between them by March, 1941.

Contact

Now, too, in the spring of 1945, the menace which those seven wayward U-boats represented was far out of proportion to their numerical strength, the number of combatants they carried, their firepower. This was why Admiral Ingram now needed four escort carriers with four composite squadrons of 76 aircraft, and 42 destroyer escorts to protect the East Coast of the United States from seven forlorn U-boats trying frantically to recoup a war their country had hopelessly lost.

Throughout March and early in April, the Tenth Fleet was furnishing Admiral Ingram with an amazingly accurate plot of the progress of the Germans who, Ingram was told by McCann, had left their bases in March and were at large, creeping towards the United States. The information enabled CINCLANT to set up a formidable defense in true Ingram style. He created what he confidently expected would be an impenetrable barrier in the direct path of the sea wolves, "to bar off," as he put it, "the entire Eastern Seaboard of Canada and the United

States to a phalanx of snorkel boats." The barrier, when completed, stretched from just south of Iceland to well south of Newfoundland. It was the backbone of a prodigious undertaking, going by the code name "Operation Teardrop."

"Teardrop" involved the escort carriers *Mission Bay* and *Croatan* in the first or northern barrier, *Core* and *Bogue* in the second or southern barrier. By the morning of April 11, the first barrier was set up and it was the eleventh hour! The Germans, long lost on their tedious approach march when no fixes or contacts could be obtained, were moving relentlessly westward in two close formations of three U-boats each, one north, the other south, with the *U-881* (the last to leave Norway) bringing up the rear.

The raw spring weather was foul, the sea heavy and running. Dense fog often rested on the water. The wind was blowing at a steady forty to fifty knots. The cruel sea rose high above the ships, then came crashing down on groaning decks. The broad and empty world of the ocean was concealed behind a curtain of drizzle. It was ideal for the furtive U-boats who could burrow themselves into the filthy weather and gain protection from it. But it was hard on Ingram's barrier forces, rolling and pitching in the angry sea. Air operations were either impossible or very hazardous, so it fell to the destroyer escorts to search relentlessly through the gloom.

There was nothing for four days. Then, at 35 minutes past nine P.M. on April 15, the destroyer escort *Stanton* made radar contact at 3,500 yards. The final battle of the Atlantic was on at last!

Suddenly silhouetted in the searchlight of the *Stanton* was a sea wolf —Oberleutnant Barsch's *U-1235*. She was on the surface because the weather was too rough for her snorkel, but as soon as the beam of the searchlight hit her, she crashdived. At once hedgehogs from the *Stanton* began plummeting after her. The sullen air was rent with a series of underwater explosions, but the U-boat remained alive, trying to escape by diving deeper. The hunt continued for eighty-five minutes and then the *Stanton* was joined by the destroyer escort *Frost,* panting in through the foul weather for the kill.

Lieutenant Commander John C. Kiley on the *Stanton* and Lieutenant Commander Andrew E. Ritchie on the *Frost* allowed the cornered U-boat no respite. At middle-watch time—but four minutes into another day—the first certain hedgehog hit was recorded by the *Stanton*. But the battle was not yet won! It took another hour and ten more minutes—until 1:14 A.M. on April 16—before the *U-1235* was sent to her final fathom. Two enormous explosions roared up from under the sea, blending, as Theodore Roscoe recorded it, "into a thunder roll that vibrated the DE's (destroyer escorts) and was felt by several of the hunter-killers ten miles away."

At 1:17, more deep-sea thunder. Then the echoes faded out, and only the crashing sea at lat. 47°56′ N., long. 30°25′W., broke the silence. Then the calm voice of Commander F. D. Giambattista, screen commander in the *Frost,* came in over radio. "That is the end of the attack," he said, adding, "and I think that's the end of the sub." It was.

Stanton and *Frost* were told to stay in the area, to search for the sisters of the downed sea wolf. It took them only forty minutes to find one—the *U-880.* At 1:55 A.M. *Frost* made radar contact. *U-880* was on the surface, apparently trying to run for her life. From the commander of the escort division came the prompt signal:

"Close the target, illuminate, fire and ram!"

It was easier said than done. The sea was too heavy for ramming. The fire of the destroyer escorts' 3-inch guns could hardly be expected to be accurate in this foul weather. The fog was so low and dense that star shells from *Frost* could not illuminate the U-boat; but her searchlight could. Its beam caught her fully surfaced. Apparently Kapitaenleutnant Schoetzau had changed his mind, because now he was closing the hunters, as if hell-bent on fighting it out.

Ritchie accepted the challenge and rose to it. He opened up with his guns, for better or for worse, and Shoetzau was quick to get the message. Abruptly he took his boat down. Following her on sonar, the *Stanton* moved in with a hedgehog pattern.

At six minutes past four o'clock in the dismal morning, four hits were scored, attested by their bangs. Then four minutes later came a terrific blast, even more violent and ponderous than the vicious explosion that had broken the back of *U-1235.* It fractured galley crockery on the *Stanton.* It shook the *Croatan,* fifteen miles away.

At 4:29 A.M., the two destroyer escorts nosed through thick oil slick. The U-boat, with all hands on board, was gone.

Admiral Ingram signalled to Captain John R. Ruhsenberger who, on *Mission Bay,* was the O.T.C. of the whole first barrier force, his gratified, "Well done." Ingram also directed him to break off and retire to Argentia in Newfoundland, leaving the next phase of Operation Teardrop to the second barrier force, then just moving in from the north and the south.

Prior to departure, on April 21, Ruhsenberger ordered Captain Kenneth Craig's *Croatan* to stage a last air-surface sweep, hoping to find the missing member of the pack, Korvetten-Kapitaen Bernardelli's *U-805.*

The weather was too foul for the *Croatan's* planes, but the destroyer escorts sailed into the sweep and four of them obtained a bead on what they confidently thought was the *U-Bernardelli*. They opened fire with hedgehogs and the DE's were rewarded with a few underwater explosions, but the sonar told a different story. Bernardelli confirmed his reputation as a master of evasion. He backed his sub into her own wake and vanished without a trace.

Yet in her escape she led the hunters to another boat, Offermann's *U-518*. Sweeping undaunted in the mountainous sea, the flagship of the DE task unit was the first to pick up the contact. Commander M. H. Harris, in charge of the group, ordered the *Carter* to hold it, then called in the *Neal A. Scott* for a creeper attack. At exactly four minutes to ten on that hideous night, the *Scott* fired her first hedgehog, then the *Carter* also attacked. Offermann apparently hoped to sit it out by diving deep down and remaining mum, but the *U-518* died quickly in that motionless position, expiring with a volcanic thunder at 10:15 P.M., less than an hour after *Carter* had first pinged her.

The first barrier force thus disposed of three sea wolves. Four more remained still at large. At least the threat to the East Coast had been cut almost in half.

Barrier No. 2

Many miles from this hot spot, the Tenth Fleet was in on these kills. Its faceless plotters, presided over by Admiral McCann, bleary-eyed and haggard from their nocturnal vigil, followed the actions blow by blow on scrambler teletypes and through a maze of incoming reports. The peculiar demise of these three U-boats had an ominous message for them.

Even if these were not necessarily the hottest anti-sub actions in the Atlantic, they were undoubtedly the loudest. You could almost hear those protean blasts roar up from the teletypes. The exceptional violence and thunderous noise with which the three wolves had succumbed now convinced the Tenth Fleet that these U-boats were carrying something very nasty and powerful, doubtless rockets, to throw at our Eastern cities. Those violent blasts stimulated everyone from Ingram and McCann down "to make special efforts to mop up the rest of the group".

Mop up, indeed!

The day before, in the morning of April 21, the second barrier force had taken up its appointed position south of St. John's, Newfoundland, extending in a long vertical line from just below the Grand Bank. Made up of the escort carriers *Core* and *Bogue*, and twenty-two destroyer escorts, with Captain George J. Dufek, USN, in overall tactical command, it was an even more formidable barrier than the first force. Both the spacing and timing of this second force was superb, for the first sea wolf of the second *Rudel* reached the patrol area of the *Core* just when the destroyer escorts became ready to snap into action.

The weather did not get any better, but now the situation became still further muddled by another storm of a different nature, blowing up thousands of miles away. Even while the issue was being joined at sea, Grossadmiral Doenitz's attention became diverted by some more urgent development much closer to home. Whatever he expected from it, *Seewolf* was a gamble, a hit-or-miss venture over which he no longer had any control. Now he was far removed from it, both physically and emotionally; and there was nothing tangible on hand to enlighten him, no news from the Atlantic.

On April 10, as the Russian and American advances to the heart of the Reich threatened to cut the country in two, Hitler had made Doenitz supreme liege lord of the northern sector of the country. On April 22, just as *Seewolf* was about to enter its second critical phase, Doenitz removed himself physically from the conduct of the war at sea. He abandoned the Koralle, his besieged headquarters near Berlin, and established himself at Ploen in Holstein, his next to last stop on his flight from disaster, where he busied himself with "civilian problems," conferring with scared *Gauleiters* and panic-stricken Nazi officials.

The Last Gasp

Doenitz remembered *Seewolf* only once during those days. On April 23, he signalled its U-boats to dissolve the groups and proceed singly to their pre-arranged patrol stations off the East Coast. It was one of the abrupt command decisions for which Doenitz was notorious. He was forever changing his mind and dispositions, often in the middle of complex operations he himself had designed, confronting his U-boat commanders with difficult new situations for which they had not been prepared and briefed.

That April 23 was an important date, not merely for Doenitz at home, but also for his pathetic little force in mid-Atlantic. The second barrier force was active, sweeping its enormous patrol area around the forty-first meridian. It was there, at quarter to seven in the morning, that the American armada of Captain Dufek was suddenly electrified by the first contact developed by no less than six destroyer escorts on a tip from the *Pillsbury*. While efforts were under way to run down the *Pillsbury's* tip, an Avenger pilot from the *Core* reported an actual sighting. What he saw was a feathery wake typical of those made by the protruding snorkel. The Avenger made a bomb run on the sighting —a tiny object way down below—and reported encouraging results. But when a couple of destroyer escorts were sent by Dufek to confirm, all they found was a dead whale.

But the U-boats were there!

They made their presence painfully known by torpedoing the destroyer escort *Frederick C. Davis*—popular "Fightin' Freddy" of Anzio beachhead fame—and sinking her in a spectacular disaster. "Men died instantly in the molten vortex of that eruption," wrote Roscoe in his official account. "A number were flung overside. Others, trapped in a mangle of bulkheads and machinery, went down with the ship."

Aside from everything else, "Fightin' Freddy" had still another distinction in her blazing end. She became the last American destroyer escort to perish in the Battle of the Atlantic.

Credit for what remained the only positive achievement of the whole *Seewolf* operation belonged to Kapitaenleutnant Paul Just, who had fired the lethal torpedo at a range of only 650 yards from the lone stern tube of his *U-546*. It was a gallant shot, fired at a risk daringly calculated in a situation that must have impressed Just as utterly hopeless. "It was a matter of life or death," the German later said, "a question of me getting the *Davis* or the *Davis* getting me."

The moment Just's torpedo turned "Freddy" into a sheet of fire, a swarm of furious wasps pounded upon the U-boat—eight destroyer escorts from "Freddy's" dismayed unit directed personally by the Task Unit Commander, Frederick S. Hall, in the *Pillsbury*.

The *Davis* was hit at 8:40 A.M. Within twenty-seven minutes, the *Flaherty* was in sonar contact with the guilty U-boat, but Paul Just was not the kind of man who gave in easily. The dramatic hunt for *U-546* lasted until 6:44 P.M. when Just had no choice but to concede defeat. Badly damaged by depth charge and hedgehog, he decided to bring up his boat and call it a day. His sudden appearance on the sea, whipped as it was by wind and explosives, was the apt climax of an exceptional sea saga.

"As the U-boat's conning tower broke water," Roscoe wrote, "all ships that had a clear range opened fire. Frantic submariners fought their way out of the hatches. Under a storm of hits the sub plunged and rolled." The *U-546* went under, after her bridge had been knocked to bits and her snorkel throat had been severed.

During his shock-interrogation, Kapitaenleutnant Just professed to know nothing about any buzz bombs or a plan to launch them against the East Coast. And he naturally refused to say anything about any of the other sea wolves. But from Washington, the Tenth Fleet signalled: "Four down, three to go!"

Now there were only the *U-805* and the *U-858* unaccounted for, as well as the supernumerary member of the group, *U-881*. It now became the turn of the straggler to feel the full brunt of Admiral Ingram's avenging anger, though it was not until dawn on May 6 that destroyer escort *Farquhar* finally found Oberleutnant Frischke's slow boat to nowhere. She was caught in the very act of maneuvering to torpedo the escort carrier *Mission Bay*, back on patrol duty from a brief rest at Argentia.

The *Farquhar* cut in with a single depth charge attack and that was that for *U-Frischke*. She sank without survivors at 4:13 A.M. on May 6. No time was now left to hunt for the remaining two sea wolves because just twenty-two hours later the whole big show was over. At exactly 2:41 in the morning of May 7—without remembering to tell his sea wolves—Grossadmiral Karl Doenitz capitulated.

Even then, Operation *Seewolf* was not yet quite over.

Bernardelli in *U-805* and Thilo Bode in *U-858* managed after all to slip through Ingram's double barrier. Cruising at snorkel depth, they made for their pre-assigned patrol stations off the East Coast, ready to execute their part of the *Seewolf* operation.

It was only on May 9, when he was standing off Cape Race, that Bernardelli found out that the war was over. He climbed up the hatch to survey the world on this balmy spring morning from the bridge, and what he saw did not make him proud of his feat. On this, his first day of peace in those alien waters, he wrapped up years of stubborn endeavor on this cruel ocean in but two bitter words:

"*Verdammter Atlantik!*" he said, with his teeth biting his lower lip. "Damned, cursed Atlantic!"

Then he made his presence humbly known by signalling CINCLANT for someone to whom he could surrender. He still had to wait four more days, until May 13, when the *Varian*, one of his recent hunters, arrived at Cape Race to collect the *U-Bernardelli*.

Kapitaenleutnant Bode took the last of the sea wolves, the *U-858*, all the way to the Delaware Capes before he hoisted a couple of olive-green blankets to signal that he, too, was ready to surrender. That closed this chapter of the Atlantic battle for good—on May 19, twenty-six days after Bode's escape from Ingram's noose. Now he was caught at last, not by the hunters, but by the inexorable finality of V-E day.

When the two surviving members of the *Seewolf* group had been examined at Norfolk with fine-tooth combs, and when Bernardelli and Bode had been thoroughly interrogated, that strange hypothesis of the buzz-bomb threat evaporated like wasted steam. Neither of the two captured U-boats had anything resembling robot bombs or rocket launchers on board; and Bernardelli and Bode assured their interrogators that there never had been a serious plan in the U-Boat Command to subject the East Coast to a buzz-bomb attack from U-boats.

Yet if that hypothesis proved to be but fancy, it was strangely supported by at least some hard facts. The Tenth Fleet's information that the Nazis had developed seagoing rockets for their U-boats was correct, up to a point. It was, indeed, the mysterious "RTG" whose existence Commander Knowles had on file.

Lessons of the Morning After

Now it became known that the ominous *Raketen Tauch-Geschoss* was a 38-cm. rocket, actually capable of being fired from a submerged submarine. It had an initial muzzle velocity of 35 meters per second. Its air-breathing rocket, turned on when the missile was in flight above the water, increased its speed to about 100 meters per second, or 225 miles per hour. Its range was limited to four thousand meters—only about two and a half miles.

Obviously, this "RTG" would have been clearly incapable of doing any appreciable damage to the East Coast. In actual fact, it was designed as an anti-aircraft missile, to enable the U-boats to combat planes from submerged positions, instead of relying solely on their deck anti-aircraft guns.

But if the robot-bombing of the United States was not the true mission of *Seewolf*, what was?

"In late March, 1945," wrote Samuel Eliot Morison in *The Atlantic Battle Won*, "when [Doenitz] dispatched these six (sic) boats from their Norwegian bases, the Nazi regime was on its last legs. . . . Group 'Seewolf' for Doenitz was a means of employing part of his large submarine fleet in a manner to annoy and defy the United States."

It is not an explanation that should satisfy the historian, or, for that matter, the Germans who would be justified in making Doenitz account for those young lives he had so recklessly sacrificed just to "annoy and defy" the United States.

And, indeed, in the broader historical perspective, Operation *Seewolf* looms up today as a most significant venture with crucial lessons to remember. Despite Ingram's tight barrier defense, despite the most efficient deployment of the protective armada, despite the assemblage of a seemingly foolproof warning system, *two out of seven U-boats still managed to slip through* to reach the East Coast and remain undetected to the bitter end. The fact that those two U-boats succeeded in breaking through the barrier is far more important than the dramatic feat of sinking the other five.

The two intrepid U-boats that crossed the finish line in the face of such overwhelming odds represented a frightening percentage—almost thirty per cent of the force that could break through, no matter how strong and broad and ingenious the defense had been. And there are indications that the situation has not changed substantially since 1945, that a comparable percentage of an attacking submarine force could still sneak through today, despite the presumably improved and far more sophisticated defenses we are now able to throw in their paths.

By mounting his futile *Seewolf*, Karl Doenitz himself perhaps merely sought to work off his bitter frustration in senseless aggression. He could not know then that he was doing more. He was, in fact, rehearsing a pattern of sneak attack that would, within a couple of decades, become as real and perilous as his *Seewolf* was inane and nebulous.

CHAPTER II

The Man Who Turned Up the Ocean

One of the deadliest doctrines of modern warfare first occurred to Karl Doenitz in the early fall of 1918 as he was taking a nocturnal swim in the Mediterranean. Although this was a balmy October night off picturesque Cape Passero at the southeast tip of Sicily, he wasn't in the water for pleasure. He was in the Mediterranean on business, having been until that moment in command of a U-boat made by the great Germania Yards with something less than perfect Teutonic workmanship.

The *UB-68* of young Lieutenant Doenitz had set out for Malta where she was expected to raise havoc with a couple of British convoys; but just when one of these convoys steamed into sight, the *U-Doenitz* was seized by a tantrum. From periscope depth, without the slightest warning, she plunged bow first until she stood on her head at about 300 feet. Doenitz managed to bring her up once more, for the last time. She broke water in the center of the convoy whose escorts hit her with everything they had.

"That was the end of my sea-going career in a U-boat in the First World War," Doenitz recalled. "That last night, however, had taught me a lesson in regard to basic principles."

By the time he was fished out of the water, Doenitz had the contours of those basic principles fairly pat in his head; and then he had plenty of time to develop them into a "system" during almost ten months of imprisonment in England. The idea inspired by the fact that the convoy got away unscathed was that if only one or more U-boats could have been there in *concerted action with the UB-68*, that *verfluchter Geleitzug* would have had its casualties!

24

But as things stood in 1918, such a balling of the fist was not possible. Primitive means of communications and other mechanical limitations forced the U-boats to operate as lone wolves. Even so, U-boats had scored impressive victories until 1917. Then, the introduction of the convoy system prevented them from remaining a major factor in the war at sea. Then, too, Britain developed what was confidently believed to be a powerful, if not decisive, antidote, an underwater listening device called *asdic*—named for the initials of the Allied Submarine Detection Investigation Committee, where it was originally developed. The early successes of asdic appeared to confirm the views of those who—taking their cue from Mahan—steadfastly refused to see a truly effective weapon in the submarine; and they shook the confidence of those who did regard it as a potentially vital factor in the war at sea. However, young Doenitz persisted in his seemingly irrational dedication to the U-boat.

"A U-boat," Doenitz wrote, "attacking a convoy *on the surface* and *under cover of darkness*, I realized, stood very good prospects of success. The greater the number of U-boats that could be brought simultaneously into the attack, the more favorable would become the opportunities offered to each individual attacked. . . . It was obvious that, *on strategic and general tactical grounds, attacks on convoys must be carried out by a number of U-boats acting in unison.*"

Thus was born the "wolf pack" concept at a time when Doenitz himself was struggling with the sea for his own survival. Thus was born, too, an obsession, a blind faith in the U-boat's opportunities, her power, and her capabilities.

Prisoner of War

Intoxicated by his ideas and raring to share his theory with like-minded officers at home, Karl Doenitz could barely endure the humiliation and idleness of imprisonment. Whether it was a wholesome yearning to get home and start again from scratch, or morbid remorse, or obsessive preoccupation with his ideas, Doenitz found it well-nigh impossible to live through his captivity in a barren region of Scotland. He was somewhat erratic and petulant by nature, a man like his ill-fated *UB-68*, not quite in control of his stability; soon his captors noticed a steady deterioration of his mental state.

He would spend all of his allowance on little china dogs at the camp's canteen, then like a child would play with them and with empty cooky jars for hours on end, isolating himself more and more from his environment. He showed other signs, too, of mental disability. His condition deteriorated so markedly that he had to be transferred to the psychiatric ward of the hospital where he was locked up in the special department reserved for raving maniacs. He was certified insane and, in the summer of 1919, was returned to Germany. He made the journey tied to a stretcher.

Doenitz himself skips over this episode of his life in his otherwise loquacious memoirs; and Wolfgang Frank, brilliant author of *The Sea Wolves* (who spent the Second World War as a correspondent covering Doenitz) presents it as a smart case of malingering. He claims that Doenitz feigned insanity to speed the day of his repatriation.

Dazed by the turmoil and the apparent hopelessness of Germany's plight, Doenitz tried to grope his way to a post-war existence. He went to Kiel, headquarters of the tiny navy Germany was allowed to maintain under the Versailles Treaty, to arrange his separation from the service. His fame as an intrepid U-boat captain had preceded him to Kiel. His psychiatric adventure in Scotland, accepted as a "darned good ruse," added to this aura. He was, therefore, received with open arms, especially by his erstwhile commanding officer in the Mediterranean, Commander Otto Schultze. Schultze, now acting as Director of Personnel, was busily recruiting a cadre of officers for the new navy of the Weimar Republic.

Doenitz

Schultze invited him to join the *Reichsmarine*, but Doenitz was skeptical. He saw his future only within a U-boat service; yet this post-war Germany had no U-boats and was prohibited from building any under the Versailles Treaty.

"The war has made me an enthusiastic submariner," he told Schultze. "Do you think we shall ever have any U-boats again?"

"Yes, I'm sure we shall," Schultze assured him, for he himself was already engaged in the vast conspiracy to breach the peace treaty.

"When?" Doenitz asked with characteristic impatience.

"Soon," Schultze replied, "in a few years."

That was enough for Doenitz! He decided then and there to serve, to avenge if possible, not merely the defeat of Germany, but even more the bitter humiliation of his personal defeat.

Who was this strange man, this dreamer of vast designs—this stubborn Don Quixote of the ocean who plotted and worked so hard to carry naval warfare deep under the sea? Who was this man destined to emerge from utter obscurity as the most dangerous single adversary the United States would encounter in World War II?

It is not simple to answer these questions, if only because Karl

Doenitz is a slippery subject for a biographer. This man—famous and notorious, yet in the final analysis little-known—is inordinately shy when it comes to a review of his family and background, probably because they were so dull and *petit bourgeois,* so landlocked and unproductive except for this single son.

During the Nuremberg days when his co-defendants produced long, self-laudatory autobiographies, his American interrogator was hard put to coax even his vital statistics from Doenitz. An "autobiographical sketch" was eventually submitted by him on November 8, 1945. Consisting of a single sheet of paper, it listed but twenty dates, beginning with "1891, born in Berlin" and ending with "1945, chief of state." What happened in between was barely sketched in the briefest of entries, mostly in one to three unavoidable words.

When Karl Doenitz was born, on September 16, 1891, in Berlin-Gruenau, a good middle-class residential district of the German capital, his family's peasant past was far behind. His own immediate forebears were all city dwellers—his father an engineer, an uncle a reputed historian. The boy was educated in Berlin, Jena, and Weimar, but his character was shaped at home by a jingoistic father whose idol was Wilhelm the First, the strict and predatory soldier-king of Prussia, and whose religion was Prussianism in its chauvinistic, militaristic, expansionistic sense. A severe and demanding master, his father imbued the son with a spirit of what Doenitz later conceded was *blind* patriotism.

When young Doenitz decided upon a career in the navy, it was not the romance of the "ageless and eternal sea" that lured him. It was rather the popular image of the Imperial Navy, evoked by Grand Admiral Tirpitz's grandiose plans of expansion, as a prime symbol of rampant German patriotism and imperialism in defiance of and in competition with England. Then, too, the Imperial Army of Kaiser Wilhelm II attracted scions of the nobility. Without the much-coveted "von" in his name, and without connections on higher social echelons, young Doenitz expected to rise faster and higher in this newer service than in the army, hoary with tradition.

Doenitz entered the Imperial Naval Academy at Flensburg on April 1, 1910, and was commissioned an ensign on September 27, 1913. He was assigned to the light cruiser *Breslau,* stationed in the Mediterranean. At the outbreak of the war, the *Breslau* was transferred to the Turkish Navy, renamed *Midilli* and assigned to the Black Sea. Her German officers were issued Turkish uniforms complete with fez, a headgear that sat rather incongruously on young Doenitz's Nordic head.

Doenitz was a highly competent officer. Distinguishing himself in action against the Russian Black Sea Fleet, he was promoted to be a lieutenant and awarded the Iron Cross, First and Second Class. For a time he served as air observer near the Dardanelles and then, despite his youth, as commandant of a naval aviation squadron near San Stefano. He thus served abroad from 1913 to 1916, and his foreign duty had a marked influence in shaping his outlook. "It was a period," he wrote many years later, "that made a deep impression on me and strengthened my feelings of patriotism. I saw Germany from afar and in perspective as an entity, and while I was able to compare my country with other lands and peoples, her internal weaknesses were shrouded from me by distance."

From War to War

Although Doenitz is known primarily as a protagonist of the U-boat, his active service in submarines was confined to less than two years all told and his close association with the U-boat arm to only ten out of his thirty-five years in the Navy

As a fighting submariner Doenitz was a sort of ninety-day wonder. His formal schooling for the U-boat service was brief, and the artillery course that was supposed to have made him a torpedo wizard was even briefer. Under the pressures of war both were crammed into a few months in 1916. His first detail as a submariner was in *U-39* under Kapitaenleutnant Forstmann, one of the U-boat aces of World War I. He received his first command, that of *UC-25*, on March 1, 1918, when the war had only seven months and eleven days to go. He exercised command, in *UC-25* and eventually in *UB-68*, for just six months and three days. *UB-68* was sunk on October 3, a few weeks before the surrender of the German fleet. As far as the record shows, Doenitz succeeded in sinking only a single vessel, the British repair ship *Cyclops*. Armistice Day found him a prisoner of war in Gibraltar, aboard H.M.S *Sapphire*, pending his transfer to a prison camp in England. The news of the armistice caught him below deck, shaving. When he heard the whole harbor burst into a noisy celebration, he ran out on deck in his underwear, his youthful face smeared with shaving lather. Brandishing a razor, he threatened to slit every British throat on board.

From 1919 to 1928, Doenitz was desk-bound, a kind of morale officer. His job was to watch for and prevent Communist and Nazi infiltration into the *Reichsmarine*—an important job because some continental navies were traditionally wide open for extreme political influences. Shipboard mutinies often served as prologues to revolutions. While thus serving as a "political officer," he evolved his attitude to both extremes in German politics—uncompromisingly negative to Communism, sympathetic to Nazis. He also learned the art of intrigue and fitted himself into the conspiracy within the German military establishment that gnawed subtly but steadily at the foundations of the Weimar Republic.

Like prophets everywhere, Doenitz had to bide his time. His daring new ideas had to be shelved after World War I when Commander Schultze's hopeful prediction (that Germany would have U-boats again "very soon") did not come true. They were revived in 1935 when Hitler's Germany received the gift of a naval agreement from Great Britain, including the permission to build U-boats again, up to 45 per cent of the Royal Navy's own submarine strength.

By then, Germany was merrily and unilaterally violating the peace treaty anyway, building U-boats, first in friendly foreign yards, and then in secret shipyards inside Germany. A group of handpicked officers and men were being trained for the pending U-boat arm in a special clandestine establishment characteristically called *Anti*-Submarine School. Even so, despite his vested interest in the U-boat concept, Doenitz was taken by surprise when on September 27, 1935, he was abruptly transferred from command of the globe-girdling cruiser *Emden* to command of the new "Weddigen" Flotilla of three little U-boats with which the Third Reich began its ambitious program.

Doenitz was the right man. "He succeeded in closing a gap of 17 years," a German naval diarist wrote in 1944, "during which no training took place, with a few months of tireless work. Day after day, night after night, week after week he stood on the bridge of one of his U-boats indoctrinating the men in his charge, by hard, thorough training, with the spirit of the men who manned the submarines during World War I. At the same time he collected new technical experience and new improvements in the development of different submarine types."

As early as 1937, he led his handful of new U-boats—mere "canoes," as they were called—into the Atlantic to exercise his concept of massed attack in an all-out *guerre de course*. He realized that he would need some 300 U-boats in actual operation at sea to accomplish the defeat of the enemy by this means alone. And, though he had only 57 of them altogether in the late summer of 1939, and only eighteen operational in the Atlantic (deployed well in advance in the firm expectation of war with England), he was elated behind his façade of equanimity when, at 1:30 P.M. on September 3, 1939, he received the order from Berlin to go to war against Britain, forthwith.

Later that afternoon, he went to his command post at the Neuende Naval Radio Station in Wilhelmshaven for an emergency conference with Admiral Boehm, commander in chief of the fleet, and Admiral Saalwaechter, the flag officer in command of Naval Group West. Awed by the stifling superiority of British seapower and overwhelmed by their new task in the face of Hitler's repeated assurances that they would never have to fight Britain, Boehm and Saalwaechter were bluntly pessimistic. Boehm in particular voiced in no uncertain terms his concern and emphasized the gravity of the German Navy's plight.

But Doenitz was confident. Before him was "Directive No. 1" of the OKW, the Wehrmacht High Command, dated August 31, 1939, outlining the basic principles of the war at sea. "The Navy," it read, "will wage *guerre de course* with emphasis against England." This was exactly as he wanted and expected it. And he knew that his U-boats would have to carry the major burden, if not the sole burden, in that kind of war.

So it was in excellent spirits and with great expectations, at exactly 5:15 P.M. on September 3, 1939, that he handed Lieutenant Fuhrmann, his young aide, his own implementation of the OKW's directive, to be encoded at once and signalled to all the U-boats at sea. It read:

"Commence hostilities against Great Britain immediately! Do not wait for attack!"

This was the exact version of the signal entered in the log of *U-30* by Kapitaenleutnant Lemp, its captain. Heeding the instruction, Lemp proceeded promptly to torpedo and sink the British liner *Athenia*, en route to the United States. Unrestricted submarine warfare that in World War I reared its ugly head only in the third year of the war, now began within the first twenty-four hours of World War II.

CHAPTER III

Puppet Show in the Atlantic

On October 1, when the war was only a month old, Doenitz sat down at his headquarters at Sengwarden near Wilhelmshaven, to take stock. It was already clear to him that neither side was ready for the war and that it would take some time to get the U-boat arm into shape. His boats had the initiative, to be sure, but there was no method as yet in their offensive. Hunting alone as best they could, they mounted their raids in hit-or-miss, hit-and-run fashion, sticking close to the Scottish and Irish coasts or foraying into the Bay of Biscay. The whole thing was, as Nicholas Monsarrat put it in *The Cruel Sea*, unpredictable and amateurish, like a game of hide-and-seek in a nursery world.

When Doenitz sized up the situation, he wrote in his War Diary: "The salient feature of our present position is the dearth of U-boats at our disposal. In view of the incorporation of enemy shipping into convoys, I do not consider it advisable to distribute the U-boats singly over a very wide area. Our object must be to locate the convoys and destroy them by means of a concentrated attack by the few boats available."

Note: I trust the reader will understand, but I would like to point out, nevertheless, that this book deals primarily with the American phase of the Battle of the Atlantic. Bear with me if I devote but passing references to its British phase. This does not mean, of course, that I underestimate the heroic part the Royal Navy played, first in the containment, and then in the subjugation of the U-boat, or, indeed gloss over the fact that theirs was the dominant and decisive part. For their historic role I suggest that the reader should consult such brilliant books as the *The War at Sea*, by Captain Stephen W. Roskill; *Max Horton and the Western Approaches*, by Rear Admiral W. S. Chalmers; and *Walker's Groups in the Western Approaches*, by D. E. G. Wemyss.

September was hot. His U-boats had sunk forty ships, including the aircraft carrier *Courageous*. But he could not keep them at that pace. Now the question was, what to do next? How to bring a semblance of control and coordination into the game, he asked himself, just when autumnal gales were turning the Atlantic into the finest hiding-place in the world?

"The finding of a convoy on the high seas is a difficult task," Doenitz answered the question in his War Diary. "Our operations therefore must be concentrated against those areas in which the enemy sea lines of communication converge and join—namely, off southwest England and in the vicinity of Gibraltar."

He dismissed the nearer target because British defenses, even in their feeble state, were more dense so close to the English coast; and although Gibraltar had the disadvantage of being remote, he opted for it. Doenitz had only three boats available for the operation west of the Rock, but they proved sufficient to confirm to his complete satisfaction the soundness of one of his "basic principles" while refuting another—a refutation, though, that did not displease him at all.

Birth of the Wolf Packs

October 17, 1939, then, was destined to become a red-letter day in Karl Doenitz's calendar. On that day his U-boats mounted for the first time a co-ordinated attack on a British convoy. The scene of this historic engagement was the Atlantic near the northwest shore of the Strait of Gibraltar, just off Cape Trafalgar where Nelson had made history almost exactly a hundred and thirty-four years before.

The overall tactical command of the operation was entrusted to one of the U-boat commanders on the spot—Kapitaenleutnant Hartmann in *U-37*. This was the acid test! The three U-boats managed to sink three ships out of a convoy that sailed ponderously westward under air cover. The soundness of his theory of the massed attack, this *Rudeltaktik*—the German word *Rudel* meaning flock, herd, or pack—seemed to be fully and triumphantly validated.

Now his vague designs were quick to take definitive shape. Instead of trying to blockade the British Isles, as Grand Admiral Raeder's master plan had envisaged it, he would sever the British lifeline far out in the Atlantic where the Allied convoys would not enjoy the advantage of land-based air cover, their strongest defense. His U-boats would be working according to his cherished plan—in teams of eight or nine, some of them hunting, others killing. Such mass attacks promised still another advantage over the lonewolf tactics of World War I.

They would break up the convoy's escort forces and enable the U-boats to strike in through the tattered screen.

The method called for surface attack under the cover of darkness, not merely because the U-boats had to use their radios to co-ordinate their actions, but also because they could thus take advantage of the higher speed produced by their Diesel engines. The convoys would be tracked down during the day by the group's reconnaissance line. Then, after sunset, the pack would strike and kill.

Doenitz no longer doubted that he was on the right track and that his *Rudeltaktik* held the answer to the enemy's convoy defense. On the other hand, his idea of leaving tactical command in the hands of one of the U-boat commanders on the spot appeared unsound. "To be able to remain on the surface," Doenitz pondered when all the facts of the Gibraltar operation were in, "in order to direct operations, the subordinate commander in tactical control had to remain far enough away from the convoy to be beyond the reach of its escorting aircraft. But if he did this he was out of sight of the convoy and was therefore robbed of the essential 'on the spot' information and power of observation. If on the other hand," he mused on, "he remained closer to his objectives, he would be forced to observe the same defensive precautions as any other U-boat in action." In addition, he felt the small number of boats available to him precluded *ipso facto* detailing one of the boats of the *Rudel* to tactical command because it meant reducing the small striking force.

Problem of Tactical Command

Here was a dilemma! The *Rudel* technique demanded iron-clad co-ordination and running direction during the attack or else it would have to be discarded altogether as impractical or unfeasible.

Suddenly it dawned upon Doenitz that he himself at U-boat headquarters could, by radio, be in tactical command of those concerted actions even though they took place hundreds of miles away. This was possible because of the rapidity with which even enciphered signals could be handled. A revolutionary new situation was thus created, unprecedented not merely in the annals of U-boat war, but indeed in twentieth-century warfare as a whole. It was reminiscent of the so-called *Feldherrnhuegel* era when supreme commanders like Napoleon and Wellington directed their battles from elevated vantage points on the spot, except that Doenitz's electronic *Feldherrnhuegel* was hundreds and sometimes thousands of miles from the scene of the battle he directed.

Doenitz accepted his new role avidly, without any pangs of false modesty. His own description of this command decision shows how vainglorious he really was and how highly he regarded himself as the tactical commander of those U-boats in action, aside from being their commander in chief: "My 'on-the-spot knowledge' [*"Milieu-Kenntnis,"* as he himself expressed it] and my ability to 'get the feel' of how things were out there in the Atlantic proved to be greater than we had hoped."

Aside from this faith in his own psychic faculties, Doenitz was forced into his gigantic blindman's bluff by one of his major operational deficiencies—his lack of intelligence data about the enemy. His personal feud with Admiral Wilhelm Canaris closed to him, largely by his own resolve, the huge *Abwehr* apparatus of secret agents and intelligence specialists; and then a running feud with Reichs Marshal Hermann Goering also deprived him of the crucial aid of air reconnaissance. This latter was the old story of jurisdiction over aircraft leading to interservice rivalries in every military establishment. The German Navy fought a long and futile battle for its own air arm, but foundered on Goering's greed. "Everything that flies belongs to me," the Marshal said when asked to let the Navy have its own planes. Instead of Doenitz getting at least a squadron or two for the reconnaissance and cover his U-boats badly needed on their sailings through the highly vulnerable Bay of Biscay by means of a sage compromise of his differences with Goering, his stiff attitude irreparably antagonized the Marshal and lost him whatever chance he had to put a permanent reconnaissance force into the Atlantic battle.

Later, in 1943, when he sought an explanation for the turn of the tide that found his U-boats at the losing end, Doenitz told Hitler: "Historians will depict the struggle at sea during the Second World War in different ways, according to their nationality. But on one point there will be complete agreement: that the German Navy, in this twentieth century, the century of aircraft, was called upon to fight without an air arm and without aerial reconnaissance of its own is wholly incomprehensible." Undoubtedly it was, even though, from time to time, Doenitz still managed to scrape up some air support, usually behind Goering's broad back.

In the end, he had principal recourse to only one intelligence auxiliary to aid the U-boat Arm. It was the so-called *B-Dienst* (B-Service), the Naval High Command's fabulously efficient cryptographic service. Those busy bees of the B-Service monitored the Allies' radio traffic, broke codes and ciphers, intruding upon many of the secrets the Allies thought were safe and sound. It is not too much to say that, insofar as his vexing intelligence problem was concerned, the B-Service saved the day for Doenitz.

Between 1939 and 1943, the B-Service succeeded again and again in breaking the British cipher and translating most of the signals concerning convoy sailings. The U-boat Command thus received, not only routing instructions signalled to the convoys, but also the Admiralty's super-secret periodic "U-boat Situation Reports" which gave the known or presumed distribution of U-boats in the different areas. The possession of those situation reports enabled Doenitz to change his dispositions and withdraw his U-boats from locations apparently known to the enemy. As Doenitz acknowledged it, "These 'Situation Reports' were of the greatest value to us in our efforts to determine how the enemy was able to find out about our U-boat dispositions and with what degree of accuracy he did so."

Yet even with the information supplied by the B-Service at his fingertips, Doenitz never had the quality and quantity of intelligence he needed. He had to fall back upon his own psychic resources—a built-in "intelligence service" of a rather supernatural character, and yet—as we shall see—not entirely useless in Doenitz's hands.

The Doenitz System in Action

He explained the system to Hitler on September 28, 1939, during one of the Fuehrer's rare visits to the U-boat Command. "Very great advances in inter-communications have been made in the U-boat arm," he said. "It is now possible to co-ordinate the movements of U-boats spread over the widest sea areas and to concentrate them as desired in accordance with any plan in a joint operation. This means that we now possess the ability to attack merchantmen massed in convoy with a concentration of U-boats. The convoy in question becomes the rallying point for all U-boats operating in the area."

Although Doenitz subsequently claimed that he had exercised tactical control only up to the launching of the attack and then left the individual commanders to their own resources during the actual attack, in practice he continued to muscle in, so to speak, on attacks in progress, literally exuding all sorts of suggestions and orders. In his innate impatience and his eager involvement in the Big Battle, he proved incapable of curbing himself on this score. He kept breathing down the necks of his commanders with both useful and useless signals, including some that proved detrimental to the operations. In his pent-up state, over-anxious to inflict the maximum damage on the foe, he demanded that the commanders radio him at once all the successes they scored, as well as estimates of their failures. He thus filled the air with endless chit-chat in crass violation of a basic tenet of sea warfare: radio silence during an operation is a sacrosanct obligation and a primary measure of precaution.

The Operations Room at Doenitz' headquarters came to resemble the radio booth at Yankee Stadium during the World Series. Excitement was at fever pitch as the boss sweated out an operation, receiving his reports and broadcasting his commentary. Doenitz gave a graphic description of the system when he wrote, "If, as sometimes occured, my 'on-the-spot picture' seemed to be insufficiently clear, I used to ask by radio for further information, and as a rule I received an answer within half an hour. Whenever I was called upon to make some special decision, which depended upon precise knowledge of any particular given circumstances, I used to speak personally in code language to one of the commanders whom I had previously informed by radio of the precise time at which I would call him."

How the Doenitz system operated in action was illustrated by a chain of victories which began early in September, 1940, when the faithful B-Service sent an intercept to U-boat Command. It was the decoded transcript of routing instructions to a homeward-bound British convoy still in the Western Atlantic, sailing slowly toward rendezvous with its escort in mid-Atlantic.

Doenitz consulted the big chart on the wall of the Operations Room that plotted the location of every U-boat he had at sea, and he found that four of his boats were in the crucial area around longitude 19° 15′ W. He directed one of them, the nearest to the convoy, to establish contact. As soon as the picket boat signalled that the convoy had been spotted, Doenitz ordered the other boats to form themselves into a *Rudel*, then guided them to their trapped target. The pack, which included one of his top aces, Kapitaenleutnant Guenther Prien in *U-47*, took five ships out of the convoy under their admiral's personal command.

The engagement over, Doenitz instructed Prien to stay in the area and radio weather reports twice a day to him at Lorient. By then, *U-47* was down to her last torpedo, a matter of considerable chagrin to Prien when another homeward-bound convey of fifteen fully-laden Allied ships sailed straight into his area. He immediately signalled the information to headquarters, then kept contact with the convoy while Doenitz rounded up five nearby boats for a *Rudel*. Relaying Prien's intelligence to each boat, he led them to the convoy. The issue was joined in the night of September 21-22, and eleven of the fifteen ships were sunk.

Although Doenitz still had some mild apprehension about the safety of his radio game, the lethal double punch he had directed blow by blow reassured him. He noted with satisfaction that the convoy had run into Prien's arms "in spite of the fact that the British must have been receiving the weather signals which he was making twice daily, and therefore should have been able to locate him." The *Rudeltaktik*, too, was working to his satisfaction. Late at night on September 22, after his boats had radioed in the score, he wrote in his War Diary: "The engagement of the last few days shows that the principles enunciated in peace time both with regard to the use of radio in the proximity of the enemy and with regard to U-boat training for offensive action against convoys were correct."

Thanks to the "method," he then scored additional victories in October. A small handful of his boats in the Atlantic managed to sink sixty-three ships, losing but one of their own, the *U-32* of Kapitaen-leutnant Hans Jenisch, one that was not involved in any of the *Rudel* operations.

His second series of victories began in the night of October 16-17, when Doenitz was raised with a signal from the area northest of Rockall Bank; Kapitaenleutnant Bleichrodt in *U-48* was reporting contact with a convoy. From intercepts he had received from the B-Service, Doenitz knew it was SC7, a fully-laden convoy bound for Liverpool from Nova Scotia.

The big chart on the wall showed that five of his boats were in the area where Bleichrodt had spotted the convoy. It was an especially formidable force. It included four of his top aces—Endrass in *U-46*, Schepke in *U-100*, Frauenheim in *U-101*, and the incomparable, imperturbable Otto Kretschmer in *U-99*. Even Kapitaenleutnant Moehle, who commanded *U-123*, the fifth member of the hastily-improvised *Rudel*, was one of his better commanders.

Doenitz as usual assumed tactical command promptly; his favorite stance made the Operations Room hum with action and excitement and enabled his staff to participate vicariously in faraway operations at sea. But just when he was alerting the boats one by one and forming them into a *Rudel*, a signal from *U-48* dampened his enthusiasm. Bleichrodt reported he had been spotted by the escorts of the convoy and had been heavily attacked with depth charges. Although *U-48* had suffered no damage, he had lost contact with the convoy. Now it became Doenitz's job, hundreds of miles from the spot, to find the convoy. He ordered the *Rudel* to form into a line abreast at right angles to what he presumed—or, thanks to the ever-helpful B-Service, had reason to believe—was the prescribed course of the convoy.

"Make sure," he radioed his commanders, "that you will be well in advance of the convoy and so placed that it will be daylight by the time it reaches you, presumably in the morning of October 18." Then he could sit back and, like a chess player who had made his move, wait for the move of his opponent. It came in the afternoon of the day he expected. A signal from *U-48* told him that contact had been re-established with the convoy at the exact spot where Doenitz had assumed it would sail into the U-boat line. The boats took up their pre-arranged positions in the ambuscade, then waited for night to fall. That night, in a series of surface attacks, they sank seventeen ships.

The morning after, a signal from Prien in *U-47* returned Doenitz to the Operations Room and to tactical command over yet another *Rudel*. *U-47* had made contact with convoy HX79, homeward bound from Halifax. Endrass, Schepke, and Bleichrodt were still in the area. Doenitz alerted *U-38* of Kapitaenleutnant Liebe and *U-28* of Kapitaenleutnant Kuhnke to join them in yet another *Rudel*. Kuhnke could not make it, but the other boats proved adequate to sink fourteen ships of the convoy before October 20 dawned. They then picked up HX79A, outward bound for Halifax, and added seven of its ships to the loot. In just three days, while gales swept the ocean with a force of eight and intermittent rain squalls darkened the starless autumn night around Rockall Bank, eight U-boats thus sank thirty-eight ships in three different convoys without losing a single boat.

It was a strange way of conducting battles and waging a war, and as we shall see, it was not destined to guarantee victory forever, certainly not the *decisive* victory Doenitz had promised Hitler. But he insists to this very day that it was a brilliant and safe system, both efficient and productive—the only way to conduct submarine campaigns and to win wars.

The U-Boat Becomes a Menace

Thus, almost from its outset, the whole U-boat campaign became a gigantic operation inexorably tied to a single indispensable man—Karl Doenitz. He acted like a master puppeteer who handled his different performing dolls all by himself in a show of dazzling diversification. In this operative arrangement, the individual U-boat commander was, for all his technical skill and personal daring, merely a cat's paw.

Out on the high seas, Doenitz' new doctrine was working perfectly in practice. At no time between September, 1939, and December, 1941, in any single monthly period, did he have more than a maximum of thirty-eight U-boats at sea; and sometimes he was able to send fewer than a bare dozen of them on *Feindfahrt* against the vast Allied tonnage moving ponderously across the Atlantic. Yet their effectiveness was dramatically evident in the number of ships they managed to sink.

Thus in December, 1939, for example, when Doenitz was down to only eight U-boats at sea, his submarines sank thirty-eight ships. They scored a record of sixty-three sinkings in October, 1940, when he had only twelve operational subs out. In a twenty-seven month period of the Battle of the Atlantic, Doenitz directed the sinking of 973 Allied ships—from the battleship *Royal Oak* and the aircraft carrier *Courageous* down to tiny trawlers—a monthly average of thirty-six ships destroyed by a corresponding monthly average of fourteen U-boats at sea.

This frightening demonstration of the submarine's effectiveness was not solely the result of the Doeniz doctrine, nor of his skill. Several historic factors not directly connected with the war at sea combined to enhance the efficiency of his campaign.

At first Doenitz's boats, because they were based in the Baltic Sea, had to inch their way into the Atlantic Ocean through perilous passages, passing necessarily through the North Sea, no matter whether they sailed slowly through the Kiel Canal or whether they sailed around Denmark through the Kattegat and Skagerrak. Then all this changed abruptly.

In the spring of 1940, the conquest of Norway gave Doenitz bases with direct access to the Atlantic, and the fall of France established him all along the wide-open Bay of Biscay. As soon as France fell, he moved the U-boat Command to Lorient and built formidable and, as it turned out, impregnable pens of reinforced concrete to shield his U-boats from air attack.

The dismal collapse of France also brought him unexpected advantages, mainly through the treachery of Admiral Darlan, commander in chief of the French Fleet, whose blind hatred of the British made him an eager informer on his recent allies. In a series of hush-hush meetings with high-ranking German naval officers—including an elaborate conference at Evvy-le-Bourg with Grand Admiral Raeder on January 28, 1942—Darlan supplied exactly the kind of information Doenitz needed to make his campaign more effective.

Darlan delivered to the Germans a number of asdics the British had entrusted to his care and urged Raeder to raid Portland where the asdic was developed and assembled. He also handed over a top secret French gear called *Metox*, a search receiver that warned against detection devices. He outlined in detail all he knew about British doctrines and methods used against the U-boats and went so far as to warn Raeder against Doenitz's spirited use of the radio for the conduct of his tactical command. He actually revealed that the British had developed a high frequency direction finder that spotted the U-boats by the simple process of tuning in on Doenitz's conversations.

Victories by Default

To a considerable extent, the U-boats' initial success resulted from the astounding failure of the British to see the handwriting on the wall. "The British Navy between the wars," Doenitz conceded, "really had lost sight of the U-boat menace and had underestimated its importance." A better witness on this score was Captain Stephen Roskill of the Royal Navy, official British historian of the Battle of the Atlantic. "The reader will naturally ask," Roskill wrote, "why the employment by the enemy of such tactics was not foreseen, and why we had concentrated our energies and attention on dealing with attacks by submerged U-boats only. When British naval training and thinking in the years between the wars are reviewed, it seems that both were concentrated on the conduct of surface ships in action with similar enemy units and that the defense was also considered chiefly from the point of view of attack by enemy surface units."

On the very eve of the war, in August, 1939, Admiral Sir Dudley Pound, the First Sea Lord, warned his colleagues on the Chief of Staff Committee against German surface raiders and described them as the major threat to British shipping, but Pound glossed over the threat from U-boats.

Even Winston Churchill, who was a Cassandra in almost all other matters, had not regarded the U-boat as a menace. "I had accepted too readily when out of office," he later wrote, "the Admiralty view of the extent to which the submarine had been mastered." His prewar opinion, duly recorded in one of his articles, was that "the submarine should be quite controllable in the outer seas and certainly in the Mediterranean. There will be losses, but nothing to affect the scale of events." When shortly afterwards he was back at his old job in the Admiralty, the man responsible to King and country for the war at sea, he could still not perceive anything in the initial U-boat offensive to warrant alarm. On September 26, 1939, when addressing the House of Commons for the first time as First Lord, he had what he called a good tale to tell: "In the first week our losses by U-boat sinkings amounted to 65,000 tons; in the second week they were 46,000 tons; and in the third week they were 21,000 tons. In the last six days we have lost only 9,000 tons. One must not dwell upon these reassuring figures too much, for war is full of unpleasant surprises. But certainly I am entitled to say that so far as they go these figures need not cause any undue despondency or alarm."

Although he sought to avoid all optimistic forecasts, he nevertheless treated Commons to an unduly cheerful picture of the situation. "Even taking six or seven U-boats sunk as a safe figure," he said, when actually only two of them had been sunk, "that is one-tenth of the total enemy submarine fleet as it existed at the declaration of war destroyed during the first fortnight of the war, and it is probably one quarter or perhaps even one third of all the U-boats which are being employed actively. But the British attack upon the U-boats is only just beginning. Our hunting force is getting stronger every day."

It may be useful to re-examine such examples of overconfidence and ignorance, for today preparations for the novel exigencies of the next war are again anchored to lessons left from the last one, to weapons that proved effective in the past, and to installations developed on the basis of bygone experiences. Even for what we call retaliation, we place much faith in conventional airpower, which in a showdown might prove as outdated as the blunderbuss.

Therein lies the lasting significance of Karl Doenitz, the man who almost single-handedly had turned up the ocean, for he had staged a persuasive demonstration of the overwhelming threat inherent in the submarine and of its destructive power in a furtive campaign. Since man is notoriously deficient in envisioning what lies immediately beyond his perceptions, the distant events of the war at sea—and especially so minuscule an event as the brief encounter of a ship with an enemy sub—fail to impress and stimulate us to appropriate action. In spite of all the evidence now on hand, the stupendous part the submarine played in World War II—its contribution to Germany's ability to stay in the war as long as she did and to Japan's inability to avert disaster—is still not recognized.

CHAPTER IV

Downbeat on the Kettle Drum

Karl Doenitz was like Samuel Johnson's Mr. Piozzo—a very good hater. In 1941, he hated the United States the most. It was different from his aversion to England. His anglophobia stemmed from bitter personal memories and professional envy—it was jealousy rather than rancor. But he detested the United States and his hatred grew into contemptuous, virulent malevolence as the war wore on. Roosevelt's America was *bête noire* to every U-boat man. The President was regarded as a cowardly meddler who, behind his bogus neutrality, made everything so much more complicated in that damned Atlantic by supporting Britain.

Undeclared War

Doenitz, a practical man of few illusions, had not persuaded himself, as had his superiors, Hitler and Raeder, that the United States would stay out of the war indefinitely. Hitler in particular was deluded on this score; he had given strict and explicit orders in September, 1939, to avoid all "incidents" that would bring America into the shooting war. He remained adamant on this policy even when the United States moved boldly to aid Britain with overt action. To be sure, much aid was proscribed by America's neutrality laws and by public opinion, which was still leaning toward isolationism; but Franklin D. Roosevelt made no secret of the fact that he did not consider himself neutral at all. As a result, the jokers were wild in the Atlantic—as the President once put it—the "jokers" being all sorts of trump cards sneaked into the Atlantic pack to stack it against the Germans, in a game involving few, if any, risks to the United States.

42

To the land-minded Hitler, this American intervention—ranging from the exchange of fifty U. S. destroyers for a string of bases in the West Indies to naval co-operation with the British in a desperate effort to keep the Atlantic lifeline open—did not seem so brazen and serious as it appeared to Doenitz. But to Doenitz, the increasingly elaborate maneuvers of the United States represented a one-sided undeclared war in which Roosevelt's America was allowed to strike at will but the U-boat Command was not permitted to hit back.

Roosevelt's all-out intervention in the Atlantic was induced by a paper drafted by Admiral Harold R. Stark on April 4, 1941, in which he described the Atlantic situation as "hopeless except as we take strong measures to save it." The U-boats lent weight to Admiral Stark's warning by sinking nearly 600,000 tons of shipping in April. That month the recommended strong measures followed rapid-fire, one by one, and resulted in innumerable incidents in the Atlantic which Doenitz came to regard as personal affronts.

In May, a German surface raider at large in the South Atlantic sank an Egyptian liner that happened to have 150 American passengers aboard; and a U-boat in the same general area torpedoed the U. S. merchantman *Robin Moor*, bound for South Africa with general cargo. In June, Kapitaenleutnant Hermann Kottmann in *U-203* sighted the U. S. battleship *Texas* in waters Washington had closed to American ships. Assuming that the battleship had been transferred to Britain in a deal similar to the destroyer swap, Kottmann mounted a furtive attack. The attack failed. In actual fact, the *Texas* was very much part of the U. S. Atlantic Fleet; until a few weeks before, she had been its flagship. Her presence in the presumably forbidden zone was one of those "jokers." Since Hitler had prohibited any overt incident involving the United States, the appearance of the *Texas* in the blockade zone forced Doenitz to order an immediate cessation of night attacks for fear of attacking an American vessel.

August was relatively quiet, but in September the tense situation came to a head. At 8:40 A.M. on September 5, the U. S. destroyer *Greer* —bound for Iceland with mail and supplies—was warned by a British aircraft that a "U-boat had been located submerged ten sea miles further to the west on the destroyer's course." It was the *U-652* of Oberleutnant Georg-Werner Fraatz. Thanks to the brilliant handling of the destroyer by her skipper, Lieutenant Commander L. H. Frost (who had received his command barely a month before), the *Greer's* sonar promptly established contact with the *U-Fraatz* and then, for several hours, "reported the submarine's position, course, and speed to all ships and planes within radio range," pinning down the U-boat for some Briton to come and finish it off.

By 12:40 P.M., Fraatz had had enough of the pinging. He turned his boat and headed straight for the *Greer*, trying to torpedo her, but the "fish" missed by about a hundred yards. The *Greer* responded with a pattern of eight depth charges. However, they failed to hit their target, as did Fraatz's second torpedo, which missed the *Greer* by three hundred yards.

The *Greer* continued the search until 6:40 P.M. when a signal from Iceland, giving the benefit of the doubt to the U-boat, ordered *Frost* to break off.

The propriety of *Frost's* dogged pursuit was, at the very least, open to doubt. "In view of the fact," wrote Langer and Gleason, the Harvard historians, in *The Undeclared War*, "that the Greer had found the U-boat, had followed it for hours and had passed on information to British aircraft to help them attack it, it would have been surprising if the envisaged victim had not in the end turned on its tormentor."

Proper or not, the *Greer* incident marked America's *de facto* entry into the shooting war. It was followed by other similar actions—by the *U.S.S. Truxton* coming up against another U-boat in the same hot area, pinning her down with sonar, then dropping depth charges; by the torpedo-sinking of the *U.S.S. Kearny;* and the subsequent loss of *U.S.S. Reuben James*—proofs positive that this was war in everything but name.

Doenitz Prods Hitler

The *Greer* incident sent Doenitz to Hitler with his woes. On September 17, he called on the Fuehrer to discuss, as he put it, "the rapidly deteriorating situation in the Atlantic."

His relations with Hitler were always formal and, at this stage, remote and spotty. Unfortunately for his admirals, the Fuehrer neither knew much about the war at sea nor was he overly interested in it. His preparation for supreme command was in the infantry and he retained a rather low terrestrial view of war. He would at any time much rather discuss shoes and sealing wax, cabbages and kings, than ships or the boiling sea.

This meeting on September 17 was their fifth. Doenitz wanted Hitler's approval for more stringent measures against "Roosevelt's piracy" and to obtain permission to deploy *immediately* a flotilla of U-boats close to the American coast to be ready when (not if) the war broke out. "I would like to have my forces in position," he told Hitler, "before war is declared. Only this way could full advantage be taken of the element of surprise to strike a real blow in waters in which anti-submarine defenses are still weak."

The prophetic streak in Doenitz was holding up, but Hitler said no. Instead the Fuehrer ordered Doenitz to divide up his boats mainly between the Mediterranean (where he wanted them to cut the British supply line to the army fighting Rommel's *Afrika Korps* in North Africa) and Norway (where he expected a British landing momentarily).

War—at Last

Early in December, Captain Godt, the slight, sad-eyed dapper chief of staff of the U-boat Command, made a trip to Berlin where he picked up gossip at the Naval High Command. He returned to Kernevel on December 6, and told Doenitz that Hitler was more adamant than ever about keeping the United States out of the war. He seemed to be right, too, because American interference appeared to be dwindling as the last fall storms slowed the Atlantic Battle almost to a standstill.

"We must not do anything," Godt told Doenitz, "that might aggravate the tension between Germany and the United States."

Five days later, the two countries were at war!

Forty-eight hours after the Japanese attack on Pearl Harbor, Doenitz was summoned to Berlin and told that Hitler had made up his mind to go to war against the United States after all. A declaration of war was scheduled for December 11. In the meantime, the lid was off. Doenitz could do as he pleased anywhere in the Atlantic, including the so-called Pan-American Security Zone which Roosevelt had declared out of bounds for U-boats.

"There is nothing I can do," Doenitz shot back, "because I don't have a single U-boat even near those American waters."

On this momentous eve, he had almost two hundred-fifty U-boats, but only ninety-one of them were operational, and thirty-three of the latter were laid up in dockyards undergoing repairs. Twenty-six of his boats were in the Mediterranean on Hitler's orders; six stood in the Atlantic between the Strait of Gibraltar and the Azores; and four were in Norway. Only twenty-two of his boats were actually at sea and half of those were in transit, either sailing to their prospective operational areas or returning home from *Feindfahrts*.

A lightning onslaught on America, no matter how he craved it, was out of the question. He needed time to organize the assault.

On December 11, the day war was declared, Doenitz was in Berlin again, lobbying to get the boats he desperately needed to use against the United States. He was uncharacteristically modest, asking for only about a dozen boats from the "goddam Gibraltar mousetrap," as he called it, and from the Mediterranean, where he thought his U-boats could no longer perform any useful service.

He went from office to office in the Naval High Command and even buttonholed whoever he could find from the Fuehrer's headquarters. He thus saw Grand Admiral Raeder and also Captain von Puttkammer, the Fuehrer's naval aide, Admiral Schniewind, Raeder's chief of staff, and General Alfred Jodl who, he thought, could influence Hitler.

But he was told he could not have those twelve boats; he could not take any from the Mediterranean flotilla; he could not withdraw any from the "Gibraltar mousetrap." Jodl just shrugged: "The Fuehrer's orders!"

"See what you can do," Schniewind told him, "without them—but hurry up! The Fuehrer demands action!"

From dockyards, from among the returning boats, from boats refitting at the bases, Doenitz managed to scrape up six for the trip to America, then had to scratch one because of trouble with her Diesels. So it was to be—five U-boats against America!

Just before Christmas, the *U-123* of Kapitaenleutnant Reinhard Hardegen sneaked out of Lorient bound for New York and Cape Hatteras by way of Newfoundland. He was followed by the *U-66* of Kapitaenleutnant Zapp, the *U-130* of Kapitaenleutnant Kals, the *U-106* of Kapitaenleutnant Rasch, and the *U-103* of Kapitaenleutnant Winter.

Their mission was cloaked in ironclad secrecy behind the code name *Paukenschlag*—"Downbeat on the Kettle Drum."

The Hardegen Operation

Buffeted by heavy seas, ignoring occasional targets he encountered on the voyage, Kapitaenleutnant Hardegen in *U-123* was proceeding steadily on his alloted course. He made the Atlantic crossing almost in a straight line, from Lorient to just southwest of Cape Race, Newfoundland.

This trip to America was unexpected, a kind of bonus Hardegen received for the dash and vim he had displayed in lesser assignments. Nobody in the U-boat arm could curse and ridicule the United States better than "Reini," so nobody was surprised when, the October before, Korvetten-Kapitaen Victor Schuetze, his flotilla commander, told Hardegen in confidence, "You'll get command of the first boat against America as soon as we get the green light." Even then, war with the United States still seemed frustratingly remote. So Hardegen took time out to get married; he was in Italy on his honeymoon the day war was declared. He left his new bride to finish the honeymoon alone and rushed back to Lorient to claim the command Schuetze had promised him. Although Hardegen was new to his command, U-123 was a seasoned veteran of the Atlantic Battle. She had been a member of the *Rudel* that sank seventeen ships out of a convoy in an all-night battle around Rockall Bank. Hand-picked by Doenitz for the American offensive, Hardegen inherited his boat from Kapitaenleutnant Moehle when it already boasted a record of 100,000 tons in sunken enemy ships. The night before his departure, Hardegen dined in style on oysters at Mme. Melainie's, a favorite hangout of the young U-boat crowd. His tongue loosened by wine, he spoke confidently of doubling Moehle's record on a single *Feindfahrt* against America.

Hardegen had received his orders personally from Doenitz. He was to begin operations off New York—as close to the city as possible—then work his way south to Cape Hatteras where Doenitz had ample reasons to believe targets were plentiful, most of them sitting ducks. His instructions were complete and explicit, except for one detail. D-Day was to be signalled to him at sea. Until then, even when in position to attack, he was to do nothing.

The eagerly awaited signal to begin was picked up on January 7. "Commence *Paukenschlag*," it read, "on January 13." That was almost a week away. A boisterous young submariner, Reinhard Hardegen found it hard to endure the enforced idleness. He became especially restive when he found, from a number of unmistakable signs, that he was sailing into a fairyland of sleeping beauties. A month after the outbreak of the war, America's coastwise radio traffic was as unmuted as the lights of the coastal cities were undimmed. Weather reports continued to be broadcast at the usual regular intervals. Although he was close to American waters, Hardegen did not see a single plane or a stray patrol craft. "Don't these people realize," he asked his gunnery officer, "that they're at war?"

Shortly after dusk on January 11, exactly a month after Hitler's declaration of war but still a couple of days from his own target date, Hardegen was just north of longitude 40°, about 160 miles south of Nova Scotia, when his lookouts reported thin smoke on the horizon. The ship turned out to be the *Cyclops*, a British freighter bound for New York carrying Chinese crews for several ships in United States ports.

It was a quaint case of history repeating itself, for *Cyclops* was also the name of the British ship Doenitz had sunk in his first command as a submariner some twenty-four years before. Now it was seven o'clock in the evening of January 11, and the itch in Hardegen's trigger finger was becoming unbearable. He had strict orders to pass up anything under 10,000 tons but the *Cyclops* was up to those standards. As far as his target date was concerned—oh, well, he thought, it was just a couple of days away. "What would the admiral do," he mused, "in my shoes?" Then he gave himself the answer: "He would attack!"

At 7:40 P.M. the *U-123* reached attack position and Hardegen let go with the first torpedo of Doenitz's offensive against the United States. The *Cyclops* was hit in the engine room. She went down within twenty minutes with the loss of eighty-seven lives. Hardegen had bagged his first 10,000 tons toward the 100,000 he hoped to chalk up on this trip. But there was more to it, too. *The American phase of the battle of the Atlantic was inexorably on!*

In the next fifteen months, the United States was to suffer a defeat compared with which Pearl Harbor was but a slap on the wrist. For truly this was a *Paukenschlag* destined to be heard all around the world.

Part Two

THE BATTLE AT THE WATER'S EDGE

. . . *let no one imagine that America will escape, that America may expect mercy, that this Western Hemisphere will not be attacked.*

FRANKLIN DELANO ROOSEVELT
speaking in Chicago
October, 1937.

CHAPTER V

Pearl Harbor of the East

"The years 1945-56 must have been a great strain on your nerves, but 1942, when you conducted your astonishing U-boat war against me in the Caribbean, was, for me, an equally nerve-shattering period."
From a letter in 1957 to Admiral Doenitz by Admiral John H. Hoover, USN (Ret), upon the former's release from the inter-Allied prison of major war criminals at Spandau.

At Pearl Harbor, the Pacific Fleet of the United States was a splintered shambles and 2,403 Americans were dead. Bloodied by this bludgeoning, but not yet knowing what had hit them, the American people went to war somewhat like O. Henry's marooned octopus: they managed to preserve their decency and dignity, but inside they were "impromptu and full of unexpectedness." The situation was somehow symbolized by a detachment of Coast Artillery in Los Angeles that jumped to war footing at once, but had to raid the prop department of Paramount Pictures to get the weapons it desperately needed.

Note: The title of this chapter is not meant to infer that the Germans attacked the United States in the Japanese manner, without warning. On the contrary, Germany had observed all the formalities of international protocol and accepted the onus of such initiative by declaring war formally in a note handed to the U.S. *Chargé d'affaires* in Berlin, on December 11, 1941. While Pearl Harbor has been subjected to searching inquests, the far worse disaster that befell America's Atlantic frontiers has escaped scrutiny. It is late to revive the issue of negligence, but it may still be useful—during this period of a comparable threat—to review the facts behind the disaster.

The mood in America was mixed of bewilderment and escapism, and both were fed by the initiated few in Washington who did not quite know whether or how to take the people into their confidence. The opaque gloom of those days was broken occasionally by cheering announcements—like the one claiming the sinking of a Japanese battleship in Philippine waters—in which truth, as usual, proved to be the first casualty of war.

Good news in another form came from Oakland, California, where Captain Will Vartnow, the skipper of the garbage disposal scow *Tahoe*, claimed he had rammed an enemy submarine on one of his dumping trips. Vartnow sent a bill to Uncle Sam asking for $2,000 for damages which he said his flat-bottomed lighter had sustained in the brief encounter.

On December 20 in Washington, D.C., Secretary of the Navy Frank Knox bested Vartnow's claim by announcing that "United States naval forces in the Atlantic had probably sunk or damaged at least fourteen enemy submarines." Even while Colonel Knox was broadcasting these glad, and totally false, tidings, Admiral Ernest J. King, new commander in chief of the Fleet, was pondering an urgent dispatch from his friend and classmate, Vice Admiral Adolphus Andrews, in whose domain those "victories" supposedly took place.

"Should enemy submarines operate off this coast," Andrews wrote from the eastern seaboard, "this command has no force available to take adequate action against them, either offensively or defensively."

Andrews' Lonely Outpost

Admiral Andrews had reason to be apprehensive. Those five eager U-boats of Admiral Doenitz's *Paukenschlag* were sailing directly against him. As commander of the North Atlantic Naval Coastal Frontier (soon to be renamed the Eastern Sea Frontier), he was responsible for the defense of the east coast from the St. Lawrence River down to North Carolina, approximately 28,000 square miles of ocean waters.

As far as appearance went, "Dolly" Andrews did not seem to be the ideal man for what so suddenly became a fighting command. In a sense Andrews' assignment symbolized the second thoughts of the Navy and the inferior attention the Atlantic occupied in the collective mind of the naval high command.

Long mesmerized by the problems posed in the Pacific by the growing and boisterous, but badly underrated, Japanese Navy, and delighted by the quasi-feudal amenities and sunny, starched-white pageantry of service in Hawaii and other such charming Asian stations, the big brass of the U.S. Navy became so preoccupied with and devoted to the mysterious East that they had little liking for the usually humdrum duty in the occidental ocean, even when the U-boats made it hot. Many regarded command in the Atlantic as distinctly derogatory, and Washington gave those jobs mostly to second-drawer flag officers, or to men who rated but a last fling in command before retirement, or indeed to the "misfits" who deserved nothing better.

Throughout the war, the various Atlantic commands produced plodding and well-intentioned, even competent flag officers, like Ingersoll, Hoover, and Kauffman, but no truly brilliant captains of the sea in the heroic mould of a Halsey, a Spruance, or a Kinkaid. This was due partly to the nature of the job and partly to the nature of the men holding down those command positions.

As far as Admiral Andrews was concerned, the war had caught the sixty-one year old Texan at the far end of a long career, a distinguished career, to be sure, but mainly for its shore assignments, many of them in highly-polished drawing rooms. Pompous and overbearing in manner and speech, he had specialized in Presidents from the days in 1903, when he served on the *Dolphin*, Teddy Roosevelt's Presidential yacht. Later he commanded the *Mayflower*, the Presidential yacht of the Harding administration, then moved into the White House as President Coolidge's naval aide.

He had an inauspicious start in his present command when the big French liner *Normandie* burned at her pier in New York while being refitted for service as a troop transport. Only his friendship with Franklin D. Roosevelt, dating back to World War I, saved Andrews from being singled out as the scapegoat for the disaster.

But he fooled his critics. He had long been bracing himself for just such an emergency and had no illusions about it. For months before Pearl Harbor, while his country was flirting with war in the Atlantic, Andrews pleaded with Washington to send him the ships and men he needed desperately to protect his sea frontier. Again and again he was told they were needed elsewhere and none could be spared for him. Andrews, who saw clearly the shape of things to come, grew caustic in the face of Washington's do-nothing attitude. Once, upon his empty-handed return from a pleading mission to Washington in June, 1941, he spoke to Captain John T. G. Stapler, his operations officer, bitterly about "the futility of a national defense policy that always finds us weak instead of strong when war starts." He also told Stapler:

"Our defenses should have been maintained in an orderly manner year by year, but remained neglected until past the time when needed."

It was fortunate that the Japanese had played it so close to their chest and mounted their attack without taking their German allies into their confidence, thus precluding a co-ordinated east-west punch against the United States. The war now found the Navy in particular even more unprepared in the east than in the west. The nerve center of this country's crucial eastern coastal defense—of the sea lanes leading to and from Boston, New York, Baltimore and Norfolk—was in downtown Manhattan, on the fifteenth floor of the Federal Building on Church Street, where Andrews had his headquarters. On that fateful Sunday of Pearl Harbor the office was virtually deserted. Andrews, his chief of staff, and his intelligence officer, Captain Roscoe McFall, heard the news on their radios at home, donned uniforms and rushed to the office, then had to put their yeomen on the phone calling the staff to report for duty until a grand total of seven officers could be assembled to start operations.

Since no master plan had ever come from Washington, and no blueprint existed to cope with the possibility of a U-boat assault, Andrews had to develop his own war plans as best he could. He divided his vast region of responsibility into several anti-submarine patrol areas, and also tried to establish liaison with the Army Air Force for air-sea co-ordination. But plans alone, no matter how elaborate or good they were, could not do the trick in the absence of ships and men. Andrews had a total of twelve surface vessels—four yard patrol boats, four subchasers, one Coast Guard cutter, and three *Eagle* boats of World War I vintage. He had one hundred and three aircraft, to be sure, but only five of them in combat-ready condition. On December 22, in another report to Washington, Andrews described this force as "woefully inadequate," even for limited action against the U-boats. There was, as he put it, "not a vessel available that an enemy submarine could not outdistance when operating on the surface," adding that "in most cases the guns of these vessels would be outranged by those of the submarine." On the morning after the commencement of *Paukenschlag*, Andrews told COMINCH in Washington that he had "no effective planes attached to the Frontier . . . capable of maintaining long-range seaward patrols." In answer to his urgent pleas for destroyers, escort vessels and at least one squadron of patrol planes, Washington told him that "any additional allocations depended on future production."

Nothing had happened yet along his sea frontier, but Andrews was getting a pretty good notion of things to come from dispatches pouring in from Vice Admiral John Wills Greenslade, his opposite number on the Pacific coast. Japanese submarines were active alarmingly close to shore, bringing the war virtually to the mainland. On December 18, one of them shelled the schooner *Samoa* and the tanker *Agwiwood*; on the twentieth, another Japanese sub sank the tanker *Emidio*; then the tanker *Montebello* was sunk, as was the freighter *Absaroka*. Others, like the *Larry Deheny*, the *Dorothy Phillips* and the *Idaho*, were shelled —some of them but a few miles off shore.

Then Andrews received word that *his* enemy subs were also on the way. Allied agents covering the German submarine bases in the Bay of Biscay had reported to London the departure of the *Paukenschlag* group. British Intelligence promptly alerted Washington and Andrews was warned in an ominous signal. "Suspected westward movement of enemy submarines now confirmed," it read, "but there appear to be more operating than at first believed. Probably several in waters in vicinity of Newfoundland." Next day came another signal aggravating Andrews' worries by exaggerating the number of U-boats he could expect. "Strong indications," the signal read, "that sixteen German submarines are proceeding to area off southeast coast of Newfoundland."

There was little Andrews could do except to mark the presumed advance of these U-boats on a huge plotting board on the wall of his L-shaped operations center and then wait to see what they had in store for him.

"Well, they are here!"

For what it was worth Kapitaenleutnant Hardegen's brash violation of *Paukenschlag's* target date did supply the tip-off that Doenitz feared would alert the American defenses. Captain Leslie Kerslie of the *Cyclops* managed to put a frantic SOS on the air after the first hit, giving his location and stating explicitly that it was a torpedo from a submarine that had hit him. Andrews was handed a transcript of Kerslie's signal on the morning of January 12, and did what he could to prepare a reception for the U-boats now indubitably approaching. He alerted the First Bomber Command, signalled a hopeful *Condition Red* to his own meager forces afloat, and then ordered the Coast Guard cutter *Duane* to proceed to the spot where the *Cyclops* had gone down. By then *U-123* was gone. All the *Duane* found was the Canadian minesweeper *Red Deer*, picking up survivors.

January 13 came and went. Though *Paukenschlag* was scheduled to begin on that day, nothing in Andrews' operations center indicated that the assault was actually on. In came intermittent reports about sightings and pick-ups on the few listening devices we had, but the random torpedoing of the *Cyclops* was not followed immediately by other sinkings. However, it was evident that the U-boat that bagged the *Cyclops* was moving southward. The pattern of the sighting reports indicated there were other subs in the area as well.

A few planes of Brigadier General Arnold N. Krogstad's First Bomber Command were out searching as best they could, against a home-made handicap. Just when Krogstad received the assignment to patrol Andrews' waters, Washington had stripped his command of its best tactical units for missions on the West Coast and overseas. To make up for the losses, Krogstad assembled everything he could from the old crates of the First Air Force, mostly two-engine types with green crews, and placed them at the disposal of the hard-pressed admiral. Krogstad likened this force of about a hundred motley aircraft to Marshal Joffre's legendary taxicab army which had saved Paris and turned the tide on the Marne in 1914. But Krogstad's planes could not even stem the tide.

Welcome though it was, the help did not amount to much. Krogstad could maintain his patrols only at the rate of six flights daily, two each from bases in Massachusetts, New York and Virginia, with a total of eighteen planes, three in each flight. The patrols operated only during daylight hours, and after darkness fell Andrews did not have a single craft out.

The admiral spent the whole of January 13 at his headquarters on Church Street, sifting the reports as they tumbled in, but finding nothing tangible in any of them to warrant even a search. He continued his vigil into the long winter night, waiting helplessly for the U-boats to show their hand. Shortly after midnight he joined the brass of his command for a coffee break, and Lieutenant Commander Harry H. Hess, his submarine tracking specialist, handed him a sheet torn from a teletype. It was an SOS from Captain Harold Hansen, Norwegian master of the Panamanian flag tanker *Norness*, reporting that she had hit a mine and was sinking. Hansen gave his location as latitude 40° 28′ N., longitude 70° 45′ W., and that gave Andrews a jolt. For one thing, he knew there wasn't a mine in those waters; for another, the spot was only sixty miles southeast of Montauk Point, the easternmost tip of Long Island, barely two hundred miles from the very room he was in.

"Well," Andrews said with almost a sigh of relief, "they are here." Then turning to Captain Stapler, he gave orders for his tiny armada to sail. The hunt that followed was enormous for those days. It comprised the destroyer *Elson*, the Coast Guard cutter *Argo*, a minesweeper, a few planes from the Salem Air Station in Massachusetts, and the Navy blimp K-3. They found the wreck, its bow projecting about forty feet into the air, then sighted a raft and a lifeboat with sixteen members of the tanker's crew. They worked over the area for hours, but could not find even a trace of the sub.

The *Norness* was Hardegen's second victim. He finished her off with three torpedoes as he was moving stolidly south on something resembling a sightseeing tour. "I always wanted to see New York," he wisecracked to his crew in *U-123*, "and now this is our opportunity." Amazed and emboldened by this absence of American defenses, he maneuvered his boat close to New York, sinking the British tanker *Coimbra* just twenty miles off Southhampton, Long Island. Then he turned south again to complete his mission with a brief sojourn around Cape Hatteras.

The Rampage of U-123

Hardegen's journey was typical of the first *Paukenschlag* group. At no point on the mission covering the whole length of Andrews' sea frontier was he molested by the pathetic American forces. He reached Hatteras on January 17, and bagged his first American victim, the Esso tanker *Allen Jackson*, within an hour and a half of his arrival, just as the tanker was raising Winter Quarter Lightship northeast of Diamond Shoals. He turned around and wasted one of his precious torpedoes on a little freighter, the *Norvana*, then took his boat down to spend the day idly on the bottom off Hatteras, confident that the next night would see the completion of his mission.

That night of January 18 to 19 was destined to be his busiest, for the weather was ideal and the sea was full of ships. His chances were unexpectedly enhanced by the astonishing fact that most of his targets sailed into view fully lighted.

Hardegen surfaced shortly after dark and cruised about at a leisurely pace, giving his men a brief respite in the fresh air. He sampled his prospective victims one by one until the pre-dawn hours. Then he began to strike—one, two, three—in rapid succession.

His first victim was the *City of Atlanta*, an old freighter that had seen better days as a passenger steamer on the regular New York-Savannah run. Without bothering to observe the *Atlanta's* final agony, Hardegen turned to survey a fantastic nocturnal scene. There were three ships moving slowly around the light buoy that marked the northeastern end of Wimble Shoal, and another group of five, all of them fully lighted, coming toward him in a single row. He had only two torpedoes left—two torpedoes for eight ships—so he decided to go after one of the ships that looked like a medium-sized tanker with his gun. After setting her on fire, he left her to burn out, explosions rending the cold air.

The *U-123* turned again, racing for what Hardegen reckoned was a fat 6,000 tonner, but he lost her before he was ready to fire. Engine trouble slowed him down, then stopped him altogether. He made the repairs with impunity; although his presence must have been known by then, there was still nothing to indicate that anybody was looking for him. Even as he was cruising at half speed with that patched-up engine, his radioman handed him a signal he had intercepted. It was from the tanker that he had shelled and left, but that apparently refused to die. The signal read in such explicit detail that it invited disaster, "Tanker *Malay*, on fire after being shelled. Fire under control. Am making for Norfolk."

"Have you looked her up?" Hardegen asked the radioman.

"Yes, *Herr Kaleu*," the man replied. "The book says the *Malay* is an 8,000-ton tanker."

"My God!" Hardegen exclaimed. "I didn't think she was that big! *Los!* We've got to get her!"

He brought the *U-123* around again; but even in turning in the crowded sea, he almost bumped into another ship literally poised for his next to last torpedo. The subsequent distress signal identified her as a Latvian freighter, presumably the *Ciltvaria*; when the radioman checked her in the book, he called excitedly to Hardegen:

"She's a 5,000-tonner, *Herr Kaleu*."

"Splendid," Hardegen shot back, for now he figured he had the 100,000 tons of his own he had come to get—and he still had one more torpedo for the *Malay*. It was five-thirty A.M. on January 19 when *U-123* fired her last torpedo into the crippled tanker. Without waiting to check the result, Kapitaenleutnant Reinhard Hardegen yelled out the command:

"Right full rudder! Set course for home!"

According to his reckoning, and there was nobody around to contradict him, the *U-123* had bagged over 100,000 tons—an exuberant exaggeration, for his exact score was eight ships, 53,360 tons. The *U-66* of Kapitaenleutnant Zapp got five ships of about 50,000 tons; Kals, in *U-130*, three tankers and one freighter, 30,748 tons. The toll taken by the other two totalled 60,000 tons.

The first *Paukenschlag* was over. In just ten days of action, it had scored twenty-five ships of about 200,000 tons; not a single U-boat was as much as shaken by a stray depth charge.

And this was only the beginning!

On February 6, 1942, Churchill sent an urgent note to Harry L. Hopkins in the White House. The message was really meant for Roosevelt, but Churchill felt it was more politic to send it to Hopkins for it was a pointed little note and the President could be somewhat touchy at times.

"It would be well to make sure," the Prime Minister wrote, "that the President's attention has been drawn to the very heavy sinkings by U-boats in the Western North Atlantic. Since January 12, confirmed losses are 158,208, and probable losses 83,740 and possible losses 17,363, a total of 259,311 tons."

The message drew no answer, probably because Hopkins could not work up any interest in the Atlantic battle, whose overwhelming significance for the war effort he could never fully comprehend. There was no real apprehension in the White House, not even when the situation that impelled Churchill's note continued unabated. On March 12, now sorely tried by disappointment and anxiety, Churchill sent another message, again to Hopkins, although it was clearly meant for Roosevelt.

A Warning Note

"I am most deeply concerned," he wrote, "at the immense sinkings of tankers west of the fortieth meridian and in the Caribbean Sea"— in other words, in waters for which the United States bore sole responsibility. He pointed out that in only two months, in those waters alone, some sixty tankers had been sunk or damaged, a staggering loss of some 600,000 dead-weight tons. "The situation is so serious," the Prime Minister wrote, "that drastic action of some kind is necessary."

Hopkins talked to the President, and on March 18, Roosevelt answered in a self-critical mood, saying candidly that "we might as well admit the difficult military side of the problems." He conceded that the United States was not doing too well along her own Atlantic sea frontiers. "My Navy," he wrote, "has been definitely slack in preparing for this submarine war off our coast." He singled out for blame naval officers who, he said, stubbornly refused to "think in terms of any vessel of less than two thousand tons," the kind of ship now urgently needed to combat the U-boats.

"I have begged, borrowed, and stolen," Roosevelt added, "every vessel of every description over eighty feet long"; and pointed out that he had organized a "separate command against the U-boats" under Vice Admiral Andrews.

Then, on March 19, Roosevelt discussed the matter with his admirals, and after that he was no longer so sure that responsibility for the disaster rested entirely with the United States Navy. In a brief and formal note that sounded like a reprimand, he now told Churchill, "Your interest in steps to be taken to combat the Atlantic submarine menace as indicated by your recent message to Mr. Hopkins on this subject impels me to request your particular consideration of heavy attacks on submarine bases and building and repair yards, thus checking submarine activities at their source and where submarines perforce congregate."

It was a testy little note in which Churchill detected annoyance and the strain on Roosevelt. It also hinted to him the thinking of Roosevelt's admirals about the whole U-boat situation. He rejected the contention in words that reflected both indignation and amazement. "It is surprising indeed," he noted, "that during two years of the advance of total war towards the American continent more provision had not been made against this deadly onslaught." He conceded that the war in the Pacific had pressed heavily on the United States Navy, but added: "Still, with all information they had about the protective measures we had adopted, both before and during the struggle, it is remarkable that no plans had been made for coastal convoys and for multiplying small craft."

As he followed events in this distant sea teeming with defenseless American and Allied shipping, including precious tankers moving to and from the oil ports of Venezuela and Mexico; and as he watched the American defense system developing slowly, "with painful, halting steps," he feared the worst. This was one of the hinges of fate. When, much later, he looked back on it, he admitted that this one-sided contest had well-nigh brought the Allies an indefinite prolongation of the war: "Had we been forced to suspend, or even seriously to restrict for a time, the movement of shipping in the Atlantic, all our joint plans would have been arrested."

Balance Sheet of the Disaster

In that same March of 1942, when the shadow of recrimination thus darkened the intimacy of Anglo-American collaboration, the U-boats continued unchecked their rampage in American waters. They sank 74 ships of 424,547 tons, most of them well inside the sea frontiers of the United States, the area within three hundred miles of the American coast. The situation became still worse as the year wore on; the weather became better and the Germans threw more of their U-boats into this sudden and unexpected breach. The month of May saw the sinking of a record 91 Allied ships along the sea frontiers; and by the end of July, sinkings in the so-called U.S. Strategic Area totalled 519 ships of 2,800,000 tons. This represented an appalling and embarrassing ninety per cent of all sinkings in all combat areas at sea, aside from the tragic loss of eight hundred lives.

America's first year in the war ended with the loss of 1,027 Allied ships to U-boat action. This was more than half of all the ships lost by all the Allies in the U-boat war, in all areas, all through the war years from 1939 to 1945.

The true magnitude of this defeat becomes clear only when the loss of a single freighter or tanker is viewed in the context of the war effort. In terms of cargo potential, the loss of the average freighter equals the destruction of cargo carried by four trains of seventy-five cars each. According to a U. S. Navy manual, the sinking of two 6,000-ton freighters and one 3,000-ton tanker equalled the loss of forty-two tanks, sixty-eight 6-inch howitzers, eighty-eight 25-pound guns, forty 2-pound weapons, twenty-four armored cars, fifty Bren-gun carriers, some 5,000 tons of ammunition, 600 rifles, 428 tons of tank supplies, 2,000 tons of stores, and 1,000 tanks of gasoline. The enemy would have had to make some 96,000 air-bombing sorties to destroy the amount of war material carried by the ships and tankers sunk in January and February in American waters alone.

Computing the loss of a single fully-loaded tanker in terms of civilian supplies, the American Merchant Marine Institute figured out that the loss of a standard tanker resulted in the destruction of gasoline that would have been enough to supply the holder of an "A" ration book with gas for thirty-five thousand years!

The Germans scored this astounding victory with a tiny cog of their huge war machine, and at an infinitesimal cost to themselves. In January, when *Paukenschlag* opened for business, the five submarines Doenitz had managed to throw into the breach represented but twelve per cent of all the U-boats he then had at sea; yet they succeeded in destroying almost 70 per cent of all the Allied tonnage that was sunk in that month. This staggering total was attained without the loss of a single U-boat.

The Strategic Situation in 1942

This was a phenomenal and unprecedented episode in the whole history of warfare—a major and potentially decisive victory being scored by a tiny force of submarines. It showed how even formidable oceanic barriers will crumble if a skilled and determined onslaught on them is not matched by defenses comparable in skill and determination; and it showed how the safety of the United States can be jeopardized by a furtive attack from the sea, across thousands of miles of waters presumably controlled by us.

Doenitz's U-boats wrought havoc, not merely with the material strength of the Allies during this crucial period of their build-up, but indeed with their whole planning and the grand strategy of the war.

Only a few weeks before he had written his first warning note to Roosevelt via Hopkins, Churchill met the President in a hastily summoned conference in Washington. Code-named "Arcadia", it was called to enable the two Allied leaders to assess the situation created by the entry of the United States into the war and to plan their grand strategy anew in the light of this changed situation.

Despite the shock of Pearl Harbor and the rapid encroachment of the Japanese on British and American positions in Asia and the Pacific, the old decision—reached on March 20, 1941—to concentrate on Germany first (and to contain Japan with a war of attrition pending Germany's defeat) was upheld. While it did not seem likely at "Arcadia" that a large-scale offensive could be mounted against Germany in 1942, it was expected nevertheless that a return to the Continent would be possible in 1943. The instructions "Arcadia" produced for the British and American chiefs of staffs concluded with a paragraph that expressed this expectation in no uncertain terms: "In 1943 [!] the way may be clear for a return to the Continent, across the Mediterranean, from Turkey into the Balkans, or by landing in Western Europe. Such operations will be the prelude to the final assault on Germany itself, and the scope of the victory program should be such as to provide means by which they can be carried out."

The optimism that dominated Roosevelt's outlook persisted when Japanese successes turned out to be short-lived. The Battle of Midway in May turned the tide in the Pacific phase of the war. As a matter of fact, there was reason for optimism, despite the relentless Japanese advances, as the new year of 1942 opened. Britain was no longer alone. Since June, 1941, the Soviet Union had been irrevocably engaged, as Churchill put it, "to fight to the death in close concert with the British Empire." Now the United States was also fully committed.

In addition dissension had appeared in the *Wehrmacht* for the first time. Hitler's failure to conclude the conquest of the Soviet Union on schedule had triggered serious opposition within his High Command, not merely to Hitler, but indeed to the war itself. Hitler had also reached an impasse in his war against Britain. *Sea Lion*—the invasion of England that had been planned for September-October, 1940—had been given up. Rommel had been checked in North Africa. The *Luftwaffe's* savage blitz of August-September, 1940, had left Britain badly bruised and bent, but unbroken. And in the fall of 1941, the U-boat war also showed signs of turning into a disappointment. Although the sustained victories of the preceding twenty-three months had threatened to strangle and starve the British into submission, the U-boats now were running into stiffening British defenses that were were slowly, almost imperceptibly, but definitely, stemming the tide.

December, 1941, brought the crisis to a head in the U-boat arm. It came abruptly and dramatically in the wake of the first indubitable defeat of the U-boats: in a convoy battle west of Gibraltar three British ships were sunk, but five U-boats were lost. Five more U-boats were sunk in other operations in waters around the Azores. Only twice before had Doenitz lost five boats in a single month and never ten in a thirty-day period. For the first time, defeatism swept the U-boat Command. Doenitz's staff openly voiced the opinion, and in no uncertain terms, that the U-boats had had it and were no longer capable of combatting the reinforced convoys.

Doenitz refused to concede defeat or anything beyond a temporary setback. He closed his eyes to such omens as the appearance of the first escort carrier with a convoy, the mysterious tracking down of surfaced U-boats homeward bound at night in the Bay of Biscay, the total destruction of his little fleet of supply vessels in the Atlantic. By steadfastly refusing to recognize the sudden leap forward of British defenses and by attributing his setbacks mainly to inclement weather—"quite unsuitable for U-boat operations"—he retained his faith unshaken in the U-boat and in its ultimate victory in the Battle of the Atlantic.

Thus it happened that, by these furtive changes in the fortunes of war, Pearl Harbor found the Germans in a rather bad shape as a whole, and probably worse shape for warfare in the Atlantic. As Doenitz himself put it, "The year 1941 came to an end in an atmosphere of worry and anxiety for the U-boat Command"; yet he was able to add in retrospect, "Then 1942 began, a year that was to bring us great successes in the U-boat war."

All of a sudden, the advantages of the Allies were wiped out and the great plans of Arcadia had to be put on ice. *By June, 1942, even the ultimate victory of the Allies seemed in jeopardy.* On June 19, General George C. Marshall had the shock of his life when he at last recognized the magnitude of the U-boats' victory in American waters and its damaging effect on the Allied war effort.

"The losses by submarines off our Atlantic seaboard," he wrote in an historic memorandum to Admiral King, "and in the Caribbean *now threaten our entire war effort.* The following statistics bearing on the subject have been brought to my attention:

"Of the 74 ships allocated to the Army for July by the War Shipping Administration, 17 have already been sunk.

"Twenty-two per cent of the bauxite fleet has already been destroyed. Twenty per cent of the Puerto Rican fleet has been lost.

"Tanker sinkings have been 3.5 per cent per month of tonnage in use.

"We are all aware of the limited number of escort craft available, but has every conceivable improvised means been brought to bear on this situation? *I am fearful that another month or two of this will so cripple our means of transport that we will be unable to bring sufficient men and planes to bear against the enemy in critical theatres to exercise a determining influence on the war.*"

Despite Marshall's misgivings, no effective "means" could be brought to bear on "this situation." The U-boats continued their rampage virtually unchecked, arriving in the West Atlantic in steadily increasing numbers—seventy in July, eighty-six in August, a full one hundred in September, and a hundred and five in October—sinking 524 ships between July and the end of the year, the period Marshall regarded as crucial if the Allies were to win.

Yet it had taken even General Marshall six months to become aware of the disaster and to recognize the greater danger inherent in it. Although Pearl Harbor had etched itself upon the imagination of the American public, the people never really realized that there was a Pearl Harbor in the east as well, so much more perilous and ominous, if only because it had brought the war itself to the water's edge of the continental United States and imperiled the critical issue.

CHAPTER VI

A Bit of Pinafore

Say, why is everything
Either at sixes or at sevens?
HMS Pinafore, Act II

And raw in fields the rude militia swarms,
Mouths without hands; maintain'd at vast expense,
In peace a charge, in war a weak defense;
Stout once a month they march, a blustering band,
And ever but in times of need at hand.
JOHN DRYDEN
Cymon and Iphigenia

Democracy may be what Plato called it—a charming form of government, full of disorder. In the chaos and confusion which the shooting war had brought to the United States, the charm quickly evaporated and the disorder became compounded. Hardegen and his colleagues were sinking ships at will off Long Island. The flamboyant skipper of the *U-123* observed dancers on the gayly-illuminated roof of the Astor Hotel in midtown Manhattan and admired the multicolor glow of Times Square from the deck of his boat surfaced in The Narrows.

The Fog of Ignorance

Those dancers were somehow symbolic of the American attitude to the war at this stage. That attitude was molded by rampant confusion in 1939 and 1940, by the physical remoteness of the war and by the equivocations of American statesmen. The fantastic onrush of events

65

in 1940, culminating in the collapse of France and the lethal threat to Britain's survival, numbed Americans and somewhat calloused them to other peoples' woes. Although in 1940, Churchill had warned of the "mortal danger of the steady and increasing diminution of sea tonnage," most Americans paid little attention.

Then, as the Battle of Britain waned and the Battle of the Atlantic moved into focus—a battle, indeed, that was slowly bringing the war to the United States—the public was not told the blunt truth for shallow domestic reasons. The European emergency coincided with the Presidential election campaign of 1940, complicated as it was by the sizzling third-term issue. The evasions of the campaign obscured the situation; and the abruptness of Roosevelt's post-election shift from "the fog of his campaign speeches to the comparative clarity of his Arsenal of Democracy address" of December 29, 1940, merely deepened the public confusion.

Now the war was upon the United States itself—a war with nothing but humiliating defeats. Yet there were hardly any signs that the public was fully aware of the grim facts.

On the West Coast the average American refused to get excited. Newspaper interviews with the "man-in-the-street" showed that people were generally unaware of the seriousness of the situation and of what the war demanded of them. They were cocky and confident—shocked at the audacity of such a puny and far-off nation as Japan attacking the United States, and convinced that it would need but a few months to punish the aggressor.

On the East Coast, little if anything was done to bring home to citizens the proximity of war. As a result, the public attitude did not reflect even the cocky and defiant spirit of the West Coast. So strong was the business-as-usual sentiment and so remote were the implications of war that people steadfastly resisted the modest and half-hearted requests of the authorities to dim their seaward lights, at a time when most Europeans spent their nights in total blackouts.

Enemy submarines could thus get both solace and bearings from the illumination of coastal cities, from beacons on such precious tactical targets as oil storage tanks and radio towers. When Doenitz extended *Paukenschlag* to Florida waters, the owners of big hotels and cheap honky-tonks refused to turn off their garish neons because, they argued, it would hurt their business during the tourist season.

In some cases, refusal to take the war seriously was brazen and callous. Residents of coastal communities frequently had ringside seats at this spectacle of the war; they could hardly plead ignorance of its tragic impact, since from the beaches they could watch fires lighting up those long and tense nights. As Doenitz told Wolfgang Frank at the time: "Our submarines are operating close inshore along the coast of the United States of America, so that bathers and sometimes entire coastal cities are witnesses to the drama of war, whose visual climaxes are constituted by the red glorioles of blazing tankers." This was no idle boast. On June 15, thousands of bathers at Virginia Beach saw two large American freighters torpedoed by a U-boat. The spectacle of burning tankers was an added attraction at fashionable Florida resorts.

And yet, the people at large could hardly be blamed for their apparent callousness in the face of this disaster and danger, if only because they were never told the truth. Moreover, elaborate efforts were made to conceal from them even what they suspected.

Battle of the Bulletins

One of the bizarre features of this era was the manner in which the government handled public relations along the East Coast. In this connection it was somehow symbolic that the first wartime act of Admiral Andrews' command was the introduction of censorship: it was a negative measure (of admitted urgency) and it was especially conspicuous at a time when there was a total absence of positive measures. While it is quite certain that it did impede the enemy's ability to gain useful information, it served in an even larger measure to conceal the facts, not from the Germans, but from the American people.

Both acts of omission and acts of commission were used by government officials to prevent the people from learning the facts of this Battle of the Water's Edge. On the one hand, they sought to minimize the disaster through the suppression of news that would have indicated its full magnitude; on the other hand, they tried to magnify the effectiveness of—frequently non-existent—counter-measures with claims of victories.

The spokesman for this grandiose enterprise was Colonel Franklin William Knox, the Secretary of the Navy, who had been a prominent newspaper publisher in private life. And as a publisher, Knox would have been most vociferous in protesting the kind of campaign of befuddlement whose mouthpiece he now became. I knew Knox and admired his integrity and patriotism. I know he was an honorable man and believe that in the final analysis he was the victim rather than the villain of an ill-advised "conspiracy" to mislead the American people during this sad phase of the war. And yet it is impossible to absolve him of at least some responsibility for a campaign of half-truths and brash lies that lingers on in our ignorance today. If nothing else, it still prevents us from appreciating the lessons of a battle which occurred two decades ago and which still has enormous topical significance.

Knox frequently acted as the purveyor of transparently deceptive propaganda. Even a few days before Pearl Harbor, on December 3, he told reporters that the U. S. Navy had "found the answer to the U-boat menace in the North Atlantic." On December 20 and 21, he boasted about spectacular American successes in the U-boat war, at a time when not a single U-boat was anywhere to be found in American waters. The discrepancies between the facts of the Atlantic battle and the fictions of Washington show up graphically in any review of Navy Department pronouncements during those days. While news about the sinking of Allied ships was spoonfed to the public—thus preventing it from seeing the aggregate picture of the disaster—stories about the wholesale destruction of U-boats were bandied about with calculated cynicism. The first such communique was issued on January 23, when the rampage of Doenitz's five boats was entirely unchecked. A Navy spokesman nevertheless said that "an unspecified number of enemy submarines have already been sunk off the Atlantic Coast," adding that American "counter-measures are continuing with favorable results." When asked how many U-boats had thus been destroyed, the spokesman blandly answered, "Fourteen."

After that, the nation was electrified from time to time with colorful communiques in which the public relations officers of the Navy permitted their imagination to run amuck. The first high point of this phase was reached with the claim, issued on January 29, that a naval patrol plane piloted by Chief Aviation Machinist's Mate Donald Francis Mason had sunk one of those U-boats. The "victory" was then dramatized by the inspired stunt of an anonymous public relations officer who put into Mason's mouth the famous words, "Sighted sub, sank same."

Knowing that he had neither sighted nor sunk the sub, and embarrassed by his involuntary involvement in the hoax, Mason went to bat in a valiant effort to prove the public relations man retroactively right. His zeal and skill were rewarded on March 15, when he definitely sighted the *U-503* of Korvettenkapitaen Otto Gehricke and indubitably sank same—fifty-four days after the bogus and premature claim.

Mason was assigned to Patrol Squadron 82, flying an old PBY out of

Argentia, Newfoundland. His victim was one of the only two U-boats actually killed by United States forces during this whole period between January and March. The honor of having scored the *first* kill belonged to another member of Patrol Squadron 82, an unheralded ensign of the Naval Reserve named Bill Tepuni. On March 1, piloting a Lockheed Hudson on patrol about a hundred miles south of Cape Race, Ensign Tepuni spotted *U-656* of Oberleutnant Ernst Koenig on the surface. Koenig crash dived, but it was too late. Tepuni's depth charges followed him below. From the cockpit of the Hudson, the ensign soon saw all the telltale signs of victory—Diesel oil rising from the Atlantic, then bits of the U-boat itself. Tepuni and Mason scored their kills off Newfoundland, far from the American coastline along which *Paukenschlag* was raging with undiminished fury.

Facts Vs. Fiction

The first and only U-boat actually destroyed in specifically United States waters between January 1 and April 30, was the *U-85* of Oberleutnant Eberhard Greger. Then nothing happened for seventeen arduous days, until May 2, when the *U-74* of Oberleutnant Karl Friedrich was caught and sunk in the Caribbean. Her destruction was followed within a week by the sinking of Kapitaenleutnant Helmuth Rathke's *U-352*, the first U-boat from which prisoners were taken in American waters.

Then followed another long hiatus, until June 13, when the *U-157* of Korvettenkapitaen Wolf Henne came a cropper in the Gulf of Mexico; and June 30, when the *U-158* of Korvettenkapitaen Erwin Rostin was sunk west of Bermuda.

Total killings over a six-month period thus amounted to seven U-boats in waters extending from Newfoundland to Bermuda. Only three of them had been destroyed in waters close to the United States where Doenitz's sea wolves wrought the gravest havoc.

These were the facts. Fiction was disseminated in Washington. Thus, on February 25, when not a single U-boat had been killed, Secretary Knox announced that "three U-boats have been sunk and four probably damaged in the West Atlantic since January 1." Even prior to that, in New York, General Hugh A. Drum and Admiral Andrews had jointly decorated the six-man crew of an Army bomber, amidst flourishes of press releases that claimed they had sunk the sub that sank the tanker *China Arrow* on February 8, a claim correct only insofar as the tanker was concerned.

On April 1, the Navy anonunced that Navy fliers had killed two additional U-boats off the Atlantic Coast, adding that these kills had brought "the total sunk and presumably sunk to twenty-eight, four by Army bombers, and twenty-four by the Navy". The announcement gave Mason *two* kills in an admirable demonstration of stick-to-itiveness on the part of public relations. In actual fact, not a single U-boat had been sunk up to the date of this announcement in waters properly regarded as American.

By contrast, those same public relations officers were rather "conservative" in communiques announcing the sinking of Allied ships in those same waters. And the language of those communiques was ambiguous. In an announcement on February 25, Washington merely said that U-boats had "attacked" a grand total of 114 Allied and United States vessels between January 1 and February 13, only 55 of them in "U. S. coastal waters." In actual fact, in that time a total of 108 ships had fallen victim to *Paukenschlag* in the West Atlantic, 81 of them in American waters.

On March 11, the Navy put the lid on the Atlantic massacre, by announcing that henceforth ship sinking news would be "limited." The last announcement under the old arrangement reported the sinking of the American freighter *Malama*—in the Pacific. The new restrictions were accompanied by the statement that as far as the East Coast was concerned, a total of 28 ships had been sunk "to date"—between January 14 and March 10, that is. The actual number was 91.

After that, it was left to the press associations to keep score of the sinkings from eyewitness reports, insisting that the true figure was many times that of the Navy's tabulation for public consumption. Thus, on March 11, the United Press claimed that the U-boats had sunk 27 ships off the Canadian coast and 10 out of 17 attacked in the Caribbean. On the very day the Navy decided to keep mum about any further sinkings, the United Press announced the sinking of the Brazilian passenger liner *Cayru* only 130 miles off the Ambrose Light and the United States tanker *Gulftrade* three miles off Barnegat Light in New Jersey.

On April 7, just when *Paukenschlag* was concluding its first phase with enormous profits and was moving into its second phase, which was to yield even more staggering gains, Secretary Knox reported a marked decline in our losses. "There were only two ship sinkings, a tanker and a tug, last week," he said, "because of the increasing effectiveness of the anti-submarine campaign." His claim was contradicted by the score for the month—sixty-seven ships of nearly 400,000 tons of which sixty-one vessels of 366,000 tons were lost in waters for which Knox had primary responsibility.

On June 11, the Secretary was rewarded with an honorary degree from Harvard University. By then, the score stood at 311 Allied ships sunk by U-boats in the coastal waters of the United States and 90 more in waters of which the United States was supposed to be the guardian.

The maritime massacre caused by the Germans along the Atlantic coast in 1942, would have been considered a national disaster if the full facts had been published. I recall how shocked I was when, late in 1942, properly cleared for the facts on file in O.N.I., I had my first opportunity to learn the unvarnished truth about this tragic phase of the Atlantic battle. By then, our losses stood at 973 ships as against fifteen U-boats sunk by United States forces. I raised the issue with a commander in public relations who happened to be a former journalist and noted radio commentator, but he was scandalized by my indignation. He said the American people were far too immature and emotional to be told the truth; and besides, the campaign was necessary to mislead the enemy. I invariably heard these same rationalizations whenever the issue came up in later years.

It was never clear to me how the enemy could be misled with claims which he knew at first hand were blatantly untrue. On the other hand, morale in the United States was a genuine concern. In the White House, Harry L. Hopkins headed a school "afraid," as Robert L. Sherwood recalled, "that the flood of bad news would produce a resurgence of isolationist sentiment." In his anxiety, Hopkins inspired some of those optimistic claims and encouraged Knox, among others, in his campaign of deception.

In contrast, Roosevelt was not greatly worried about public morale. As it turned out, the President was right and Hopkins wrong. "The people," Sherwood wrote, "needed no hypodermic stimuli other than the daily doses of bad news they were absorbing." It was an insult to their maturity and intelligence to delude them still further when the truth was there, in its most potent Biblical sense, to make them free and strong.

The Issue of Responsibility

Serious as the losses were, the ultimate significance of the prolonged U-boat blitz was not reflected in the number of ships sunk and the more than seven million gross tons lost in the West Atlantic between January, 1942, and May, 1943. The United States proved strong enough to make up for these titanic losses and more than hold the line. Neither was its significance in the unexpected new lease on the war Hitler gained form this victory he himself was the last to anticipate, nor in such *sequelae* as near-famine in Puerto Rico, sugar and coffee rationing in the United States, the stoppage of fuel oil shipments for domestic consumption—not even in the postponement of the military operations the Arcadia plans had envisaged for 1943, and in the extension of the war.

Its historic significance, with lasting and current implications, was in the fact, that the U-boats could penetrate to the shores and beaches of the United States, operate with virtual impunity in our coastal waters, and stay on more or less unchecked for seventeen months. Another ominous feature was the U-boats' ability to land teams of spies and saboteurs on the very soil of the continental United States, twice in the immediate vicinity of Coast Guard stations. Thus was created a "pattern of invasion" whose long-range implications cannot be dismissed, even though these landings involved only a handful of agents who were quickly collected by the Federal Bureau of Investigation.

At his lonely outpost, Admiral Andrews felt the heavy burden of his responsibility exactly because he recognized well in advance the essential futility of his task. I have been much impressed by Theodor Taylor's remarks in *Fire on the Beaches,* where he wrote: "Day after day, Andrews and his staff studied coastal areas they were assigned to guard, fully realizing *there were miles of shallow-fathomed sea lane which could never be protected* with the forces assigned. It was sobering to know that during the First World War a foreign power had found a way to carry the fight into the United States waters. Before 1918, the seemingly endless oceans to the west and east had always been moats, physically forcing any surface fleet to fight at the very end of its supply train. But the Kaiser's *Unterseeboots* had easily swum thousands of miles in the eastern moat, virtually undetected."

The situation on this oceanic front in World War II was bluntly exposed by the historians of the Army Air Force. "That the Germans would move their U-boats into American waters as soon as practicable after the formal entry of the United States into the war," they wrote in their wrap-up report on the Battle of the Atlantic, "was implicit in the military situation as it developed from 1939 to 1941." But what was done to prepare for this eventuality? "Seemingly no one had seen fit," they wrote, "to develop comprehensive plans and forces specially designed to counter the U-boat threat."

"This writer," Morison wrote in his Navy-sponsored definitive history of the Battle of the Atlantic, "cannot avoid the conclusion that the United States Navy was woefully unprepared, materially and mentally, for the U-boat blitz on the Atlantic coast that began in January, 1942.

He further believes that . . . this unpreparedness was largely the Navy's own fault."

Blame was imputed to the Navy even more bluntly by the historians of the Army Air Force: "Whether because of its traditional concern for the problems of the Pacific or for other reasons, the crisis of December, 1941, found the Navy unable to perform the offshore patrol necessary in order to cope effectively with the submarines." They summed it up by stating without equivocation: "The weakness of the antisubmarine forces can be explained only in part by mere lack of men and equipment. It must be explained also in terms af lack of the right kinds of equipment and of properly trained men—which, in turn, points unavoidably to faulty planning in the field of coastal defense during the years before the war."

At least some of the Navy's deficiencies reflected the total unpreparedness of the nation. Responsibility for that extends from top to bottom, from Congress and the President to the people at large.

I raise the issue of responsibility for two reasons—first, to caution against the possible repetition of past mistakes; and second, to describe the causes that in the end induced Admiral King to establish the Tenth Fleet.

Total Unpreparedness

On the eve of World War II, the United States had a formidable navy as far as sheer tonnage was concerned (over 1,300,000 tons all told). But it was a lopsided force afloat because well over half of this strength (853,000 tons) was in capital ships and cruisers—vessels that could make no contribution to the efficient prosecution of an antisubmarine campaign.

This naval strength reflected tradition more than anything else, a mental state that places undue emphasis on the historic fleet rather than on pragmatic need. President Roosevelt put his finger on this weakness in modern naval thinking when he complained to Churchill that "the [U. S.] Navy couldn't see any vessel under a thousand tons." The President himself preferred smaller craft whose size was far below those thousand tons.

Therein lay one of the fundamental deficiencies of American naval forces at this historic turn—in the Navy's predilection for ships which were far too big and the President's preference for craft which were far too small. There was nobody in Washington in decisive authority to promote the ships we actually needed—escort craft of seagoing type, destroyers, destroyer escorts and cutters.

The shortage was brought to the attention of the Navy's General

Board, which had the last word in these matters, in 1940, when Admiral King, himself a member of the Board, suggested that a potent antisubmarine fleet be built as fast as possible around the *Hamilton* class of Coast Guard cutters. Plans for these cutters were on hand and production could have begun at once. What with a maximum speed of only twenty knots, and armament of only three 5-inch guns, King did not consider even this vessel ideal for the purpose; but he always sought to make the most of what was immediately available and thought that a force of cutters would do until something better could be built.

The General Board was less than lukewarm to King's proposal. When the Fleet Training Division of the Chief of Naval Operations objected to the idea on the ground that the speed of *Hamilton* class cutters was too low and their armament too light, the recommendation was shelved. King revived the issue early in 1941, after he had been transferred from Washington to command of the Atlantic Fleet. The woeful shortage of such vessels in his new command impressed him even more with the extreme urgency of his proposal. But when he tried to obtain approval for the construction of seagoing craft, from two hundred and fifty to three hundred feet in length and capable of twenty-five knots, he was told that neither the General Board nor the President was in favor of such vessels and, therefore, his recommendation could not be acted upon favorably.

The President's attitude was shaped during World War I when he, as Assistant Secretary of the Navy, was instrumental in the development of a subchaser program whose backbone was a small antisubmarine craft. Now, almost twenty-five years later, and in the face of vastly improved U-boats, he was convinced that the Navy would be able to counter the German submarines with the same kind of small patrol vessels which could be built quickly and *en masse*, even in the last moment of need. Although King did his best to point out that poor sea-keeping qualities would render such craft "inadequate for submarine work" and that their small crews could not sustain the continuous watch imperative in this hunt, the President persisted in his views, causing King to remark: "Nothing remains static in war or in military weapons, and it is consequently often dangerous to rely on courses suggested by apparent similarities in the past."

Other factors also mitigated the prompt build-up of an effective antisubmarine fleet and some of them are not pleasant to contemplate. Thus, in the background of the Navy's megalomaniac attachment to the big ships was a policy that was brought out in the investigation of the Navy's shipbuilding program by the Senate's Special Committee Investigating the National Defense Program, the famed Truman Committee.

According to Truman, "the Navy was extremely liberal with the private shipbuilders." The Committee found that the admirals, in going to bat for the big ships, surrendered to the lobby of the private shipyards. These shipyards preferred to build big ships because the profit on them was so much bigger than it would have been even on mass production of smaller craft, which they were not equipped to build anyway. The big-ship lobby of the huge private yards, which in 1940 secured 70 per cent of a four billion dollar shipbuilding program for its clients, had thus harmed this country's defenses in this predominance of the profit motive over the needs of preparedness.

Aside from the scarcity of vessels best suited to combat the U-boat, the Navy's unpreparedness showed up in other fields as well—in organization and training, in weapons and devices, in communications and intelligence. Although we cannot, and need not, consider them all here, a few of these deficiencies need to be shown, if only to demonstrate the improvement eventually brought about.

As early as World War I, the U. S. Navy had found out that the hunt for U-boats was a complex enterprise requiring specialized equipment, such as sound gear and depth charges, and personnel specifically trained and psychologically conditioned to handle them. However, after the war the Navy became primarily preoccupied with problems of the Pacific. Up to 1941, only a handful of officers had what Washington lingo calls cognizance of and training in antisubmarine warfare, and even that on a rather rudimentary basis.

This lack of interest in antisubmarine warfare was mirrored in the want of everything the Navy needed to throw against the U-boat—in ships, devices, and men. At the outbreak of the war, the Navy had only 170 vessels equipped with sound gear, the primary device for the detection of submerged submarines, and only a handful of men more or less qualified to handle it. At that time, the Navy's foremost sonar expert was a chief radioman named W. A. Braswell and he was put to work overtime to teach a new generation of soundmen. Braswell was up against odds any educator would have regarded as absolutely prohibitive—he had no textbooks nor enough sound equipment to aid him—yet he somehow managed to train hundreds of men, although his first course, which opened on November 15, 1939, had only sixteen bluejackets assigned to it.

76 The Tenth Fleet

The situation was dismal as far as radar was concerned and there was no Braswell to improve it quickly. Although the first discoveries that resulted in the development of radar had been made in 1922 by two physicists of the Naval Aircraft Radio Laboratory in Anacostia, and the British had made great progress in extensive use of it during the war, it was not until October, 1941, that the first American-built sets were installed in the fleet, and on a limited scale at that. The antisubmarine vessels in the Atlantic received radar only a year later. Personnel to handle it was not available in adequate numbers. Men resisted assignment to radar training; they regarded it as worse than KP duty. At the beginning of the U-boat blitz, and for most of its duration, the American forces had to fight the uneven battle without the benefit of this crucial instrument.

The founder of the dynasty of antisubmarine weapons was the depth charge, a barrel-like device filled with explosives that is dropped over the submarine from a ship. During World War I, depth charges enjoyed a brief span of popularity in the Navy, but after the war, their development was halted. The United States thus went to war in 1942 against the U-boat with depth charges which had been more or less antiquated, even at the end of World War I. It was not until May, 1943, that up-to-date "ashcans" were produced, together with improved devices to drop them. For some inexplicable reason, the Navy resisted improvements in this field. Early in 1942, an American naval officer stumbled upon an antisubmarine projectile mechanism that became famous later in the war under the name of hedgehog. He had to "sell" it to the U.S. Navy, but the British had to demonstrate its value in action before our Navy would adopt it.

The extreme difficulty of finding a submarine and the concerted action needed to hunt it down and kill it, placed emphasis on two collateral means of warfare—intelligence and communications. The deficiencies in both were appalling throughout the seventeen months of the U-boat blitz and were not remedied until the Tenth Fleet assigned top priorities to both activities. The Office of Naval Intelligence, a subsidiary, desk-bound division under the Chief of Naval Operations, was far too static to play an important role in as dynamic an activity as the U-boat hunt. The intelligence organizations attached directly to the fleets and the various sea frontiers embarked upon the war woefully undermanned and with personnel inadequately trained to procure and disseminate the information the hunters needed to find their quarries. It was not until a specialized intelligence agency was established within the headquarters organization of COMINCH, and promoted vigorously by Admiral Low that this gap could be filled.

The communication system aiding the U-boat hunters was far more elaborate, of course, but only a little better than the system of intelligence. Even in peacetime, naval communications involve the complex and cumbersome manipulation of difficult technical means and intricate human resources. Prior to the war, the U. S. Navy used a system known as the Fox Schedule. In that system, encrypted messages were sent to one of the three main radio stations (in Washington, San Francisco, and Pearl Harbor). The responsible station then "put on the Fox," broadcasting continuously all the messages it received. The radio operators on individual ships had then to copy the whole Fox, but they forwarded to the coding officer only what was addressed to them.

The system was certain to clog up radio traffic once its peacetime volume became tremendously increased by the exigencies of war. When other inconveniences and difficulties also developed, the usefulness of the Fox Schedule was well-nigh cancelled. Yet the Navy had nothing up its sleeves to replace it when the need for a better system became evident and pressing. During this same period, communications also proved difficult and often nearly impossible between ships, and especially between aircraft and surface vessels. These difficulties, which also needed some time to be remedied, frequently precluded concerted surface action or prevented aircraft that had spotted U-boats from alerting nearby ships and guiding them to the submarines.

To complicate things, the Navy persisted in its adherence to a communications policy in which security was trump. They steadfastly refused to realize the truism that often it is more important to get information to one's own forces than to withhold it from the enemy. "During the first year of the war," Morison noted, "the Navy Department laid such stress on security of communications that they sometimes failed of their essential purpose to communicate."

The vast complexities and highly specialized problems of anti-submarine warfare would have required years of diligent planning before the outbreak of hostilities, and the mobilization of all the resources needed in men, installations, and facilities, well in advance. As it was, virtually nothing had been done on this score.

Since it is a military truism that the relative strength of a belligerent reflects the weakness of his adversary, the freakish victory of the U-boat in American waters was not entirely the result of Doenitz's excellent planning and the intrepidity of his U-boatmen. The task we neglected and the opportunities we missed in the carefree years of peace inevitably showed up as a major factor contributing to the U-boats' success so close to our shores.

From such a historical review as this, certain crucial issues emerge to haunt us. The compartmentalization of national defense, the divergent allocations of the hardware of war to different segments of the war machine, inter-service rivalries and professional jealousies intrinsically undermine the efficiency of the military establishment. History clearly shows that these factors continue to exert their harmful influence even after the outbreak of war.

Modern war with its stress and strain, and especially with its fantastic new weapons, leaves little margin for error and virtually no time to remedy a bad situation or make up for past neglects. This was recognized by General Marshall during the difficult early stages of World War II, when he ruefully remarked: "We used to have all the time in the world and no money, now we've got all the money and no time."

The Impact of the Disaster

When the U-boats struck, President Roosevelt was preoccupied with what he regarded as weightier problems and projects—the token Doolittle raid on Tokyo and the Pearl Harbor investigation, for example, trouble with Vichy France, and above all else, the effort of keeping the Soviet Union in the war. Later he showed livelier interest in the fate of the Arctic convoys to Murmansk than in those moving up and down the American coast, the latter without adequate escorts because the vessels Andrews and the other Sea Frontier commanders needed for escort duty had been diverted to those convoys to Russia. This is certainly not meant to impugn the President's patriotism or to question his leadership in the war—but it is an irrefutable fact that he first underestimated and then glossed over the U-boat menace in his contemplation of and preoccupation with aspects of the war further away from home. According to Admiral King, this was one of the President's blind spots, for he was, as King put it, "somewhat short of realistic in assessing the submarine menace."

To the admirals—even to the brilliant and energetic King who eventually conquered the menace—this was a technical problem of tactical and logistic details that had to be solved, to be sure, but only in due course in their own unhurried ways, along established professional lines, and within the strict bureaucratic and jurisdictional confines of the military establishment. As we shall see presently, there was considerable fiddling in the Navy Department and the Pentagon while the ships burned.

The impact of the disaster can best be fathomed in its simplest human terms in the grand manner of Nicholas Monsarrat: the contest between the lonely individual and the cruel sea. To the ordinary seaman, in his deadly struggle in the boiling oil trying to escape from his torpedoed tanker, the U-boat blitz was a highly personal matter. To men and women in lifeboats tossed by angry storms or sucked to their doom by the sinking ships, this was an intimate and macabre adventure.

When the American-South African motor ship *City of New York* was torpedoed in a heavy March gale, only one of the big ship's four lifeboats could clear. It carried away twenty survivors, among them a three-year-old girl with her mother and a young woman in the last stage of pregnancy. The baby was delivered in total darkness, only to die forty hours later when his mother also succumbed.

One by one, eight of the men also died and had to be buried at sea. The boat carried no weights and so the corpses kept bobbing up and down around the boat until they floated away. When, on the tenth day of this ordeal, her mother also died, the little girl burst into hysterical sobs and pleaded with the men, "Please don't throw my mummy into the water, please don't!" On the thirteenth day, the little girl also died. In the end, only a single man—an ordinary seaman named Pat Peck —was left to bury her and then, when the lifeboat was found at last, to tell her story.

When the Standard Oil tanker *W. L. Steed* was torpedoed in February, 1941, eighty-five miles off the Virginia Capes, all four boats were launched, even though two U-boats surfaced to slug the mortally wounded tanker from their deck guns at point-blank range. The weather was bad. There was a snowstorm to complicate things and the boats pitched crazily in the running seas. Conditions in the boats were chaotic because there had been no time to observe the abandon ship bill. In the abruptness of the emergency, most of the men scrambled into the boats hatless against the wintry winds and in shirtsleeves.

But every man got into the boats—the captain even carrying his briefcase with the ship's papers—and now they did not let any panic grip them. The shore was only a hundred miles away. The boats were in busy ship-lanes. They expected to be picked up soon since the radioman had signalled their position just before the end.

And yet, the sea held out slight promise for these brave men. The slow agony of their gradual death now stands as one of the great sagas of this uneven battle.

No. 1 lifeboat vanished without a trace. There were no survivors from No. 4 when it was eventually found. Only one of the fifteen men in No. 2 lived through the ordeal.

No. 3 lifeboat cleared with five men, apparently the fittest of the lot, for they put on a stiff and ingenious struggle against their fate. They rigged up an auxiliary anchor from a broken water keg; they bailed out whenever the heavy seas mounted over the gunwales; and they kept warm to some degree by hovering over a flame in a bucket, in which they burned wood chopped from the boat, destroying, board by board, the little craft they hoped would preserve them.

Even so, when No. 3 was found at last by a Canadian cruiser, only three of its five passengers were still alive—four survivors all told from the *Steed*, whose whole crew had managed to get safely into the boats.

The eastern part of Central Florida is separated from the open Atlantic by a long and narrow landstrip that runs like a thin ribbon from Daytona Beach to the red brick tower of the light on the north shore of Jupiter Inlet. Isolated from the mainland most of the way by the Indian River, whose rich valley to the west grows juicy citrus fruits, this barren strip juts out into the ocean below but once, at Titusville. An old lighthouse, erected on the cape in 1854, traditionally warned shipping of this abrupt protrusion.

This wild area was picked by Doenitz in February, 1942, as destination for another *Rudel* of his U-boats. Oberleutnant Hermann Steinert, one of the youngest skippers in the U-boat arm, was sent straight for the cape in *U-128*. Others—like Kapitaenleutnant Hans Poske in *U-504* —moved into waters as far south as the sprawling luxury suburbs of Miami.

Although the carnage further north should have alerted this exposed Florida coast to the imminence of danger, little if anything seemed to indicate here that any U-boats were expected at all. Lookouts kept watch around the clock at the various Coast Guard stations, but the seaward windows of the beach cottages were all lit and the honky-tonks of the tourist row glowed with neons. Both business and pleasure proceeded as usual, for this was February, the height of the season.

The morning of February 19 was sodden, with line squalls on the horizon. Traffic at sea was proceeding as usual. The slow British tanker *Elizabeth Massey* had just passed the light of the cape, followed ponderously and then overtaken by an old American freighter, the *Pan Massachusetts*. At 1:45 P.M., the Coast Guard lookout on the cape suddenly sighted flames and thick black smoke rising over the horizon, about twenty miles out at sea. They came from the *Pan Mass*. She had sailed straight into Steinert's *U-128*. Struck amidship by two torpedoes, the ship was quickly enveloped by flaming gas that set her rafts and boats on fire. The U-boat surfaced boldly in broad daylight to finish her off by shellfire.

Further south, the tanker *Republic* sailed into the ambush of the *U-504* of Poske. She was stopped dead by two of his torpedoes and sank by the stern in minutes. The freighter *Missouri* was the next to go; then the tanker *Cities Service Empire;* followed by another tanker, (the *W. D. Anderson),* the freighter *Norlavore,* then a four-master from Cuba, and finally a Brazilian straggler.

Another U-boat front had opened up in American waters. Although its future significance could not be recognized at that time, it now looms up with an added measure of apprehension in the light of more recent history. The desolate spot the U-boats had reached with such impunity and had made into their happy hunting ground is now world-famous as the sanctuary of angry, fire-spewing birds.

Its name? Cape Canaveral.

CHAPTER VII

Days of Indecision

> *'Be bold! be bold!' and everywhere*
> *—'Be bold!*
> *Be not too bold!'*
> HENRY WADSWORTH LONGFELLOW,
> "Morituri Salutamus"

On the Monday morning after Pearl Harbor, an aide of Secretary Knox called Admiral King at his headquarters in Newport, Rhode Island, and asked him to come to Washington at once. King left immediately, but the mode of his travel to the capital illustrated the leisurely pace at which such business was still transacted. Wearing civilian clothes, he motored to West Kingston on the other side of Narragansett Bay, caught the afternoon express from Boston, and arrived in Washington after midnight.

After his arrival, however, the pace of events quickened. Knox told King that Roosevelt had decided to reorganize the Navy and to give King command of all the fleets. For the next couple of weeks, King commuted between Newport and Washington as he prepared to relinquish his Atlantic command.

Then at 4:30 P.M. on December 16, in the Oval Room of the White House, Roosevelt himself told King: "Well, admiral, I'm working on an Executive Order that will bring about a revolutionary change in the archaic organization of the Navy and, I am confident, will have a telling effect upon its future operations. I am redefining the duties of the Commander in Chief, United States Fleet. Henceforth he will have supreme command of the operating forces which comprise, not merely the Pacific Fleet, but all the fleets, and the forces of the Frontier Command. He will be directly responsible to me."

The President then said, "I intend to appoint you to that supreme command."

Even before Pearl Habor, Roosevelt had come to rely heavily on King; he had increased his responsibilities until the admiral complained, "You're giving me a big slice of bread, but damn little butter."

Later, when a number of ships were transferred from the Pacific to King in the Atlantic, Roosevelt had asked him, "Well, admiral, how do you like the butter you are getting?"

King had answered wryly, "The butter is fine, Mr. President, but you keep giving me more bread."

Now he had the whole loaf.

The Executive Order (No. 8984) was issued on December 18, and two days later King was formally named Commander in Chief, United States Fleet. The very first thing he did in Washington was to change the abbreviated name of his new command from CINCUS to COMINCH because the old shorthand had, as he put it, undesirable connotations in the light of Pearl Harbor.

King came to Washington from his austere headquarters on the cruiser *Augusta* (on which Roosevelt and Churchill had met for the Atlantic Conference), but since he now moved into shoes made especially for him, he found no space in the Navy Department where he could establish himself. He was assigned a single third floor room from which, as one of his aides remarked, "someone had moved out in a hurry, taking the furniture with him, but not the dirt." In the midst of a two-ocean war, the new Commander in Chief's most immediate task was to "liberate" a big desk and a couple of chairs. Even before the leftover dirt was swept from his office, he was working at one side of the desk, with his new Chief of Staff, Admiral Willson, working with him at the other side of the same desk.

King had brought with him to Washington Captain Francis S. Low, USN, his indefatigable, self-effacing and exceptionally competent Operations Officer; and he had summoned Rear Admiral Richard S. Edwards, USN—a "remarkable man who combined penetrating intellectual abilities of the highest order with an immense capacity for hard work"—from command of submarines in the Atlantic Fleet to act as his Deputy Chief of Staff. Edwards and Low now sat at an old table they had borrowed "from a friend who was out to lunch," in a corner of King's own one-room office. "I recall thinking," Edwards later remarked, "that as the headquarters of the greatest navy in the world it fell somewhat short of being impressive."

King had no time to contemplate the quality of his new quarters. Accompanied by a huge professional staff, Winston S. Churchill had arrived in Washington for what became known as the Arcadia Conference, to plot the joint grand strategy of the Allies. It was King's first participation in top-level military diplomacy. From December 24, 1941, to January 14, 1942, he stood by to represent the Navy.

Before the chores of Arcadia removed him temporarily from the business of conducting the war at sea, King took stock and reoriented himself, both mentally and physically. It reflected the exacting diversity of his commitments that, within a single forty-eight hour period in December, he sent four crucial directives to as many distant addressees who now depended on his orders. In one he told Admiral Chester W. Nimitz, USN, what he was expected to do in the Pacific. In another he informed Admiral Thomas C. Hart, USN, of the strategy designed for him as Commander in Chief, Asiatic Fleet. In the third and fourth, he took up the U-boat problem with the British Admiralty and Admiral Andrews respectively.

The U-boat had been foremost on King's mind and the paramount consideration of his mission when he was CINCLANT and was waging an undeclared war. Now it inevitably receded in the background as the Pacific war moved to the fore. This was natural. In the Pacific, it was the United States Navy that was fighting virtually alone against a major sea power intoxicated by its phenomenal victories; in the Atlantic, it was the Royal Navy which bore the brunt in a tricky battle, to be sure, but they opposed an inferior sea power whose strength derived solely from its mammoth submarine force.

This was a distribution of labor King regarded as proper, professional and efficient. His overall attitude to the U-boat war was far from ambiguous, but his plans had not yet jelled. According to a quip in the Navy Department, Old Blowtorch really liked this U-boat business because it took his mind off the war.

But, of course, the U-boat menace could not be ignored. In his dispatch to the Admiralty, King predicted in so many words that a U-boat attack on the Atlantic seaboard was an "imminent probability" because, he said, he assumed that the Germans would "take advantage of the well-known weakness of our coastal defense force." To Andrews, who was expected to be hit first by the German onslaught, he sent a general directive in which he urged his old classmate to "do the best you can with what you've got." It was the famous maxim of the eighteenth-century French Admiral Pierre Andre de Suffren de Saint-Tropez. King had adopted the maxim and now he worked it to death.

King was still busy with the Arcadia Conference when the Germans struck. On January 19, 1942, he met with the President to review the rapidly developing U-boat situation. He was frankly desperate, and his despair showed in what became one of the first offensive measures he adopted against the U-boats, not upon his own initiative, but at the President's eager suggestion. They were discussing the scarcity of ships suited for antisubmarine warfare, when Roosevelt suddenly asked King:

"Do you remember the so-called Q-ships?"

"Yes, of course," King said somewhat suspiciously because he had come to recognize a special twinkle in Roosevelt's eyes whenever the President was trying to sell him something. "What about them?"

"Well," Roosevelt said, "let's have a few of our merchant vessels converted into Q-ships and send them against the U-boats until we have something better to throw at them."

War on the Q.T.

The pressure from the U-boats and the lack of means to combat them made those days fertile for offbeat ideas, some developed in the Navy, others pouring in from armchair strategists. Many of them, brewed in the pressure cooker of the emergency, were little better than crackpot schemes, like the proposal to defend the East Coast by anchoring "a chain of small boats five miles off shore, within hailing distance of one another, all the way from Maine to Florida." A proposal that we barricade off the entire coast behind booms and nets was receiving serious consideration.

In deepest secrecy, the Bureau of Ships was drafting plans for a vessel whose inner hull was to be encased in twelve feet of ice produced and maintained by a refrigeration plant on board, the idea behind this icecapade being that a torpedo exploding in such a solid ice mass would cause damage but could not sink the ship. On other draftboards were plans for giant cargo-carrying submarines and unsinkable barges.

Roosevelt's suggestion revived the measure of a former despair. The idea to pattern fighting ships on the legend of the Flying Dutchman was first suggested to Churchill in 1915, and the buccaneer-minded First Lord eagerly accepted the proposal. He then vigorously promoted a small fleet of apparently defenseless Lorelei ships whose mission was to lure unsuspecting U-boats onto themselves. At the proper moment, the naval crew of the Q-ship was supposed to unmask their ordnance, open up on the U-boat and wipe it off the face of the ocean.

Despite the gallantry of their venturesome crews, the Q-boats had been duds. When three of them were sunk in August, 1917, the Admiralty decided to scrap them. The United States Navy also experimented with a Q-ship, called *Santee*, but the experiment ended abruptly when she was torpedoed and sunk on her maiden voyage.

The British revived the ruse in the early days of World War II, but by the end of 1941, they had again had enough of it. However, so great was the pressure of the U-boat blitz on the United States that we decided to use Q-ships despite the Royal Navy's dismal experience. Called Project LQ, it became the quaintest venture of our anti-U-boat campaign.

Projects like "LQ" neither amused nor satisfied King in his relentless search for sound professional solutions, but he was willing to go along with the President's romantic suggestion for want of anything better. On January 20, 1942, King instructed Andrews to get himself a few Q-ships if he approved of the idea. Andrews, who would have done anything to harm the U-boats, was persuaded by Commander Louis C. Farley, USNR, his Operations Officer, that the Q-boats were "well worth trying" and had a "reasonable chance of success." Farley was sincere in his advocacy of the mystery ships and professionally competent to make this assessment. A 1905 graduate of Annapolis, he had commanded a destroyer division in World War I, and had been recalled to duty from private business to serve on Andrews' staff.

When Andrews agreed to go through with the scheme, Project LQ was quietly launched. Its supervision was assigned to Admiral Horne (who kept all data concerning it in his personal custody), while Andrews received "complete authority to implement the Project."

The Mystery Ships

Project LQ began in earnest on February 19, at the Riggs National Bank in Washington, with the appearance of a mysterious stranger who deposited $500,000 to the account of two other mysterious strangers going by the names of F. J. Horne and W. S. Farber. Upon closer scrutiny, the two last named turned out to be not so mysterious after all. "Horne" was Vice Admiral Frederick J. Horne, USN, soon to be named Vice Chief of Naval Operations, and "Farber" was his principal assistant, Rear Admiral William S. Farber, USN. The money came from secret funds at the disposal of the Chief of Naval Operations.

Various sums of the deposit were allocated to three dummy corporations. Thus $50,000 went to an Eagle Fishing Company; $100,000 was allocated to the Asterion Shipping Company; and another $100,000 was transferred to the account of the Atik Shipping Company. The three "companies" owned three vessels—the *Wave,* a Diesel-powered New England trawler, and the *Carolyn* and the *Evelyn,* two old black-and-tan Bull Line freighters of 3200 tons each.

Some time in February, they were moved to the Portsmouth Navy Yard in New Hampshire. There, under the supervision of still another mysterious stranger—actually Commander Gerald Thompson, USN—the *Wave* became the *U.S.S. Eagle,* the *Carolyn,* the *U.S.S. Atik,* and the *Evelyn,* the *U.S.S. Asterion.* They were equipped with camouflage nets, false bulwarks, and a bristling array of concealed ordnance, as well as sonar. Then they were given still another set of names and bogus call letters and became Q-ships in fact, ready to decoy the U-boats.

While the three ships were at Portsmouth undergoing their conversion, Commander Farley was busy at 90 Church Street giving instructions to three handpicked lieutenant commanders—Harry L. Hicks, USN, G. W. Legwen, USN, and L. F. Rogers, USNR—in the science and art of operating Q-ships. Finally, on March 18, their skippers boarded their respective vessels, and on March 23, the *Wave*-alias *Eagle*-alias *Captor,* the *Carolyn*-alias-*Atik*-alias-*Villa Franca,* the *Evelyn*-alias-*Asterion*-alias *Generalifa,* sneaked out of the Navy Yard, and were on their own.

Three days later, the *Atik* had the misfortune to sail into the arms of the ace of aces Doenitz had on this side of the Atlantic—the victory-flushed Hardegen on *U-123.* It became a pathetic and uneven battle. We know only from Hardegen's log how it ended, because the *Atik* vanished without a trace and without any survivors.

It was after sunset on March 26 that Hardegen fell for the ruse, and sailed up to the decoy ship about 300 miles east of Norfolk. Contrary to our expectations that such a tramp would not be considered worth a torpedo and would draw only fire from the U-boat's inferior guns, Hardegen, obviously ignorant of Q-boat protocol, started out by hitting the target with a fish. Then he waited to see what would happen. The *Atik* sent out an SOS and then, it seemed, it was "Abandon ship!" Hardegen saw her crew taking to the boats. But it was only the "panic party" whose part in the play was to feign distress. Her naval crew remained at general quarters. When the U-boat surfaced they whisked off the false bulwarks, opened the gun ports, and went for it with everything they had.

It was Hardegen's turn to panic. When a midshipman he had on board was hit by a shell from the *Atik,* he withdrew to give the mortally wounded youngster first aid. But the boy died and Hardegen, hopping mad, returned to the *Atik* and finished off the helplessly drifting Q-ship with another torpedo.

The *Atik's* SOS—sent under her real name *Carolyn*—did not mean anything special to the unitiated duty officer at Church Street. He logged the signal and filed it because there was nothing he could do even if he had known who the strange vessel actually was. All the surface craft of the Sea Frontier were out on patrol, none in the vicinity of the *Carolyn's* mishap.

The SOS, routinely routed to COMINCH in Washington, reached Project LQ during the night. A call was then put through to Church Street and the duty officer was asked:

"Have you notified the admiral or the Chief of Staff?"

"No, sir," the duty officer answered. "They're in Norfolk."

"Then, for God's sake, notify Commander Farley!" Washington ordered the startled ensign. "And please, hurry!"

Farley was called and he rushed to Church Street. He scraped up the destroyer *Noa* and the tug *Sagamore* for a rescue mission. Rough weather forced the *Sagamore* to return to port, and the *Noa* ran out of fuel, but it made no difference. The brave little *U.S.S. Atik*, with Commander Hicks and all hands aboard, had been gone since 8:55 the night before.

The *Atik's* misfortune caused King to review the project but, so grave was the situation and so limited the means, he agreed to continue it. Then another mishap—of an entirely different nature—created some apprehension even among the advocates of this war on the Q.T. The Gulf Sea Frontier had also moved into the act and converted a vessel called *Alice* into a mystery ship for operations in the Caribbean. Early in June, while the *Alice* was at sea, the *U-584* landed four German agents at Ponte Vedra, near Jacksonville, Florida. When the agents were apprehended, the FBI found the *Alice's* specifications and conversion plans on them. Admiral Kauffman was notified, and the *Alice* was recalled and decommissioned.

Aside from this mysterious breach of the *Alice's* secret, the source of which was never found, the B-Branch of Naval Intelligence had some reason to suspect that the mystery of the other ships had also been penetrated. Those "gumshoes" of the ONI had information that during their conversion in Portsmouth, the *Eagle*, *Atik*, and *Asterion* were the subjects of considerable loose talk in the various boarding houses where many of the civilian workers at the Navy Yard lived. It was assumed that some of those conversations—that included details of the conversion job and identified the three ships as decoy boats—had reached the German Intelligence Service.

While Project LQ seemed to be thoroughly compromised from several angles, it was continued nevertheless and several additional vessels were converted. One of them was the tanker *Gulf Dawn*, chosen because it was assumed that a big tanker would be certain to attract the U-boats and, thanks to her superior equipment, that it would succeed where the little tramps failed. Renamed the *Big Horn* for her secret mission, she never even met a U-boat and wound up as a weather ship.

None of the Q-ships managed to sink or even so much as damage a single U-boat, and even their sightings proved to be erroneous. On the other hand, they frequently sailed into predicaments from which the Navy had to extricate them.

Last of the Q-ships was the *Irene Forsyte*, a handsome three-masted schooner, under Lieutenant Commander Richard Parmenter, USNR, an expert in antisubmarine warfare. Parmenter was the ideal man for the job and he had an exceptional crew, all of them volunteers. However, the jinx of the Q-ships followed the *Forsyte*, too. She sailed into a hurricane off Bermuda and was so badly damaged that she had to put into Hamilton Sound for repairs.

Parmenter pleaded that he be permitted to return to sea, but by then Admiral King had had enough of it. He was sorry he ever agreed to the launching of the project. He sent a round-robin dispatch to the Sea Frontier commanders telling them that they would no longer be given "uncontrolled authority to implement projects of this nature."

That sounded the death knell for Project LQ.

Despite its futility, and even though it claimed the lives of one hundred and forty-one officers and men in an unproductive adventure, the project stands out as one of the sagas of the anti-U-boat campaign. It was mounted when we had nothing better to throw into the breach— when it was our sole aggressive effort to harm the marauders. The mystery ships demanded the utmost in seamanship and courage from their officers and men. If nothing else, they created an offensive spirit when the defensive was trump and defeatism was still rampant on the East Coast.

CHAPTER VIII

The Issue of Leadership

In the evening of January 24, 1942, Harry L. Hopkins dined with Franklin Delano Roosevelt and afterwards jotted down a note of their conversation. It sketched graphically one of the cruel problems confronting the President.

"It is perfectly clear," Hopkins wrote, "that the President is going to have ... many of the same problems that Lincoln had with generals and admirals whose records look awfully good but who well may turn out to be the McClellans of this war. The only difference between Lincoln and Roosevelt is that I think Roosevelt will act much faster in replacing these fellows.

"This war can't be won with ... men who are thinking only about retiring to farms somewhere and who won't take great and bold risks and Roosevelt has got a whole hatful of them in the Army and Navy that will have to be liquidated before we really get on with our fighting."

In the person of Admiral Harold R. Stark, USN, the Navy had an able, scholarly, self-effacing, and dedicated Chief of Naval Operations who, moreover, clearly foresaw the trends and tried his best to provide for the needs. However, he "lacked the quickness and the ruthlessness of decision required in wartime." Thus was created under Stark a *status quo* of inadequacy, partly by the influence of the General Board whose power during those days accrued directly from "Betty" Stark's humane weakness. The board was dominated by superannuated admirals. They used this last chance before final retirement to perpetuate in the Navy their own outmoded concepts and doctrines.

The *status quo* was terminated abruptly when President Roosevelt moved Admiral King into what critics of the Navy's sweeping reorganization called a "virtual naval dictatorship." But Roosevelt had no qualms. The nation hardly knew the stern-visaged, taciturn, sinewy naval officer to whose hands he had entrusted such enormous power, but King had proved to the President's complete satisfaction that he was a strict disciplinarian, a superb organizer and, above all else, a grim realist.

Under King, the Atlantic Fleet had been "operating and training twenty-four hours a day under battle conditions, no lights at night, the responsible officers watching with suspicion every uncharted speck on the radar screen, the crews constantly ready for the sounding of GQ." In sharp contrast, the Pacific Fleet under Admiral Husband E. Kimmel, USN, had been "meticulously careful to avoid all semblance of awareness of tension."

King of the Navy

Ernest Joseph King, a single-minded sailor from Ohio, was not only the greatest chief the United States Navy ever had, but one of the authentic naval geniuses in history. He resembled Sir John Jervis (one of his two acknowledged heroes) rather than Drake and Nelson or Farragut, because his greatest strength was in fighting the war from behind his desk rather than from the bridge of a flagship.

A classmate of Andrews (Annapolis, 1901) and nearing retirement age when history afforded him his greatest opportunity, King brought to his new job a youthful vigor and energy, and a capacity for hard work and fresh ideas that never ceased to amaze his much younger colleagues and subordinates. He had served in World War I in the Atlantic Fleet as a top aide to Admiral Mayo (his other idol), then, after the war, he had acquired a versatility second to none by spending tours of duty on both surface ships and submarines, qualifying as naval aviator, and holding down a succession of jobs in various bureaus.

After a brief and discouraging tour of duty on the General Board, he was appointed commander in chief of the revived Atlantic Fleet—in 1941 when the "undeclared war" against the Nazis made it America's sole fighting force. That King had no illusions, either about the march of events or of the demands they had imposed upon the United States, was clear in his first message to his new command, in which he said:

"We must all realize we are no longer in a peacetime status and have no time to lose in preparing our ships and ourselves to be ready in every way for the serious work that is now close aboard."

Tall, gaunt and taut, with a high dome, piercing eyes, aquiline nose, and a firm jaw he looked somewhat like Hogarth's etching of Don Quixote but he had none of the old knight's fancy dreams. He was a supreme realist with the arrogance of genius. He had unbounded faith in himself, in his vast knowledge of naval matters and in the soundness of his ideas.

Unlike Stark, who tolerated incompetence all around him, King had no patience with fools. And where Stark had been inclined to procrastinate in the face of the onrushing events, King was decisive and adamant in his decisions. He was a grim taskmaster, as hard on himself as on others. He rarely cracked a smile and had neither time nor disposition for ephemeral pleasantries. He inspired respect but not love, and King wanted it that way, for he held with Troilus that to be wise, and love, exceeded man's might.

Somehow emblematic of the sentiments he evoked was the spontaneous remark of a chief petty officer who, it seems, remembered him from their salad days in 1903, when they had served together on the cruiser *Cincinnati* at Chefoo in China. Bumping into the heavily gold-braided King (who had just been upped to full admiral) on the third "deck" of the Navy Department, the old chief blurted out: "Look who goes there—*Ensign* King! A *mean* man!" But I never met anybody who did not admire his intelligence, integrity, and energy, even though many of his admirers were annoyed by his narrow chauvinism and blind devotion to his Navy. King, of course, was by no means unique in possessing these sentiments. It was what Henry L. Stimson called the peculiar psychology of the Navy Department. That department, Stimson wrote, "frequently seemed to retire from the realm of logic into a dim religious world in which Neptune was God, Mahan his prophet, and the United States Navy the only true Church."

King could be most difficult at times and extremely stubborn in his views and ways. An authoritarian personality, King was bent on keeping the reins firmly in his own hands, and he was trying to run the enormous COMINCH organization in the tight and comparatively simple manner of a command at sea. He organized his headquarters in bureaucratic Washington along spartan and taut lines. He persisted throughout the war in the grand illusion that he had actually succeeded in keeping COMINCH headquarters a "small, closely knit organization," imbued with "the fleet point of view"—preserving, as he wrote, "a certain seagoing character throughout the war quite unfamiliar to Washington."

The illusion was carried over into King's arrangements for his personal environment. Although he had his office on the third floor of the Navy Department building (the Navy had refused to join the Army at the new Pentagon although King had favored the move), he maintained his headquarters as COMINCH aboard PG 53, his sleek little flagship, the *U.S.S. Vixon*, riding at anchor in the Navy Yard in Washington. She had the warlike atmosphere of a flagship of a combatant fleet. On the *Vixon*, and later on her sister ship, the *U.S.S. Dauntless*, King surrounded himself with a small *côterie* of hand-picked aides who had to stand watch and actually drew sea pay.

Various stories and legends that floated about illustrated his strict adherence to the stifling protocol of the regular Navy. Although nobody would swear to their authenticity, they did indicate the atmosphere that prevailed at COMINCH. The resulting tension and discontent were not exactly conducive to making King's domain a "happy ship."

One such story clearly illustrated his condescending attitude to officers of the Naval Reserve from whose ranks more and more of his own co-workers had to be drawn. According to the (probably apocryphal) story, King once entered an office in the Navy Department and stopped at a desk behind which a lieutenant junior grade was completely engrossed in his work. The young man did not see the admiral enter and paid no attention to the mighty visitor who waited impatiently and stiffly for a sign of proper recognition.

The embarrassing situation was terminated when someone in the room yelled out, "Attention!" It brought the eager beaver promptly to his feet and then shook him out of his shoes. Those present believed that they saw an expression of contempt on King's stern face and heard him mutter, "What can you expect of a reserve officer?" True or not, the story of this strange encounter got around quickly and went far to undermine the reserve officers' devotion to their commander in chief.

Another such story averred that King, on his high and secluded perch, was willing to commune only with officers of flag rank and that he would not condescend to get his reports from anyone below the rank of rear admiral. At one point, a new Director of Naval Intelligence, who also headed the Combat Intelligence Division of COMINCH had to be promoted quickly to flag rank in order to gain Admiral King's personal attention for him.

At the same time, King was extremely strict even with the top-ranking admirals closest to him. An austere man who frowned upon anything ostentatious, he introduced a stern gray uniform into the Navy and insisted that it be worn at all times. The drab gray became extremely unpopular in the Navy, which was long used to its blues, but each time anyone in King's entourage dared to revert to the old color, he was promptly reprimanded.

Exasperated by the rule, Vice Admiral Russell Willson, USN, King's Chief of Staff, sought to solve his dilemma by wearing the new regulation gray, but restoring to it the gold braid of the old uniform. He arrived in his office one morning in this resplendent gray-and-gold. King looked at him with unbelieving eyes, then told his Chief of Staff:

"Willson, go home and change!"

Worst of all, King stubbornly resisted some of the very innovations the anti–U-boat campaign needed desperately, especially in ships best suited for this kind of specialized warfare at sea. He thus opposed the construction of the "jeep carriers" Henry J. Kaiser, the West Coast shipbuilder, proposed, first to the Navy's Bureau of Ships and then, when he could get no hearing there, directly to President Roosevelt. The President overruled King and ordered the Navy to accept Kaiser's baby flattops. Several of them—notably the *U.S.S. Guadalcanal* and *Mission Bay*—were destined to make major contributions to the defeat of the U-boats, a fact King was prepared to acknowledge ungrudgingly.

Otherwise King's relations with the President were excellent, because Roosevelt knew how to handle his invaluable but difficult COMINCH-CNO. Roosevelt was the only man in Washington the admiral was willing to defer to, probably because he realized that his whole professional destiny was in the President's hands.

King's noble life ambition was to remain at his high command post for the duration, to become one of the architects of victory, but he was apprehensive that the length of the war and his own passing years would disqualify him. When, in the fall of 1942, he neared retirement age, he decided to bring this prospect to the attention of the President. On October 23, in a characteristically curt note, he told Roosevelt:

"It appears proper that I should bring to your notice the fact that the record shows that I shall attain the age of 64 years on November 23rd next—one month from today."

Roosevelt promptly returned the note with the remark scrawled in his own hand across the bottom of King's letter:

"So what, old top? I may even send you a birthday present!"

That settled the matter to the final and perfect satisfaction of both men. Yet after that King must have felt, if only subconsciously, that he was serving in the great job he coveted body and soul in the best interest of his country, but at the grace of the President.

Behind the martinet was the man—a proud but essentially sensitive human being, far more attractive than this harsh description of his professional personality intimates. I once asked Admiral Low, "Could you describe in a few words how it was to work for Admiral King?"

"I can describe it in a single word—*difficult*," Low answered with a serious mien, but he added quickly: "Yet I never found him unkind, unpleasant, or vindictive. Though he would never relax completely, not in my company, he could laugh uproariously now and then. I found him curt but courteous, exacting but considerate, and occasionally even humorous."

That King had a sense of humor is evident in some of his private correspondence and off-hand remarks. In a bread-and-butter letter to General George S. Patton, Jr., after a visit to his headquarters in Casablanca, King added the impish postscript: "I trust that when you appear, the lions continue to tremble in their den." He did cherish his reputation as a "formidable old crustacean" but he was not disinclined to view it with a sense of proportion and, occasionally, even poke fun at it. He especially enjoyed Roosevelt's guip that "old Ernie shaves every morning with a blowtorch and I'm trying to verify the rumor that he trims his toenails with a torpedo net cutter."

In January, 1943, he allowed a rare insight into his private life, in a charming little note to an eighth-grader in Brooklyn who was doing his biography as part of her English work in school.

"I drink a little wine, now and then," he confided to her. "I smoke about one pack of cigarettes a day. I think I like Spencer Tracy as well as any of the movie stars. My hobby is cross-word puzzles—when they are difficult. My favorite sport is golf—when I can get to play it—otherwise, I am fond of walking."

He was an avid reader. I know this from personal experience, because he once sent for me and asked me to prepare a list of books on propaganda and psychological warfare for him. A few weeks after I had submitted the list, he summoned me again (after my own office hours) to discuss at length the books he had diligently read by then. On another ocacsion he called me in to clear up a certain passage in *Axis Grand Strategy,* a book I had compiled and edited. The range of his literary taste extended from Captain Hornblower to Douglas Southall Freeman's great biographies. *R. E. Lee* was King's favorite.

That his spartan regime was not necessarily innate but something he had imposed upon himself was indicated by Whitehill when he wrote, "Although by temperament no enemy to conviviality, Admiral King had, with simple logic, gone on the wagon so far as spirits were concerned in the spring of 1941 and remained there until the end of the war."

Now in 1942, he had brought to his new job firm ideas along both strategic and tactical lines, but the plan needed to deal with the U-boat menace was still vague and only fermenting in his mind.

In one of his rare moments of mirth King recalled a typically Churchillian distinction in referring to the underwater craft of World War II. During a discussion of submarine operations, the Prime Minister ven-

tured the suggestion that German underseas boats should be called
"U-boat" at all times, to distinguish them from Allied "submarines"—
thus to make clear that "'U-boats' are those dastardly villains who sink
our ships, while 'submarines' are those gallant and noble craft which
sink theirs." Now that he was up against the U-boats, King found them
potently villainous, mainly because, as he put it, available means to
deal with them were inadequate.

Confusion was compounded by both omissions and commissions.
Some of these mistakes were petty oversights, yet they proved serious
in their consequences. Thus, for example, the headquarters of the Gulf
Sea Frontier was established at Key West, although its sole connection
with the mainland consisted of a bridge and causeway which U-boats,
had they been aware of their opportunity, could have breached with
gunfire. Far more serious was the fact that communications at Key
West were unbelievably bad. If, for example, a U-boat was sighted
off Palm Beach, the commander of the Gulf Sea Frontier, at his isolated
Key West post, had to call the Third Army Bomber Command at
Charleston, S.C., *by commercial telephone,* and request that Army planes
based at Miami begin a search.

Omissions and Commissions

At this stage, for want of other defenses, the Navy decided to guard
our various anchorages with elaborate mine fields, hoping that the
U-boats would either perish in them or would be kept away by them.
The result was just short of catastrophic. Far from entrapping the U-
boats or discouraging them, the mine fields rendered navigation still
more hazardous for our own harassed freighters and tankers.

Thus in December, 1941, preparations for the reception of the anticipated U-boats were virtually confined to the laying of a protective
field of 365 mines off the Capes of the Chesapeake. Then, between April
24 and May 2, 1941, a huge field of 3,460 mines was laid around the
anchorage on the Gulf side of Key West. This latter field forced all
westbound shipping to steam an additional eighteen to twenty hours
around Rebecca Shoals before making the mine field entrance. It was
so difficult to navigate that "during the first ten weeks of its operations
U.S.S. *Sturtevant* and three merchantmen fouled mines and were sunk."

On July 25, while trying to extricate his damaged ships from the
encounter with *U-576* (which I will describe in some detail in a following chapter), Captain Newton Nichols, USN, led the tanker *Mowinckel*
and the freighter *Chilore* squarely into a mine field supposedly protecting the Norfolk approaches. The *Chilore* was blown up and capsized in

the field. When the tug *Kenshena* was sent to haul the *Mowinckel* out, both struck mines, the *Kenshena* sinking in twelve minutes, the *Mowinckel* barely making it to Norfolk. Many more ships were also destroyed or damaged by our own mines, their freakish fates lengthening the list of our maritime losses.

Today we realize that it was a mistake to continue business as usual in those hard-pressed shipping lanes. It would have been much wiser to confine the tankers to their ports, until such time as the escorts became available and they could proceed in protected convoys. However, the abrupt stoppage of all tanker traffic along the coast would have cut short the flow of oil to the United States and necessitated a strict embargo on fuel. This was a move Washington was reluctant to make, if only because it would have dramatized the true gravity of the situation and depressed civilian morale.

Throughout the darkest months of the U-boat blitz, the tankers were allowed to proceed, soloing up and down the burning lanes, and falling easy victims to the U-boats. The German skippers soon coined a picturesque name for this area. They called it "U-boat paradise." The decision to let the tankers sail on resulted in the loss of twenty-two tankers in February, 1942, alone, out of a fleet of 350 tankers the United States had. In March again, 57 per cent of all sinkings were tankers, at a time when 450 ships, including tankers, made the trip across the Atlantic in convoy—without the loss of a single ship.

A firm believer in the convoy system—which he regarded, as we shall see, as the *only* answer to the U-boat menace—Admiral King hoped to commence coastal convoys at once. But he found that they could not be organized, for he had neither escorts to screen them nor planes to patrol overhead. All he could do for the time being was to expand the Navy organization. He did it by setting up the Gulf Sea Frontier, first under Captain Russell S. Crenshaw, USN, and then under Rear Admiral James L. Kauffman, USN; and the Caribbean Sea Frontier with headquarters in Puerto Rico, under Rear Admiral John H. Hoover, USN.

In retrospect it must be said that while both "Reggie" Kauffman and Hoover were competent flag officers with outstanding administrative abilities, they were not exactly the best men the Navy could—or maybe would—spare for these crucial jobs, if only because, in the unspoken opinion of the Navy high command, the best men were needed in and assigned to the Pacific. What Kauffman and Hoover lacked was that flexibility and dynamism the situation demanded. The result was that static principles and a somewhat inert spirit came to be pitted against the kinetic warfare of a spirited foe. Hoover in particular was somehow incapable by nature of infusing his command with a genuine fighting spirit. He was an aloof and pedantic man, something of an introverted martinet and a stickler for naval protocol. In his own command, he was dubbed "Gentleman John," in the manner in which Americans like to nickname a fat boy "Skinny" and a tall guy "Shorty."

The Navy's failure even at the outset to delegate young and vigorous men to the Atlantic command to fight the U-boat on Doenitz's own terms, to imbue the fight with the spirit of the hunter, was in the final analysis one of the causes for our defeat at this stage.

On the other hand, it must be conceded that it was not only dynamism and a buoyant fighting spirit Kauffman and Hoover lacked. Although it was in their specific domains that the U-boats were soon to show "the utmost insolence," they were considerably worse off materially than Andrews, who had managed to coax seven destroyers from King. In May, 1942, when Doenitz shifted *Paukenschlag* into high gear, Kauffman's whole antisubmarine force consisted of two Coast Guard cutters, a small converted yacht, a 125-foot cutter, a couple of ancient Army B-18's, and a six-plane squadron of unarmed Coast Guard aircraft. They had to take care of the vast coastal area extending from Jacksonville, Florida, to the Mexican boarder, covering the whole Gulf of Mexico. Hoover had a couple of destroyers, three submarines, a few small craft (including Ernest Hemingway's yacht), and a dozen old PBY's, for the protection of the entire Caribbean region.

The Tale of Two Feuds

It was King's job to improve the situation in all its vast ramifications, by planning at the top, organizing our defenses, and then obtaining the immense hardware the Navy needed. Gradually the plan was taking shape in King's mind. It was no panacea. It needed time and means for its translation into action, but King pursued it relentlessly, without the slightest deviation, demanding total acquiescence, not merely from his own Navy but also from the Army and his Allies.

A clash with other peoples' concepts became inevitable. Thus very soon, when the war pressed hardest on his mind and soul, King became embroiled in two major feuds. He tangled with the United States Army and the British Admiralty.

Of his two feuds, King's running skirmish with the British was the more nebulous and the more difficult to justify. Its sources must have been mostly emotional because it could not be comprehended or explained on any purely rational grounds.

In his innermost mind, he harbored a dormant prejudice against anything British. It was aggravated by jealous resentment of Britain's long predominance (and occasional arrogance) as a seapower; and probably it also was a subconscious compensation for the humiliation King felt his Navy suffered when it was so badly bested by Doenitz just as the British appeared to be gaining the upper hand. I believe these intangible sources of his anti-British sentiment played as great a part in his mind as such strictly professional considerations as his insistence upon a vigorous prosecution of the war in the Pacific for which, he thought, the British had but tepid enthusiasm.

The emotional undertone was apparent in his relations with colleagues from the Royal Navy, war-hardened, heroic admirals like Sir Andrew Cunningham and Sir Percy Noble. In the late summer of 1942, when he headed the British Admiralty Delegation in Washington, Cunningham called on King with the suggestion that additional escort-type United States vessels be detailed to assist in convoy operations in the North Atlantic. Although King strongly felt the need and spent sleepless nights worrying about the dearth of such vessels, now he resented the suggestion which he interpreted as a "needle" directed at him and a reflection on the U. S. Navy.

King sternly reprimanded the baffled British admiral. "Although the British had been managing world affairs for some three hundred years," he said he had felt obliged to remind Sir Andrew, "the United States Navy now had something to say about the war at sea, and the fact should be faced, whether palatable or not."

The British on their part did not count Admiral King among their best friends in Washington. On July 15, 1942, in a moment of exasperation, Field Marshal Sir John Dill told Churchill, "King's war is against the Japanese." Churchill was similarly exasperated with King, but initially he attributed the admiral's thinly-concealed hostility to his newness in the rarified air of high command. On January 3, 1942, he wrote to Prime Minister Curran of Australia: "Admiral King has only just been given full powers over the whole of the American Navy, and he has not yet accepted our views." Later, when King invariably registered objections to anything Churchill proposed, the Prime Minister recognized this strange streak in the chief admiral of his foremost ally, but accepted it without demur. He knew full well that ultimate decision rested, not with King, but with Roosevelt, and that King was too good an American and an officer to rebel against civilian control.

As soon as the U-boats struck at the far end of the West Atlantic, the British rushed to the United States twenty-four of their best antisubmarine trawlers and ten corvettes with trained and experienced crews. They were sent unasked, on Churchill's initiative. More would have been sent—including planes, sonar and radar equipment, and personnel, anything at all from the British arsenal—but the United States did not ask for any such help. Moreover, the Navy under King showed no signs whatever that it was eager at all to benefit from the vast British experience in the Battle of the Atlantic.

This inane hostility to the British was probably most marked at the big Argentia base in Newfoundland. The strained intra-allied atmosphere at Argentia was described graphically by Captain Donald Macintyre, one of the Royal Navy's ace U-boat killers, on the basis of his personal experience at the big base.

"As the solitary 'Limey' in the place—my staff were at first all Canadian—I was looked on with the utmost suspicion," he wrote. "Had I come to try to teach the Americans their jobs? Or would I claim the right to participate in the operational control of the British ships which, in the western half of the Atlantic, came under U. S. Naval control?" His welcome was anything but cordial and he was advised to stick to his purely administrative desk, leaving operational matters alone. "I confess," Macintyre wrote, "that I was somewhat chilled by this reception" —a chill felt by many an officer of the Royal Navy who, at this hectic early stage of the war, had to be insinuated into, rather than detailed to, American naval units fighting the common enemy.

Even as late as January, 1943, at the Casablanca Conference, King persisted in his pique. During one of the high staff meetings, Admiral Sir Dudley Pound, Britain's genteel, soft-voiced First Sea Lord, discussed antisubmarine operations at some length, stressing the need for more long-range air protection and additional escort vessels. King, very sensitive on this score, took Pound's remarks as a thinly veiled criticism. He brusquely dismissed the First Sea Lord's businesslike suggestions and introduced a bit of acrimony into the discussion by reviving the old rationalization he had succeeded in palming off on Roosevelt the previous March. He said the U-boats could break through to the United States only because the British had been derelict in failing to exterminate Doenitz's wolves at their bases. His impression was, he added, that attacks on those bases had been sporadic and haphazard, for lack of what he called any planned program.

Such petty hostility vis-à-vis the British undoubtedly damaged our ability to cope with the U-boats, but whatever disagreements there were, they were resolved harmoniously in the end. That there remained no hard feelings was eloquently documented in an illuminated scroll the British Chiefs of Staff sent King on December 15, 1945, the day of his retirement. Written in exquisite calligraphy and bound in blue Morocco, it was signed by Field Marshal Lord Alanbrooke, Admiral of the Fleet Lord Cunningham of Hyndhope and Air Chief Marshal Lord Portal of Hungerford, and assured King that all was forgiven.

"We have watched with admiration and heartfelt gratitude," the British chiefs wrote, "the energy and order with which this unequalled expansion has been carried through. . . . We are anxious that you should know how deeply we have appreciated, throughout our association in the higher direction of the war, your keen insight, your breadth of vision and your unshakeable determination to secure the defeat of our enemies in the shortest possible time."

The Navy-Air Force Clash

Admiral King's long "battle" with the Army Air Force in general, and with General Henry H. Arnold in particular, had none of the nebulous undertones of the British feud nor the redeeming denouement of mutual admiration. It was a deadly serious business; it was also preposterous, for this strife within our own military establishment was carried on in the face of the enemy.

The controversy harked back to the early 1920's when the Air Corps of the Army, emerging from its baptism of fire in World War I, began to arrogate to itself more and more power, trying to pre-empt the air for its own planes and even to evict the Navy from some of its functions at sea. In 1921, Colonel William F. Mitchell sank some old battlewagons in an over-publicized test of air power versus sea power. Air enthusiasts promptly claimed that navies had become obsolete because none of their surface ships could survive bombardment from the air. After that, Air Corps extremists attempted to gain control of all land-based aircraft, leaving to the Navy only carrier-based planes.

When the Navy's unpreparedness left much of the burden of the coastal defense to the First Bomber Command, the Air Corps was not much better off. To begin with, it had only a limited number of planes and most of them were unsuited to antisubmarine action. Virtually nothing had been done before the war to train or equip any Army units for this kind of work or to establish a system of Army-Navy cooperation.

The Army planes that now flew against the U-boats carried demolition bombs instead of depth charges. They were manned by green crews totally untrained in naval identification or in the techniques of attacking such an elusive target as the submarine. None of the planes had any detection devices and their crews could never know whether the dark object they spotted from the air was a U-boat or a whale.

Even so, the Air Staff in Washington was highly pleased by this turn because it showed nevertheless how important air power was in anti-submarine warfare. As soon as this became evident, a spirited controversy broke out about jurisdiction over AAF units engaged in the U-boat war. Since the U-boat was, for all practical purposes, an integral part of the war at sea, the Navy took it for granted that over-all jurisdiction should be vested in it.

The controversy began quietly and politely on January 14, the morning after the commencement of *Paukenschlag*. Rear Admiral John H. Towers, chief of the Navy's Bureau of Aeronautics, wrote to General Arnold, requesting that about two hundred B-24's and nine hundred B-25's and B-26's be transferred to the Navy as soon as they came off the assembly line. It speaks well for the Navy that it recognized at the very outset of the U-boat blitz this urgent need of planes. But the Air Staff believed it detected in Admiral Towers' request an attempt on the part of the Navy to muscle in on the Air Corps' domain. They ignored the request altogether.

When no reply was received by February 20, Admiral King decided to send a note of his own to Arnold, asking for four hundred B-24's and nine hundred B-25's. Arnold replied five days later in a brief statement. He sent King a long dissertation about the AAF's responsibility to "operate land-based aircraft against suitable targets, wherever found." He insisted that "regardless of the ever increasing importance of air power and the consequent need of the Navy for the protection and assistance of land-based aircraft when operating in close waters, this basis of organization should be carefully observed."

King continued the exchange on March 5 and Arnold replied on March 16, then King wrote again on March 18, the correspondence becoming increasingly acrimonious. Arnold quoted remarks made in Congress in 1920 (!) by the late Senator Wadsworth, recommending the establishment of a Coastal Command within the Army Air Corps, a reference which King promptly dismissed with ill-concealed contempt.

When Arnold remained adamant in his refusal to assist the Navy, King took the matter to General Marshall. By then it was May 6 and the U-boat blitz raged unabated. The leisurely pace at which this burning matter was handled was demonstrated by Marshall who answered King's note only after a hiatus of sixteen days. Then the general merely stated he had not gotten around to the subject but "when he had returned from a trip, and, after taking up the question of allocation of planes to the British," he would concentrate on a solution.

The log jam was broken at last in July when Marshall agreed to allo-cate "a fair proportion of land-based planes" to the Navy for antisub-marine work.

There may have been much to justify the stand of both sides in this debate, but there was nothing to justify the delay in its solution. The jurisdictional part of the controversy had its lasting adverse effect, not merely on the strategic, but also on the tactical problems of the U-boat war, and especially on the problem of command. When there was an urgent and critical need for immediate offensive air operations out of Bermuda, the Navy directed the commander of the Eastern Sea Frontier to send Army aircraft to Bermuda. This was done, but when the planes landed at Bermuda, their pilots refused to take orders from the Navy's operational commander there or from any naval authority anywhere. This bit of *Pinafore*, as King later referred to it, was re-solved by King's giving orders to the Commander, Eastern Sea Frontier, who, in turn, gave them to the Army commander in New York, who, in his turn sent them to Bermuda.

Strategically, the situation was made odious by a basic difference of opinion as to the best means of combating the U-boats. The Navy had a preventive approach to the problem, concentrating on the protection of convoys and leaving offensive action to escort vessels, mostly when the U-boats mounted their attacks. The Air Force thought this approach was far too defensive, if not defeatist. It advocated an offensive ap-proach to seek out and attack the U-boats wherever they were and destroy them before they could attack.

King was scandalized by the Air Force's concept, partly because it was proven wrong by British experience, partly because it was patently inferior to the Navy's concept, and chiefly because he resented the fact that the Air Force was arrogating to itself doctrinal planning for the war at sea which was clearly the Navy's prerogative.

Consequently, even the settlement of the dispute over the allocation of planes settled very little. In the words of the Air Force's own his-torians, "it left undefined the nature and extent of the operational con-trol to be exercised by the Navy; and it left untouched the problem of duplication, the parallel of two landbased air forces for the same task".

In retrospect, both of King's feuds seem petty, especially in the light of the magnitude of the stakes. One was triggered by his myopic nationalism, the other by service rivalry. Neither should have been al-lowed to intrude upon the conduct of the war.

I believe that history's verdict will find him right in his struggle with Secretary of War Henry L. Stimson and the AAF, and wrong in his feud with the British. Right or wrong, the feuds had a bad effect on our conduct of the anti-submarine campaign and substantially delayed our victory over the U-boat. While they were being fought, an important part of the antisubmarine campaign was at a virtual standstill and thousands of tons of shipping, and hundreds of lives, were being lost in the Western Atlantic.

☆

★

CHAPTER IX

"The Situation Is Not Hopeless"

*Do the best you can with what
you have.
Do not worry about water that
has gone over the dam.
Difficulties exist to be overcome.*
—Maxims attributed to
Admiral King

June 21, 1942, was the first Sunday of another summer, but Room 3047 in the Navy Department, the crowded office of Admiral King's Flag Secretary, was busy as usual. Its full complement of officers and yeomen was present, despite the Sabbath, to attend to the admiral's multitudinous clerical needs.

Around two in the afternoon the buzzer summoned Ship's Clerk Jack McCoy across the hall to spend the next couple of hours in King's inner sanctum, sitting at unrelaxed attention as he took down one of the most important memoranda his exacting boss was ever to dictate. Addressed to General George C. Marshall, Chief of Staff, United States Army, it was the answer to a memo Marshall had sent King two days before.

Majestic Memorandum

In this long and carefully worded memo, King set down on paper his innermost thoughts about a subject that was intriguing and burdening him—his thoughts about the U-boat menace.

I propose to reprint it here almost in full, because it is simple, lucid, and comprehensive, and sums up better than any words of mine ever could the entire problem in all its staggering complexity.

I have long been aware, of course, of the implications of the submarine situation as pointed out in your memorandum of 19 June. I have employed—and will continue to employ—not only our regular forces but also such improvised means as give any promise of usefulness. However, it is obvious that the German effort is expanding more rapidly than our defense, and if we are to avoid a disaster not only the Navy itself but also all other agencies concerned must continue to intensify the antisubmarine effort.

As you are aware, we had very little in the way of antisubmarine forces in the Atlantic at the outbreak of the war except the fleet destroyers which were committed to troop escort duty and other services that made them unavailable for the protection of shipping in general. We had to improvise rapidly and on a large scale. We took over all pleasure craft that could be used and sent them out with makeshift armament and untrained crews. We employed for patrol purposes aircraft that could not carry bombs, and planes flown from school fields by student pilots. We armed merchant ships as rapidly as possible. We employed fishing boats as volunteer lookouts. The Army helped in the campaign of extemporization by taking on the civil aviation patrol. These measures were worth something, but the heavy losses that occurred up to the middle of May on our east coast give abundant proof, if proof were needed, that they were not an answer to our problem.

Concurrently with these extemporized operations we are building up our regular and reserve forces. Shortly after the war started our antisubmarine building program began to produce a trickle of submarine chasers. We also obtained some suitable vessels by borrowing from the British and also—I regret to say—by robbing the ocean escort groups. With these increments we were able to establish on 15 May a coastwise escort system between Key West and northern ports. At about the same time your valuable contribution to the cause—the First Bomber Command—became effective. Since 15 May our east coast waters have enjoyed a high degree of security. It should not be assumed, however, that this state of security will continue. We made it pretty hot for the Germans and they spread out to areas where the going was easier, but our east coast convoy system is still far from invulnerable and we may expect the Germans to return to this area whenever they feel inclined to accept a not-too-heavy risk.

"A Reasonable Degree of Security"

Though we are still suffering heavy losses outside the east coast convoy zone the situation is not hopeless. We know that a reasonable degree of security can be obtained by suitable escort and air coverage. The submarines can be stopped only by wiping out the German building yards and bases—a matter which I have been pressing with the British, so far with only moderate success. But if all shipping can be brought under escort and air cover, our losses will be reduced to an acceptable figure. I might say in this connection that escort is not just one way of handling the submarine menace; it is the only way that gives any promise of success. The so-called patrol and hunting operations have time and again proved futile. We have adopted the "killer" system whereby contact with a submarine is followed up continuously and relentlessly—this requires suitable vessels and planes which we do not have in sufficient numbers. Large numbers of small local patrol craft are required to prevent mining of harbor entrances, to keep lookout and to reinforce escorts at focal points, but no system of patrol will give security to unescorted vessels. We must get every ship that sails the seas under constant close protection.

It is not easy to create an adequate and comprehensive escort system. Our coastal sea lanes, in which I include the Caribbean and Panama routes, total 7,000 miles in length. To this must be added the ocean convoy system to Great Britain and Iceland (which is already in effect) and extensions which should be made to protect traffic to the east coast of South America (and perhaps to the Cape of Good Hope), not to mention our Pacific Ocean commitments. An enormous number of seagoing vessels is required, as well as very large air forces. Aviation for ocean coverage must be taken along in auxiliary carriers. For convoys moving close to land the air should operate from shore bases. While observation planes can be used for certain limited missions, the bulk of the shore-based aviation should be of the patrol or medium bomber type. Land type planes are essential in freezing weather because sea planes ice up on the water. All planes must have radar. All must have crews specially trained in the technique of antisubmarine operations and must be able to operate at night as well as by day.

King then dealt briefly with aviation requirements for antisubmarine operations, estimating that a joint effort would need a total of 1,350 planes (of which the Army was supposed to contribute 500 medium bombers). He continued (with a mixed metaphor):

The following steps are in hand:

(a) The convoy system is being extended as rapidly as possible. It is expected that Surinam-Trinidad-Aruba-Key West convoys can be started about 1 July to give protection primarily to oil and bauxite vessels. As escorts become available the system will be extended to cover the following routes, not necessarily in the order listed:

    (a) Panama-Key West
    (b) Guantanamo-New York
    (c) Guantanamo-Puerto Rico-Trinidad
    (d) Trinidad-South America
    (e) Key West-West Gulf ports
    (f) Possibly the route to the Cape of Good Hope

(b) The Navy components of shore based aviation are being augmented as rapidly as possible.

(c) Auxiliary carriers are being obtained to reinforce appropriate ocean escorts.

(d) The small craft organization is being augmented.

(e) The sweeper force is being increased as rapidly as possible to deal with the menace of mine laying by submarines.

(f) Every effort is being made to train personnel in the technique of antisubmarine warfare.

Birth of a Blueprint

This majestic memo with its broad and brutal assessment of the problem (and its hopeful listing of those "steps in hand") was the end product of the Army-Navy controversy over their divergent concepts of antisubmarine warfare. It drew scorn and sarcasm from Secretary Stimson of the Army, a much older man than King, yet one who showed much greater aggressive spirit than was apparent in the Navy's approach, which Stimson regarded as obsolete and defensive, if not defeatist.

"The War Department," Stimson wrote, "fortified by a comprehensive and extremely able report prepared by [Dr. Edward L.] Bowles [the distinguished physicist who was Stimson's scientific adviser in the matter], began a final effort to win for Army aircraft the autonomy and full naval co-operation needed for a prosecution of offensive operations."

The effort failed. Stimson suggested to Knox the establishment of an autonomous, offensive air task force for antisubmarine work. The suggestion was rejected. Then Marshall urged in the Joint Chiefs of Staff the creation of a new over-all antisubmarine command embracing all air and surface units, and responsible like a theater command directly to the Joint Chiefs. King rejected this solution, and so forth.

Even if the controversy caused substantial harm, it had this one salutary effect: it stimulated King to a minute exploration of the problem and became a catalytic agent in guiding him towards its best possible solution.

Careful study of the memorandum brings to light the five major themes underlying King's personal antisubmarine creed:

(1) Strategic: All-out attack mounted from Britain on German building yards and submarine bases.

(2) Operational: Bring all shipping under escort and air cover.

(3) Tactical: Introduction of the hunter-killer system.

(4) Institutional: Training of personnel in the specific techniques of antisubmarine warfare.

(5) Organizational: Unification of all antisubmarine warfare activities under control exercised by himself.

Here was the crux of the matter—the first intimation in so many words of the master plan that the situation needed. Unfortunately at this stage, much of what King called "steps in hand" was not yet in hand, but merely in the planning stage (at best). Almost another year was needed before the ideas so forcefully and clearly expressed in this blueprint could be translated into action.

In the meantime, King continued to extemporize, in accordance with his favorite maxim: "Do the best you can with what you have."

CHAPTER X

Skipjacks and Hooligans

On a breezy but hazy mid-July day in 1942, the KS-520—one of the first coastwise convoys worthy of that name—was nearing Ocracoke Inlet just south of Cape Hatteras. A motley assortment of nineteen ships, it was sailing southward at eight knots, bound for Key West and hoping for the best.

Captain Newton Nichols, USN, convoy commander in the tanker *J. A. Mowinckel,* had every reason to be apprehensive. At the final briefings at Lynnhaven Roads, he was told that, according to Combat Intelligence, there were sixteen U-boats vertically deployed against the area through which his convoy was to pass.

KS-520 was not only slow, it was also green. Its escort consisted of but five ships—the destroyers *Ellis* and *McCormick,* two patrol craft, and the Coast Guard cutter *Triton.* Its "air cover" consisted of a couple of Navy planes that flew over from the Marine Corps' station at Cherry Point.

This was a pitifully weak escort to pit against those estimated sixteen U-boats, if only because, according to the book, the break-even point of a convoy's safety needed at least 50 per cent more escorts than the maximum number of subs likely to attack. Fortunately for KS-520, Combat Intelligence was way off with its estimate. Although Doenitz had some seventy U-boats at sea in the Atlantic, there were only six of them in Admiral Andrews' entire Sea Frontier and, as it turned out, only a single sub in this particular convoy's path. Even so, KS-520 was destined to make history. For one thing, its experience showed—even though it was not immediately apparent then—how little Doenitz needed to get cold feet and run. For another, it demonstrated how effective a handful of greenhorn reservists could be, even when left entirely to their own meager resources.

The Saga of KS-520

The escort the Navy could spare for KS-520 represented an impressive force when compared with the "bucket brigades" of the previous months. That was what Andrews called the partial convoy system he had inaugurated on April 1, using whatever local craft were available at the various Naval Districts to escort ships from one anchorage to another. Each day between February and June, some 120 to 130 ships required protection; but Andrews, as he himself recorded it in his War Diary, still had only twenty-eight surface vessels that could be used on convoy work. Thus the protection now enjoyed by KS-520 on its Hampton Roads-Key West run was relatively formidable—the result of a more recent doctrine, issued on May 15, under which seven escorts were supposed to be assigned to each coastwise convoy. Ships were still too scarce to meet this minimum quota. But with five escorts it could call its own, KS-520 was better off than most.

Everything went well until 4:00 P.M. on July 15, when the *Triton* suddenly picked up a sound contact on the convoy's starboard beam. A search was on within seconds and, within minutes, the *Triton* followed down the contact with two attacks. The U-boat responded by firing an effective spread of four torpedoes. One hit the big *S.S. Chilore,* another the small *Bluefield,* and two the *Mowinckel* that had the convoy commander on board.

Captain Nichols was bracing himself for the worst when the unexpected happened. Instead of pursuing his attack against the disorganized convoy, Kapitaenleutnant Hans-Dieter Heinicke—for he was the attacker in *U-576*—suddenly blew to the surface bow first, in broad daylight at that, exposing himself to the fury of all the escorts racing in for the kill.

It was evident to all, and to Heinicke most of all, that *U-576* had been badly hurt by the *Triton's* ashcans and that she was no longer bending to her skipper's will. Closest to the U-boat when it darted up was the S.S. *Unicoi.* Her Naval Armed Guard under Ensign M. K. Ames, USNR, needed less than a minute to open up with their 5-inch gun at a hundred yard range and hit the conning tower of the German. The boat was also spotted by the two planes overhead. Their pilots, Ensign Frank C. Lewis, USNR, and Ensign Charles D. Webb, USNR, swooped low, straddled the conning tower with their depth bombs, and sent the *U-576* to its doom.

It was the only kill of the month in Andrews' Sea Frontier—one of a total of three U-boats sunk by United States forces in July out of eleven destroyed all told—but it caused a celebration at Church Street. Admiral Andrews wrote in his War Diary:

"This month is the most significant in operations in the history of this Frontier since it demonstrates that the increasing success of past weeks rests upon a solid basis of strong forces properly used."

If this now seems to have been a premature and unduly optimistic entry in the light of the continuing holocaust, Andrews' enthusiasm proved to be justified as far as his own frontier was concerned. Within that fortnight, Doenitz had lost three of his U-boats in this general area—not only the *U-576*, but *U-701*, also the *U-215*. The latter had vanished unrecorded and unclaimed by anyone on our side, but it shows up as "*Totalverlust*" or total loss in the German roster, which gives July 3 as the date of its demise and "off the American coast" as the location last heard from. The loss of *U-701* represented an especially heavy blow to Admiral Doenitz because its commanding officer, Kapitaenleutnant Horst Degen, was one of his younger skippers from whom he had expected great things. But on July 7, Degen was caught on the surface off Hatteras and his *U-701* killed by a young American, Second Lieutenant Harry J. Kane, USA, who disposed of him with three Mark-17 depth charges dropped from an altitude of fifty feet.

Although in the six months of his *Paukenschlag* Doenitz had lost only six U-boats (out of a total loss of thirty) in American coastal waters, the loss of the *U-701*, *U-576*, and *U-215*, as well as heavy damage to *U-402*, had a sobering effect on him. He was determined from the very outset to conduct this campaign at the doorstep of the United States on a hit-and-run basis. Now he confided to his War Diary that he considered the time ripe to run. The introduction of the convoy system, however weak and haphazard, and the appearance of air and sea patrols (which he described as "strong") made him quit. "There seemed to be no justification for keeping boats there any longer," he wrote, "and so I withdrew them. Thus the operations off the North American coast," he added, "which had been started in January, 1942, now appeared to have come to an end."

This was a significant concession of defeat, for it went far to show how easily Doenitz could have been discouraged from the very beginning and how he could have been persuaded to abandon *Paukenschlag*, had the limited forces we could pit against him in July, 1942, been available even a few months before.

These crucial triumphs were scored, not by seasoned, meticulously-primed veterans acting upon carefully-drawn doctrines in finely-honed machines, but by a handful of young Americans, all of them new-comers to war and, so to speak, free-lancing at it.

Ensign Ames, an accountant in civilian life, was one of the "ninety-day wonders," picked more or less at random and hastily trained for a job that required courage, quick thinking, and great skill. He displayed these attributes in superabundance in his first moment of truth. The two Navy pilots who finished the job Ames had begun and the Army second lieutenant who avenged the sinking of the big tanker *William Rockefeller* by destroying her nemesis, the *U-Degen*, were all reservists in their twenties, but perfunctorily prepared and equipped for their struggle with a shrewd and skilled foe, wise in the ways of the U-boat war.

The Ensigns' War

Consider for a moment the grave disadvantages under which these young men had to go to war:

They had to be hastily trained for naval warfare's most exacting and difficult job—antisubmarine warfare—and that job demands innate aptitudes and physical and psychological conditioning well beyond the functions normally expected of the fighting sailor.

They were given outdated or inadequate weapons, then they had to economize even with what they had because there was not enough of anything.

They had primitive means of communications to guide them in action; and detection gear—both sonar and radar—proved far from being perfect or reliable at this stage.

Most important was the lack of a set of rules to operate by. The Navy had failed to develop a definite antisubmarine doctrine; what doctrines there were, were exasperatingly contradictory. Thus each of the four destroyer training centers of the Atlantic had a different set of attack instructions. And while the Atlantic Fleet's Anti-Submarine Warfare Unit in Boston counseled audacity, Vice Admiral Richard M. Brainard, USN, at Argentia, urged caution.

In this welter of contradictory "doctrines," these young men had to exercise independent judgment and draw upon their own common sense. In their ignorance of doctrine, problems became magnified and this contributed to the impunity with which the U-boats could operate. A sonar man, for example, fresh from a brief course at Key West and never yet told about even the most common escape tactics of U-boats, had to discover (when it was too late) that the enemy he had on his sonar was forcing him to take ranges on his wake rather than his hull, or that the U-boat was fooling him with "knuckles" in the water, conjured up by a sudden revving of the propellers.

The predicament of the inexperienced Naval aviator thrown to the wolf-packs with his quickie training was even greater. To spot a tiny submarine required special conditioning and a bag of tricks, lest the airmen go after whales (as they frequently did) instead of the raiders.

Yet the ensigns grew into their tasks and, after an initial period of hesitation and bungling, they soon performed with astounding competence.

This was the bright side of this uneven bout during these days of disaster—this demonstration of ingenuity, initiative, finesse, and competence by young men derided by die-hard Regulars and viewed with some skepticism even by their commander in chief. While their admirals and generals wrestled and wrangled, prevaricated and procrastinated, the actual physical conduct of the U-boat war shifted to their lay hands. For months in 1942 and 1943, while the U. S. Navy groped frantically for means and doctrines, these green youngsters carried on the war with whatever they had. It was they who produced the only victories of those days in the Atlantic battle.

The Armed Guards

When on May 21, 1941, Kapitaenleutnant Ulrich Graef's *U-69* sank the American freighter *Robin Moor* in the South Atlantic, she performed a far greater service to the United States than to the Fuehrer. At that time the United States still had seven months of an uneasy peace, but Graef's greedy trigger finger showed the United States Navy what American merchantmen could expect from the U-boats in a regulation war.

The sinking of the *Robin Moor* persuaded the Navy that armed guards were needed on merchantmen and if Pearl Harbor found them unarmed it was not the Navy's fault. Since our neutrality statutes outlawed the arming of our merchantmen, Congressional sanctions were needed. It took Congress until November 17—but three weeks before Pearl Harbor—to pass Public Law 294 whose Chapter 473 authorized the President to put guns and guards on American merchant vessels.

As soon as the act was passed, Roosevelt telephoned Admiral Stark and instructed him to put it into effect immediately. The Navy was ready with a plan, but it did not have enough of the guns needed and could not spare men for guard duty. So, until the end of 1942, only about a hundred ships a month could be equipped and manned. The shortage remained so acute throughout the year, and so few of the dual-purpose 5-inch 38-caliber guns were available, that they had to be shared by removing them from the incoming ships that had them and putting them on the outbound vessels that needed them.

There were other difficulties, too, and the most delicate of them was the ambivalent attitude of the National Maritime Union to the armed guard business. Joseph Curran, president of the union, was a tower of strength and a paragon of co-operation with the Navy, aiding the war effort with such diverse contributions as the prevention of maritime strikes, the removal of drunks and troublemakers from the ships, and the integration of Negroes into the merchant marine. But in the matter of the armed guards, he was reluctant to go along with the Navy's plans. He sought the protection of guns, to be sure, but he demanded that gun crews be composed of merchant seamen, with only an ensign or a gunner's mate of the Navy over them. The problem was solved in the end when only a few of the civilian crews volunteered to handle the guns and Curran had to accept the bluejackets or see the guns left unattended.

The Naval Armed Guard—that was to come under the Tenth Fleet in due course—was organized under the Vice Chief of Naval Operations, with an energetic and ruthlessly effective reserve officer, Commander Edward C. Cleave, in charge. While on December 31, 1941, only fourteen merchantmen flying United States colors had guns and guards, by December 31, 1942, thanks to Cleave's efforts, over sixteen hundred had them, in addition to 204 American-owned vessels sailing under foreign flags, and the big British and French liners carrying our troops to Africa.

The commander of a ship's Armed Guard was a usually young ensign of the Reserve. These lads—barely out of their teens and fresh from the Navy's various quickie courses—had a complex job in which they had to cover the whole spectrum of wartime seamanship from gunnery to diplomacy. As Captain Al Brown, a veteran master of World War II, told me, "These boys had to mould their own men into disciplined crews, and they had to do it entirely on their own, without any chief petty officers to aid them. They had to operate in the unbuttoned atmosphere of our merchant vessels, establish working relationships with us masters and our officers, and prove to the seamen that they were 'regular guys'."

Their job was complicated by the fact that those guns aboard the merchantmen had more symbolic than practical value. As the seamen were becoming increasingly restive, and even mutinous, in the light of the maritime massacre, the presence of the Armed Guards was supposed to reassure them by giving them, if not absolute safety, at least a feeling of protection.

It was the primary job of the ensigns to impress the apprehensive seamen with their own fighting spirit and prowess, their technical skill, seamanship, and leadership. This was recognized by the Navy when it prescribed for the Armed Guard a set of exacting General Instructions that sounded almost like a Samurai's code.

"There shall be no surrender and no abandoning ship so long as the guns can be fought," they read. "In case of casualty to members of the gun crew the remaining men shall continue to serve the gun. The Navy Department considers that so long as there remains a chance to save the ship, the Armed Guard should remain thereon and take every opportunity that may present itself to destroy the submarine."

The vast majority of the Armed Guards lived up to these expectations. By the end of the war, they were the toasts of the merchant marine.

Case Histories of Courage

The actual job of the Armed Guards was both exhilarating and frustrating. The constant tension and the unpredictability of the U-boat war, its sudden flare-ups and furtive ambuscade, made the job exhilarating. The inherent limitations of the Armed Guard system made it frustrating. This frustration was pathetically described by Ensign J. K. Malo, USNR, commander of the Armed Guard on the freighter *Deer Lodge*, in his action report describing the loss of his vessel in the South Atlantic, on February 17, 1943.

"The ship listed sharply to port but righted herself considerably and went down by the bows somewhat," Malo wrote. "I ordered the gun trained to a bearing of 300°, and myself and my crew made every effort to spot the submarine. But it was too dark, all we could see were many shadows on the heavy swells.

"By this time the ship was completely out of control; the crew were abandoning ship, but the ship still had some headway. About fifteen minutes after the first torpedo hit, I gave the order, through the battle phones, for the 20-mm gunners to abandon ship; the rest of us remained aboard waiting for the submarine to show itself.

"About forty minutes after the first attack the second torpedo hit in practically the same place on the port side. This time she listed heavily to port but didn't come back and was settling well down forward; I gave the order to abandon ship as it appeared she was going under. My coxswain and pointer threw the small doughnut raft, that we had ordered left behind for us, off the poop deck, and we all went over the side."

Less than five minutes later the ship went down, bow first. Malo and his men were on their raft about thirty-two hours before a fishing trawler found them and took them to Port Elizabeth.

Ensign Ames's crew on the *Unicoi* was the only Armed Guard officially credited with participation in the actual destruction of a U-boat, but I believe the *U-215*, which only the Germans ever listed as lost, also succumbed to a merchantman's gun crew. On July 3, 1942, the day Doenitz said the *U-Hoeckner* was sunk without survivors, the tanker *Gulf Belle* was attacked by a submarine that fired a single torpedo from below, then surfaced. While it was crossing the tanker's stern, the *Belle's* gun crew fired a round from their 5-incher at 300 yards, forcing the boat down in a hurry. It was what followed that now convinces me that the mysterious attacker was Kapitaenleutnant Fritz Hoeckner in *U-215:* in the confusion after the first torpedo hit, the merchant crew abandoned the tanker, giving the submerged U-boat free rein to deliver the *coup de grâce*. But nothing more was heard from the raider.

In exemplary observance of their General Instructions, the Armed Guard remained aboard and continued to spray shellfire on the spot where the U-boat had vanished. When nothing more was heard from the U-boat while the *Belle* stayed afloat, the crew returned and made Port of Spain safely in tow—somewhat embarrassed by their haste to abandon ship and full of praise for their Armed Guard.

Other Armed Guards had the satisfaction of seeing their charges saved by their prompt and effective intervention. Thus on June 16, 1942, the *Columbian*, a thirty-year-old freighter plodding southward in the Atlantic en route to Basra with lend-lease cargo for Russia, ran into a U-boat on the surface. For hours afterwards, the *Columbian* felt the hot breath of the sub. The U-boat stalked the old lady while its master, Ed Johnson, tried to outwit the raider by taking his vessel on evasive courses in the treacherous moonlight.

At midnight, the U-boat opened fire. This was the cue for Ensign Merrill R. Stone, USNR, to order his gun crew into action at point-blank range. The very first shot from their 4-inch stern chaser was a direct hit. Then Stone's 20-mm machine guns also opened up, and the stern chaser scored another hit. A great volume of orange flame lit up the night, and the U-boat, still on the surface, seemed to have lost its taste for a fight. "The last we could see him," Johnson wrote in his report, "he was lying still at right angles to our course, and seemed to be getting low in the water." There is no record of this sub's fate, but the *Columbian* reached Basra without any more incidents.

The saga of the Armed Guards shone brightly in the encounter of the 9,000-ton Socony tanker *Brilliant* with an anonymous U-boat. She was hit by a stealthy torpedo on November 18, 1942, while sailing in convoy from New York to Belfast. The torpedo started a fire.

"The master, first, second, and third mates, also the cook and the steward, abandoned ship in a lifeboat," wrote the Port Captain at St. John's in his report. "This prompt action of the Master and the others struck the Armed Guard officer, Lieutenant (j.g.) J. R. Borum who was observing it, so humorously that the fourth officer, Mr. Cameron, checked himself on going overside and decided to wait awhile. The Armed Guard officer asked him why he didn't try to put out the fire, so the fourth officer, who remembered the layout of the Lux fire-fighting system from recent study, turned on the system."

When the fire was brought under control, muster of the crew showed nine men missing, including the master. That left Mr. Cameron in charge.

"The fourth officer," the Port Captain's report continued, "thereafter relied on the Armed Guard officer. Neither claims to be proficient in navigation, but between them they managed to bring the ship, at three knots, back to the Newfoundland coast, and finally located themselves after stormy weather in Bonavista Harbor, where they anchored. The day following the ship got underway again, and on 24 November was safely brought into St. Johns."

In the end, their sacrifice proved vain. On January 20, 1943, while the *Brilliant* was being towed to Halifax in a heavy sea, she broke up and sank. Borum and Cameron went down with her.

The Hooligan Navy

When Shakespeare wrote, "Light boats sail swift, though greater hulks draw deep," he could not know of course that his lines from *Troilus and Cressida* would attain a certain pertinence in the United States Navy during World War II. However it was a curious clash between swiftly sailing light boats and deeper drawing great hulks that, in the end, led to the establishment of what became known as the "Hooligan Navy." Already in 1941, foresighted American yachtsmen urged the Navy to organize them and their boats into a branch of naval defense, to be ready for whatever need a future emergency held. One of them was a New Yorker named Alfred Stanford, commodore of the Cruising Club of America.

In the summer of 1941, Stanford began to haunt the Eastern Sea

Frontier staff, buttonholing Captain Thomas R. Kurtz, USN, Admiral Andrews' chief of staff, and his ASW officer, Captain Ralph Hungerford, USN. He hoped to convince them that pleasure boats and their owners could contribute mightily to the nation's defenses. Andrews and his staff seemed to be receptive but could not act upon Stanford's suggestion without Washington's approval; and the powers in the Navy Department flatly refused to take the proposal seriously.

The big brass of the Navy was not swayed from its negative attitude by the British example at Dunkirk or in the Battle of the Atlantic in which, as Monsarrat so graphically put it, "the pinched circumstances of the Royal Navy necessitated the employment of anything that floated including tugs and yachts and fair-weather tubs." Since there were neither more nor better ships to be had, skill and luck and a makeshift armada of feeble boats had to fill the gap to "bring about what a rational probability could not hope to effect."

Stanford found no such spirit in the United States Navy and no inclination to accept his armada of amateurs and auxiliaries. On March 5, 1942, when sinkings in the Sea Frontier reached alarming proportions and it was evident to all in the know that Andrews could not cope with the situation unless he had more ships, Stanford appeared at Church Street with a concrete and binding proposition. On behalf of the Cruising Club, he volunteered to loan the Eastern Sea Frontier "thirty auxiliary sailing yachts between 50 and 90 feet long, with experienced skippers and skeleton crews." He further suggested that "this fleet be placed in commission immediately, and operated by the Navy as an experiment in patrol duty and anti-submarine warfare."

Although his offer was not accepted in so many words, Captain Hungerford voiced the Sea Frontier's agreement with Stanford's scheme, but delayed final decision pending Washington's approval. On April 27, Stanford raised his offer to seventy seagoing yachts and 100 smaller ones. He came fully prepared to hand them over right away. But he was now told, "The Navy's construction plan for small craft had been so accelerated that a yachting patrol is no longer needed."

This was just a brush-off foisted upon Captain Hungerford by COMINCH that did not want any part of those "bloody amateurs." There was, to be sure, a legitimate clash of honest opinion about the value of these sailing yachts and their white-flannelled owners in the protection of the seaboard against 500-ton submarines and their seasoned crews. The Navy was sincerely apprehensive that, far from being any help, they would become a nuisance, getting into all kinds of predicaments from which the Navy would have to extricate them.

Instead of arguing out the case, the Navy chose to turn them down bluntly with a transparent subterfuge, the callousness of which infuriated Stanford and his eager fellow yachtsmen. They carried their woe to their Congressmen and the press, and kicked up such a fuss that Admiral King, foremost opponent of their scheme, had to change his mind. He still did not want them in the Navy proper; but on May 4, he sent a note to Rear Admiral R. R. Waesche, USCG, commandant of the Coast Guard, requesting the Coast Guard Auxiliary to take over and organize this volunteer effort.

Admiral Waesche went to work at once and, with the help of his district officers, organized a substantial armada of these vessels—auxiliary sailing yachts, motorboats, converted fishermen and small freighters. Thus was born the Coastal Picket Patrol or, as the Coast Guard called it, the Corsair Fleet. Its own personnel, mostly amateur yachtsmen, preferred to refer to it as the "Hooligan Navy," calling themselves the "Hooligans." They did their best under difficult and often humiliating circumstances to aid the war effort against the U-boats.

The Navy in its continuing pique refused to commission most of the skippers of these picket patrols—experienced yachtsmen and substantial citizens, or else they could hardly afford this de luxe pastime. Thus the schooner *Primrose IV* was commanded by a sixty-year-old Harvard professor, a naval reserve officer in World War I, now reduced to the rating of chief boatswain's mate. Most of the time the owners of these yachts stayed on board, satisfied with the same rating. Even Al Stanford, who was *Commodore* of the Cruising Club, made only lieutenant commander, a rank which he cheerfully accepted and proudly bore.

The personnel of the "Hooligan Navy" was a motley assortment of seagoing buffs—Great Lake navigators, college boys and Sea Scout leaders, also beachcombers, former bootleggers and ex-rum-runners, in additions to pedigreed yachtsmen. The foremost celebrity who served a stretch in the "Hooligan Navy" was Ernest Hemingway, an episode in the late great writer's adventurous life I am reprinting here from Milt Machlin's fascinating book, *The Private Hell of Hemingway.*

"At the start," Machlin wrote, "he had approached Spruille Braden, then U.S. Ambassador to Cuba and offered his powerful, fast *Pilar* for the conquest of submarines in the Caribbean. The 42-foot sportsfisherman, rigged up with special radio and other equipment, worked undercover for Naval Intelligence as a Q-boat. Throughout 1942 and much of 1944, it patrolled the north shore of Cuba with a crew of nine, a machine gun (in addition to Hemingway's Thompson), a load of big explosives and other lethal paraphernalia.

"'Hemingway's objective,' Braden says, 'was to be hailed and ordered alongside by a Nazi submarine, whereupon he would put a plan into operation which was designed to destroy the U-boat.

"'This,' Braden comments, 'was an extremely dangerous mission, as certainly a fishing boat under normal circumstances would be no match for a heavily armed submarine. However, Ernest worked out the plan intelligently and, I believe, would have won the battle had he been able to make the contact.'

"The scheme, which was described as 'suicidal' though probably workable by Navy experts, was never put into action, though Hemingway's crew was able to report many valuable sub-sightings. 'In fact,' Braden recalls, 'he would have made the contact had not my naval attache called him into Havana one day when he was on a location he himself had picked, and where a submarine did show up within twenty-four hours.'

"So worthwhile was Hemingway's contribution that Braden put him in for a naval decoration. All of this, of course, was carried on in strict secrecy."

Hemingway's one-man naval war ended, and the threat of his terrible wrath was lifted from the U-Boat Arm in 1944, when he became bored with patrolling the Caribbean waters from which the U-boats had prudently departed. He decided to hell with the Gulf Stream and accepted an assignment from Collier's magazine as war correspondent in Europe.

The Navy's somewhat petty and petulant apprehension that delayed for so long the integration of the "Hooligan Navy" into the nation's seaborne defenses was destined never to be proved or disproved, certainly not insofar as the employment of this makeshift armada in the anti-submarine campaign was concerned. If the Picket Patrol met no conclusive test of its value, it was because the U-boats departed from the Eastern Sea Frontier before there were enough pickets on hand to throw into the fracas. Even so, in several "incidents," they proved both their value and their limitations.

Thus on August 13, 1942, the Army Air Base at Westover, Massachusetts, sent out a flight of airplanes to test the Army's aircraft-warning system. No advance notice was issued about the flight and no naval vessel or shore station made contact with them. But four vessels of the "Hooligan Navy" reported the planes promptly and accurately. They were the ketch Sea Roamer, the schooner Sea Gypsy, the power cruiser Willidy II, and the motor fisherman Dorado. They picked up the sneak-flight as soon as it swung across Cape Cod, south of Nantucket, before it turned west and south, heading for its destination at Philadelphia.

Several Picket Patrol boats managed, if not actually to sink U-boats, at least to keep them down. Thus the *Edlu II* sighted a U-boat on September 15, 1942, south of Montauk Point. The former yacht had no depth charges on board and could, therefore, mount no effective attack on the U-boat it had spotted less than a hundred yards away. But its enterprising crew attacked nevertheless with the machine gun and forced the U-boat to submerge. On the other hand, a motor cabin cruiser-turned-Hooligan vessel shied away from a U-boat it had sighted at 450 yards, although it had the depth charges it needed for attack. In his moment of truth, the motorboat's owner-commander became confused and zigzagged away, then even failed to report the encounter.

The glory of these Hooligans was destined to be short lived. By January 1943, Coast Guard cutters were coming out in sufficient numbers to justify a thirty-five per cent reduction in the picket force. And on October 1, 1943, the "Hooligan Navy" ceased to exist. Summarizing its history and value in World War II, Morison feelingly wrote: "The Coastal Picket Patrol is another of those things which should have been prepared before the war came to America. It would have been slight protection against submarines, but might have saved many a merchant seaman's life at a time when survivors from torpedoed freighters and tankers drifted about for days within sight of the coast, unseen by aircraft or surface vessels.

"More of the Dunkirk spirit, 'throw in everything you have,' would not have been amiss in May and June 1942, when regattas were being held within Chesapeake Bay while hell was popping outside the Capes," he concluded. "The yachtsmen, or some of them, were eager to stick their necks out; but at the time of greatest need, the Navy could not see its way to use them."

CHAPTER XI

The View from OP-16-W

The winter of 1942-43 was one of the foulest on record in the North Atlantic. Its bone-chilling cold spread torture over the ocean as if God had decided to disavow the adage that He always tempered the wind to the shorn sheep.

The Atlantic was full of ships, all of them trying to get behind the weather. But there was no escape. Whole gales blew continuously as battered convoys sailed through icy rains and snow squalls. The sea whipped over the bows and froze on the weather decks until the vessels looked like giant icicles. During those months, it seemed, the savage weather was our foremost enemy at sea. Between November, 1942, and March, 1943, our marine casualties amounted to an unprecedented 166 ships of which 91 succumbed to the Atlantic's frantic mood.

Early in December, 1942, the cheerless weather had even Washington in its grip. Gloomy and dark from overcast skies, the city looked unkempt under a blanket of stale, dirty snow. And yet, as I drove down the broad avenues on my way to the Navy Department, I thought I saw a dim glow over the massive government buildings. Pearl Harbor was only a year past but things looked amazingly good to our side. The Russians were holding fast at Stalingrad. The Japanese were definitely checked in the Pacific. General Alexander A. Vandegrift's Marines seemed to have decided the issue on Guadalcanal.

In October, enormous convoys had ferried tens of thousands of American troops across the ocean—unmolested by the 105 U-boats Doenitz had at sea—and the Allies were now firmly established in North Africa where Rommel had reached the end of his desert road.

Everywhere it seemed that Axis had their back to the wall and they had it, too—everywhere except in the Atlantic.

Coming from imperturbable, flippant New York, and having been fed a steady diet of optimism by the press, I was not aware of this exception. Believing every word I had read in the papers, I now thought the U-boats were also on the run and that the Battle of the Atlantic was as good as won. I was not alone in this untutored cheer. "Even in naval cricles," Theodore Roscoe recalls, "some of the more hopeful were encouraged to think that the U-boat menace was nearly liquidated."

The Washington Scene

That distant and mysterious battle of the ocean was now to become a personal and immediate concern for me, because I was in Washington on a "secret mission" against the U-boats. A so-called "special warfare" branch was being formed within the Office of Naval Intelligence to add a new dimension to our antisubmarine campaign. It was a purely intellectual dimension, for the new branch was shrewdly designed to attack the U-boats, and weaken the morale of their crews, with words especially tailored for and beamed mostly to them. A specialist of propaganda and a student of morale in the German Navy, I was hired by ONI to research and plan this campaign. Never before had this kind of weapon been given any scope and opportunity inside the United States Navy, and it was only the bold new spirit Admiral King had introduced that made the establishment of such a branch possible. We were to talk directly to the enemy over the din of war, using "ammunition" that came from the classified files of the ONI.

December 7, 1942, was my first day in Op-16-W, as the Special Warfare Branch was labelled on CNO's table of organization. ("Op" standing for Chief of Naval Operations, "16" for the Office of Naval Intelligence, and "W" designating our branch; it was, as the letter indicated, way down in the table.) It was a portentous day for more reasons than one. It was the first anniversary of Pearl Harbor. It was the beginning of a convoy battle in the course of which the *U-611* was sunk. For me personally, it was a day of occult thrills that filled me with excitement. For the first time in my life, I was allowed into the inner sanctum of an intelligence service and given access to its mystery-shrouded paraphernalia kept in the big steel safes with intricate combination locks holding reams of secret reports.

I had been in Op-16-W about a week when Commander Cecil H. Coggins, USN, brought to my desk a sheet of blue paper torn from the teletype. It was the transcript of a German broadcast from U-boat headquarters which the FCC's Foreign Broadcast Monitoring Service had intercepted.

"Things look awfully bad," Coggins said darkly in his usual staccato manner. "They're claiming they sank a million gross tons in November."

This was the high water mark of what the Germans called *Tonnageschlacht*, the Battle of Tonnage. Doenitz contended that if he could sink our merchantmen faster than we could build them, Germany would nullify American aid and win the war. According to his calculations, his U-boats had to sink a steady one million tons a month to accomplish this. He drove his U-boat commanders ruthlessly to sink, sink, sink— and in 1942 they responded beautifully. In May, for example, they sank 120 Allied ships (of which forty were American), when otherwise we lost a total of only twenty-three ships to all our enemies by all other causes in all parts of the world. In the crucial record month of November, the U-boats sank 106 ships, when our losses by all other causes were but thirteen vessels.

Since October, the U-boats had concentrated on ships that carried supplies to our forces in North Africa, as if Doenitz tried to compensate for his failure to prevent our troops from initially getting there. It was already apparent to us in Op-16-W that it was a historic blunder and in an analysis we prepared about its long-range significance, we bluntly expressed the opinion that this mad *Tonnageschlacht* would not make up for the opportunity he had missed. Had he succeeded in sinking our troopships en route, his U-boats would have scored a victory Hitler's generals could never have been able to match in their land battles. He would have made a decisive contribution to the war as a whole, not merely by the massacre of the troops consigned to their overseas posts, but especially by a demonstration that he had control of the sea and our efforts to move overseas were too costly and maybe even futile. It is truly incalculable how American public opinion would have reacted to such a massacre at sea and how our entire war effort would have been affected by a decimation of our expeditionary force.

As it was, the U-boats were singularly ineffective against the transports. They managed to sink only three in all, bound for Iceland. Doenitz waged his campaign with self-seeking opportunism. Since he assumed that the troopships had lavish protection, he refrained from attacking them (if he actually knew that they were en route) and went after the easy plums from which he could expect a spectacular showing at negligible cost to himself. Worse still, instead of balling his fist for a single brutal blow, he spread his fingers for a series of slaps. In November, for example, his U-boats operated in five major areas—

along the North Atlantic convoy routes, to be sure, but also in the South Atlantic, the Caribbean, in the Azores-Freetown area, and off Brazil. They scored fantastic successes in each of these areas, but their dispersal took the pressure off our solar plexus.

In October-November, 1942, Doenitz had his decisive strategic chance, but he failed to recognize it and nobody in the German High Command called his attention to it. In this was reflected a critical deficiency of the German war machine, the ultimate inadequacy of Hitler as a war lord. His inability really to comprehend that strategic capability of the U-boat, and his failure to devise a master plan for its decisive role *ipso facto* reduced the importance of the U-boat arm. Its victories then looked wonderful in the *Sondermeldungen*—the special communiques of the Wehrmacht High Command in which Hitler bragged of spectacular victories amidst flourishes of trumpets—but did not make a contribution to the ultimate decision as an absolute weapon.

Deceptive Halcyon Days

On September 3, 1939, Doenitz was told to wage a *guerre de course*. He waged it with superb determination, ingenuity, and skill, but his part in the greater order of things remained confined to what was a limited naval war at best. At no time during the whole war was the U-boat's role broadened to include this strategic mission. This was clearly the fault of Doenitz's boss, Grand Admiral Raeder, a surface admiral of the old school who was forever awed by the task of waging a naval war against the world's great seapowers. Logged as his mind was to traditional warfare at sea, he tried to stretch his limited means and assigned to the U-boat its limited task within his makeshift strategic concept. Raeder was avidly aided in all this by Hitler.

In the summer of 1942, flushed by the enormous victories of his U-boats, Hitler appeared fleetingly to grasp the true potential of his submarines. He told some luncheon guests at his headquarters: "The decisive factor in any war is the possession of the technically superior weapons. Our main preoccupation today must be to maintain the lead we have already gained in this respect, which has been the foundation of our great victories up to date. If we do, we shall be able to wage— and win—this war at a third of the cost, in casualties, which we inflict on our foes.

"It would therefore be the height of folly to insist on retaining in the army specialists in submarine construction. The net result would be," he mused, "that the British would be able to blast their way through to Archangel with a convoy carrying a thousand tanks and as many aircraft; and then the Army and the Air Force would have to destroy them all in bloody and single combat, and with losses many times greater than the number of men demanded from the Wehrmacht for the construction of submarines."

But these were only musings. He refrained from ever really implementing his own ideas. How little he truly understood the crux of the issue was shown when he lumped the construction of U-boats with that of minesweepers and ventured the opinion that the building of both was of "equal importance."

Working under an infantryman and a mediocre surface admiral, Doenitz played the lone wolf throughout the war. He hugely enjoyed being allowed to make his own designs and operate more or less as he pleased. He was never firmly integrated into that greater design that would have enabled him to give Hitler the victory they both so eagerly sought.

The *Tonnageschlacht* was like all his other campaigns. It was a vast measure of expediency rather than a carefully thought-through plan. It was not developed on Hitler's echelon in the highest councils of the Wehrmacht. It was Doenitz's idea in which, as usual, Hitler merely acquiesced and to which Raeder, as usual, had no serious objection. It did a lot of damage. But it had in it the seeds of Germany's eventual inevitable doom.

Now Doenitz had his halcyon days and his *Tonnageschlacht* was going just fine. That broadcast Coggins had brought to my desk about a million gross tons having been sunk in November was calculated to show how right he was and how well he was doing. He hoped to prove with it that he had reached the breaking point at which the defeat of the Allies could be assured.

If he really believed his own hypothesis—that was based on a woeful underestimation of American capabilities—he further deceived himself by padding his figures. His U-boat commanders were notoriously unreliable with their sinking claims and even Doenitz conceded that "the reports from the boats were sometimes somewhat exaggerated." This, too, was really his fault. Driven as they were by their boss's insatiable greed, they had to make up victories when their actual scores did not come up to Doenitz's expectation. Since this was only too evident to us in Op-16-W, we composed several broadcasts in which we cited figures and facts in a continuing effort to document the congenital mendacity of the U-boat commanders. Thus on October 16, 1942, a *Sondermeldung* proclaimed the "destruction" of a convoy by sinking "eleven ships out of forty." We checked the claim with the Convoy and Routing Section of CNO and found that the convoy the *Sondermeldung* had "annihilated" was SC-104, that it actually consisted of forty-seven ships of which only eight were lost. On March 20, 1943, a special communique of the U-Boat Command claimed that "in an action lasting from March 17 to 19, thirty-two ships of 186,000 tons and one destroyer were sunk, and hits were scored on nine other ships." The convoy was SC-122, it was made up of fifty-one ships of which it lost only eight.

Doenitz had claimed the magic million tons several times, although in actual fact that total was never reached in any single month and he knew it. In November, 1942, he thus let it go with the trumpeted *Sondermeldung*, claiming a million tons when his own tabulation at Lorient added up to only 750,000 gross tons, and our true losses totalled 637,000 tons. The Atlantic was still the "U-boat paradise" but Doenitz was living in a fool's paradise. We already knew that we could no longer lose the whole war to the U-boat, but we still doubted that we could win it in the face of their interference. If his own figures were not enough for him, they were still far too much for us.

The Burning Ambush

Only the exceptionally violent storms of December spared us even greater losses, and then it was our turn to indulge in a delusion. Doenitz had ninety-seven U-boats at sea in the Atlantic but now they managed to sink only fifty-four of our ships totaling 287,730 gross tons. January was then highlighted for our side by the Russian victory at Stalingrad, but in the Atlantic, too, the picture continued to look better. Just when we began to hope that the U-boats had expended their sting, an exceptionally painful convoy battle taught us otherwise. Though it remained an isolated action in January, it showed how dangerous the U-boat could still become to our ability to maintain our forces overseas.

It began on January 3. At 9 A.M. on that day, when he arrived in the Operations Room of the U-Boat Command to preside over the daily situation conference, Doenitz was handed a signal that had come in during the night. It was from Kapitaenleutnant Hans-Juergen Auffermann in *U-514*, sent from a spot near Trinidad where he was on what he called his Calypso Patrol.° Auffermann reported that he had sighted a convoy consisting entirely of tankers, proceeding without escort at high speed in a northwesterly direction. From this germ of information Doenitz developed one of his most brilliant victories.

The convoy had been put together in great haste in the Dutch oil

---

° Auffermann was killed six months later, on July 8, 1943, when his boat was sunk in the Bay of Biscay with all hands on board.

ports of Curaçao and Aruba in the West Indies in answer to urgent pleas from Eisenhower for fuel for his tanks and armored columns stalled in North Africa. It was a calculated risk to mass this many tankers in a single convoy and send them on their way without proper protection—but the need for the fuel was great and pressing, and it was hoped that the fast new tankers would outrun any U-boat that might come up against them.

Of course, these facts were unknown to Doenitz when he perused Auffermann's signal. All he knew was that an apparently precious and important Allied convoy was at large in the Atlantic. But, putting two and two together, using whatever pertinent data his staff could assemble, as well as his educated hunches, he decided the convoy must be en route to North Africa with oil for Eisenhower. He correctly guessed that it had been assembled in Curaçao and Aruba, and even that it had made a last stop at Port of Spain in Trinidad before starting the race across the ocean for what he further conclued would be Gibraltar, passing the Azores on the way.

He resolved at once to intercept the convoy at a point he assumed it would have to pass. He needed a *Rudel*, but the nearest pack of U-boats he had in the Atlantic was the "Dolphin" group, stationed on the great circle track from New York to the Canary Islands, standing about a thousand miles northwest of the spot where the *U-514* had sighted the convoy. Doenitz radioed the "Dolphin" group to proceed at once to a definite spot on the Great Circle route off the Azores, quite as if he had inside information of the convoy's exact routing.

It was a fantastic shot in the dark!

On January 5, after two days on its problematical course, the "Dolphin's" reconnaissance boat sighted a fair-sized *westbound* convoy steaming at fourteen knots, a very high speed. The sighting, signalled to the U-boat Command, confronted Doenitz with a dilemma. In situations like this he was wont to preach that a bird in the hand was worth two in the bush; but in this particular case he was not sure whether the fast convoy the "Dolphin's" reconnaissance boats had sighted was a fair substitute for the phantom convoy his boats were chasing. It did not take him long to make up his mind. He instructed the "Dolphin" commanders to ignore the convoy and proceed as ordered originally.

His decision was not as arbitrary or whimsical as it seemed. Because of the high speed achieved by the westbound convoy Doenitz calculated it must have been made up of ships sailing in ballast; he expected the other was a fully-loaded prize.

January 6 came and went and nothing happened. Nothing happened on the seventh either. Out on the broad ocean byways the "Dolphin" group was sailing steadily toward its problematical target. In the Operations Room in Doenitz's little chateau in Kerneval near Lorient, France, the suspense was becoming nearly unbearable, with Doenitz alone remaining calm and composed.

At 2 p.m. on January 7, Doenitz signalled the Dolphins to deploy in patrol line west of the Canary Islands, south of the Azores. The line was to consist of eight boats proceeding on a 245° course at a speed of seven knots, thus covering a front of about 120 miles. That same night, after the moon had set, he sent another signal ordering the Dolphins to turn and proceed at nine knots on a reciprocal course—a course his intuition told him the tanker convoy was following to its doom.

The pay-off came on January 8!

At 6:38 a.m. Doenitz was roused by his flag lieutenant, Fuhrmann, with the decoded message a signalman had just brought over to the villa from the communications shack. It was from "Dolphin," Korvetten-kapitaen Guenther Seibecke of *U-436* reporting. His lookout had just sighted *the* convoy, exactly where Doenitz predicted it would be. Then came another signal, from Kapitaenleutnant Mehlmann in *U-571*, then still another, from Kapitaenleutnant Guenther Heydemann in *U-575*.* Both reported the convoy had been located.

The battle was joined on January 9. It lasted until the eleventh. Not a single U-boat was lost, but of the nine tankers only two escaped. Recalling this victory which he had contrived in a tour de force of deductions and hunches, Doenitz pointed out "how often we could do little more"—in the well-nigh total absence of hard intelligence and air reconnaissance—"than make an intelligent guess and plan our operations accordingly."

The loss of those tankers and the threat which their loss represented to our ability to supply our forces overseas left a deep impression on Admiral King. More than any other single engagement in the Atlantic, it convinced him that the U-boats had to be stopped, as soon as possible, once and for all.

Aside from that disaster, January was not too bad. There were still over ninety U-boats on *Feindfahrt* in the Atlantic, but now they could

---

*Seibecke fell four months later when *U-436* was sunk without survivors in the North Atlantic. *U-571* perished on the first anniversary of this engagement, west of Ireland; and the *U-575* was sunk on March 13, 1944, almost at the exact spot where the tanker convoy was eventually attacked.

sink only twenty-nine ships. Their aggregate of about 180,000 gross tons was the lowest since January, 1942. Had the U-boats really lost their touch? Or was the abominable weather responsible? However, what seemed to be an abrupt end to the holocaust was quick to prove deceptive. The U-boat arm was not yet defeated. Unknown to Allied Intelligence, it was merely in the process of redeployment. Doenitz was moving his U-boats again, this time back to mid-ocean, for a vicious new series of wolfpack attacks against our ships sailing in those North Atlantic convoys.

In February they struck! Our losses rose abruptly to fifty ships of 312,000 gross tons. By March, Doenitz had a record number of 116 U-boats at sea. That month we lost ninety-five merchantmen and tankers of 567,401 gross tons, while Doenitz paid the forfeit of only fifteen U-boats, still overcompensated for by twenty-three new constructions.

How the center of gravity had shifted was shown graphically on the big charts of our plot room that featured a different pin for every one of our ships lost. Back in August, the American waters of these charts blossomed with forests of those pins. Now in February and March, the forests moved out to sea.

All of a sudden, the situation was devastatingly dismal again. In the five winter months, our losses totalled almost two million gross tons, while the Germans paid with but fifty U-boats for their fantastic victory. Roscoe summed up the true seriousness of the situation when he said, "If the wolfpacks were not squelched in the near future, Hitler would win the Battle of the Atlantic."

Part Three

THE PHANTOM FLEET

> *Nothing remains static in war or in military weapons, and it is consequently often dangerous to rely on courses suggested by apparent similarities in the past.*
>
> FLEET ADMIRAL KING
> A Naval Record

CHAPTER XII

Stemming the Tide

~~~~~~

At the time of the tanker disaster, Admiral King's attention was focused on the inter-Allied conference in Casablanca at which Roosevelt and Churchill proclaimed the "unconditional surrender" formula. The one-sided convoy battle was at its height on January 9, 1943, when King left Washington, hopscotching to Morocco where he arrived on the twelfth.

At Casablanca, all the broad questions of grand strategy came under survey and major decisions were made about plans in the Pacific and the Eastern Mediterranean and about aid to the Soviet Union. However, the pressing problem of the U-boat kept hovering like a pall over the conference. King was still somewhat petulant and testy when Admiral Sir Dudley Pound, his British colleague, reviewed the U-boat situation. King again raised his stock argument that "in his opinion the most favorable targets were the assembling yards and the submarine bases," and added pointedly that "it was his impression that the attacks against these had been sporadic, and that there had been no planned program."

The Legacy of Casablanca

Judging by his actions in the immediate wake of the conference, this was the last flare-up of his petulance and also of his habit of relegating the U-boat menace to second place in his global considerations.

In their final report at Casablanca, the Combined Chiefs of Staffs stated unequivocally that "the defeat of the U-boat must remain the first charge on the resources of the Allied Nations." King concurred loyally in the resolution, then moved swiftly and with his accustomed vigor to implement it.

This change of heart was probably the result of some timely missionary work Churchill had decided to do on King. On January 22, the American admiral received an invitation to lunch with the Prime Minister. When he arrived at Churchill's villa, he found that the lunch was for just two. At this tête-à-tête, Churchill was at his most eloquent. He spoke so persuasively that King was moved to say afterwards:

"I kept my hand on my watch all the time. Had the Prime Minister asked me to give him that cherished possession of mine, I would not have known how to refuse him."

After that luncheon, King appeared to be a different man. On January 24, in Algiers, he went out of his way to pay his respects to Admiral Sir Andrew Cunningham, his old adversary and sparring partner from Cunningham's Washington days. He was so mellowed, indeed, that during a stopover in Dakar on his return trip, he agreed to take a hitch-hiker back to the States on his plane. This was significant, not merely because the hitchhiker was only a lieutenant commander, but especially because he was a reserve officer.

The admiral arrived in Washington on January 30, in a snowstorm, invigorated by his Casablanca experience and by two notable victories of our side. After almost six months of bitter fighting Guadalcanal had finally been secured; the first Japanese base that threatened our position in the Southwest Pacific had been eliminated. And at Stalingrad, the German Sixth Army of Field Marshal Paulus had surrendered.

The Ingersoll Era

King was now preoccupied with the pressing question of how to implement the Casablanca resolution concerning the U-boats. He recognized that the antisubmarine activities of the United States Navy were still in an unsatisfactory shape at a time when a new Doenitz offensive demanded strict order in these things. Long merely irritated by the antisubmarine problem, he now realized that operations against the U-boats "were not only growing in scope but also getting a bit out of hand."

"Some naval commands, as well as other agencies that were assisting in the antisubmarine campaign, with laudable intent but with only meager knowledge of governing considerations, were issuing directives not based on sound doctrine," he wrote, adding that "new and comprehensive general directives needed to be promulgated and there had to be closer watch over what forces afloat were doing."

Though King probably did not mean this to imply any criticism of Vice Admiral Royal Eason Ingersoll, USN, his successor in command of the Atlantic Fleet, it put a finger squarely on the crux of the trouble—on Ingersoll's inability to deal with the problem and evolve the overdue remedies for it.

Despite the fact that he had managed American participation in the Battle of the Atlantic from January 1, 1942, to November 15, 1944, Admiral Ingersoll remained World War II's most obscure and enigmatic senior flag officer. "The public knew nothing of him," Morison wrote in a melancholy tribute to a cherished friend; "even to most of the Atlantic Fleet, he remained a shadowy, almost legendary figure. But," he added with his customary generosity, "to Admiral Ingersoll's sagacity and seasoned 'sea-cunning,' to use an Elizabethan phrase, the Allies owed in large measure their progress in 1942-1943."

Nobody who ever came under the spell of Ingersoll's impressive personality questioned his sagacity, which, I presume, Morison applied in the word's dictionary sense as the quality of discernment, judgment, shrewdness. A sad-faced, quiet, and somewhat rumpled man, he was, indeed, a wise and learned man, a percipient naval officer, a great teacher, and an outstanding staff officer. He finished fourth in the 1905 class of the Naval Academy, three places ahead of Chester W. Nimitz. Ingersoll was by nature and disposition the staff officer par excellence—intense, purposeful, diligent, pedantic, with a real passion for anonymity—and it was in that capacity that he became exceptionally popular among the admirals who always competed for his invaluable services.

Ingersoll performed a herculean job in building the Atlantic Fleet into a gigantic force, in maintaining it in top form under the stress and strain, and utilizing it with dispatch and efficiency. But the subtle intricacies of antisubmarine warfare somehow eluded him. He lacked that extra finesse the activity demanded and which Admiral Low, under King's remote control, was soon to bring to it.

For sixteen months, however, until the establishment of the Tenth Fleet, Ingersoll was the *de facto* head of antisubmarine warfare. While it cannot be denied that those sixteen months had produced a certain number of antisubmarine measures and the beginnings of a doctrine, it must be said nevertheless that Ingersoll was not able to inspire anything original and definitive along these lines. In the final analysis it was his fault if the situation, as King put it, got a bit out of hand.

Ingersoll's failure was implicit in King's sudden personal interest in the U-boat menace and in his search for someone to whom he could entrust the task of finding a solution to the problem.

Such an interest was, of course, a little late on King's part as well. In the beginning, King's regular staff was given the added duty of handling antisubmarine matters "as part of the general task of getting on with the war." Even when the unique nature of this antisubmarine business was recognized, King merely added the task of coordinating the scattered activities to Admiral Edwards' innumerable duties and responsibilities.

In early 1943, on the eve of still another U-boat blitz, it became at last evident to him that his makeshift arrangements could no longer be prolonged.

The Man from the "Wichita"

Busy as he himself was with the over-all conduct of the war at sea, King properly realized that he had neither the time to spare nor the necessary minute knowledge needed to devise a specific blueprint against the U-boat menace. He needed someone he could trust without reservation, someone with a quick and flexible mind, with profound analytical and administrative abilities—someone who was also versed in the peculiar problems of the submarine.

He looked around but could not find immediately the right man in his own entourage. Suddenly he remembered an officer he regarded as ideal for the job. That exceptional officer happened to be thousands of miles from Washington, in the Solomon Islands area. At that particular moment, he was commanding officer of the cruiser *Wichita*, helping to cover a transport group moving from Noumea to Guadalcanal.

The man was Captain Francis S. Low, the former Operations Officer in the Atlantic Fleet he had brought with him to Washington when he became COMINCH. In September, 1942, Low had gone to sea in the *Wichita* and showed that he was as gallant and intrepid a leader in combat as he was erudite and industrious on the staff. He had distinguished himself in the Battle of Casablanca, in November, 1942, by his accurate bombardment of shore batteries at Point El Hank and Table d'Aukusha. During the sortie of Admiral Darlan's misguided fleet he had dealt energetically and effectively with the swiftly maneuvering French destroyers.

King's order to report to him in Washington reached Low late in February, in Efate. On March 5, after an absence of only five months, he rejoined his former chief. He was named Assistant Chief of Staff (Antisubmarine) on the staff of the Commander in Chief and was advanced to rear admiral.

Admiral Low did not step into a complete vacuum when, with his customary vigor and industry, he threw himself at the problem. Despite the chaotic state of our antisubmarine warfare affairs and the anarchy that was rampant in their management, much had been done in the field to provide at least a few of the stones he needed in building his mosaic. There was, for instance, the Convoy and Routing Section, firmly established within CNO; there was an antisubmarine warfare unit inside the Readiness Division of King's staff; there was a mysterious group of civilian scientists known as the Asworgs working on the solution of the pressing technical problems of the U-boat war; there were several operational units inside the Atlantic Fleet specializing in antisubmarine warfare; and there were two supersecret branches in the Office of Naval Intelligence which operated on the periphery of the U-boat war.

Let us now, before we follow Admiral Low on his road to the Tenth Fleet, look at all that had been done prior to his assignment to introduce at least a semblance of control over the U-boat.

Bristol's Brain Trust

It is impossible to establish exactly when the idea was originally hatched and by whom, but I believe credit for the innovation that eventually became the Tenth Fleet should go to Vice Admiral Arthur LeR. Bristol, USN, one of the unsung heroes of this still inadequately appreciated effort of World War II. His preoccupation with the problem long preceded our involvement in the shooting war and the mental and physical labor he invested in it cut short his exceptional service. Just when he was indispensable for the management of our share in the Battle of the Atlantic, the strain brought on a heart attack. He died on board his flagship, the destroyer tender *Prairie*, on April 20, 1942.

Bristol was an extraordinary man and even his coming to the Atlantic was somewhat exceptional. He came from the Pacific when the majority of the Navy's most-gifted flag officers travelled in the opposite direction. He was summoned from Honolulu in January, 1941, to take care of an appalling variety of jobs—to organize a special force from units of the Atlantic Fleet to escort convoys from North America to Scotland and to supervise the building of a string of advanced bases in Newfoundland.

While Newfoundland was being prepared for its role, Bristol had his headquarters in Norfolk; but on September 19, he moved to Argentia—a ghost village a few months before, now a bristling naval base—and plunged immediately into the U-boat campaign. A generous and genial man who inspired devotion in his subordinates and stimulated their independent thinking, he assembled a fine staff of naval officers. Amidst his enormous administrative duties as senior naval officer at Argentia and commander of the Support Force, commandant of the naval air base at Quonset, the destroyer base "Sail" at Casco Bay in Maine, and of the United States forces in Iceland, somehow he still found time for the step-by-step development of a badly needed antisubmarine doctrine.

Three days before his arrival at Argentia, the HX-150, the first trans-Atlantic convoy assisted by the United States Navy, had sailed from Halifax. That was two months and twenty-one days before the United States was officially at war with Germany. An American escort group commanded by Captain Morton L. Deyo, USN, took charge of the convoy at about 150 miles south of Argentia and stayed with it until September 25, where Deyo handed it over to a Royal Navy escort at the pre-arranged "Momp," the mid-ocean meeting point.

Captain Deyo went on his escort mission—indeed, into the lions' den—with such perfunctory and rudimentary instructions that they could be called an escort doctrine only by a generous stretch of the imagination. He had some "prescribed procedures" in the General Instructions of the Atlantic Fleet, and they were aptly named, because they abounded in such generalities as "the guiding principle shall be that, whenever it is possible, escorts will be so disposed that no submarine can reach a successful firing position without being detected." But the instructions did not include any set pattern for the disposition of the escorts.

In the "special instructions" he received from Admiral Bristol, Deyo was told that his "first duty was to protect the convoy" and was cautioned against "pursuing a submarine contact for more than an hour." If Captain Deyo managed to carry out his mission without any untoward incidents, it was because no U-boats happened to be on his course.

The situation was dramatically demonstrated in all its appalling and perilous primitivity in the harrowing experience of another convoy, the ON-67. Crossing westward during the full moon of February 1942, with thirty-five ships in eight columns, ON-67 was to rendezvous with its all-American escort south of Iceland, but Commander A. C. Murdaugh, USN, experienced some difficulty even in finding the convoy.

Murdaugh's group consisted of four destroyers—the *Edison, Nicholson, Lea,* and *Bernadeau*—and all had radar, but only the *Nicholson's* radar was in working order. It was she who eventually picked up the convoy, a full day after the pre-arranged date. There was a high-frequency direction-finder on the rescue ship *Toward* and at 5:30 P.M. on February 21, it monitored a U-boat signal. Murdaugh sent the *Lea* to run down the bearing. She searched for about an hour, as prescribed in the instructions, then rejoined the group without making contact. However, the HF/DF proved right. A U-boat was in the area, a fact that became painfully evident ten hours later when two ships of ON-67 were torpedoed and sunk from outside the screen by a German who was neither sighted nor heard.

An energetic search Murdaugh ordered in the afternoon produced no clues whatever, although it was somehow sensed by everybody in ON-67 that the convoy was being trailed. Then, between midnight and 6:45 A.M. on February 24, four more ships were torpedoed. Later that day, the *Toward's* Huffduff picked up more suspicious signals, and when Murdaugh sent the *Lea* and the *Nicholson* to search out the bearing, the latter sighted two U-boats idling on the surface about fifteen miles from the convoy. Murdaugh now had a good chance to go after them but his instructions proscribed the hunt.

As a matter of fact, the escort commander had but limited powers to cope with a situation like this and had to gain consent from Washington for every change he proposed to make in his dispositions. At about noon on February 24, Murdaugh sent a message to CNO in Washington suggesting that, in view of the enemy's dogged shadowing, the convoy be dispersed or its course be changed. He then had to wait seven hours for the answer. It was affirmative and Murdaugh then ordered a drastic 68° change of course.

Even so, he could not shake off the U-boats. The *Edison* sighted two of them in quick succession—one at a distance of only two hundred yards—and mounted a six depth-charge attack, but both boats eluded her. On the other hand, the spirited search kept the U-boats down and the convoy reached Halifax without any further incidents or losses.

On March 4, Captain Wilder D. Baker, USN, an escort commander who blossomed into an antisubmarine warfare specialist in the pressure cooker of the campaign, reviewed the experience of ON-67 with Murdaugh, in order to pinpoint the lessons gained. Although Murdaugh went strictly by his instructions, everything he did turned out to be wrong, simply because his instructions were not adapted to the realities of the anti-U-boat campaign. The initial one hour search by *Lea* was far too brief. The escort commander's dependence on Washington seriously interfered with the efficiency of his operation. Failure to make contact with the Germans whose presence was indicated conclusively by the Huffduff showed the urgent need for better sonar training. The ineffectiveness of the *Lea's* depth charge attack proved there was an equally urgent need for a definite doctrine for ashcan attack. Most important, Murdaugh's experience indicated that the injuction against leaving the convoy and hunting down a U-boat whose presence had been established in the area was a crippling factor, not merely in an offensive against the enemy, but even in the defense of the convoy. "You've got to go out," Captain Baker summed up the review, "and run them down!"

Even at this stage, no definite plan existed for the disposition of the escorts with the convoys. In December, 1941, for example, Argentia prescribed a patrol distance of three to five thousand yards from the convoy in daytime and less after dark. Captain Baker, who was then commanding Destroyer Squadron 31 in the Atlantic Fleet, wrote to Admiral Bristol and suggested that destroyer escorts patrol "out as much as six thousand yards" at night. His was the voice of experience, but it required several months of discussion before Baker's recommendation became doctrine in 1942.

Similarly there was no accepted pattern for escort disposition until Captain H. C. Fitz, USN, another escort commander acting on his own initiative, developed one. It was then eagerly adopted by other escort commanders.

Bristol realized he would never be able to develop a definite antisubmarine doctrine from the haphazard suggestions of escort commanders and could never liquidate the U-boat menace by pursuing an emphatically defensive approach. While he could not yet afford an abrupt change-over to an offensive approach, he decided to explore the path to it. He called a series of staff conferences at Argentia in which the various ramifications of antisubmarine warfare were reviewed from all angles. It was an informal night school in which the small band of American practitioners of the U-boat hunt learned antisubmarine tactics and techniques somewhat in the manner Leo Rosten's eager beaver Hyman Kaplan learned English—by trial and error, and mostly by error.

By January, 1942, Bristol's night school was ready to produce its most important recommendation—one that contained the seed of the Tenth Fleet seventeen months before its establishment and which must have stimulated Admiral King when he got around to exploring the problem from close quarters, exactly a year later.

The recommendation was incorporated in a letter Captain Robert B. Carney, USN, Admiral Bristol's operations chief, sent to Commander William B. Moses, USN, Gunnery Officer of the Atlantic Fleet. Carney suggested that an antisubmarine warfare unit be established within the Atlantic Fleet, preferably at Boston, "located where the dope can best be collected on the spot while it is hot, free from any other duties, working from practical experience, and furthering the aims of

COMINCH without further cluttering up COMINCH's own staff. I feel sure," Carney added, "that such a unit commanded by the right officer would work in perfect harmony with Fleet Training, and at the same time furnish hot material for the Atlantic Fleet and its task forces daily engaged in antisubmarine warfare."

Carney's letter was dated January 27, 1942. Commander Moses, in hearty agreement with the recommendation, lost no time in implementing it. A conference of interested officers was arranged for February 5, at the Boston Navy Yard. It was unanimous in seconding Carney's proposal, then elaborated upon the original recommendation. On March 2—only thirty-four days after Captain Carney had penned his note—an Anti–Submarine Warfare Unit was established within the Atlantic Fleet, with headquarters in Boston. The "right officer" of the Carney letter was quickly found in the person of Wilder D. Baker.

Baker's Dozen

This was a giant step and the influence of the unit was immediately felt in a sudden interest in antisubmarine warfare as a discipline, so to speak, distinctly apart from traditional and conventional procedures, tactics, and doctrines of the Navy. Captain Baker was a gregarious, articulate, and aggressive officer who brought to his job considerable practical experience.

Baker's unit became the first ASW information collection and analysis agency in the United States Navy. It studied, collated, and evaluated the intelligence reports pouring in from London and Washington; scrutinized the action reports and combat narratives to analyze the tactics of the U-boat commanders; and embarked upon a long neglected task, the training of teachers for American antisubmarine warfare schools which began to mushroom after the outbreak of hostilities.

Baker quickly assembled a congenial staff of experts—the celebrated Baker's Dozen—whose specialties covered every facet of antisubmarine warfare—communications, air activities, submarines, training, intelligence, material, and liaison.

When he found that our lack of standard operating procedures was mainly responsible for our weakness in antisubmarine warfare, especially in search and attack, Baker set out to develop a specific and uniform system to replace a wide variety of techniques. Thanks largely to his initiative and the efforts of Baker's Dozen, the first American general submarine manual was issued on July 9, followed on August 2 by the first manual of standardized search and attack procedure—eight and nine months after Pearl Harbor respectively—but better late than never!

Probably his most enduring contribution was the integration of scientists into the ASW effort on the operational level. On March 12, only a week after the commissioning of his unit, Baker wrote to Dr. John Terrence Tate, professor of physics at the University of Minnesota, who was then chief of the Subsurface Warfare Section of the National Defense Research Council, and asked him to organize a group of scientists and engineers to conduct a new kind of pragmatic research for antisubmarine warfare. Tate responded avidly. Such was the effect of the Baker whirlwind that Tate had a group of physicists, chemists, mathematicians, actuaries, and engineers available to Baker at Boston —within a week. What distinguished the work of this group from that of other scientists engaged in the war effort was their function as *operational researchers*. They worked closely with the sailors and the aviators, mostly at sea or at their bases, checking the equipment they used and their operating procedures, then analyzing the efficiency factor in both. In effect their job was to show the naval commanders and aviators how to use their ships and planes, sonars and radars, and all the paraphernalia of antisubmarine warfare, to get optimum results. Although scientists had worked previously in research and development, and in production, Baker utilized them in actual operations. His pioneering system survives today, booming more than ever, in what is now actually called "operations research."

After only a few weeks in Boston, Baker was called to Washington to head the Antisubmarine Measures Unit of COMINCH's own Readiness Division. The ASW Unit in Boston continued under Commander Thomas L. Lewis, former commander of the destroyer *Wainwright* and a veteran of "William Sail," the legendary Convoy WS-12X, that sailed from Halifax to the Orient in November, 1941, and of which Morison said, "It is doubtful whether any convoy had ever been escorted so far with so few mishaps."

In the end, both Baker and Lewis faded from the picture, when all antisubmarine activities came under Low, even before the formal establishment of the Tenth Fleet. The era of trial and error ended. The pioneer was to be replaced by the planner.

It was a remarkable feature of this *Sturm-und-Drang* period that the outstanding accomplishments of the pre-Tenth Fleet era were closely tied to outstanding individuals. Just as Baker was almost singlehandedly responsible for the gratifying success of his unit, another forceful and ruggedly individualistic naval officer became the key to the effectiveness of another important institution—the Sub Chaser Training Center in Miami, Florida.

When the U-boat blitz broke in January, 1942, the Navy's woeful lack of small vessels was badly felt because they were needed, if not to destroy, then at least to locate and keep down the U-boats. There was an urgent need for a World War II counterpart of World War I's gallant mosquito fleet of patrol craft and subchasers. A. Loring Swasey, a noted naval architect, had designed the old PC's and SC's. Now a captain, USNR, on duty in the Bureau of Ships, Swasey again became responsible for the quickest possible build-up of a great number of improved craft for what became known as the "Donald Duck Navy."

McDaniel's Donald Duck Navy

They were tough little vessels and they were hard on their crews. Since older men could not be expected to stand the hardship of service on them, a group of sturdy young officers had to be trained, all of them reservists. In order to harden them for those vessels, and impart to them at least a rudimentary knowledge of their craft—in both meanings of the word—the Sub Chaser Training Center was commissioned on March 26—and then hit a snag. The Bureau of Personnel could not find any qualified officer who was willing to take over this "Annapolis of the Donald Duck Navy." Just then, a lieutenant commander named Eugene F. McDaniel—"a lean, mean, thin-lipped officer whose eyes burned with hatred of the enemy and whose heart glowed with devotion to the Navy"—happened to put into port after a strenuous tour of escort duty in the destroyer *Livermore*. The job was offered McDaniel. He grabbed it—and became a legend!

He opened the school on April 8 with about fifty pupils. By 1944, he had trained 10,396 officers and 37,574 men for the Donald Duck Navy. Fired by his own fanatical zeal, assisted by two professional educators from the University of Chicago, the "Old Man" operated the school on a seven-day basis, with instructors who all had personal experience in antisubmarine warfare. "McDaniel's Academy" became Miami's "biggest business" as it overflowed into ten hotels on Biscayne Boulevard and extended over a dozen piers of the waterfront below.

I am singling him out of the many fine teachers of antisubmarine warfare in a great number of special schools that came into being under an elaborate training program because he was the dean of all these ad hoc "professors." He also was by far the most popular amateur educator inside the ASW program. Low recalls him as one of the architects of our victory over the U-boat because he produced what was even more important than the ships—the gallant boys who manned them.

Walter T. Flynn, a lawyer in his civilian life, was one of the graduates of McDaniel's high-pressure prep school and *PC-565*, the 173-foot patrol craft he had the honor to command, a typical vessel of the "Donald Duck Navy." "Like other young reserve officers," Morison wrote in his description of the Eastern Sea Frontier's bitter battle against a swarm of "nuisance" U-boats, "Flynn had been laughed at for errors due to overeagerness and lack of experience, and he had taken these things to heart."

Early in the afternoon of June 2, 1943, *PC-565* was escorting a Guantanamo bound convoy when, about eighty-five miles southeast of Five Fathom Bank Lightship, Flynn and his crew were suddenly electrified by what sounded like contact with a U-boat, apparently sneaking up on the convoy. In actual fact, it was a U-boat Flynn's sonar had detected, but the German was blissfully unaware of the convoy's presence, its skipper relaxing in his bunk, reading a German translation of the Lynds' *Middletown*.

Flynn put an end to the German's study of decadent American society by dropping five ashcans that exploded so close that they forced the U-boat to the surface. It was the *U-521*. Its studious skipper was Kapitaenleutnant Klaus Bargsten, one of Doenitz's aces who had recently been awarded the Knight's Insignia of the Iron Cross, for his claim of having sunk nearly forty-thousand tons of Allied shipping on a previous 79-day cruise.

As soon as the sub broached, Bargsten rushed to the bridge and then, seeing the *PC-565* (now ably assisted by *PC-89*) bearing down on him to ram, he ordered all hands still below to abandon ship. Bargsten was the first to heed his own command and thus became the only survivor from *U-521*. Before anyone else could follow him into the water, prodded by five more depth charges from *PC-565*, the U-boat went to the bottom. During his subsequent interrogation, the Kapitaenleutnant seemed to worry little about the loss of his boat and crew. What bothered him really was the ignominious fact that his conqueror had been "a landlubber lawyer only two years before."

Mavericks of the ONI

On November 6, 1941, the light cruiser *Omaha* was on patrol duty between Trinidad and the hump of Brazil, looking for U-boats and German raiders, when she unexpectedly ran into a German freighter, the *Odenwald*, trying to run the British blockade. Disregarding the legal nicety that we weren't at war, she took the German into custody and brought her into San Juan, Puerto Rico.

Thus, unexpectedly, the United States Navy came into possession of a batch of "prisoners of war" even before this country was at war. As soon as the *Odenwald's* crew was safely caged in Camp Upton, Long

Island, N.Y., a stern-looking but suave naval officer flew in from Washington and closeted himself with the ·Germans.

He was Lieutenant Commander Ralph G. Albrecht, USNR, a distinguished and successful international lawyer in private life. He spoke German faultlessly and that was what had brought him to Camp Upton in such a hurry. He came from a mystery branch of the Office of Naval Intelligence whose very existence was known only to a handful of insiders. It was called Op-16-Z or "Special Activities Branch," and that "special" in its designation—a handy all-purpose word in Intelligence lingo—covered a multitude of "sins." Prisoner interrogation was one of them. And now that the Navy had its first batch of prisoners ahead of the war, Albrecht was sent into action to pump whatever information he could from the Germans.

His effort was rewarded beyond our fondest expectations. Aside from some tactical data of immediate value and a lot of what was called incidental intelligence, his skillful questioning of the Germans also produced invaluable strategic material. From the intelligence Albrecht had coaxed from the *Odenwald's* scrubby crew, the analysts of OP-16-Z then managed to develop the first definite clues to German blockade running procedures.

When later in 1942, the cruiser *Somers* of Task Group 23.2 captured the *Anneliese Essberger,* a five thousand ton blockade-runner en route from Bordeaux to Yokohama, additional clues were obtained and *Asworg* prepared a plot that exposed the exact pattern of German blockade-running through the Narrows of the Atlantic. This triumph enabled the Navy to capture another blockade-runner, the former Dutch freighter *Kota Napan,* on February 4, 1943; and then virtually to stop the running in either direction. After 1942, only two of eighteen runners managed to sneak through on the Japan-Biscay route—thanks primarily to Op-16-Z's stupendous coup.

Behind this practical triumph of intelligence as, indeed, behind the whole of Op-16-Z, was a tall, broad-shouldered, smartly groomed officer in his early fifties, John Lawrence Riheldaffer by name. A West Virginian by birth and a cosmopolitan by temperament and outlook, Riheldaffer was a graduate of the 1910 class of the Naval Academy and a veteran of World War I, having served as navigator on the U.S.S. *New Orleans* in the Atlantic. When physical disability forced him to retire in 1921, the former lieutenant commander—a specialist in ordnance with an excellent business head—joined General Motors and moved to Germany, where he organized the European headquarters of GM's Frigidaire division.

Riheldaffer learned to speak German fluently, became familiar with the German way of life, and developed many important German acquaintanceships—qualifications that in due course attracted the attention of the ONI. Although on the retired list and with but little time to spare for such extra-curricular activities, Riheldaffer kept up a tenuous connection with the Navy. It was tenuous because, in times of peace, ONI was not much interested in tapping even so qualified an informant as he was.

On the whole, the Office of Naval Intelligence, suffering from a rapid turnover of directors who were not always qualified for the job, was a static and bureaucratic organization. It subsisted mostly on information gathered by the Naval Attachés, and worked on such humdrum tasks as the preparation of the silhouettes of alien ships and the listing of the biographical data of foreign admirals, including their foibles. It kept tab on ship movements and tried to draw up the order of battle of foreign navies from all sorts of telltale evidence.

To the outsider, ONI appeared to be a musty organization with an exaggerated air of secrecy and protocol. But it was, even at this slipshod stage, a tight and intelligent agency in OpNav, as bright and good as any Naval Intelligence bureau could be in times of peace, and much better than its German counterpart.

In 1941, its German Desk was already at the peak of its efficiency, thanks largely to a highly gifted and thoroughly experienced civilian specialist, Harold Bennett, a permanent fixture amidst the continuously rotating uniformed personnel. In his long years of service, Bennett built up excellent files in which the curious could discover anything from the exact caliber of the *Bismarck's* new guns to the date of Admiral Doenitz's marriage. It was the kind of latent information that, although invaluable in both war and peace, lags behind the wartime needs of the Navy.

In preparation for the imminent war, ONI did streamline its organization and added a few functional branches, such as a superb technical branch and a multilingual translation branch. But by and large it remained static—more like a research organization at some university than the lively secret service of a Navy at war. However, it was recognized as early as 1940 that the ONI needed a dynamic annex within its static set-up. Admiral Stark was persuaded to authorize the establishment of a truly warlike branch for the specific exigencies of the pending conflict. It became the Z-Branch of Riheldaffer.

It was "the first of its kind in the history of the United States Navy," assigned to "critically important and diverse activities concerned with captured enemy equipment and its operation." The word "equipment"

was another word like "special". It included prisoners of war and all sorts of enemy documents that fell into our hands.

In January, 1941, Riheldaffer was recalled to active duty, promoted to commander on the retired list, and told to build up this Special Activities Branch. His success was attested by the citation that went with the Legion of Merit he received after the war. It must have been composed by someone who had had an opportunity to observe Riheldaffer at close quarters, because it was both dramatic and accurate:

"As a result of his clear understanding of his mission and his meticulous attention to the most effective techniques to be followed, the information furnished by this unit throughout the war and particularly during its latter stages, served as one of the principal sources upon which Combat Intelligence based its appreciation of the enemy, especially in the evaluation of the U-boat campaign. His unique analytical skill, sound judgment and professional ability were contributing factors in the final defeat of the German U-boat fleet in the Battle of the Atlantic."

Riheldaffer kept Op-16-Z out of the Tenth Fleet because he believed he could maintain liaison with his British opposite numbers on a more congenial and fruitful basis if he remained in ONI. Even so, the Special Activities Branch became an essential annex of Admiral Low's organization.

*War of Words**

A great conflict like World War II needed and developed all kinds of weapons. One of the quaintest was, I submit, a phonograph record a yeoman of the United States Navy named Nelson bought in a downtown Washington music shop, on a snowbound January day in 1943. It was a recording of Richard Wagner's *Flying Dutchman Overture,* and it was needed in a confidential operation against the U-boats.

Yeoman Nelson was attached to another one of ONI's wartime annexes that was lumped with Op-16-Z at the bottom of OpNav's table of organization. Called Op-16-W (or, by its full and proper name, Special Warfare Branch, Intelligence Division, Chief of Naval Operations), it came into existence through the efforts of Dr. Cecil Henry Coggins, a Missourian who ranged far and wide on the magic carpet of his fertile imagination.

Coggins was a naval surgeon—a lieutenant commander, Medical Corps —but he was practicing his profession infrequently at this time. The

---

* For a fuller description of this operation, see *Secret Missions,* by Ellis M. Zacharias (New York, 1947), and my *Burn After Reading,* (New York, 1962), pp. 276–302.

doctor was an espionage buff. With his heart in intelligence work, he made a name for himself among the cognoscenti during the Thirties when he trapped two wayward Americans who spied for Japan. At the outbreak of the war, he went to sea with Captain Ellis M. Zacharias, USN, in the cruiser *Salt Lake City*, and organized the first combat intelligence unit aboard a warship. Upon his return to terra firma, impressed with the Germans' fiendish use of propaganda in war, he hit upon the idea of organizing a "psychological warfare" office in the United States Navy, to conduct the war with words to weaken the enemy's morale and bend him, if possible, to our will.

Some of the officers to whom Coggins had submitted the idea looked at him incredulously as if he had proposed to organize a knitting circle for admirals, but he also found supporters, including Captain Zacharias, who took Coggins' brainchild directly to Admiral King. Probably thinking that such a unit could not do much harm and might even do some good, King promptly approved it. When King was for a project nobody in his right mind dared to be against it. Thus, in the late fall of 1942, the Special Warfare Branch came into being with Commander Coggins as the Officer in Charge.

That record of the *Flying Dutchman* Nelson had bought was needed for its very first operation—a series of broadcasts to the German Navy, and more specifically to the U-boat crews in the Atlantic. It was thought appropriate to introduce the broadcasts with those majestic strains to symbolize that the ultimate fate of the U-boat men was not much different from that of the shadowy sailors in that fully-rigged ship of legend, who were doomed to sail forever around the Cape of Good Hope because their captain had made a blasphemous oath.

The Tenth Fleet was only indirectly involved in the operations of Op-16-W, mostly by just tolerating them. The unit functioned throughout the war as a branch of ONI, partly because nobody else in the Navy was willing to take it, and mostly because we used the data Bennett of the German Desk and Commander Riheldaffer of Op-16-Z were willing to dole out to us. But as the war progressed, 16-W survived despite all prophecies to the contrary. When we scored several impressive successes, the branch became accepted in this naval world and even attained a certain respect and popularity. It was a valuable cog in the antisubmarine machinery of the Navy and it was so recognized by Admiral King when he accorded us his coveted "Well done" at the end of the war. We received special citations also from the Office of War Information and the Office of Strategic Services.

Throughout the war, Op-16-W performed all the functions of psychological warfare except one. We never indulged in what is called black propaganda. Our opposite number in the British Admiralty, a branch of the Division of Naval Intelligence called 17-Zed, was participating in a phenomenally successful propaganda coup called the *Atlantik Sender* (Radio Atlantic). It was a full-scale radio transmission going on the whole day that pretended to be somewhere inside Germany, operated by some patriotic but anti-Nazi Germans, although it was actually operated at Woburn Abbey, the palatial seat of the Duke of Bedford, which Britain's Political Warfare Executive had taken over for the duration.

Envious of the *Atlantik Sender's* extraordinary appeal, we wanted to mount a similiar operation. When the plans were presented to Admiral King, he disapproved of them scornfully, with words that I cherish to these days.

"I don't want any deception in the United States Navy," he said.

Our major operation was, from our inception to the end of the war, that series of radio talks which became well known in propaganda circles as the Norden broadcasts. Observing strictest security (over which watched a succession of captains delegated for the job by COMINCH), intelligence material was woven into purposeful radio scripts, each of which was supposed to persuade the German listener of the error of his cause and the futility of his struggle. This was not an easy task in 1942 and 1943, when the dice were heavily loaded against us, but we became both persuasive and popular from 1944 to the bitter end, when our broadcasts deeply impressed the U-boat men both at home and in the Atlantic.

The voice of Op-16-W was Commander Albrecht, the ingenious reserve officer from Op-16-Z who had cracked the secret of the blockade runners. His German was fluent, his delivery perfect, and he had a commanding tone that had its impact on the Germans who savored authority. He was, of course, far more than just our "voice." A deputy to Commander Riheldaffer in the management of Op-16-Z, he was privy to a great number of German secrets. It was left to his discretion to cull from them those we were permitted to beam back. He conducted ceaseless research among transcripts of the prisoner interrogations and captured documents for material we could use. He was personally our most important and productive source, and he also assumed responsibility for policy matters, a thankless and ticklish task.

In the course of our existence, we prepared 609 scrips of which more than 300 went on the air, all of them spoken by Commander Albrecht. The effectiveness of our operation was attested to us by a number of straws in the wind, including a number of letters we received from our German "fans" via Switzerland, Argentina, and other neutral countries. One letter mailed in Portugal advised us to change our schedule because the writer, who craved to listen in, had to stand watch when we went on the air and could not very well listen to the enemy. Another inquired whether it was really true that German prisoners were served pork chops and sauerkraut in camp, as we averred in one of our broadcasts, because if it was really true, he might consider surrendering, if only because pork chops with sauerkraut happened to be his favorite dish. A third requested us to broadcast from time to time certain tunes by Irving Berlin which he had come to love during a sojourn in the States.

We found out how popular our operation really was in the summer of 1943, when we received first-hand positive proof that Albrecht—who broadcast under the *nom-de-guerre* of Robert Lee Norden, *Fregatten-kapitaen der Amerikanischen Kriegsmarine* (Commander in the United States Navy)—was not only heard over the din of war but was avidly listened to and very much liked by the officers and men of the U-boat arm.

The proof came at the end of a chain of events that began on July 19, 1943, off the Brazilian coast north of the Amazon estuary. That day a southbound convoy of eighteen ships, the TF-2, was picked up by the *U-662* of Kapitaenleutnant Heinz Eberhard Mueller, about whom we had some interesting biographical data on file. We knew he was an aggressive, Nazi-minded U-boat fanatic, one of Doenitz's pets, but a competent skipper well-liked by his crew. We also knew that he was hellbent on collecting tonnage because he suffered from what the U-boat men called the "neck itch"—the burning ambition to be awarded the Knight's Insignia to the Iron Cross (nicknamed the "*Halsband*" or necklace, since it was worn around the neck). We also knew that he had had a very successful *Feindfahrt* the March before when, in co-operation with the *U-400* of Kapitaenleutnant von Buelow, he added four ships of some 23,000 tons to his collection.

But we did not know, of course, that he was back in the Atlantic and that very soon we would have the pleasure of his company. Now on this nineteenth of July, he was stalking the convoy until a Surinam-based Army Liberator forced him down and chased him away. The *U-662* was caught again next day, by an old Bolo—a B-18—just two hundred miles east of Cayenne. Mueller escaped again. But his luck was running out. On July 21, he was attacked for a whole hour by Lieutenant "Stan" Auslander, USN, in a PBY, and was then sent to the bottom by another Catalina piloted by Lieutenant (j.g.) R. H. Howland, USNR.

The *U-662* had only four survivors. Her skipper was one of them, but he was in very bad shape. If I remember correctly, he had both of his arms and one leg broken and had severe internal injuries, the results of his dogfight with Auslander. Yet he was kept afloat and alive by his chief mate, one Horst Gaertner, a strong and dedicated sailor from the Hanseatic waterfront. Gaertner swam about with Mueller in his arms for seven days, until they were picked up by a patrol craft.

We heard that Mueller was a prisoner through the 16-Z scuttlebut, and that he was in the hospital in Fort Meade, Maryland, in a very serious condition. Then all of a sudden we heard from Mueller himself. He was badly broken up, but still worse, he had the blues. In his despair, he craved companionship, if only a comforting word or a friendly pat. There was only one man he "knew" in America—Commander Norden. He asked Norden to visit him in the hospital.

Elated as we were by this unsolicited testimonial, we also faced a problem, even if it was purely sartorial. Norden pretended to be a full commander, but the real man behind his voice, Ralph Albrecht, was only a lieutenant commander. The problem was solved by "promoting" Albrecht for the duration of this temporary duty.

There was a lot of philanthropy in Albrecht's visit to Mueller's bedside, but it was not entirely without its ulterior motives. He had to get whatever information he could from Mueller because otherwise the hapless Kapitaenleutnant was not supposed to be interrogated.

Prisoner interrogation as devised by Riheldaffer utilized a complex psychological technique that became apparent to the prisoners only after it was all over. Disabled prisoners like Mueller, who had a chance of being sent home under the stipulations of the Geneva Convention, were excluded, because Riheldaffer feared they might enlighten the U-boat command about our interrogation techniques upon their return home.

Mueller went out of his way to butter up Albrecht. He pulled out all stops as he described Norden's popularity with the U-boat men and the alleged benefits they gained from his talks. He talked without restraint and behaved like a starry-eyed fan bumping into Frank Sinatra.

Albrecht then mentioned his visit to Mueller's bedside in a special broadcast, in which he dwelt mainly on the saga of his survival, describing in blunt terms Mueller's injuries, his fight against sharks, his agonies while preparing himself for what appeared to be imminent death. Never in his broadcasts did Albrecht ever talk down to his audience or belittle the accomplishments of the U-boat men. His talks reflected a kind of international comradeship that continued despite the war. The Mueller broadcast was in this vein—paying unstinted tribute to the brave foe—and yet it had, like all the Norden broadcasts, its dose of what we called the Mickey Finn. While bemoaning Mueller's fate and sympathizing with him, Albrecht also described the vicissitudes of the U-boat service, in terms a U-boat man on the eve of his next *Feindfahrt* or on actual war patrol could not misunderstand.

This heartwarming yet functional encounter had a sequel. Mueller was sent home in due course and was apparently taken to task by Doenitz for his fraternization with the hated Norden. Mueller then spent the rest of the war conducting a propaganda campaign of his own—against Norden. He went on a lecture tour of hate, depicting his bedside companion and samaritan friend in abusive language and warning his comrades not to be taken in by his siren song.

The Henke Incident

If the Germans listened to us on their own volition, for enlightenment or entertainment, we listened to them only because it was part of our job. Usually I had a strong stomach when listening to their foolish and arrogant Nazi propaganda, but one particular broadcast made me sick. I happened to catch one of our distant "friends," the U-boat ace Werner Henke, bragging on the radio about his sinking of the British ship *Ceramic*. She was an old passenger liner doing the England-Australia run the hard way, around the Cape of Good Hope, and was left on her regular run even during the war. She carried civilians who had a legitimate reason to book passage in her, and a sprinkling of military personnel. She was usually crowded with women and children uprooted by the war.

The *Ceramic* had left on her last voyage late in November, 1942, bound for Australia but starting out with a westbound convoy to enjoy its escorts' protection through the U-boat infested waters. She stayed with the convoy as far as Cape Farewell, then broke off and headed south. She did not get very far. On December 7, near the Azores, she was spotted and accosted by Henke in *U-515*. He stalked the *Ceramic* for hours through the night in a rapidly rising wind, then maneuvered his boat into attack position and at midnight fired his first torpedo into the old lady. She shuddered and began to wallow but she showed no sign that she was seriously hurt.

Henke let go with two more torpedoes. He had the *Ceramic* in sinking condition, but he was a perfectionist; in his impatience with the sinking ship, he fired a fourth fish that broke the *Ceramic's* back.

It was 1:02 A.M. of December 8. She expired noisily as her steel plates tore apart. The screams of women and children shattered the silence of the night.

Kapitaenleutnant Henke then did what criminals sometimes do. He returned to the scene of the crime. Moving up and down among the crowded lifeboats, illuminating them with his searchlight, he was looking for a prize. This was a big catch . . . 18,800 tons . . . maybe even a troopship. . . certain to get for him a *Sondermeldung* and the Oak Leaves for his *Halsband* . . . promotion to Korvettenkapitaen. He was now looking for the captain of the *Ceramic* in the crazily bobbing boats, because he wanted to take him to Germany to prove to Doenitz that he had really sunk the *Ceramic*.

When his search for the captain remained futile, he called out to a uniformed figure his searchlight caught squatting on a raft:

"Sie da drueben!" Henke yelled at him. "Who are you?"

"Sapper Munday, sir," came back the answer. "Royal Engineers."

Henke spoke excellent English but he did not know what sapper meant and that the RE was part of the British Army.

"Are you a soldier?" he asked Munday.

"Yes, sir."

"Heave him a line," Henke shouted to his men. When Munday was aboard the *U-515*, Henke called out: "Full speed ahead."

Soon there was a deathly silence where the *Ceramic* had gone down. There were no survivors—except Sapper Munday, to verify Henke's tonnage claim.

It was this Henke I now heard on the radio. He was not alone. He had a witness appearing on the show to attest to his triumph. It was poor Munday, whom the Nazis had brainwashed, mumbling some silly propaganda into the mike.

I sat down while my anger was still fresh and wrote a script for Norden in which I accused Henke of the cold-blooded murder of women and children. I called him "War Criminal No. 1" and assured him that he would be tried for his crime after the war.

The broadcast was monitored as usual by the U-Boat Command. It included an account of the *Ceramic's* demise—the facts which Henke had concealed from Doenitz. The admiral was visibly upset when the script was shown him. Upon his return a few weeks later, Henke found orders waiting at his flotilla directing him to report to headquarters at once.

At Kerneval, he was received by the polished Fuhrmann, Doenitz's overworked Flag Lieutenant, who handed him an envelope and said: "The admiral's orders. Read the contents of this envelope, then report to the Chief of Staff."

Henke found the transcript of our broadcast in the envelope, and the big, blonde bully paled and trembled as he read it. Then confronting Captain Godt he denied everything. He showed Godt the entry in his log—"Wind NW, Force 10, Sea 8 [very rough], rain and hail"— to prove that the howling gale had prevented him from offering any help to the stricken *Ceramic*. He pointed out that the liner had been armed with a 3-inch gun and claimed that, with hundreds of soldiers aboard, she was really a troopship. He recalled that the *Ceramic* had sent out an SOS when hit by the first torpedo, forcing the *U-515* to run before the British arrived.

Then he changed his tune and became arrogant again. He begged Godt to send him to sea at once—Godt let him go.

In the spring of 1944, his number came up.

In the morning of April 8, the Tenth Fleet sent a high priority signal to Captain Daniel V. Gallery, USN, commander of an escort carrier group in the *Guadalcanal*, one of the first two baby flattops Henry J. Kaiser had built over Admiral King's "dead body." The message reported a fix on a U-boat, about 200 miles northwest of Madeira. The carrier group peeled off at once and its Avengers began to stalk the sub. Gallery also sent the destroyer escorts *Pillsbury* and *Flaherty* after the boat and at 7:15 in the morning, the *Pillsbury's* sonar made contact. Two other destroyer escorts, the *Chatelaine* and the *Pope*, then joined the hunt that lasted until around two in the afternoon. At 2:05 P.M. the U-boat suddenly snorted to the surface in a gush of white water that splashed all over the *Chatelaine*.

All hell broke lose at once. On the U-boat, the hatches snapped open and the crew spilled out on deck to man the guns and fire with desperate fury at everything in sight. The destroyer escorts opened fire at point-blank range, an Avenger peppered the U-boat with rockets, Wildcats strafed it—and to top it all, a Wildcat exploded a *Zaunkoenig*, an acoustic torpedo, that seemed to be chasing the *Pillsbury* around.

At 2:13 P.M. it was all over. Shaken by an internal explosion with smoke streaming through its conning tower hatch, the U-boat sank, leaving six officers and thirty-seven men of her complement of fifty-three in the swirling water. Kapitaenleutnant Werner Henke was in our hands.

"Some of our skippers in the Battle of the Atlantic," Gallery later wrote, "treated rescued U-boat captains as guests. I didn't agree with this idea and figured it was better for all concerned to treat U-boat survivors as prisoners of war regardless of rank." And so, the Herr Kapitaenleutnant was in the brig of the *Guadalcanal.*

He did not like the idea and demanded an audience with Gallery, whose wonderfully Irish dander was now all the way up. To Henke's glib and guttural protest, he simply said:

"Captain, we are going to refuel in Gibraltar about ten days from now. If you don't like the way I'm treating you, I'll be glad to turn you and your crew over to the British. Maybe they will treat you better."

His words had a shattering effect on Henke. He paled and a beaten look came into his eyes. He had none of his arrogance when he now told Gallery, "It isn't that bad. I can put up with this treatment for a few more weeks. I withdraw my protest."

While in his cell below, Henke cuddled up to Gallery's chief master-at-arms and in a weak moment told the CMAA why he did not cherish the idea of going to Gibraltar. "The British are gunning for me," he said, "because they are angry that I sank the *Ceramic.*"

Gallery now began to wonder just how far he could push the idea of unloading Henke at the Rock after all. He had a message to the *Guadalcanal* written up on an official dispatch blank, purporting to have come from CINCLANT. It read:

> BRITISH ADMIRALTY REQUESTS YOU TURN OVER CREW OF
> U-515 TO THEM WHEN YOU REFUEL GIBRALTAR X CONSIDERING
> CROWDED CONDITION YOUR SHIP AUTHORIZE YOU USE
> YOUR DISCRETION X

He then drew up a statement on legal foolscap with the ship's seal on it, ready for Henke's signature. It read:

"I, Captain Lieutenant Werner Henke, promise on my honor as a German officer that if I and my crew are imprisoned in the United States instead of in England, I will answer all questions truthfully when I am interrogated by Naval Intelligence Officers."

Then he sent for Henke. Confronted with the dispatch and the draft, Henke blushed and asked with that beaten look back in his eyes, "Why do they want me?" And when Gallery gave him his choice, a scene followed that reminded Gallery of a Hollywood production.

"I knew nothing of the real story of the *Ceramic* at the time," he recalled, "but I'm sure now that all the harrowing details with which he was so familiar ran through his mind again. He knew that no impartial court would punish him for what he had done, but he believed a British court martial would hang him."

In the end Henke picked up a pen, signed the paper, looked at Gallery defiantly, and went back to the brig. Gallery then circulated a photostat of the paper among the petty officers and non-rated men, then invited them to sign another agreement that went into much more detail as to what they would say. At first they refused to believe that Henke's signature on the paper was authentic. But when Gallery supplied the proof, every man in the *U-515's* crew signed up to tell all he knew.

Upon their arrival in the United States, Op-16-Z took over and while the crew talked a blue streak, Henke reneged on his agreement. "My signature was obtained under duress," he told Captain Riheldaffer's boys, "and so I am not bound by it."

Probably stimulated by Gallery's make-believe, 16-Z decided to continue the Henke melodrama. During one of the interrogations at Fort Hunt, in which 16-Z could not make any headway with Henke, a gentleman arrived whose British accent made the German apprehensive. The stranger was introduced as an officer of the Mounted Police, in from Canada—to collect Henke for transfer to England. In actual fact, the British-accented visitor was one of 16-Z's civilian employees.

But the Kapitaenleutnant remained adamant and began to show symptoms of a morbid depression. He was then transferred to the Army's P/W camp at Papago Park near Phoenix, Arizona, "pending," as he was told, his "shipment to England", but by then Henke had enough. The drama which began when I happened to tune in on his boastful broadcast was now nearing its tragic climax.

He was out walking in the exercise compound of the camp when the idea of his final exit must have occurred to him. It was broad daylight, there was a high barbed fence all over the compound, and armed sentries all around the fence. He waited until the sentry closest to him looked straight at him, then he started to climb the high fence.

"Halt!" the sentry called to him, and repeated the warning twice more, but Henke just kept on climbing. The sentry raised his submachine gun, aimed perfunctorily, and fired. Henke was killed instantly. His death was certified with the usual phrase—"shot while trying to escape"—and it was true, too, as far as it went. I am convinced it was this cornered man's desperate way of committing suicide.

☆

★

CHAPTER XIII

The Tenth Fleet

What the discordant harmony of
circumstances would and could effect.
Horace, Epistle I, 12, 19

The stage was now set for the establishment of the Tenth Fleet, but before it emerged into actual existence a division between the Allies' divergent approaches to antisubmarine warfare had to be resolved; and yet another Doenitz offensive had to be subdued.

On a murky, quiet morning in 1943, answering a call from topside, I found the office of the Deputy Director of Naval Intelligence in a blaze of excitement. Handing me a message he had just received, Captain Zacharias, the Deputy Director, told me: "Drop everything you're doing and write a Norden about this. We've just sunk five U-boats in a single operation—*five of them in one fell swoop!*—with a new secret weapon."

A man of abundant enthusiasm and imagination, Zacharias was sometimes trapped in snap decisions. A glance at the message now persuaded me that he was off again on one of his climbs out on a limb. But I did as I was told. Then Commander Albrecht cut the record. A few hours later, the Office of War Information put it on the air.

The victory of which we thus bragged was scored by a British Support Group of six sloops under Captain Frederick John Walker who was, as Churchill called him, the Royal Navy's most outstanding U-boat killer. He not only devised effective tactics against the U-boats but, in personal command of Support Group 2, also carried his ideas into deadly execution.

The Admiralty was so peeved by our crossing of the international demarcation line of propaganda that they launched a formal protest and Admiral King had to apologize in a little note for our trespass.

I mention this silly little incident to illustrate on an extreme example one of the basic weaknesses of the anti-U-boat campaign—a division along national lines. From the Allied point of view, there were two battles of the Atlantic—one waged by the Royal Navy, another by the United States Navy. The ocean was divided down the line by the "Chop"—short for "Change of Operational Control"—east of which was the British Atlantic, and to west of which was the American Atlantic.

The "Chop" was not just a thing of geography. The concept that created it permeated the Allies' entire antisubmarine effort. They used widely divergent tactics and methods in this great joint venture to defeat the U-boats. How far this dual control of the Battle of the Atlantic was adverse to our cause is difficult to assess, but it certainly did not enhance our efficiency. Confusion was especially rampant when a convoy's screen was of mixed British, Canadian and American escorts because they had no uniform procedures, tactics, gunnery instructions. Even worse, they used two entirely different sets of signals.

Several times during the dark hours of the Atlantic battle, suggestions were advanced that a uniform system of procedures and signals be devised, and even to bring the whole gigantic operation under unified command patterned after Nimitz's command in the Pacific. Thus in September, 1942, Air Chief Marshal Sir Philip Joubert, commander-in-chief of the RAF Coastal Command, "proposed a single supreme control for the whole anti-U-boat war, with a central planning staff to coordinate the separate and often conflicting policies of the British, Canadian and American naval and air authorities."

A similar recommendation was put forward by Captain L. Hewlett Thebaud, USN, from his vantage point as U.S. naval control officer at Londonderry. His proposal was seconded by several officers on the staff of Admiral Stark in London. They went so far as to suggest that a combined naval staff be set up under a single admiral who would exercise operational control over all phases and forces of the Allies' anti-U-boat effort. There was widespread agreement that something along these lines was badly needed. However, the proposals went too far. Such a supreme command would have had to be given to a British admiral but this would have been, as Morison put it, *politically* impracticable. President Roosevelt could not have turned over responsibility for "the support and supply of the United States Army overseas to an Englishman".

There was, moreover, a wide and emotionally charged disagreement within the Allies regarding the divergent procedures. The British, steeped in naval traditions, regarded American procedures as immature, while Americans thought those of the Royal Navy were obsolete. There was some justification for both views. Several of the U.S. doctrines had been improvised by escort commanders on the spot, while some of the British signals harked back to Admiral Lord Howe and the Eighteenth Century.

Even before the partnership in the shooting war, the United States Navy was sometimes appalled by the tradition-bound and outmoded procedures of the senior member. When, for example, Churchill met Roosevelt on the *Prince of Wales* during the Atlantic Conference of 1941, typewriters had to be supplied from the U.S.S. *Augusta* because the brand new British battleship had none on board. Typewriters may not be imperative for the conduct of the war at sea but their absence on the newest British battle wagon somehow impressed even the youngest American naval officer in attendance that his British ally was a bit overdoing tradition. The old four-stackers we exchanged for British bases in the West Indies had to be "de-modernized" to adapt them to "traditional" British standards.

In the wake of the Casablanca Conference, an attempt was made to standardize procedures and signals. Two inter-Allied boards were created, one to survey the situation and make recommendations, the other specifically to devise a uniform system. The Allied Antisubmarine Survey Board worked from March to September, 1943, then petered out; the other, called hopefully Combined Procedures Board, went out of business in June, without accomplishing anything.

The British made Admiral King chiefly responsible for the failure of these boards and charged in effect that he had sabotaged them because, as the official history of the Royal Air Force put it, "he did not view the Battle of the Atlantic in the same light as General Marshall viewed the invasion of Europe."

It must be said that King had commanding reasons to oppose a sweeping standardization. In view of the fact that the United States Navy had to rotate destroyers and other antisubmarine vessels between the Atlantic and the Pacific, it would have been confusing to introduce two different procedures. The situation was remedied after March, 1943, when mixed escorts were discontinued on specific convoy routes so that each Navy could use its own procedures without confusion.

King was further justified in his stand by the fact that there was no clear-cut uniformity even within the British antisubmarine war effort.

Although the Coastal Command was supposed to be under Admiralty control, its commander-in-chief characterized this arrangement as "polite fiction". There was diversification and duplication throughout the British antisubmarine establishment, certainly up to the appointment of Admiral Sir Max Horton, RN, to the command of the Western Approaches, in November, 1942. It was then mainly his forceful personality, enormous professional skill and dominant influence that made it seem there was, if not specific unity of command, at least unity of purpose in British antisubmarine warfare.

However, by the spring of 1943, King recognized that something had to be done to improve ASW organization. To this end, he decided to call a conference to Washington to review the U-boat situation and make recommendations to remedy it.

The Conference met on March 1, in the ominous shadow of a new Doenitz blitz. Britain was represented by Admiral Sir Percy Noble, RN, recently appointed chief of the British Admiralty Delegation in Washington, Horton's predecessor in command of the Western Approaches and second only to him as an authority on antisubmarine warfare. The chief American delegate was Admiral Edwards.

King opened the Conference in a board room of the Federal Reserve Building with a thoughtful speech in which he reiterated his absolute faith in the efficacy of the convoy system and expressed some reservations about the practicability of the hunter-killer groups unless "used directly in connection with the convoy routes." He concluded with what for him was a rhetoric flourish. "A ship saved," he said, "is worth two built. Think it over!"

The Enemy Is Listening

Even as the Convoy Conference pondered the problems of the Atlantic, the very convoys it was designed to safeguard were getting into more and greater troubles. Now followed a brief flare-up of the battle when it seemed that cloak and dagger became the decisive implements of the U-boat war. The formidable B-Service of German codebreakers scored its greatest triumphs during those days when it seemed to be reading the signals of the Allied convoys almost at will.

This was a grievous leak whose existence became known only after the war when we captured the archives of the German Naval High Command intact and found in them reams of intercepts which showed that the U-Boat Command had been privy to some of our most closely guarded secrets. The B-men had managed to decrypt virtually every Allied signal over the Atlantic and passed on to Doenitz everything he needed to know about the convoys—the number of ships in each, sailing date and speed, and—most important—their course and destination. Although in January the weather continued to be dismal, making a systematic search for convoys virtually impossible, Doenitz was enabled nevertheless to deploy his U-boats and go after our ships.

In January, 1943, though, this phenomenal feat was overshadowed by some circumstantial evidence that the Allies actually had a dark intruder inside the U-Boat Command. Just when Doenitz sat back rather smugly awaiting reports from his U-boats that they were shadowing the convoys, they told him that they were not able even to locate them. The mystery was deepened by fresh intercepts which showed that the convoys had radically altered course immediately after Doenitz had directed the U-boats to them. This was the result of exceptionally skilled routing that took full advantage of a fairly comprehensive knowledge of U-boat dispositions, gained from an almost foolproof saturation coverage of their transmissions. But Doenitz—who refused to concede that he himself was supplying telltale intelligence to the Allies by insisting on reports from his boats—was convinced that the Allies were getting "dope" from someone inside his Command.

Counter-espionage agents from both the *Abwehr* and the Gestapo were called to Lorient and for days everybody at the "Sardine Can" was suspect. However, no positive proof of treachery was found as, indeed, it would have been almost impossible even for the best Allied agent to supply such information on an hour by hour basis.

However, very soon it looked that, quite on the contrary, it was Doenitz after all who had someone on this side of the Atlantic attending our own convoy briefing sessions. In reality, he did not have to risk a live spy on such a precarious mission. He had the B-Service to cater to his needs, and what it accomplished in a single week in March, 1943, must sound like the climax of a Hitchcock thriller.

This halcyon week of the German cryptoanalysts began on March 9, when the B-Service intercepted and decrypted a signal that revealed to Doenitz the precise position of eastbound Convoy HX-228.

Then on March 10, SC-121 was identified and located.

On March 13, decrypted signals located HX-229 south-west of Cape Race, sailing on a course of eighty-nine degrees.

On March 14, the B-Service identified Convoy SC-122. It was also able to advise Doenitz on the basis of still another decrypted signal that, according to orders the convoy had received the night before, it would stear a course of sixty-seven degrees as soon as it reached a certain point in the ocean.

Thanks to those intercepts, Doenitz knew everything about this "large mass of shipping," as Captain Roskill put it, "in a relatively confined space of ocean." He immediately organized three wolfpacks consisting of thirty-eight boats and sent them with explicit directions against the 208 merchantmen and some thirty odd escorts of the four convoys. Assuming that the convoys would counter by radically changing their courses, he spread out his U-boats as widely as possible, to deceive the enemy as to his real intentions, but also to give his commanders a better chance of stumbling upon the convoys.

The issue was joined on March 10, and when the multiple engagement ended on the seventeenth, the U-Boat Command proclaimed in a jubilant communique, that listed thirty-two ships and one destroyer as sunk, and nine additional ships as damaged: "This is the greatest success ever achieved in a convoy battle and is all the more creditable in that nearly half the U-boats involved scored at least one hit."

The claim was wildly exaggerated, but the battle was a dazzling spectacle. The U-boats made the most of Hoyle's advice that when you are in doubt, win the trick. They used every trick in the book.

They attacked at night from periscope depth, from several directions simultaneously, to confuse radar. They used decoy subs to befuddle the Huffduff and succeeded in sending our escorts on wild goose chases. They created confusion within the convoys by breaking into their voice-radio circuits with phony messages. They tuned in to intra-convoy radio traffic and gained useful information that often determined their tactics.

The savage violence of the battle can be guaged from a single-sequence of fast-moving events in the course of a single one of its engagements. On March 11, the Senior Officer of HX-228 in HMS *Harvester* sank *U-444* of Oberleutnant Langfeld, then the *Harvester* was sunk in turn by *U-432* of Kapitaenleutnant Hermann Eckhardt which was then sunk by the French corvette *Aconit*.

Doenitz's bravura performance created something akin to panic in the Admiralty. "In the first ten days [of March], in all waters, we lost forty-one ships," wrote Roskill; "in the second ten days fifty-six. More than half a million tons of shipping was sunk in those twenty days; and, what made the losses so much more serious than the bare figures can indicate, was that nearly two-thirds of the ships sunk during the month were sunk in convoy."

The British naval staff went so far as to actually voice the opinion that convoys might not be "an effective system of defense" after all. And Roskill asked: "Where would the Admiralty turn if the convoy system had lost its effectiveness? They did not know; but they must have felt, though no one admitted it, that defeat then stared them in the face."

Doenitz wrote: "After three and a half years of war we had brought British maritime power to the brink of defeat in the Battle of the Atlantic—and that with only half the number of U-boats which we had always demanded."

The United States was remote from these events. The public knew nothing of the sudden deterioration of the Atlantic situation and had no inkling of the fact that victory itself was in the balance again. But Admiral King knew it, and he was especially concerned because these events seemed to mitigate against his own firm belief that the convoy was "the *only* way that [gave] any promise of success."

The Convoy Conference—that went far beyond its name to explore all aspects of the antisubmarine problem—produced a number of important results. It laid the groundwork for the regular employment of escort carriers in the protection of convoys. Its discussions stimulated the studies in King's headquarters that led to the establishment of the hunter-killer groups. But even in the face of what Roskill in retrospect called "a serious disaster to the Allied cause," it still left two major problems suspended in mid air:

It did not provide for a unification of the Allied antisubmarine command; and it did not even attempt to develop the specific organization that was woefully needed to render our antisubmarine measures more efficient and more effective. The Conference left it to each country to unify ASW and create the organization its Navy regarded as the most likely to succeed.

The Fleet Without a Ship

However, there was a significant bright spot even in this dark picture. After having lost only six U-boats in January, the Germans lost twenty in February, and fifteen more in March.

The tide appeared to be stemmed. Now Admiral King decided to dedicate himself body and soul to the task of turning it.

On May 1, 1943, he sent a terse three-paragraph message across the street to the Joint Chiefs of Staff which began with the statement: "It is arranged to set up immediately in the Navy Department an antisubmarine command to be known as the Tenth Fleet."

The statement was characteristic of King and remarkable on several counts. For one thing, it presented as an accomplished fact something that was still congealing inside his staff and which, when brought into the open, could raise a first rate controversy. For another, it spelled out for the first time the designation King had chosen for an institution that was to be anything but a fleet.

For what is a fleet?

Every dictionary defines it as a "number of vessels." William Falconer, the hapless poet-mariner who had learned the meaning of nautical expressions the hard way, interpreted the word as a "collection of ships sailing in company." To the sailor, a "fleet" can also be a locality of shallow tidal water. To fleet is to move aft or forward, or to overhaul a tackle. It could mean any of these things but it was never meant to mean a number of naval officers who would *not* sail at all and whose job was to tackle an overhaul rather than overhaul a tackle.

Why did King chose such a bizarre name for a landlocked organization consisting of a handful of shore-bound Navy men and women? This question is best answered in a description of the Tenth Fleet's final evolution.

King made his first "gingerly step" toward the unification of the American antisubmarine effort when, on April 6, he named "Frog" Low assistant chief of staff to be concerned exclusively with ASW matters and transferred to his control the scattered antisubmarine warfare units and sections of the Navy. However, in spite of the existence of those diverse units, ASW was still but a bead on a string of confusions and King, therefore, instructed Low, a cerebral trouble-shooter whose specialty was to *think* King out of his troubles, to draw up an "appreciation of the antisubmarine situation."

Low then looked at the situation and did not appreciate too highly what he saw. Somewhat like a drowning man who sees his whole life flash by, he had a broad historic view of the problem, and realized that the old and gray-headed errors of the past were responsible, not only for our unpreparedness in 1941-1942, but also for our troubles in this spring of 1943.

Though he began his career in the battleship *Connecticut*, Low spent the best years of his life in submarines and knew intimately the specific problems of underseas warfare. He always regretted that the dominant powers of the United States Navy—the big battleship-oriented admirals and the big-bang buffs of the "Gun Club" (as the powerful clique in the Bureau of Ordnance was called) could never work up any real interest in either the submarine or antisubmarine warfare.

In preparation for his memo to King, Low waded through a mass of British and American literature, trying to pick the best of everything and to synthesize it into a working design. He found much that was useless and much that was good or even excellent. But probably he was most influenced in his approach by Admiral Horton because his findings and recommendations seemed to be closest to Horton's philosophy and tactical principles.

Like Horton, Low emphasized the need to focus in on the fundamentals and to make them work with ruthless determination; like Horton, too, he believed that training and experience counted more than numbers; and like Horton again, he advocated a tight organization with overriding powers and with coverage for all aspects and phases of antisubmarine warfare, its operational procedures evolving from the minute analysis of the U-boats' tactical and operational patterns.

On April 20, Low submitted his memorandum. "The prosaic answer to the problem is," he wrote, "*enough* escorts *and* aircraft, recognition of fundamentals, and pressure to make them work."

The rock-bottom philosophy of this grass-roots approach was then summed up in the words: "Improvement in the present situation will result if all officers in the chain of command require that fundamentals be *learned* and *applied*."

King approved the memorandum, then superimposed on Low's proposed plan his own ideas. A firm believer in the classic fleet organization as the most efficient organizational pattern in the Navy, whether ashore or afloat, he concluded that what the anti–U-boat campaign needed was a similar set-up. "I am now convinced," he told Low, "that a fleet organization for antisubmarine warfare is a military necessity."

Taking his cue from this remark, Low recommended on April 25, that all units and sections King had recently shifted to his control (but had not yet "delivered" in his hands) be united under Admiral Ingersoll in the Atlantic Fleet, but King rejected the proposal. He had the organizational solution all worked out in his mind, including the contours of the set-up with four major points dominating all his considerations:

(1) Antisubmarine warfare needed a commander of the highest rank whose prestige and influence would be paramount and who could make his decisions prevail.

(2) The organization he had in mind would have no ships of its own, but would have recourse to every vessel of the United States Navy with inherent and explicit power to commandeer whatever forces when and where needed for antisubmarine operations.

(3) It had to be a small organization with assured and easy access to any and all agencies of the Navy, and especially to the various existing intelligence services and their resources.

(4) It had to have the status of a fleet, partly to simplify its per-

sonnel and administrative structure in a headquarters-type organization, partly to function along operational lines, and mainly to be able to use the channels of fleet communications.

The Problem of Command

King then instructed Low to draft, first, the preliminary statement for the Joint Chiefs (which he intended more or less as a trial balloon but was prepared to defend to the hilt); and, second, the basic directive of the Tenth Fleet. While King was then busy with *Trident*—that included the taxing exposition of his vast Pacific plans before the Combined Chiefs—Low completed the basic directive (in which he defined the primary function of the Tenth Fleet as the "destruction of enemy submarines") and gained for it King's approval. Now there was but one point to be settled—the question of who would be Commander Tenth Fleet, whose overpowering and total functions King had outlined in his statement to the Joint Chiefs as follows:

"The Commander Tenth Fleet is to exercise direct control over all Atlantic Sea Frontiers, using sea frontier commanders as task force commanders. He is to control allocation of antisubmarine forces to all commands in the Atlantic, including the Atlantic Fleet, and is to reallocate forces from time to time, as the situation requires.

"In order to insure quick and effective action to meet the needs of the changing antisubmarine situation, the Commander Tenth Fleet is to be given control of all LR [long range] and VLR [very long range] aircraft, and certain groups of units of auxiliary carriers, escort ships and submarines which he will allocate to reinforce task forces which need help, or to employment as 'killer groups' under his operational direction in appropriate circumstances"—the whole works and no holds barred.

King assigned to the new command a vast area of operational control and arrogated to it well-nigh total discretionary powers, virtually independent of all other commands. It was evident that such an exalted command needed a senior officer of the highest rank, indeed, if it was to function at all. King had two officers specifically in mind as best qualified for this super-command, but neither was immediately available. The search seemed to be hitting a snag when, on May 15, Low happened to mention to King:

"Admiral, Commander Tenth Fleet should be a naval aviator."

"He is," King said.

"Who?" Low asked.

"Me," King answered, and that settled it.

It was an inspired and fortunate decision that had the seeds of the Tenth Fleet's eventual success in it. While afterwards King himself exercised but rarely the actual physical functions of this command, he hovered over all its proceedings and infused them with his authority. Everything was issued in his name, and from King's orders there was no appeal. Not only was thus the utmost in unity-of-command automatically assured but acquiescence was also secured in it *ipso facto*, guaranteeing the prompt and faithful execution of the orders.

The designation "Tenth Fleet" was picked out of the hat, as Low put it. On March 15, King had introduced a new naval shorthand for the designations of fleets by numbers and assigned the odd numbers to the Pacific, even numbers to the Atlantic. When now a number was needed for the new phantom fleet, King picked "ten" because it was a nice round figure, easy to remember, and because no numbered fleet in service was close to it.

The Tenth Fleet, now officially so named, was formally established on May 20, 1943. Its coming was heralded only in a classified dispatch announcing that "it was to exercise [under the direct command of COMINCH] unity of control over U.S. antisubmarine operations [sic] in that part of the Atlantic under U.S. strategic control." These lines pointed up two important aspects of the issue. They clearly stated that the "fleet without a ship" was envisaged as an *operational* force. And they showed that the "Chop" had prevailed.

What, then, was this Tenth Fleet in specific terms and how was it supposed to function?

At that stage, in the summer of 1943, few people outside King's own entourage knew enough about it to be able to answer the question. Aside from being a phantom fleet, it was also one of the mushrooming mysteries of the war because, for the time being, King was playing his cards close to his chest.

He had several reasons for this, some strictly rational, others maybe emotional. He was confident that it would work—especially in the capable hands of Low as Chief of Staff—but so intricate was the challenge it was designed to meet and so shrewd the enemy with whom it had to deal that even King could not be certain. He also assumed that his phantom fleet might evoke misunderstandings or antagonism from timid and conservative souls, and provoke criticism for being too novel, sweeping and arbitrary. Moreover, this Tenth Fleet was stepping on many toes—a cardinal sin in any military organization—and nobody could tell how the vested interests would react to their sudden "unification."

Even weeks after its establishment—in mid-July, for example—the shroud was so thick that officers outside Washington with actual responsibilities in the anti—U-boat campaign were mystified by it. They buttonholed knowing friends with lines to Washington and asked them to find out "what the hell this Tenth Fleet" was.

It became better known within the Navy on July 29, when a general announcement introduced it, described its exact functions, and arranged for the mass shift of all ASW units and groups to the control of the Tenth Fleet. Among the agencies thus transferred—or, in some cases, abolished or superseded—were the Antisubmarine Warfare Unit of the Atlantic Fleet that still had its headquarters in Boston; the Antisubmarine Measures Unit of COMINCH's Readiness Division; the ASW Operational Research Group of civilian scientists (the ASWORG); and the mammoth Convoy and Routing Group of Admiral Metcalf.

A few months then sufficed to persuade Admiral King that the Tenth Fleet was doing its job and was there to stay. On November 19, he therefore, agreed to make it publicly known through a special Navy Department communique that revealed its evolution, organization and functions in simple but comprehensive terms.

The "Fleet" in Being

While thus taking the wrap off the Tenth Fleet, the businesslike communique did not make it either widely known or even moderately popular. Since it was not a combat organization *per se*, and whatever glamor it had was subtle and inherent, it never came in for the familiar ballyhoo treatment by Public Relations. This was welcome to Low, who had a genuine passion for anonymity and was inclined to view his unique organization with an acute sense of proportion.

From the captured files of the *Kriegsmarine* we now know that the Germans, although somewhat intrigued by this phantom "force," had but the haziest notion of the Tenth Fleet and never fathomed its unique concept nor understood its peculiar status. In his post-war memoirs Admiral Doenitz chose to ignore it completely. Such neglect was not confined, however, to the former enemy. Even the American historians of the war at sea dealt sparingly and superficially with it, a reflection of their failure to grasp its greater implications and enduring influence, and to recognize the peculiar genius that created and managed it.

As fleets go the Tenth was a fleet-in-being at best, but true to its name, it operated around the clock. There was something urgent and vibrant about it that filled its crammed premises occupying part of a single wing on the third floor of the Navy Department with the close-hauled air of a fleet organization afloat. Its "lookouts" scanned the ocean.

Its operations officers moved the ships and the planes assigned to antisubmarine work. The Battle of the Atlantic was a full time enterprise and the new men now delegated to conduct it by remote control had to adapt their hours to those of the opposing forces at sea.

The organization was relatively small. The charter was, as far as possible, patterned after the COMINCH Headquarters Organization, adding the Convoy and Routing Division, a scientific advisory council, and providing for close liaison arrangements with two major ASW organizations left intact in the Atlantic Fleet. The Cominch Headquarters Organization consisted of four major divisions: Plans (F-1), Combat Intelligence (F-2), Readiness (F-3), and Operations (F-4). Inside the Tenth Fleet, however, the first had no division status because planning was done by Low and his top-level associates in close—almost daily—consultation with Admiral King. Low had broad discretionary powers to make use of COMINCH Plans Division for strategic guidance and facilities.

Similarly the Tenth Fleet did not have an intelligence service strictly of its own but utilized F-2, the Combat Intelligence Division of Cominch, to take care of its own crucial and enormous intelligence requirements. However, the Atlantic Section of F-2 soon became an integral part of the Tenth Fleet and also operated its plot.

Within the Tenth Fleet, the functions and responsibilities of the Cominch Readiness Division were assigned to the Anti-Submarine Measures Division that was thus charged with research, material development and training. It further included units engaged in statistical and analytical work which was found to be imperative and indispensable for operational calculations in the development of doctrines. The Tenth Fleet also maintained its own Operations Division whose function was to move the ships into action. It kept a constant check on the fleet organization, the allocation of ships, the adequacy of ships to carry out given ASW operations, and the capabilities of all types of ships suited for ASW. But it left to Admiral Ingersoll's Atlantic Fleet to implement its "recommendations" by alerting and assigning the vessels and planes needed for the *physical* phase of operations.

This basic function, in which the Tenth Fleet became operational, was an immensely delicate task requiring as much savvy in tact as in tactics. In the course of the war, the Tenth Fleet's messages to Admiral Ingersoll employed an impressive variety of semantic artifices to avoid the impression that the Tenth Fleet was giving orders to CINCLANT. Thus the action messages usually began with "Suggest that you . . ." or "It is recommended that you . . .", or were expressed in question form such as

"Would it be possible for you . . .?" or "Would you concur in . . .?" Of course, the only answer Ingersoll was expected to give to these politely formulated questions was affirmative. Protocol worked out extremely well, to the complete satisfaction of all concerned. Although the Tenth Fleet was authorized to take operational control, it never had to resort to such blunt and drastic measure except in a single instance when Admiral King himself did not like a certain disposition in the Atlantic and signalled an *order* to CINCLANT in so many words.

This strict adherence to etiquette, and the urbane ingenuity and modesty with which Admiral Low practiced it, proved an important element in the Tenth Fleet's effectiveness. The fighting men of the Navy, after all, naturally resented any kibitzing, especially by people who were hundreds of miles from the hot breath of war and proffered their gratuitous advice from the comforts of their safe port. Much sooner than they cared to concede, those fighting men came to depend on prompting by the Tenth Fleet and cherish its counsel even in low-level tactical matters. But they were loath to admit that any of their successes had originated in the brain of some chair-borne Washington meddler using a weapon no more lethal than an adding machine.

Captain Gallery, in his vivacious book *Clear the Decks*, never gave credit to the Tenth Fleet for guiding him to the *U-505* which his gallant escort group captured. In private, however, he was quite lavish with his acknowledgment and even sent a picture of the captured German, with an appropriate inscription, to Commander Knowles whose accurate and timely plotting had made the coup possible. Admiral Ingram's chief of staff once visited the Tenth Fleet plot and inquired about a certain marker on the chart. The duty officer told him, "It marks one of our kills."

Though the Tenth Fleet plotter meant the "our" in its broad generic sense, the visiting fireman took exception to it and reprimanded the young officer with pointed sarcasm.

"Since when are *you* killing U-boats?!" he asked.

The Anti-Submarine Measures Division was the "egghead" of the Tenth Fleet, not merely because it harbored the civilian scientists and actuaries who analyzed the U-boat war, but especially because it published the "Yellow Peril." That was the Navy-wide nickname of the secret *U.S. Fleet Antisubmarine Warfare Bulletin*, a superb periodical published once a month from June, 1943, to June, 1945, in which the Tenth Fleet disseminated its ideas, conclusions, doctrines, as well as information about weapon developments, the tactics and capabilities of U-boats—simply everything even remotely connected with antisubmarine warfare. It was a running and self-renewing, always up-to-the-minute and comprehensive manual of ASW, so edited and written as to attract even those who normally find the reading of a tabloid a chore. The "Yellow Peril" was the Tenth Fleet's major means of direct communication with those it was to serve most directly—the skippers of the escort carriers, destroyers and destroyer escorts, and the pilots, whose job was the actual destruction of the enemy.

Another series of its publications was called *Tenth Fleet Incidents*, of which several thousands were issued during the war. They reconstructed actions and operations in a graphic manner to stimulate their readers to original ideas and to teach them how to benefit from the experience of others. Admiral Low used both media most considerately, proffering advice in the circumspect and inspiring manner of the self-effacing educator. On October 4, 1943, Commander Charles L. Westhofen, USN, in a Navy Ventura, sighted the *U-336* of Kapitaenleutnant Hans Hunger about 200 miles southwest of Iceland and was in turn sighted by the German who promptly submerged. Westhofen applied unusual tactics. He feigned ignorance of the *U-Hunger's* presence, retired behind the horizon, then flew back hoping to find the boat back on the surface. When his expectation was fulfilled, he dropped three depth charges through the U-boat's dense anti-aircraft fire, then ordered his turret gunner to rake the German from stem to stern. The depth charges almost blew the *U-336* out of the ocean, then sent it to its final fathom without survivors.

Westhofen's feat rated a *Tenth Fleet Incident* and it carried Low's comment that the action was "worthy of emulation by all aircraft engaged in antisubmarine activities." What was in fact an admonition sounded like a pat on the back in Low's phraseology.

This was the inner core of the Tenth Fleet. Its outer layer consisted of the Convoy and Routing Division, functioning as its integral part but with a great deal of autonomy; and the group of some seventy civilian scientists, known as the ASWORGS. Beyond that, the Tenth Fleet maintained close liaison with the Operational Training Command and the Antisubmarine Development Detachment of the Atlantic Fleet.

Convoy and Routing was grafted on the Tenth Fleet for reasons of accommodation rather than unification. It long predated the Tenth Fleet as, in fact, it was one of the first agencies the Navy had organized specifically for the impending war. It was established in 1941, as a section in the Ship Movement Division of OpNav, when the Chop Line was first drawn and the United States Navy assumed responsibility for the routing and diverting of convoys and troop movements in the western half of the Atlantic. Later King incorporated C & R into COMINCH Headquarters, finally he moved it into the Tenth Fleet.

At least one of the reasons for this was a peculiar dilemma presented by the director of C & R. From its inception, a retired captain (later rear admiral) named Martin Kellog Metcalf, a Californian who was sixty years old in 1941, headed C & R. He earned the Navy Cross for chasing U-boats, escorting troop convoys and conducting rescue operations in World War I. Now in World War II, he ran C & R with well-oiled efficiency, thanks to two Reserve officers, Everett Alexander Rhodes and Charles E. Ames, whose know-how gained in the Merchant Marine proved extremely useful in the management of the section.

By the very nature of its mission, Convoy and Routing had to work closely with the Admiralty, but unfortunately for all concerned, Metcalf belonged to that faction of the Navy whose members viewed the British with jaundiced eyes. His anglophobia resulted in several lively breezes and squalls where smooth sailing was a *conditio sine qua non.* It was, therefore, largely to accommodate the British by curbing Metcalf's anti-Limey regime that King decided to throw C & R in with the rest when the Tenth Fleet was established. Low on his part was a past-master of inter-Allied cooperation and maintained the friendliest relations with his opposite numbers of the Royal Navy. The British no longer had any reason to complain. The U-boat was not yet licked, but at least Metcalf had been subdued.

There now remained only two organizations outside the Tenth Fleet with exclusive responsibilities in ASW—the Operational Training Command under Rear Admiral Donald Bradford Beary, USN, and the so-called Asdevlant of Captain Aurelius B. ("Abe") Vosseler, USN, a pioneer naval aviator, developer of the high-altitude oxygen mask, and charter member of the first antisubmarine fraternity under Captain Baker in Boston.

Beary's Command operated as an "antisubmarine university" on the Oxford pattern, with independent "colleges"—several sound schools and fifteen antisubmarine training and refresher centers. The alumni were expected to spread the know-how they had gained in the rough-and-tumble world of the Atlantic.

Vosseler's Asdevlant—short for Antisubmarine Development Detachment Atlantic Fleet—brought together in yet another "college" naval pilots and crewmen, technicians and scientists, to explore and improve the air aspects of antisubmarine warfare. They tested equipment, developed their optimum operational use, and worked out coordinated ASW tactics and communication procedures between aircraft and surface vessels, in accordance with the Navy doctrine that "aircraft and ships should operate as one team."

Though not an integral part of the Tenth Fleet, it worked in exceptionally close association with it. It was one of the Navy's ASW units that predated the Tenth Fleet, but it was neither adequate in scope, nor properly coordinated. Located at Quonset, it consisted of a handful of Navy planes. Low, who had the highest respect for air aspects of antisubmarine warfare, recognized the great value of the Detachment and recommended several improvements to Captain Kilpatrick, Admiral Ingersoll's Chief of Staff. Among others he recommended that Asdevlant be given its own surface vessel section to make it self-contained in its experiments.

The proposals were promptly accepted. When after that the Tenth Fleet sought to develop new air-surface cooperation tactics, and wanted to test them, Low would call Kilpatrick and ask him to initiate the tests. They were then carried out immediately, often on the basis of telephoned instructions.

Time was the essence and the Tenth Fleet had none to lose. It was the urgency of the problem and the immediacy of its solution that dominated all considerations and motivated all decisions. Once Low was offered a device that looked promising and which he could use to excellent effect againts the U-boats. But he turned it down when he was told that it would take two years to produce it. "What is the use of the best weapon," he said, "if it won't be ready till 1946? The criteria of our acceptance of anything offered us are whether it is good and whether it is immediately available."

It was the pragmatic formulation of King's dictum, "Do the best you can with what you have." But Low was tireless in cutting red tape, and using his influence up and down, to get the best to do his best with. This principle was applied to the whole Tenth Fleet and especially to its human equation.

CHAPTER XIV

The Human Equation

In the conquest which is service,
In the victory which is peace!
F. L. Knowles (1869-1905)
The New Age

The Tenth Fleet was broad in scope, sweeping in power and virtually absolute in influence, yet it was astonishingly small and tight. Aside from the Convoy and Routing Division (that perforce needed a large staff which Tenth Fleet had inherited) and ASWORG (that employed about a hundred civilian scientists and technicians), the Tenth Fleet operated with about fifty officers and enlisted personnel. Most of the latter were Waves. Its entire budget was below that of a destroyer. It could be so small, of course, because it had recourse to the whole of Cominch and the Sea Frontiers, and had the power to commandeer anything afloat and ashore over which the United States Navy had control. Even so, the very compactness of this operational organization represented a daring new concept in naval thinking.

Team of Virtuosos

This was how Admiral King envisaged it and Admiral Low wanted it. Low in particular was so frugal in personnel matters that he himself managed to get along without aides or flag lieutenants, without any of the uniformed retainers the brass is entitled to. He had but one secretary, a Wave ensign named Mary Elizabeth Cummings, but she was the paragon of a Girl Friday. Among other qualifications, she held the degree of Bachelor of Secretarial Studies from Carnegie Tech.

The staff of the Tenth Fleet was assembled from all over the globe. The few top people were selected for their special qualifications and, therefore, there was a preponderance of destroyer, submarine and air specialists. Low had still another overriding personnel policy. He insisted on rotating the heads of his divisions, partly to bring fresh blood into the Tenth Fleet straight from the combat zones and partly to train a handful of "missionaries" who would spread the Tenth Fleet gospel in the fleets.

Since Low was determined to use existing facilities but make a new beginning, he bypassed the small clique of antisubmarine specialists—whose pioneering work was notable but whose efforts had produced "only a system of incoherent and haphazard units"—and recruited for the Tenth Fleet a very small group of aggressive and intelligent officers with a reputation for rugged individualism and independent thinking.

The first head of his Operations Division was Captain William Dodge Sample, USN, one of the Navy's greatest aviators who finished the war with four Gold Stars on his Legion of Merit. When in the spring of 1944, Sample was transferred to the Pacific, his place was taken by one of the Navy's keenest young captains, Arnold J. Isbell, fresh from a remarkable tour of duty in command of the escort carrier group in USS *Card*. "Buster" Isbell was severe and something of a martinet, but he was full of vim and practical ideas, and knew his business as a naval aviator with a masterly sense of air-surface teamwork.

The Antisubmarine Measures Division's first head was a veteran submariner, Captain John Meade Haines, USN. Just this side of fifty, this life-long Navy man (he was actually born at the Boston Navy Yard) came to the Tenth Fleet from command of Submarine Division 42 whose job was to ferry Carlson's Raiders to their destinations on Japanese-held islands in the Pacific. Haines was succeeded by Captain Harold Carlton Fitz, USN, one of the Navy's most versatile officers. First a torpedo specialist, then a radio communications expert, still later a student of both mine and chemical warfare, Captain Fitz was the kind of man who got a law degree from Harvard on the side while he served a tour of duty in the office of the Judge Advocate General. Before joining the Tenth Fleet, he made a great name for himself as commander of a Destroyer Division on escort duty during the darkest days of the Battle of the Atlantic.

The section that drew up the pattern of the U-boat war through a continuous analysis and statistical evaluation of combat operations, and on whose findings Tenth Fleet developed the tactics and doctrines of our antisubmarine effort, was headed by Captain Ross Forrester Collins,

USNR, whom Low had found at COMINCH headquarters. Collins was a
a graduate of the Naval Academy and saw service in the Navy as a
regular until 1921, when he transferred into the Naval Reserve and
went into business as an investment broker in Kansas City, Missouri.
He was a commander of Reserve in his late forties when, on February
6, 1942, he was recalled to active duty. He first organized and then
supervised a "statistical group which collected, correlated and analyzed
information relating to technical operational details of antisubmarine
warfare" and was eventually awarded the Legion of Merit for a difficult
job "exceptionally well done."

On the distaff side, a comely young lady from Chicago, Illinois, headed
a contingent of Waves, she herself holding down one of the most responsible and interesting jobs in Tenth Fleet. Lieutenant (j.g.) Virginia
Mildred Louise Hill, USNR (W), was working on a Chicago newspaper
when she decided to enlist in the Navy almost exactly a year after Pearl
Harbor. From the Waves' Midshipmen's School at Smith College,
Northampton, Massachusetts, she moved directly into the Tenth Fleet
and stayed with it to its dissolution in 1945. She edited the *U.S. Fleet
Anti-Submarine Bulletin*—the famous "Yellow Peril."

The "Yellow Peril" had to be a lively and well-written journal in order
to attract readers far too busy with the bloody job at hand to devote
much effort to the printed word prepared for them in the relative comforts of Washington. Virginia's experience and skill as a newspaper-
woman enabled her to produce a periodical on a rather non-feminine
subject with such journalistic know-how and flair that the monthly
became so popular that it had a long waiting list of authorized readers.
Admiral Low attributes the success of Tenth Fleet to the widespread
and effective diffusion of its findings and ideas to a broad professional
audience and to some extent, to the competent editorial job Lieutenant
Hill did with the "Yellow Peril."

Another permanent fixture of Tenth Fleet was Ensign Cummings,
the admiral's secretary. An attractive brunette from Waynesburg,
Pennsylvania, who was in her late twenties when she joined the Navy—
two days after Pearl Harbor, Mary—as everybody called her in the
office—joined Tenth Fleet in August, 1943. She was typical of the
people Low attracted to and cultivated in his organization. Miss Cummings showed how competent she was when she moved on to increasingly responsible assignments after her tour of duty in Tenth Fleet.
During her seven years in the Navy, which she entered as yeoman
second class and left a lieutenant commander, she served as administrative officer of the Joint Intelligence Center's Translation Section in

the Pacific, District Communications Officer at Pearl Harbor, and eventually in the Judge Advocate General's Legislative Division.

It was not solely their ability for good and devoted service but especially Low's ability to get the best and the most out of his subordinates and inspire them to work hard cheerfully that characterized the human equation in the Tenth Fleet.

Admiral Low

Francis Stuart Low, the son of a naval officer and a proper Bostonian (although he was born in Albany, New York), spent all his adult life in the United States Navy in which he rose from midshipman to full admiral in forty-five years. A bookish-looking man with some bulk in his build and a ponderous big head, he resembles more the dean of men in an Ivy League school, or my image of Samuel Johnson, than the professional naval officer he was. He never sought the limelight and made every grade on the way up so quietly and effortlessly that his growth was hardly noticed.

Even today, there are two mysteries about Francis Low. One is why he is called "Frog" by an obscure nickname. The other, who he really is.

As for that nickname, there are several versions abroad and nobody seems to know for certain which one is closest to the facts. According to one version, he was so dubbed by his fellow midshipmen at Annapolis because there was something froglike in his appearance or because he spoke in a rolling slow baritone that reminded one of the underwater sounds in Aristophanes' *Frogs*. According to another version, he gained the nickname because he attended the French class at the Naval Academy whose members were called "Frogs".

Although "Frog" Low's ideas spark-plugged historic events and his management of the shipless fleet produced a notable American victory, he is less known to the public than any current commandant of a neighborhood Naval District. He would be filed and forgotten if judged solely by the humdrum references of his biography on file in the Navy's Office of Information, except for certain intriguing facts in his background. He evidently excelled at both kinds of jobs the Navy alternates for its officers. He played a gallant part at sea, as in the Okinawa invasion in which he commanded a Cruiser Division; and he topped a distinguished career in shore assignments as Deputy Chief of Naval Operations. At the time of his retirement in 1956, Low was Commander Western Sea Frontier and Commander Pacific Reserve Fleet.

Aside from his own country's Legion of Merit, Distinguished Service

Medal, the Bronze Star and other decorations, he is also a commander of the Order of the British Empire in the Military Division, a commander of France's Legion of Honor, a commander of the Legion of Honor of the Philippine Republic, and a grand officer of Italy's Al Merito della Republica Italiana.

What did Low do to merit these assignments and accolades, and how did he manage to keep himself so anonymous?

He had the good fortune to spend the most important years of his service at the side of a towering figure, Admiral King, whom he served faithfully and quietly. Behind it all was a vibrant and fully realized career, because Low filled every assignment he ever had with a creative genius that lent another dimension even to his most routine jobs. It was King who brought out the best in Low and it was Low who helped King, in his own modest and self-effacing manner, to become a better Commander in Chief and a greater historic figure.

Low was forty-five years old and a commander in August, 1939, when he first came to King's attention. He was one of the most promising younger men in the Navy. His keen mind was dissatisfied with the state of affairs in the naval organization and, recognizing clearly the direction in which the United States was moving, was groping for a massive reorientation of the Navy to adapt it to the needs and realities of modern war. At that time, King was a vice admiral with but three years left of active service. He had just been moved from command of all the carriers of the United States Fleet to the relative sinecure of the General Board where, he feared, he would conclude his years in the Navy by accomplishing little, if anything.

Originally established during the Spanish-American war to do the Navy's strategic planning, the General Board had gradually deteriorated into a mere deliberative body in which a group of senior officers without any administrative or executive functions acted as nominal advisers to the Secretary of the Navy. The Secretary was free to approve or disapprove, alter or simply ignore the Board's recommendations. Unlike his colleagues, who regarded the Board as just a sterile debating society, King was determined to make it an effective and influential agency, to deal energetically with the Navy's urgent problems of rejuvenation and reorganization.

He was assigned to a personnel board whose job was to modernize the antiquated laws and regulations that governed the promotion of staff officers. Later he reviewed the urgent problem of antiaircraft weapons on the ships—a situation that, bad as it was because of inferior and inadequate equipment, was further complicated by a sharp controversy between three different schools of thought, each of which advocated a different gun for use against planes.

Familiar with Low's work in the Maintenance Division of the Chief of Naval Operations, with his modern ideas and with his ability to express them concisely and forcefully, King invited Low to join him on both boards. When in December, 1940, King moved into the Atlantic as the Navy's top man in the "undeclared war", Low was taken along as his Operations Officer. He continued in that same capacity upon King's appointment to supreme command of the United States Fleet.

Low proved to be an outstanding aide in all these jobs, but his greatest usefulness to King was as an idea man who catalyzed and concretized his chief's own ideas. It was during Low's tour of duty as King's Operations Officer in Washington that he came up with an idea that invigorated, not merely King's own lines of thought, but the whole nation and, in one fell swoop, placed a different complexion on the American people's attitude to the war.

It was the protean idea for the Doolittle raid on Japan.

In January, 1942, the United States was deep in the doldrums of its recent defeat, only gradually recognizing the true magnitude of the Pearl Harbor disaster and but slowly grasping the difficulties of the task ahead. Captain Low was as gloomy as anybody else contemplating the cruel problems of those days, but his restless mind was searching for some positive accomplishment that would restore confidence in American ability to strike back and would, in a spectacularly dramatic way, demonstrate the power of his country.

On January 9, he happened to be in Norfolk, inspecting at the Navy Yard the construction of the aircraft carrier *Hornet*. As he was leaving the yard on the flight back to Washington, he looked out of the window of his plane and saw below a strip about the size of a carrier's deck marked out on the ground for practice take-offs. That gave him the idea he was so desperately seeking.

The next day, at dinner aboard King's flagship *Vixen*, Low broached his idea to his chief. Aircraft carriers could not get near enough to Japan for short-range Navy planes to carry out a successful bombing raid—but could longer-range Army planes take off from a carrier? King was interested and told Low to explore the idea with his air officer, Captain Donald Duncan, USN.

The details of the story are outside the scope of this book. Let it only be said that Duncan found the idea feasible, King talked to General Henry H. Arnold and, as the cliche has it, the rest is history.

King took it for granted that his associates had good heads on their shoulders and that they would come up with great ideas. Low's idea was accepted and acted upon, but never acknowledged or praised in so many words. As a matter of fact, it became known only many years later, in 1953, that the raid had been originally thought up by Francis S. Low, when Quentin Reynolds researched it for his biography of Lieutenant General James H. Doolittle and stumbled upon Low's part in it.

Admiral King was Commander Tenth Fleet in fact as well as name, for he kept an eagle eye on it and demanded to be kept posted on all its various activities. He also retained in his own hands liaison with the British and lent his supreme authority to all major decisions.

For practical purposes, however, Admiral Low conducted the business in the way he knew King wanted it to be conducted. By some peculiar osmosis or empathy, Low was able to think his way into King's lines of thought; but anyway, King expected the men he had delegated to execute certain major jobs for him to act independently, then left them alone as long as they were doing the job effectively and to his satisfaction.

Low drove himself very hard and demanded competence, diligence and dedication from all his associates. The clock-watcher and the goldbrick had no place or future in the Tenth Fleet. But unlike the austere King, Low mellowed an iron rule with the traits of his own personality. He was always kind and considerate, urbane and cordial, in his relations with his subordinates. He conducted the business with a kind of grim determination, but in a highly civilized and courteous atmosphere. While King would return a memo he disliked with an ominous "No, K," leaving it to the unfortunate subordinate to figure out for himself what was wrong with it, Low would write on the margin of such papers "See me about this," then discuss in his deliberate monotone the changes he wanted.

"Frog" Low held with King George VI that service to others was the highest distinction. This was what endeared Low and made him invaluable to King and Edwards, his two superiors; and this was, too, what assured for him the absolute loyalty of his subordinates. As Morison put it, "He had the respect of his subordinates who were never allowed to doubt what he wanted, and were never let down."

There was still another feature in his relations with his staff that made the Tenth Fleet one of the "happiest ships" in the Navy. Low tolerated no distinction between the regulars and the reserves, and even went out of his way to make the reserve personnel on his staff comfortable.

Low's courtesy did not mean any tolerance of incompetence, slack discipline or boondoggle. He was a hard task master, but not a difficult boss. The Tenth Fleet was a "fleet" in that it worked around the clock. Individual officers, including and especially Admiral Low, spent sixty to seventy hours at their desks each week, and most of them forgot about leave. Once Commander Knowles happened to step from his office into the corridor and was startled to see a crowd milling down the wing, toward the exit. On first impulse he thought it must be an air raid alarm because he had never seen so many people in that corridor before.

Suddenly he realized it was five o'clock in the afternoon! Those people were going home! Nobody in the Tenth Fleet ever went home just because the five o'clock whistle signalled the end of a work day for almost everybody else in the Navy Department!

CHAPTER XV

The Magic Summer

*Now conscience wakes despair
That slumber'd—wakes the bitter memory
Of what he was, what is, and what must be
Worse.*

JOHN MILTON
Paradise Lost

On May 20, Rear Admiral Francis S. Low's first day in his new job, it almost appeared that his long journey from Efate to Washington was not necessary after all. Now it seemed that anything he could still do would be an anti-climax after what the British had done while he had been busy setting up the Tenth Fleet. When he first arrived at the Navy Department, the U-boat war had been still harsh and ominous. During the first four months of the new German offensive, there was a daily average of 111 U-boats at sea in the Atlantic. Although their campaign was losing the savage force of the March slaughter, they were still doing reasonably well. By sinking forty-four Allied ships in April, they brought the year's score up to 218 ships of better than 1.3 million gross tons.

According to the Admiralty's conservative assessment, the Germans lost only forty-four U-boats in those same four months. In actual fact, their losses totalled fifty-five boats—but even that higher number seemed to be bearable in the face of the results achieved and eighty-three new constructions.

May broke with what threatened to become a vicious flare-up of the Doenitz offensive, but without Doenitz. The new Gross-admiral, now burdened with all the woes of the whole lopsided *Kriegsmarine,* had to confine his contribution to the sending of such encouraging signals as "Don't overrate the enemy!" and "Strike to kill!" Tactical command of the May operations was exercised by his protegé, Konteradmiral Godt, from U-boat Command's new headquarters at a Berlin hotel to which it had been moved to be closer to Doenitz.

Although the quality of the offensive suffered, quantity showed no signs of falling off. Thanks to the ever-helpful B-Service, Godt had three major targets on his dart-board to keep his U-boats busy. They were Convoys ONS-5, HX-237 and SC-129. ONS-5 had left the Irish Channel on April 22 for Newfoundland and New York and Godt assembled a formidable force of fifty-odd U-boats in three wolfpacks —*Star, Specht* and *Amsel*—to deal with it. There was the usual optimism at the Hotel am Steinplatz. Godt himself voiced confidence that the three *Rudels* would "wipe out that poor *Geleitzug*".

He was using the radio as avidly and freely as "Papa" Doenitz used to, but Godt's coaching of the wolves lacked the touch of the master. The convoy was first contacted on April 27 by the *Star* pack, just as it was skirting the Denmark Strait, but only a single merchantman was taken out of it. On May 4, therefore, Godt re-formed *Star* and *Specht* into a single 30-boat Rudel named *Fink* (after the finch family of birds), assigned twenty-one boats to the *Amsel,* and ordered both to attack the convoy plodding south from Cape Farewell. The issue was joined the same day, after nightfall. The big battle lasted for thirty-six hours continuously, until 9:15 a. m. on May 6, resulting in the loss of thirteen merchant vessels out of the convoy's forty-three. Returning to the attack on May 9, the U-boats then sank five merchantmen out of Convoys HX-237 and SC-129,

Judging solely by that scoreboard, the tide was still running against the Allies. But this was only the twentieth of May, and though our losses kept adding up at an average of about six thousand tons for each day in May, U-boat losses now accumulated at an amazing and unprecedented rate. Before long, the air over the Atlantic was rent with signals growing more frantic with every passing day, as U-boat headquarters called desperately into the wilderness:

". . . *U-Huetteman,* please report! . . . *U-Tippelskirch,* report! . . . *U-Winkler,* report! . . . *U-Happe,* report! . . . *U-Wolf,* report!"

There was no answer The macabre rollcall went on: ". . . *U-Stau-dinger,* report! . . . *U-Folkers,* report! . . ." and so on, the U-Boat Command trying with evident frenzy to raise the silent boats: ". . . *U-Schramm, U-Heinsohn, U-Neckel, U-Bothe, U-Schmid, U-Lohman, U-*

Teichert, U-Rabenau . . ." A seemingly endless stream of messages squirted from the antennae of *Goliath*, the unmistakable indication that panic had suddenly seized the U-Boat Command.

"By May 22," Doenitz later recorded, "we had already lost thirty-one U-boats since the first of the month, a frightful total, which came as a hard and unexpected blow."

The drama was not played out yet. On that same May 22, the *U-Johannsen* was added to the month's roster of losses. Then next day, just before dawn, Kapitaenleutnant Karl Schroeter in *U-752* went on the air to "talk" to Berlin and was picked up promptly by the Huffduff of a British destroyer nearby. Within moments, the *U-Schroeter* was under attack by the destroyer and a couple of planes. Schroeter was doomed by his own folly, and when his end came at last, at 8:50 a.m. on May 24, it proved the last straw. The fatal mishap became known in Berlin later that same day, when *U-91* signalled from the spot: "Have picked up ten survivors from *U-752*." Doenitz had enough! He instructed Godt to remove his U-boats to other parts of the Atlantic, but the bitter cup was still not full. During the remaining week of May, Doenitz lost eight more. May thus ended with the almost unbelievable loss of forty-one U-boats. Thirty-eight of them perished in the Atlantic. It was a British victory; only six of those forty-one boats had been killed by Americans.

Enigmatic Calamity

Doenitz could be unnerved by the loss of even a single boat if it perished in a set-up he considered foolproof. Now the fantastic disaster of this May overshadowed all the brighter aspects of his campaign and set him literally quaking. His frame of mind in the face of the sudden catastrophe could be described best with the words of the Athenian orator: "Men, having often abandoned what was visible for the sake of what was uncertain, have not got what they wanted, and have lost what they had—being unfortunate by an enigmatic sort of calamity."

Doenitz, outwardly undaunted, went on the air to reassure his U-boat men. "You alone can, at the moment, mount an offensive against the enemy and defeat him," he broadcast to them. "The time will soon come when you will be superior to the enemy with new and more powerful weapons, and will be able to triumph over your worst foes— the aircraft and the destroyers." But he was whistling in the dark. For the first time in the war, defeat and doom glared ruthlessly into his face.

"The thunderbolt—so long and so fearfully awaited—had fallen at last," wrote Wolfgang Frank, the war correspondent assigned to cover U-boat headquarters. "The figure of thirty-eight represented more than thirty per cent of the boats at sea and was well above the average monthly delivery of new ones . . . Worst of all, there was no clear-cut explanation for the disaster, no certainty as to why one boat after another had failed to answer signals from headquarters."

Doenitz's fatal failure to organize an intelligence service that would have kept him posted of developments within the Allied camp had come home to roost. He knew nothing of the establishment of the Tenth Fleet, of course, and could not anticipate the influence of that new American organization mobilized specifically against him. Such want of knowledge of the Allied organization was characteristic of the U-boat Command. To them, as Harold Busch put it, the enemy was no more than an anonymous mass. Doenitz never really tried to find out what that "anonymous mass" was doing to take the wind out of his sails. In his strange inability to appreciate the importance of *total* intelligence, he was smugly satisfied with sheer *target* intelligence and did not deign it necessary to learn anything about the enemy beyond the movements of his convoys.

The *Abwehr*, the German High Command's central intelligence agency, was headed by an admiral, Wilhelm Canaris, and had its I-M, a special naval intelligence division to cater exclusively to the needs of the *Kriegsmarine*. But Doenitz bitterly complained that it had "failed completely . . . throughout the war . . . to give U-Boat Command one single piece of information about the enemy which was of the slightest use to us." That was not true. *Abwehr* agents, especially in southern Spain and South America, observed the assembly and departure of Allied convoys, for example, and Doenitz had frequently used their reports in making his dispositions. If there was little if anything in the other reports Canaris was sending to him about developments behind the scenes at the various Allied antisubmarine agencies, Doenitz on his part did nothing to fill this fateful gap.

U-Boat Command at the Hotel am Steinplatz was completely at sea. Godt presided over a dumbfounded staff that was but a handwringing group of mourners engaged in endless and futile debates about the cause of death. Godt's own first inclination was to call every boat home from the North Atlantic pending the clarification of the situation, but that was patently impossible. For one thing, there were only 110 berths available in the U-boat bunkers and any boat left unprotected would have been bombed to bits. For another, it would have been an admission of total defeat after the first major setback of the U-Boat Arm.

The ugly reports finally reached Hitler. He sent for Doenitz and the conference took place on May 31, in the Fuhrer's big living room at the Berghof behind closed doors in an atmosphere of unmitigated gloom. It was attended by five pale men: Hitler and Doenitz, Field Marshal Wilhelm Keitel, Major General Walther Warlimont and Captain von Puttkammer, the Fuehrer's naval aide.

Doenitz, in the shroud of his ignorance, double-talked his way out of his predicament. "We must conserve our strength," he said, "otherwise we will play into the hands of the enemy." He showed his own panic when he concluded on a melancholy note: "It is impossible to foretell," he said, "to what extent submarine warfare will again become effective."

He attributed the sudden crisis to three major causes—to what he called a "substantial increase of the enemy air force in submarine warfare"; to the use of aircraft carriers in conjunction with North Atlantic convoys; and he added vaguely: "The possibility that the enemy is using a new and efficient type of locating device cannot be ruled out." In the absence of hard intelligence, he could only ad lib.

His gloom was contrasted with exuberant cheer in the Admiralty where Admiral Max Horton, new Commander-in-Chief of Western Approaches, squatted behind the victory. When his codebreakers gave him Doenitz's decrypted signal of May 24, ordering the departure of all U-boats from the North Atlantic convoy route, Horton signalled to his own forces:

"The tide of the battle has been checked, if not turned," adding somewhat more cautiously, "The enemy is showing signs of strain in the face of the heavy attacks by our sea and air forces."

What Happened?

Although the showdown of May was spectacular in its abruptness, it had, of course, been long in the making. Years of the most intensive brainwork in the hidden recesses of Britain's huge scientific and antisubmarine establishments produced, one by one, more effective tactical doctrines, more dynamic operational approaches, and a string of new weapons and electronic instruments.

"Radar," the stunned Doenitz wrote ruefully, "and particularly radar location by aircraft, had to all practical purposes robbed the U-boats of their power to fight on the surface." Hitler was duly impressed by a device which Doenitz could not even sketch for his benefit and, according to the transcript of the conference, told his Grossadmiral: "I am worried that the new detection device might involve principles with which we are not familiar."

He was right, too, because the mystery device was a new *microwave* radar. In what Baxter called "the boldest jump in the history of radar," British scientists went directly from radar set on a meter-and-a-half to 10 centimeters. The possibility of such a jump had once occurred to Kapitaenleutnant Hans Meckel, Doenitz's communications officer, but when he checked with competent scientists, they assured him unanimously that radar in the region of the microwaves was "*unmoeglich*" (impossible). The Germans were not the only ones to voice such emphatic skepticism. When the idea of the microwave radar was first submitted to an eminent British scientist, he dismissed it with the succinct comment, "It stinks!"

Professor N. L. Oliphant, an imaginative physicist at Birmingham University, nevertheless persisted in exploring the possibility of producing an effective radar in that region. When, in collaboration with his British and American colleagues, his efforts succeeded, he decided to code-name the end product "H_2S" for hydrogen sulphide, a malodorous gas smelling of rotten eggs. According to Busch, the U-Boat Command came upon the "scent" of the "H_2S" in due course and took measures to "deodorize" it, so to speak, but "they never realized until after the war that it had been the culprit all along."

In actual fact it was not. There was no single "culprit", but rather a number of "culprits". Among them were such diverse implements as the *Leigh light,* named after Squadron Leader H. deV. Leigh, RAF, who had suggested as early as 1940 that powerful searchlights be installed in Wellington bombers to be used for spotting U-boats at night; the *hedgehog,* the device for *throwing* depth charge patterns instead of *dropping* them; vastly improved *high-frequency direction finders;* antisubmarine *rockets;* more powerful *explosives* like the Torpex; the 500-pound depth bomb and "*Fido*", a homing torpedo designed for use by planes; the so-called "*Support Groups*" of U-boat killers consisting of up to six sloops especially primed for antisubmarine work and using ingenious tactics developed by the celebrated "Johnnie" Walker; *Long Range* and *Very Long Range* land-based aircraft; and, last but not least, the *escort carriers* to close the wide gap in the mid-Atlantic beyond the range of even the longest-range land-based planes, and the *escort carrier groups,* the last word in hunter-killers. They appeared one by one, to put teeth into the Allies' antisubmarine effort, including still others like the sono-buoy, a baseball-looking device that enabled a man in an aircraft to "listen" to U-boats moving under water, and the "Foxer" that upset the "electronic brain" of one of the Germans' secret weapons, their acoustic "homing" torpedo. The sono-buoy was produced by American scientists to become one of the decisive implements of the Allied antisubmarine effort. It was a buoy with a hydrophone and a radio set installed in it. Searching aircraft dropped them in the sea and then listened-in to U-boats under the water, so that they could locate and attack them unseen.

Scientists also provided special gear for all the major Allied ports. These delicate instruments on the sea-bed gave protection, not only against prowling U-boats, but also against the *Kriegsmarine's* midget U-boats and frogmen, Johnny-come-latelies of the U-boat war.

What's more, these devices represented only the tangible factors in what was a generic change in the whole U-boat war. In November, 1942, the gallant and able, but spent, British Admiral Noble was replaced by the dynamic and ruthless Admiral Horton, and though Horton commanded only the Western Approaches, his influence and spirit were promptly felt throughout the entire British antisubmarine effort. Then the frustrated Sir Philip Joubert was replaced by Air Chief Marshal Sir John Slessor at the head of Coastal Command, and again, the kinetic approach of the new man was felt everywhere.

Doenitz's Dilemma

In January, 1943, Doenitz was given charge of the whole *Kriegsmarine;* soon the many-sided tasks of his new command led to his almost complete departure from the conduct of the U-boat war. In May, Admiral King assumed personal responsibility for the United States Navy's diffused antisubmarine war effort and appointed Rear Admiral Low as his Chief of Staff to synthesize it in the Tenth Fleet.

While thus in the United States, the Navy's big boss moved into closest intimacy with the anti-U-boat effort, in Germany, the *spiritus rector* of the U-boat war was removed from its conduct. And while in the United States, King's deputy was a man of broad, scientific knowledge and an innate ability to orchestrate the diverse activities of his "fleet", Doenitz's deputy—the pathetic Godt—was merely a diligent and loyal mediocrity whose ken did not extend beyond the operational problems of his job.

Thus did tangible and intangible factors combine to bring a sudden change in the fortunes of the U-boat war, confronting Doenitz with a dilemma he tried to dramatize out of all proportions after the war.

"In June, 1943," he wrote in his memoirs, "I was faced with the most difficult decision of the whole war. I had to make up my mind whether to withdraw the boats from all areas and call off the U-boat war, or to let them continue operations in some suitably modified form, regardless of the enemy's superiority."

In actual fact, Doenitz had no choice. He was but a hired hand and, no matter what he now says, a pliable and humble servant of his Fuehrer.

Doenitz was inclined to quit the game and was supported in this groping determination by Godt and some of his closest advisers. He told Hitler on May 31 in the Berghof, "The enemy's antisubmarine defense on water and from the air will be improved. That entails many uncertainties and unknown factors." But Hitler would not or could not take the hint.

"There can be no talk of a let-up in submarine warfare," he said. "The Atlantic is my first line of defense in the West."

Doenitz equivocated by recommending a series of offensive moves in which his U-boats could still play a part without being thrown to those big, bad Allied wolves. His suggestions were far-fetched, bizarre in concept and useless to Hitler's precarious war effort.

First he proposed that the U-boats be employed for amphibious operations in North Africa, to land assault troops and cut our lines of communications, but both Hitler and Keitel dismissed the suggestion as impractical. Then he recommended that a surprise attack be made on Gibraltar with the budding guided missiles of the *Luftwaffe,* in order to compensate for "the falling off in U-boat operations," but Hitler could see no advantage in becoming involved in such an adventure. Then Doenitz advocated the mining of Port Said and Alexandria to interfere, as he put it, with British movements through the Mediterranean. Hitler replied that he had no planes to spare for such an operation in which he could not perceive any practical purpose anyway.

Each time Doenitz tried to take the heat off his U-boats, Hitler put it on again. Then, raising his voice for extra emphasis, he told Doenitz in terms that tolerated no contradiction:

"There can be no talk of a let-up! Even if I have to fight a defensive battle in the Atlantic, that is preferable to waiting to defend myself on the coast of Europe. The enemy forces tied up by our submarine warfare are tremendous, even though the actual losses inflicted by us are no longer great. I cannot afford to release these forces by discontinuing submarine warfare."

On June 15, Doenitz was back at the Berghof on another fishing expedition. He tried to obtain Hitler's consent for a suspension of the U-boat campaign by maneuvering him into a corner and coaxing the suggestion from the hard-pressed Fuehrer. In one breath he said, "I am convinced that submarine warfare must be carried on," but then confronted Hitler with demands he must have known the overburdened

German war economy could not possibly meet. Two weeks before he had persuaded the vacillating Fuehrer to approve the monthly construction of, not thirty, but forty U-boats. It was a totally unrealistic program to begin with and, Hitler's signature under the plan notwithstanding, it remained a pipedream throughout the rest of the war. In not one single month was this quota reached and even the construction of thirty boats was attained but once, in December, 1944.

Now Doenitz pestered Hitler with further demands. This time he asked for more men.

"How many men do you need?" Hitler asked in some exasperation.

"Two-hundred thousand at the present and 334,000 when the U-boat building program is increased to forty a month."

Hitler blew up. "I haven't got this personnel!" he cried. "The anti-aircraft and night-fighter forces must be increased in order to protect the German cities. It is also necessary to strengthen the Eastern Front. The Army needs divisions for the protection of Europe."

Doenitz turned on his old phonograph record. "Consider, my Fuehrer," he said, "the consequences if submarine warfare ceases," and Hitler shouted, "No, no, no! A cessation of submarine warfare is out of the question! I'll see to it that you get what you want."

If this was not a den of knaves it was surely a paradise of fools. Hitler, naive in naval matters and hard-pressed on all fronts, allowed himself to be deluded by Doenitz who was, at best, fooling himself. Caught in the dilemma of his own making, the Grossadmiral realized his only option was to fight on—but at what price?

"*Ich kam zu dem Schluss,*" he spelled out the eventual resolution of the dilemma, "*das wir vor der bitteren Notwendigkeit standen, weiter-kaempfen zu muessen.*" He then revealed in so many words that he was fully conscious of the price his U-Boat Arm would have to pay for his decision:

"*Auf der anderen Seite war es wirklich so,*" he wrote, "*dass wenn wir weiterfuhren, die U-Bootverluste nunmehr eine erschreckende Hoehe erreichen wuerden, auch, wenn wir alles taten, um ihnen durch schnelle Verbesserung der Abwehrwaffen mehr und wirksameren Schutz zu geben. Es war kein Zweifel moeglich, die Fortfuehrung des Kampfes wuerde ein wirklicher Opfergang sein.*"

He thus said, "I came to the conclusion that we were confronted with the bitter necessity of continuing the fight"—a conclusion he reached after he himself had prepared the balance sheet, and stated:

"On the other hand it was evident that, if we continued the fight, U-boat losses would reach a frightening height, even if we did everything to give them additional and more effective protection by a rapid improvement of their defensive weapons."

I describe the fateful decision in Doenitz's own words, in the original German, to leave no doubt that they were, indeed, his own words. Their English translation cannot properly mirror their hypocrisy and barbaric callousness. Even so it shows conclusively that Doenitz had acquiesced in the continuation of the U-boat war although he realized full well that (1) it would be a futile struggle, unlikely to alter the issue, and (2) it would entail the senseless waste of young Germans.

This whole grim episode is significant because it shows (1) how Doenitz had actually improvised the *whole* U-boat campaign rather than conducted it on the basis of a careful plan in which provision had been made for both victories and defeats: (2) how he carried it on from one success to another in scattered and uncoordinated battles, not only by his own absolute superiority, but by the default of his enemies; and (3) how relatively easy it was to scare him and drive him into untidy retreat, even to a point at which he appeared to be willing to give up the fruits of his past efforts and abandon the whole struggle—in the wake of his first and, up to that date, only major defeat.

The decision Hitler and Doenitz had reached left the U-boats in the Atlantic to fight World War II to the bitter end. In January-April, 1945, when the issue was certainly no longer in doubt, the Germans still had a monthly average of fifty U-boats at sea in the Atlantic and several hundreds in reserve. On the very last day of the war, Doenitz had twice as many U-boats on actual *Feindfahrt* as on the first day of the war.

There is a tendency among historians to regard the difficult phase of the U-boat war as concluded on May 31, 1943, and to speak somewhat slightingly of the campaigns that followed. "The battle," wrote Roskill, "never again reached the same pitch of intensity"; and Morison wrote at the conclusion of the first volume of his narrative that ended with the events of April, 1943, "Although Doenitz still had a number of tricks up his sleeve, he was destined never to recover the initiative."

No, the U-boat war did not "virtually end" with the showdown of May! No, Doenitz did not lose the initiative forever, or else how are we to explain his successive come-backs with such remarkable new devices as the Snorkel, for example, and the various phenomenal designs built into vastly improved U-boats? The next two long years of the U-boat war—from June, 1943, to May, 1945—were as tricky, perilous and bitter as anything that went before. The only difference was that the opposing forces became more evenly matched and that the Allied losses were more in line with normal casualties in war, rather than the perverse maritime massacres of 1939-1943.

On May 24, even before the full magnitude of the disaster was known to him, Doenitz signalled all U-boats at sea: "The situation in the North Atlantic now forces a temporary shift of operations less endangered by aircraft." He ordered them to "proceed, using utmost caution, to the area south west of the Azores." That decision moved the wolves from the lion's den to the tiger's cave. The area was on the eve of becoming the least safe from aircraft in the whole Atlantic. The hunter-killer escort carrier group was about to appear in action, to close all gaps left in the ocean—to place an umbrella of Wildcats and Avengers over the sea, and create a fast and flexible surface force from the screens of the new baby flattops.

The first test of the Tenth Fleet was at hand!

"Trutz" Versus the Tenth Fleet

"After forty-five months of unceasing battle of more exacting and arduous nature than posterity may easily realize," wrote the historian of the Royal Navy about the May showdown, "our convoy escorts and aircraft had won the triumph they had so richly merited."

The Americans, engaged in that same exacting and arduous battle, had not been doing as well. In the eighteen months of their war, the antisubmarine forces of the United States Navy and Army had succeeded in killing but thirty-two U-boats all told out of a total of 189 destroyed. In the first five months of 1943, when ninety-six U-boats had been killed, Americans were responsible for the demise of only sixteen. Their contribution to the May slaughter was six U-boats—only fifteen per cent in a battle in which, by then, the burdens and responsibilities were being shared fifty-fifty.

Then with startling abruptness, everything changed for the better! On March 26, 1943, when the Doenitz offensive was at its height, Kapitaenleutnant Purkhold in *U-260* reported to Berlin that "an aircraft carrier inside the screen of a west-bound convoy" had foiled his attempt to close the convoy. Doenitz thus had his warning in ample time, but he failed dismally to draw the proper conclusions from Purkhold's report and, in the absence of properly evaluated intelligence about this crucial innovation in the American anti-U-boat effort, he failed to anticipate its decisive influence on the outcome of the Atlantic battle.

The aircraft carrier Purkhold had seen was the USS *Bogue*, the forerunner of a fleet of baby flattops, escorting Convoy SC-123 enroute from the United Kingdom to Halifax. It was the second mission of the *Bogue* group that consisted, aside from the carrier, of twelve Wildcats and eight Avengers, and of a screen made up of the destroyers *Belknap, George E. Badger* and *Greene*. The group was commanded by Captain Giles E. Short, USN, who had commissioned the *Bogue* at Puget Sound and taken her, with a keen crew composed mostly of survivors from the USS *Lexington,* to the Atlantic.

The *Bogue* group accomplished little on its first three missions. On April 25, therefore, it was thought advisable to move the green group to Liverpool for some brisk antisubmarine training and to install a high frequency direction finder on the *Bogue.*

By May 19, *Bogue* was back in harness near Iceland where it picked up a west-bound convoy of thirty-nine ships, the ON-184. Then, from May 20 on, the safe passage of the convoy was guarded, not merely by its escort, but also by the Tenth Fleet whose monitors, just assembled at their battle stations, kept up a steady lookout for any U-boats in the convoy's path. On its very day of inception, the Tenth Fleet thus learned from its network of Huffduffs that a school of U-boats—maybe as many as forty or more—was maneuvering stealthily between the Grand Bank and Greenland. The plot was evaluated and Tenth Fleet advised CINCLANT in one of its high-priority action messages that a wolfpack was in the process of being formed, presumably to pounce upon ON-148 and probably also on HX-239, a fast east-bound convoy of forty-three ships about to sail into the U-boat-infested area.

The *Bogue* was ordered to leave her station with the convoy and to run down the various bearings. At 9:10 p.m. on May 21, the Tenth Fleet's tip was first confirmed when Lieutenant Commander William McC. Drane, USN, the *Bogue's* air squadron commander flying one of the carrier's blue-and-gray Avengers, spotted a U-boat some sixty miles ahead of the convoy. Then other boats of what did turn out to be a powerful wolfpack merged of two *Rudels*—the *Donau* and the *Mosel*—also showed up one by one. However, they were kept below by the *Bogue's* planes and her screen, and were effectively prevented from ever reaching attack stations.

The Tenth Fleet stayed tuned to the wolfpack that was trying to deploy for the attack and, on May 22, located several U-boats in the *Bogue's* general area. Following one of the fixes, Lieutenant (j.g.) William J. Chamberlain, USNR, sighted a boat, dropped four bombs which exploded close to its conning tower, then saw it submarge, but he stayed on until relieved by Lieutenant Howard S. Roberts, USNR, in another Avenger. At 5:40 p.m. the air-borne vigil was rewarded. The U-boat shot to the surface, straight into a shower of Roberts' depth charges whose blasts sent it back to a depth of 350 feet. The boat was now irrevocably doomed. Its skipper blew the tanks and surfaced to abandon ship. He was received by a hail of fire from the Avenger that could not be shaken off.

It was the *U-569* of Kapitaenleutnant Johannsen, a sensible and thoroughly chastised skipper who seemed to have had the notion of surrendering to whosoever would come to pick up the crew. Johannsen ordered his men to hoist the time-honored symbol of surrender but the hapless submariners could not find anything white on the boat whose curtains, tablecovers and sheets were all made of some oil-resistant drab green cloth. They waved what they had, but those improvised green surrender flags, whose color blended with that of an angry sea, could not have been made out by Roberts who kept up his fire. However, they were spotted by the Canadian destroyer *St. Laurent* and such evident eagerness to surrender induced her skipper to make preparations for boarding the sub to capture. Johannsen's engineer officer spoiled the scheme. In the last moment he slipped below, opened the flood-valves and went down with the boat, leaving but twenty-four U-boat men for the *St. Laurent* to capture.

The sinking of the *U-Johannsen* was a historic feat. It was the *Bogue* group's very first kill. It was the first U-boat to be sunk by an American escort carrier group in the Battle of the Atlantic. And *it was the first sinking in which the Tenth Fleet had a hand.*

We in Op-16-W celebrated the event with a special Norden broadcast whose cue came from Johannsen's willingness to surrender. We did not deceive ourselves by accepting appearances for fact or by assuming that morale in the U-Boat Arm had been so badly shaken that surrenders would become common henceforth. Therefore, we did not call on our audience to surrender, not in those blunt terms. We merely put a flea in their ears, as the Germans say, by describing without comment the best procedures for a surrender. Citing the *U-Johannsen's* fate, we recommended that the U-boats carry something white on board because our pilots could not be expected to distinguish any green cloth waved at them from the level of the green sea. Our suggestion was promptly heeded. A few weeks later the *U-460* was in Johannsen's predicament. Its crew waved that "something white" we had recommended to keep handy for such emergencies. The "surrender flag" turned out to be the skipper's dress shirt. It was the only "white" he dared to smuggle on board without exposing that he was heeding Norden's proposal, just in case.

Though he was badly shaken, Grossadmiral Doenitz still had fight left in him. On May 26, he assembled seventeen of his battered boats and sent them south to form a patrol line along the 43rd meridian. Their mission was to try to accomplish on the Central Atlantic Convoy Route what apparently could no longer be done in the North Atlantic. Teeming with merchantmen and troop convoys in transit, this was an area of solely American responsibility. If the United States Navy now failed to protect them from the marauders, there would be a massacre comparable to that of 1942.

Doenitz showed his mood when he named the new *Rudel—"Trutz."* It is a truculent German word meaning stubborn insolence or bold obstinacy, and especially *defiance.* The first order he signalled to the boats of *Trutz* was to deploy for attack around the Azores, then wait for further instructions. Just then, *Abwehr* spies in Spain reported to Berlin the departure of a convoy from North Africa presumably bound for the United States. Then the B-Service told U-Boat Command that, according to decrypted intercepts, it was Convoy GUS-7A, routed to sail along longitude 43 degrees, between latitudes 37° 17′ and 30° 36′ N.

Doenitz promptly ordered *Trutz* to form a barrier for the reception of GUS-7A. But just as his spies and codebreakers had tipped Doenitz off to the convoy, the Tenth Fleet now told Admiral Ingersoll all he needed to know about *Trutz.* On May 30, the *Bogue* group was ordered to sail from Argentia at full speed to intercept the Germans. On June 4, Captain Short arrived at the exact spot where the fixes of the Tenth Fleet indicated he would meet *Trutz* in a head-on clash.

That same afternoon Short was handed a message from Tenth Fleet via CINCLANT, advising him of the position of *Trutz.* It was a fantastically accurate plot. Short sent his Avengers to find the U-boats and sure enough, they sighted them one after another, on the surface, in compliance with instructions they had just received from Doenitz not to run from the planes but to fight it out with them.

The *U-127* of Korvetten-Kapitaen Bruno Hansmann was sighted, first by a Wildcat, and then an Avenger. Before Hansmann could put up the fight Doenitz had told him to make on the surface, he was at the bottom, with all hands.

The *U-Hansmann* was the southernmost boat of *Trutz* and it seemed its fate had scared off the rest of the *Rudel.* But while they could evade the *Bogue's* search, they proved incapable of eluding the Tenth Fleet. On June 9, the *Rudel's* position was again established from a series of fixes and the tab thus kept on the pack seemed to indicate that *Trutz* was running from a fight. While thus looking vainly for more defiant U-boats, *Bogue's* patrol team came upon a juicy target that just happened to be there. It was the *U-118* and though it proved hard to sink, the result was worth the effort. The boat turned out to be one of the three 1,600-ton milk cows Doenitz had recently sent to the area to refuel his combatant boats.

The events of the week represented a startling new experience for both the U-Boat Command and the United States Navy. *Trutz* was the first wolfpack not able to sink even a single ship out of three convoys it was sent to "strike dead." And though the *Bogue* group had managed to take only a single U-boat out of *Trutz*, it had succeeded in giving one hundred per cent protection to two convoys.

But Doenitz was not yet through with *Trutz* and neither was the United States Navy. Fifteen boats left in the *Rudel* were ordered to form three lines some twenty miles apart, with center of gravity about 850 miles east of Bermuda, to intercept whatever convoys might cross their path. However, the spasmodic arrangements to shift *Trutz* again and again necessitated a lot of radio traffic between Berlin and the boats, and so it was not too difficult for Tenth Fleet to obtain a rough plot of its new dispositions. On June 13, seventy ships of Convoy UGS-10 departed New York for North Africa, so routed by Tenth Fleet as to evade the *Trutz* barriers. It was one of the weirdest convoys of the whole war, badly plagued, not only by the ill discipline of its masters, but also by some mysterious crew members on board several of its ships. The Germans—through a real coup of wartime espionage—had succeeded in planting a number of secret agents on several merchantmen. They created confusion and breaches of security throughout the convoy's passage. Several ships broke station, others showed lights; radio silence was repeatedly broken, with several transmissions which clearly showed that intrepid spies were trying to give direct aid and close comfort to the enemy. On June 22, one such clandestine transmisssion was picked up by Oberleutnant Guenther Kummetat in *U-572* and he boldly answered the call by making straight for UGS-10, breaking through its screen and sinking the French tanker *Lot* with two torpedoes.

But the *U-Kummetat* was not even a member of *Trutz!* Exasperated by the failure of the *Rudel*, the Grossadmiral dissolved it into three small packs of four boats each, taking out what defiance was still left in *Trutz*.

The sortie of the *Trutz* was a carefully prepared operation—yet its failure was total: the formidable *Rudel* did not sink a single ship and did not even sight one. On the other hand, it lost a total of five boats, two in its operational area and three more on the way home. The conclusion Doenitz then drew from the experience of *Trutz* startled even his own associates. After having toiled and fought to introduce the wolfpack system into the U-boat war, and having scored his most resounding triumphs with the *Rudels*, the Grossadmiral now ordered that the wolfpack system be abandoned in waters around the Azores.

This was June 29, 1943. The Tenth Fleet was but forty days old. And even if it had but a partial influence on these remarkable events and decisions, it showed to Admiral King's perfect satisfaction that it was the best thing that happened to the United States Navy in a long, long time in the Atlantic.

The July Massacre

The U-boats were still out in their Sunday best but all of a sudden they had no place to go. So Doenitz, for want of what he considered a "safer area," left sixteen of his eighty-four U-boats at sea in the broad area around the Azores, to refuel or to make preparations for the homeward journey or simply to shift for themselves by picking up whatever morsels they could at this pathetic feast of Lazarus. Then he directed some more to move still further southward into an area where he knew the Americans held sway and where he expected no serious trouble. But again his ignorance of current developments in the Allied camp trapped him into a costly blunder.

July began as another British month. On the third, they killed the *U-126* in the North Atlantic and the *U-628* off the Bay of Biscay, then the *U-535* inside the Bay on the fifth. The first American victory of the month was scored on July 7, by an Army Liberator that caught the *U-951* on the surface somewhere west of Lisbon and dispatched it promptly. Next day, another Army Liberator patrolling in the same general area was guided to *U-232* by its new microwave radar. Though badly hurt by the accurate AA fire of the Germans, the B-24 managed to plant two of its bombs so squarely on the boat that it split in two, each part sinking separately.

The British winning streak then continued with the sinking of *U-514* in the Bay of Biscay and of *U-435* west of Portugal. Seven U-boats down in the first nine days of the month—and what was more, every kill was a *Totalverlust*: there wasn't a single survivor from any of the boats.

In the meantime the Tenth Fleet was not idle by any means but it was somewhat knocked off base by a confusing dispersion of the fixes its monitors were getting on wayward U-boats apparently straggling in the ocean without a clearly perceptible destination. Its pedantic precision had left the U-Boat Command. Instead of following a clear-cut operations plan with the concentration of U-boats, now it scattered its shots and sprinkled the Atlantic with tiny groups or lone wolves. Even so, the fixes of the Tenth Fleet came mostly from two major areas—from around the Azores (where the *Trutz* had just come a cropper) and from further south and to the west in the Atlantic. The latter bearings gradually developed into a pattern as recurrent fixes indicated that about a dozen U-boats were moving in the general direction of the Brazilian coast.

Leading the invasion was the *U-513* and we might as well follow it down, first, because its commander was Kapitaenleutnant Friedrich Guggenberger, one of Doenitz's few remaining aces (he had sunk the aircraft carrier *Ark Royal* in 1941); and, second, because its fate demonstrated again how invaluable the Tenth Fleet's contribution had become even at this early stage of its existence.

Guggenberger's orders called for operations in the South Atlantic along the Brazilian coast between Rio de Janeiro and Rio Grande, to pick vessels out of the motley Coffee Coast convoys for which protection was supplied mostly by the old crates—including some antiquated German aircraft—of the Brazilian air force. He arrived on the outskirts of his operational area on June 21 and made his presence felt by sinking a Swedish vessel so quickly that her radio operator had no time even to put a single distress signal on his radio. Then he moved south and on June 25, torpedoed the American tanker *Eagle* a few miles off Cape Frio.

It was like the good old days! The *U-513* was briefly seen by a Brazilian bomber, but Guggenberger escaped without much difficulty and, on June 30, sank a small coastwise freighter, then, on July 3, the Liberty ship *Elihu B. Washburn*. On July 16, he was off Florianopolis, in southern Brazil, where he sank an American freighter that tried to solo it from Buenos Aires to New York. Encouraged by the easy pickings, he let down his guard. When he found that a survivor from his last victim was a native of Brooklyn, Fritz inquired genially how the Dodgers were faring. Then he went on the air with a long dissertation, giving Berlin his estimate of the situation and the benefit of his counsel. He suggested that they send more U-boats into the area because, as he put it, they had nothing to fear from the thoroughly incompetent Brazilian pilots who patrolled those waters.

That was all the Tenth Fleet needed to cut short Fritz's pleasant sojourn. A perfect fix was obtained on *U-513*, Admiral Jonas Ingram was notified, and he sent a newcomer to his command, Lieutenant (j.g.) R. S. Whitcomb, USN, in a Mariner, a two-engine patrol bomber seaplane, to look for the gabby German. Whitcomb found his quarry on July 19, almost exactly where the Tenth Fleet had said the U-boat would be, and sank the *U-513* with two direct hits. The boat went down bow first, with only seven members of its crew surviving. Guggenberger was one of them. At Fort Hunt, he proved as jovial a prisoner-of-war as he had been in command of his boat. Claiming that he had spent seven happy years in Brooklyn, he sought special considerations for himself, not on the grounds that he was such a celebrity, but because he was an inveterate Dodgers fan.

Admiral Ingram was quick to become the Tenth Fleet's most appreciative customer. Still but inadequately equipped to deal with Doenitz's blitzes and needing help from whatever quarter he could get it, he greeted the birth of the Tenth Fleet with genuine enthusiasm and instructed Captain Clinton E. Braine, USN, his alert and erudite chief of staff, to work closely with those "new bastards in Washington." Braine did and thanks to this perfect teamwork between the Fourth Fleet in the South Atlantic and the Tenth Fleet in Washington, the so-called "July blitz of Brazil" could be checked and foiled before it could do any real damage. While the dozen U-boats Guggenberger had called into Ingram's bailiwick succeeded in sinking eleven ships of about 65,000 gross tons, they paid for it with the loss of eight of their own, causing Konteradmiral Godt in Berlin to declare still another segment of the Atlantic out of bounds for U-boats. "As is apparent from the losses," he wrote in the War Diary, "the Brazilian Coast has shown itself to be a difficult and dangerous operations area."

This was but a sideshow of this magic summer. The real drama of the month was played where now the escort carrier groups began to congregate. The *Bogue* had been joined in the area Doenitz had described as "less endangered by aircraft" by the *Core* group of Captain Marshal R. Greer, USN, the *Santee* group of Captain Harold F. Fick, USN, and eventually by "Buster" Isbell's *Card* group—a formidable force of almost a hundred Wildcats, Avengers and Dauntless dive bombers, screened by twelve destroyers, most of them veterans of the Atlantic battle.

Although the escort carrier groups formed an integral part of Admiral Ingersoll's Atlantic Fleet, they were in reality—and more than any other force afloat—the "executive branch" of the Tenth Fleet. Observing strictly the sacrosanct chain of command and channels, Admiral Low cooperated most closely with the group commanders whose Combat Intelligence Centers were more or less extensions of the Tenth Fleet intelligence organization. Out at sea, the "recommendations" of the Tenth Fleet (a euphemism for orders) were accepted and carried out promptly by all the brilliant commanding officers of the groups.

It was characteristic of Admiral Ingersoll that he never quibbled over jurisdictional matters when the common good required the removal of some of his forces from his own personal command. As soon as Tenth Fleet was established, he virtually relinquished his authority over the escort carrier groups and shifted them to close coordination with Low. In this new arrangement the carrier groups and the Tenth Fleet occupied positions of equal importance, with the latter holding the power of ultimate decision, by pulling—in extreme cases—Admiral King's rank on the groups' commanding officers who were mere captains. The Tenth Fleet always formulated its dispositions as politely as possible in war, but it never left any doubt in any group commander's mind that they were orders in fact and had to be carried out.

Most of the time, the arrangement made this implicit, for the vast majority of the Tenth Fleet's day by day communications to the forces afloat consisted of plots obtained from a variety of sources, mostly from Huffduff, tipping off the groups to U-boats located in their vicinity and giving them chances of victory. But the Tenth Fleet guidance was followed also explicitly in techniques and doctrines, developed by its analysts in Washington and disseminated to the forces afloat by various means, mostly in the "Yellow Peril." After May 20, 1943, there was no doubt who was boss in antisubmarine warfare.

One who suffered from this unprecedented new arrangement was *U-487*, an important catch because it was the second to be sunk of a flotilla of three milk cows Doenitz had sent to the Azores to supply his hungry U-boats. The brain-brawn operation that led to its sinking survives as an outstanding example of carrier group-Tenth Fleet cooperation:

The Tenth Fleet obtained a firm fix on the milk cow by monitoring a transmission of Oberleutnant Kostantin Metz in the morning of July 13. The fix was developed and evaluated—the boat was located northwest of Cape Verdes—then sent in a high priority operational message to the Atlantic Fleet, all within one hour. Closest to the fix was Captain Greer in *Core*, so he was given the assignment to deal with *U-Metz*. A Wildcat-Avenger team was sent to run down the tip, sighted the boat in the afternoon—with its crew sunbathing in the balmy weather— and sunk it with four bombs. The whole operation, from the pick-up of Metz's fatal transmission to the sinking of his boat, needed less than ten hours, pointing up still another advantage of the new arrangement— one that is of supreme importance in war—speed!

Up to this date, July 13, the combined American anti-submarine forces had sunk but five U-boats, against seven killed by the British, and the month's total score stood at an even dozen. But now the massacre began and U-Boat Command was soon compelled again to fill the air over the Atlantic with anguished cries calling on a growing number of muted U-boats to "report."

On July 14, in mid-Atlantic, Captain Fick's *Santee* group sank *U-160*, on the maiden voyage of its new captain, Oberleutnant Gerd von Pommer-Esche. Next day the *Santee* struck again, sinking Kapitaen-leutnant Werner Witte's famous *U-509*. That July 15 established a new record for the American antisubmarine forces: they sank three U-boats within twenty-four hours, the *U-Witte* northwest of Madeira, the *U-Luther* (135) around the Canary Islands, Oberleutnant Heinz Beck-mann's *U-159* in the Caribbean. All three were total losses.

On July 16, the Tenth Fleet picked up the eager signals of a U-boat seeking direction from Berlin to a milk cow to refuel after a long but fruitless *Feindfahrt* between the Caribbean and the Chesapeake Capes. Now it was the *Core* group to catch the ball. A search team of her planes followed down the fix, found the thirsty boat before it could find the milk cow, and dealt with it conclusively. It turned out to be the *U-67* of Kapitaenleutnant Guenther Muller-Stockheim.

Three more U-boats perished that month by the hands of the fresh-as-a-daisy escort carrier groups, the *Bogue* people sinking *U-613* and *U-527*, both within one day south of the Azores. The *Santee* caught another oldtimer-ace, Kapitaenleutnant Hans-Joachim Schwandtke in *U-43* en route to Lagos on the Gold Coast on a mining mission carry-ing the mines on its deck. Two bulls-eyes from an Avenger exploded them and the *U-43* literally disintegrated.

As for the others, the B.d.U. gave away their ultimate plight as the roll of their names was called: "... *U-Krech*, report! ... *U-Muller*, report! ... *U-Holtorf*, report! ... *U-Friedrich*, report! ..." It was May all over again, the *reprise* of disaster. The names of the victims resounded on the air, the U-Boat Command searching for them in plain, un-encoded German: "Foerster ... Schoenberg ... Jeschonnek ... Straeter ... Koenenkamp ... Stiebler ... Kraus ... Queck, please report!"

The month ended with the downing of thirty-seven U-boats—twenty-five of them sunk by American forces. For the first time in the Battle of the Atlantic, the United States had bested Britain!

On August 4, Grossadmiral Doenitz was in Hamburg, inspecting damage to the Hansa city after a devasting air raid, when a courier brought him the latest bad news from Godt in Berlin. The little

Konteradmiral reported that "twenty-two U-boats [had been] lost in the last ten days of July" and urged Doenitz to institute a thorough investigation of the mystery because there was still "no reliable indication of the precise cause."

Doenitz responded by cancelling all operational cruises and instructing homeward bound boats to creep back to their bases by hugging the Spanish coast. As a result the average number of boats at sea that had already dropped from an all-time high of 118 in May to eighty-four in July, was radically reduced to but fifty-nine in August, the lowest number at sea since July, 1942. And yet, the disaster of this fantastic summer continued unabated to shake and uproot the U-Boat Arm. During the four months of the Allies' first counter-blitz, out of 347 U-boats at sea one-hundred and twenty were wiped out—or thirty-four per cent—a far higher percentage of casualties than ever suffered by any military organization of any nation anywhere in the whole history of war. Then came August and losses rose to fifty per cent!

Yet what was Doenitz's answer? He gave it on August 5 when, after a quick visit with the Fuehrer, he signalled all boats at sea:

"Do not report too much bad news, so as not to depress the other boats."

If he himself was depressed, he did not show it. Although he had lost one of his children in the counter-blitz, he never mentioned his personal loss or showed his grief. He tried with a stiff upper lip to re-assure and invigorate the U-boat men and inspire them to new sacrifices.

The crews of the seagoing boats were becoming restive. Flotilla commanders reported this growing restivenesss to Berlin, but were merely instructed to put up a fearless front and assure the U-boat men that everything would turn out alright. So, as they waved adieu to their departing boats in what used to be a flamboyant ritual, they continued to say, "Good luck and good hunting!"—but that farewell cry had lost its sex appeal.

Doenitz used to give the impression that he was open and frank with his U-boat men. But he was never forthright about their casualties, and was especially unscrupulous about keeping his losses from the German people. With the help of fawning correspondents at his headquarters, the U-Boat Arm was presented to the nation in the guise of an apparently invulnerable Teutonic hero. In three years of war, Doenitz permitted the announcement of the loss of only six boats, but since the real losses were amazingly low, nobody bothered to correct the impression.

Now the situation became different. While Doenitz's security smoke-screen prevented the men at the bases from learning precise details, a disaster of such magnitude could not be kept a secret. Wild rumors magnified the catastrophe and a thick pall of gloom descended upon the whole U-Boat Arm, creating a distinct spirit of defeatism. We found out about this from captured U-boat men and thought the time was ripe to make Doenitz's faithless refusal to take his men into his confidence the major theme of our propaganda transmissions.

In a special broadcast in May, we revealed that Doenitz was hiding his casualties in a blatant breach of faith, then gave him an ultimatum: "Unless you, *Herr Grossadmiral*," said Commander Albrecht in his role as Norden, "tell the truth regarding the casualties of the U-Boat Arm, it will be my sad and unpleasant duty to reveal your true casualty list!"

Doenitz did not respond to the challenge and so, four weeks after Norden's initial appeal, we started broadcasting the casualties. To tell the truth, we did not have too long a list to begin with (for we were confined to losses inflicted by the American forces)—but then, in the fall of 1943, we had more than enough to broadcast a casualty list every week, week after week, each list identifying ten U-boats that would never return from *Feindfahrt*.

The broadcasts had, as Kapitaenleutnant Zapp, commander of the Third Flotilla, put it in a special report to Berlin, "a devastating effect on the morale of the men." But, like Doenitz himself, the men had no choice. In Frank's words, "They had to go on ... Pride it was that urged them on—and maybe a secret shame at the thought of being afraid; but they also had a sense of honor to inspire them, and their own resolution to sustain them." That resolution remained strong throughout the U-Boat Arm and made it a dangerous foe to the bitter end. The victory-flushed warriors of the once triumphal *U-Waffe* became the moribund gladiators of a last-ditch suicide weapon.

The Balance Sheet

In August, American forces sank ten of the twenty-five U-boats destroyed—six of them by the hunter-killers of *Card* and *Core*. There was only one American kill in September, the *U-161* of Kapitaenleutnant Albrecht Achilles off Bahia, but October-December saw the destruction of fifty-three U-boats, eighteen of them by Americans, and eleven of the eighteen by the jeep carrier groups.

The year's score was 237 U-boats destroyed—seventy-five of them by American forces: *seventy-five* down in 1943, as against a total of *sixteen* in 1942! The year before, the American share of U-boat sinkings was a little under twenty per cent. Now the percentage rose spectacularly to thirty-two per cent, reflecting the ratio of American forces in the Battle of the Atlantic.

In as vast an enterprise as was the United States Navy's anti-U-boat campaign in World War II, it is difficult if not impossible to allocate credit between the components of the joint effort. It would be hazardous, therefore, to single out the Tenth Fleet as the organization that was primarily responsible for the victory of 1943. The real beauty of it was not the virtuoso performance of individual units, but the perfect teamwork that produced the results.

Even organizationally, the Tenth Fleet was but one of several agencies sharing both the responsibilities and the fruits of the anti-U-boat campaign. There was, for example, Admiral Bellinger's "Comairlant," Air Force Atlantic Fleet, another think factory and administrative type command dedicated to the air aspect of antisubmarine warfare in areas not covered by the Tenth Fleet. Then there were all those "existing agencies"—the various divisions of COMINCH and the bureaus of CNO—on which Admiral King had drawn in the establishment of the Tenth Fleet and on which Admiral Low then leaned.

However, the sheer chronology of events and the scoreboard of the results indicates conclusively that the Tenth Fleet had a prominent, and maybe dominant, part in coordinating old endeavors and activating new ones, in infusing the American antisubmarine war effort with a purposeful and scientific spirit, and in creating the climate and the means which were indispensable for success in this arduous venture.

The dividing date for making a comparison is, of course, May 20, 1943, when the Tenth Fleet came into being. In the eighteen months before, American forces sank a total of 36 U-boats—but by the end of 1943, when Tenth Fleet was but six months old, our sinkings totalled one hundred and one.

There is another comparison. Between January and June, 1943, the U-boats sank 229 of our ships in the Atlantic, an aggregate gross tonnage of 1.5 million. But during the six months immediately following the establishment of the Tenth Fleet, these sinkings dropped to sixty-six ships of but 342,000 gross tons!

In an almost literal sense, the Tenth Fleet was the electronic brain of the American anti-U-boat effort. Fed intelligence obtained by great ingenuity and industry from a variety of sources, this human computer produced the answers the forces afloat needed to meet the challenge of the U-boats. What they needed most were (1) pinpoint knowledge of the enemy's positions in the Atlantic; (2) uniform doctrines for the various operational exigencies of the campaign; and (3) physical implements to kill the U-boats.

The Tenth Fleet was now there to give them all three—intelligence, operational research, and the weapons to kill—the tools they needed to finish the job.

CHAPTER XVI

The Tools of Victory

~~~~~~

The U.S.S. *Buckley* needed only about fifteen minutes to kill *U-66*, but that quarter of an hour demonstrated all the intricacies of the U-boat war—the meticulousness of its intelligence effort, the technique of the battle, and the decisive importance of the human equation in this war of mechanical monsters. It also illustrated—in the chase, the pin-down and the pay-off—how the Tenth Fleet paved the way for members of the huge American sea-air armada in the Atlantic to deal with the U-boats decisively.

The fast and furious action in the mid-Atlantic was a microcosm of combat in which war was miniaturized down to the destruction of a tiny object displacing less than a thousand tons of oceanic mass, in an encounter that was more akin to a barroom brawl than to an armed clash in modern war.

The Pattern of Destruction

The moonlit nights around the Arquipelago de Cabo Verde have changed little since Luigi da Calamosto, the Venetian navigator in the service of a Portuguese king, discovered them in 1547. The sea, laced with silver ribbons and strewn with stray phosphorus, kept twinkling down the centuries, its temperate waters ruffled only by the light currents of the balmy air and the pectoral fins of flying fish.

It was on a calm and clear tropical night in April, 1944, as the moon was filling up again, that the *U-66* sailed eagerly toward a certain spot west of the Verdes. A seasoned veteran of the Atlantic that had chalked up 50,000 tons on a single *Feindfahrt* during the first *Paukenschlag*, it was the charmed boat of the Third Flotilla. Bounced about and amply bruised, it always managed nevertheless to extricate itself from all its predicaments, thanks mostly to the skill of its successive skippers. But this was the spring of 1944 when the U-boats no longer had the ocean all to themselves. The luck of *U-66* was also running out. Commanded by Oberleutnant Gerhard Seehausen on a long and disappointing patrol in the Gulf of Guinea, now it was homeward bound at last, but was experiencing some difficulty. Both boat and crew were fatigued. The men suffered from what they called *Blechkrankheit*, a quaint disease they attributed to their long confinement in the steel hull, but which doctors diagnosed simply as vitamin deficiency. They needed fresh vegetables and fruit, and their diesels needed oil, badly.

In the night of April 19-20, Seehausen surfaced and told Berlin about his plight. U-Boat Command then directed him to rendezvous with one of the milk cows, the *U-488* of Oberleutnant Studt. Time of the date: the night of April 25-26. The place: 720 miles due west of Santo Antao, biggest of the Verde islands.

On the appointed night, *U-66* was on the surface, sailing at twelve knots toward the pinpoint and then, at exactly 4:42 a.m. on April 26, caught a fleeting glimpse of the milk cow. But *U-488* was not alone. It was under attack by four American destroyer escorts. A moment after Seehausen had spotted the big boat, Studt took it to a depth of 560 feet and then, after two more hedgehog attacks, she went to the bottom.

The intrusion of the Americans on what was supposed to be a strictly German *Treffen* was not accidental by any means. The Tenth Fleet was in on Seehausen's secret from the second he had radioed Berlin five days before. The transmission was picked up and, though it produced no firm bearing, the Tenth Fleet alerted CINCLANT nevertheless. The message wound up on "Old Crow", Captain John P. W. Vest's *Croatan*, whose hunter-killer group, the plot showed, was closest to *U-66's* position at the time of the transmission.

The first tip proved futile. But the refueling arrangements Berlin had to make required so many transmissions to and fro that at least a tenuous contact could be maintained with the straggler. While *U-66* eluded the hunters, the search for Seehausen led the *Croatan* to Studt.

From then on, the *U-66* had a definite Tenth Fleet tab on it. After the inconclusive search, the *Croatan* was withdrawn and the *Block Island* group was sent into the search, with Captain Francis M. Hughes, USN, in command. Hughes had night-owl Avengers to search around the clock, and four destroyer escorts, including the *Buckley*, with Lieutenant Commander Brent M. Abel, USNR, on the bridge.

On May 1, Hughes received the latest Tenth Fleet fix that now located the *U-Seehausen* within a narrowing radius about 550 miles west of Santo Antao. It was a firm fix at that because, in the meantime, Seehausen had to do a lot of talking with Berlin to get himself another milk cow. He was told to wait where he was. Then Kapitaenleutnant Siegfried Luedden in *U-188* was directed to go and accomodate him, on the night of May 5-6.

Tenth Fleet was getting additional bearings from Seehausen's daily transmissions and could thus guide the *Block Island's* sweeps. Even so, four days of steady search yielded no results—but *U-66* now lived on borrowed time and Seehausen knew it.

Shortly after 11 p.m. on May 5, he came up to breathe and to recharge his batteries. He was desperate and in a signal to Berlin said so: "Refueling impossible under constant stalking! Mid-Atlantic worse than the Bay of Biscay!"

It was one of the "squirt" transmissions in which lengthy messages were compressed into brief signals to hamper our Huffduffs in getting fixes on them. This particular one was on the air for less than fifteen seconds. But now, with the whole Tenth Fleet network alerted to it, twenty-six HF/DF stations of the Atlantic network obtained bearings on Seehausen's latest transmission. The coordinated and evaluated fix reached the *Block Island* within an hour!

Captain Hughes sent the *Buckley* to run down the bearing. At 2:15 a.m. on May 6, Lieutenant Jimmie J. Sellars, USNR, in an unarmed night-owl Avenger, reported radar contact at twenty miles due north, and then, moments later, the sighting of a U-boat on the surface. It was the *U-66* at last! Jimmie told the carrier he would stay on top of it.

Seven miles from the spot, Abel sounded General Quarters and prepared to join the issue. The *Buckley* was looking for the U-boat when all of a sudden, three red flares purpled the whitish-blue of the moonlit scene. It was exactly eight minutes past three in the morning. The flares came from *U-66*. Seehausen had seen the silhouette of the DE and, mistaking it for the milk cow he was expecting, he ordered the flares to guide the *U-188* to their rendezvous.

3:15 A.M. Seehausen realized his mistake and opened up on Sellars. who circled over the scene planning to help the *Buckley* with advice. That was the best he could do. The Avenger was unarmed.

3:16 A.M. Jimmie was now in voice radio contact with *Buckley* and told Abel on the TBS: "The sonofabitch is taking potshots at me and how I wish I had something to throw back at him."

3:17 A.M. Sellars to Abel in a voice whose pitch indicated by itself that the showdown was at hand: "Sub is turning towards you—sub is now turning away from you—sub's course is parallel to you." Then at

3:18 A.M.: "He is moving across from port to starboard at a 40-degree angle at 3 o'clock on the watch."

Two minutes later he was telling Hughes that the issue had been joined. "*Buckley* has opened fire," he shouted, somewhat like old Clem McCarthy at Churchill Downs, "sub is returning fire. Boy! I have never before seen such concentration! *Buckley* is cutting hell out of the conning tower." Then to Abel: "Turn your sights up a little!"

It was a classic fight, the only one in the whole Atlantic battle to feature a command that had not been heard in the United States Navy since the day of cannon and cutlass.

3:29 A.M. Abel ordered hard right rudder to ram. A moment later the destroyer escort's bow crashed across the U-boat's foredeck. Seehausen's crew came boiling out of the conning tower and deck hatches. Several of them tried to scramble onto the *Buckley's* forecastle. One German had managed to reach the *Buckley,* when Commander Abel shouted the ancient command:

"Stand by to repel boarders!"

The "Yellow Peril" later gave the following account of the weird battle:

"Ammunition expended at this time included several general mess coffee cups which were on hand at ready gun station. Two of the enemy were hit in the head with these. Empty shell cases were also used by crew of three-inch gun No. 2 to repel boarders. Three-inch guns could not bear. *Buckley* suffered its only casualty of the engagement when a man bruised his fist knocking one of the enemy over the side. Several men, apparently dead, could be seen hanging over the side of the sub's bridge at this time. One German attempting to board was killed with a .45 pistol by the boatswain's mate in charge of the forward ammunition party.

"Men fell back over the side. Midships repair party equipped with rifles manned the lifelines on the starboard side abaft light lock, and picked off several men on the deck of the submarine. Chief Fire Controlman used a tommy gun from the bridge with excellent results."

One German almost made it. He got below and tried to enter the wardroom, but was repelled by a steward's mate, armed with a coffee pot.

3:35 A.M. The *U-66* slid under the *Buckley's* keel and heeled to such an angle that the destroyer escort's crew could clearly see the conning tower on fire. Then the U-boat went totally mad. It raced off at high speed, wreathed in flames and out of control.

3:37 A.M. Thirty-six men—half of its total complement—abandoned the crazed sub that went down sizzling.

The operation that really began on April 19, 1944, when the Tenth Fleet obtained its first fix on *U-66*, thus ended seventeen days later, although the *Buckley* on her part needed only fifteen minutes to win the epic battle. Seehausen's U-boat was killed in a *combined* operation and its fate, from that first fix to the final fathom, clearly delineated, step by step, the modus operandi of the Tenth Fleet in cooperation with the forces afloat and aloft.

Step 1: U-boat spotted by Huffduff, bearing obtained, plot developed and evaluated.

Step 2: Plot flashed to fleet for immediate forewarding to unit or units closest to U-boat's presumed position.

Step 3: Search initiated and bearings ran down.

Step 4: If sighted or contacted, U-boat attacked and, if possible, destroyed.

Step 5: Detailed action report submitted to Tenth Fleet for analysis and statistical evaluation; conclusions drawn from aggregate of analyzed actions developed into doctrines.

Step 6: Lessons of U-boat war disseminated to all concerned in a never-ceasing educational and indoctrinational process.

Step 7: Members of operational research staff loaned to forces at sea to test their own conclusions in action and/or teach pilots and sailors the best possible application of conclusions.

Step 8: New weapons developed on the basis of practical experience gained in action and evaluated in operational research.

It was a perennially rotating cycle, both for each individual encounter, and for the sum total of the U-boat war. It always began and ended with the basic premise—Intelligence.

The *U-66* was but one of the 863 operational U-boats the Allies had to dispossess in this war. The effort it needed to sink that single prowler illustrates what tedious a job it was. In a systematic encroachment, the primary task was, of course, to find the target. It was a super-human task! The theater of this campaign—indeed, its consecutive battlefield—was some fifty million square miles of ocean covered by billions of tons of sea-water. The targets were tiny floating specks ingeniously designed and camouflaged to blend into the ocean and to make the most of its innumerable natural hide-outs.

Even today we know less about our oceans than about the moon. Roughly accurate maps exist for only about two per cent of the deep sea regions. Definitive information is lacking about the various oceanic layers and sea mounts which can either hide or betray an intruder. The caprice of the sea is infinite. On the one hand, so-called deep sound channels of the ocean serve as ducts for very-long-distance sound transmissions. On the other hand, sound propagating in the depths is reflected or refracted when the sound waves strike the interface between two layers of sea water at different temperatures and densities, and submariners have learned how to exploit this phenomenon to hide their boats.

Depth is still an unexplored dimension of the sea. As a matter of fact, it was recognized only recently that the ocean has three rather than two dimensions. The parameter of depth presents new challenges and offers new promise that attention only to the surface and boundaries of the sea could never satisfy. During the Battle of the Atlantic, however, our working knowledge of environmental, meteorologic and topographic conditions in off-shore areas was woefully inadequate, at a time we had to wage war in a region whose nature not only baffled but actually defied us.

Finding the Needle in the Haystack

The oceanic war of 1939-1945 posed far more questions and raised greater problems than our hydrographic preparedness and oceanographic competence could answer and solve. The British were the first to make a deliberate and elaborate effort to find the U-boat in the ocean, by a variety of detection methods ranging from espionage to asdic. Their secret service worked to procure all sorts of information about the organization and personnel of the U-Boat Arm; to monitor its scientific and technological progress; to gauge its material strength and physical capabilities; and to find out, as far as possible, its leaders' intentions. Considerable progress was made along these lines through the employment of coast watchers, for example, the infiltration of spies into key regions and organizations, and through aerial reconnaissance. It became possible to follow the U-boats all the way from their launching pads to their operational bases and then on to their points of departure on war patrols. But there the surveillance hit a snag. The U-boat had no difficulty in eluding its shadows by blending into the ocean.

The British proceeded from the scientific truism that the oceans are more transparent to sound than any other form of energy and that sound travels great distances under water. They developed ingenious underwater acoustic devices—hydrophones to listen passively, and asdic which emits sharp pings of sound and depends on echoes to reveal otherwise silent targets.

These efforts began in World War I. Later other revolutionary new detection devices were added—like radar, for example, to locate the

U-boat on the surface—and the old devices were refined. The Germans, though usually late in finding out about them, were always quick and smart in devising counter-devices, either to mislead or to detect the detectors. The *Aphrodite*, for example, was a radar decoy balloon that simulated the reflective reaction of the U-boat's conning tower. The *Alberich* was a rubber coating of the submarine's hull to prevent sonar detection when submerged. The Teutonically-named *Funkmess-beobachtungsgeraet* (or FuMB for short and known as "Fu Man-Chu" to the Americans) warned against radar. The *Pillenwerfer* emitted the *Bold*, a cartridge that was supposed to fool our sound gear by producing bubbles reflecting the sonar waves in a way similar to the hull of the U-boat.

By the time the Tenth Fleet appeared, the British had advanced the job of finding the U-boats both on and under the water, from a somewhat impressionistic art to an exact science. The activity was centralized in a fantastically complex organization occupying Hollywoodish premises deep underground, the Admiralty's central U-Boat Tracking Room. It was headed by a "civilian", Rodger Winn by name, a barrister by profession, whose keen legal mind and natural curiosity made him an ideal boss of Tracking. He was aided by the Divison of Naval Intelligence, first under Admiral Godfrey, then under Commodore Rushbrook, who had a somewhat livelier approach to the job of procuring the enemy's confidences than their American counterparts; and by all Allied intelligence organizations tuned to the pertinent secrets of the Germans. The plot of Winn's Tracking Room was the last word in U-boat dispositions. Often Winn had a better idea just where all those U-boats were than Doenitz himself.

The effectiveness of the British intelligence network was attested by Doenitz's panic fear of it. From time to time, he was seized by the obsession that British agents operated inside his own office and that every U-boat base in Germany, France and Norway was honeycombed with British spies—which they presumably were. "An efficient enemy intelligence service," he wrote, "must in any case have been able to ascertain the distribution of U-boats among various bases, the dates of their sailing and return to port, and possibly also the sea areas allotted to boats proceeding on operations."

Whatever information spies supplied, the yield from prisoner interrogation was continuous. It was a highly scientific enterprise using all sorts of electronic devices from which no U-boat-prisoner could hide. The methodology was diabolic, including subtle psychological means akin to brainwashing and also touches of melodrama. It enabled the British to squeeze the last bit of intelligence from their U-boat prisoners by putting them through the wringer three times. The procedure began in the moment of truth, with the so-called shock interrogation on the rescue ship while the prisoners were still soaking wet or had their first cup of tea while wrapped in blankets after an ordeal in the water. It continued with systematic and specialized interrogation either at a carefully camouflaged interrogation center maintained at Kensington Palace Gardens in London for elite prisoners or at the Cockfosters Interrogation Center in Hertfordshire. It was concluded in a sort of post-graduate course at the camp at Bowmanville, on Lake Ontario in Canada, to which the U-boat prisoners were later shipped.

The Atlantic Section

When Admiral Low was drawing up the chart establishing the Tenth Fleet, it was evident to him that Intelligence would be the cornerstone of the unique new edifice. But he also realized that it was patently impossible to build an intelligence service from scratch. Fortunately for the Tenth Fleet, there already existed an excellent coverage of the waterfront.

First of all, the Tenth Fleet had unrestricted access to the Admiralty's U-Boat Tracking Room and the various antisubmarine warfare research and intelligence agencies of the Admiralty. Invaluable though the British contacts were, the Tenth Fleet found most of what it needed inside the United States Navy, partly in the Office of Naval Intelligence and especially in a division of COMINCH, the Combat Intelligence Division.

This division was also a King innovation. In January, 1942, Admiral King—pointedly ignoring ONI (and not caring if he hurt them)—established a Fleet Intelligence Officer of his own in the Plans Division of his headquarters organization. This officer then directed the COMINCH Chart Room—the major war plot of the United States Navy—and headed the important Operations Information Section of the Division, aiding in the preparation of estimates and plans.

In the spring of 1943, when King was pondering the necessity of a separate agency to coordinate and tighten antisubmarine warfare, he also mulled over the need of a Naval Intelligence Service so-called, because he felt that ONI was insufficintly stimulated by the war and remained too musty and muscle-bound in a global conflict.

Just then, his old classmate Vice Admiral William S. Pye, USN, was making a study of King's headquarters organization and came up with the suggestion that Intelligence be set up as a fourth Division in COMINCH. King seized upon the recommendation and established a Combat Intelligence Division to "consolidate the functions of keeping the Commander in Chief and his staff supplied with information of our own and enemy forces." On July 1, 1943, he named Rear Admiral Richard E. Schuirman, USN, Assistant Chief of Staff (Combat Intelligence), then persuaded Secretary Knox to make Schuirman also director of ONI, thus creating in fact, through a personal union, a Naval Intelligence Service.

The Combat Intelligence Division became more than just the usual bureau to prepare the orders of battle and take care of the plot. It developed quickly into a dynamic intelligence service. Combat Intelligence was coequal with the Tenth Fleet and King decreed that the two should live happily ever after. Accordingly, he decided, and Low concurred, that the Tenth Fleet did not need an intelligence division of its own but could obtain its intelligence requirements from Combat Intelligence which acquired an Atlantic Section (formerly the Antisubmarine Section) almost exclusively dedicated to the German U-boat problem.

Commander Knowles

The section was headed by Commander Kenneth Alward Knowles, USN, a retired officer of the regular Navy who had been recalled to active duty the year before. It was an exceptionally fortunate choice. Knowles expanded and improved the Anti-Submarine Section to the point where it became the obvious organization to cater to the intelligence needs of the Tenth Fleet. He then reorganized it into an Atlantic Section, now properly so-called, and headed it for the next two years, until June 12, 1945, with such competence and success that he was awarded the Legion of Merit for a job extremely well done, the citation saying: "He carried out duties of great responsibility by evaluating enemy combat information pertaining to German, Italian and other Axis submarine strength, dispositions, capabilities and intentions. His estimates were of incalculable value and assistance to the Navy High Command and in direct support of operations."

Though nominally outside the Tenth Fleet (while actually its most permanent fixture), Knowles was destined to become, next to Admiral Low, chiefly responsible for the excellence and success of the phantom fleet. As a matter of fact it was exactly because Commander Knowles headed the Anti-Submarine Section that Low decided he needed no intelligence division of his own. He knew from past experience that he could cooperate closely and well with "Kennie" and that he would get from him, not only loyal service, but top performance.

They had been shipmates in the Asiatic Fleet on the destroyer *Paul Jones* which Low commanded and whose gunnery officer Knowles was. They remained close even after some minor trouble with his eyes forced

Knowles, then a lieutenant, into retirement in 1936. They met again in Washington and it was Low who recommended Knowles to Admiral Willson for the job at the head of the Anti-Submarine Section.

A native of Wisconsin, "Kennie" Knowles studied at Cornell, then went to Annapolis and graduated with the Class of 1927. At the Naval Academy, he swam, played soccer and captained the rifle team. Later, at the Asiatic Station, he made a name for himself as a gunnery expert.

Though Knowles was, indeed, a very good athlete, he was more remarkable for his brain than his brawn. Upon his retirement in 1936, he became editor of *Our Navy*, a widely read professional magazine, where he attained influence and an intellectual reputation.

A tall, lean, severe-looking and intense, but genial and sensitive man, he combined in himself the high professional qualities of a competent naval officer and the erudition and curiosity of the intellectual. He needed both sets of qualities in his wartime job. He had innumerable opportunities to put his foot in his mouth by misreading the mass of intelligence passing through his hands and coming up with the wrong conclusions. His job needed a man who dared to risk being wrong on occasion and who did not shrink from putting up his career and reputation as collateral in a venture that abounded in calculated risks. Knowles was such a man. He had the ability to worm his thinking into that of the enemy, to separate the good from the chaff, and to handle intelligence with the skill of a master chess player.

Since his kind of intelligence activity was a novel experience for the United States Navy, he had no precedent to go by. He started building from scratch, modelling his unit on the British pattern, utilizing their experience, example and knowhow. He had some dismal failures and some remarkable successes to begin with, but as the American forces grew, and the antisubmarine effort hit its stride, so Knowles' failures became fewer and his successes more frequent.

Taxing though the task was, Knowles had an easier and more rewarding job than most intelligence chiefs inside the military establishments. In most army, navy and air force organizations, intelligence is regarded as an ancillary activity that is superimposed upon but only rarely integrated in operational agencies. *The outstanding feature of the Tenth Fleet was that intelligence and operations were completely welded.* The intelligence effort was indispensable and was recognized as such. Unlike most intelligence chiefs, who had to work hard to peddle their wares, Knowles never had to "sell" his products. He had eager customers for everything he had and, in fact, he had a tough time to procure the supply needed to meet the demand.

The Atlantic Section could have developed into a big and rambling organization, but Knowles frowned upon boondoggle and beadledom. Under him the agency operated with but four male officers, eight Wave officers, a couple of first rate yeomen, and a handful of enlisted Waves. Working directly under Knowles was his "Number One", Lieutenant Commander John E. Parsons, USNR, a young New York lawyer and yachting enthusiast, who had no specific qualifications for the job when he first drifted into it but became second only to Knowles himself as the American intelligence wizard of the U-boat war.

Knowles' day began long before eight A.M.—when most officers on duty in the Navy Department went to their "battle stations"—seven days a week, three-hundred sixty-five days a year, sixty-six in 1944— that was a leap year. By nine o'clock he was ready to impart his knowledge to the rest of the Tenth Fleet and others in the Navy authorized to benefit from it. At nine sharp, the brass and sundry assembled in the Plot Room to watch Knowles reading his crystal ball.

Combat Intelligence in Action

This was the daily situation conference—a Hollywoodish affair—in front of the huge map on which the entire Battle of the Atlantic was laid out. On the map were the convoys in transit, their progress ingeniously indicated by elastic bands stretched between two pins, arrows showing the direction of the convoys, moved every eight hours. Other pins marked the U-boats—those presumed to be at large at their assumed positions, those definitely located and some even identified, and those who no longer could do any damage—the kills.

There, too, was the whole disposition of our own forces. Whenever a fix was obtained on still another U-boat, its presumed position was entered on the plot at once, several Waves continuously busying themselves with the changes. This was the Navy Department's busiest plot. The situation changed virtually by the minute.

The conference started off the day in an informal but brisk and disciplined manner. It began as soon as Admiral Low seated himself in the center chair of the first row and nodded to Knowles. Knowles then reviewed the events of the previous night, enumerated the more important bearings, and summed up the situation in a concise intelligence estimate. A brief discussion followed, questions were asked and answered, and decisions were occasionally made right then and there. Usually it was all over in ten to fifteen minutes.

Admiral King never attended the briefings (he was briefed by Low) but the Navy-wide importance of the Knowles plot was attested by frequent visitors from King's staff. Vice Admiral Charles M. ("Savvy") Cook, Jr., head of Plans and later King's Deputy Chief of Staff, was an almost daily visitor. Others who dropped in regularly included Admirals Edwards and DeLany. The Convoy and Routing Division had its own Plot, but Admiral Metcalf regularly attended the Knowles briefings, flanked by his staff.

Knowles carried a burden that frequently bore down heavily on this sensitive man. He was aware of the departure of every convoy, was cognizant of their routes, and knew, too, just when and where they might bump into a U-boat concentration waiting in ambush. Several times during the war, the perils of those journeys across the embattled sea kept Knowles awake as he sweated out the passage of certain convoys through U-boat infested waters. He would pace the living room of his home in Arlington, Virginia, unable to sleep, waiting for the good word or the bad news, as the case might be, and hoping that the information the Atlantic Section had been able to supply would enable the convoys to evade the wolfpacks. Worse still, his agony was a top secret whose burden he could not lighten by sharing, not even with Velma Sealy Knowles, a Texan belle, his lovely and beautiful wife.

Operation Bolero

The frightful responsibility his job entailed, and the manner in which it was met, may best be illustrated by what was one of the Tenth Fleet's most important assignments. Between May and September, 1943, it had to secure *Operation Bolero,* the American build-up in Britain for the Allied invasion of the Continent. Participating in *Bolero* were the big Cunard Queens—the *Mary* and the *Elizabeth*—also the *Mauretania* and the *Aquitania,* the French passenger liner *Pasteur* and the Canadian *Empress of Scotland.* The two Queens carried 30,000 troops in each crossing. They sailed at a steady twenty-eight and a half knots, and, therefore, had to go it alone because no escort vessel could keep up with them.

This was an entirely American responsibility: all troop convoys and transports were routed and controlled by the Tenth Fleet. Knowles in particular held one of the keys to the secret of their safe routing. He had extra watch officers assigned to clear a path for the Queens and the troop convoys. They made special plots of the U-boats presumed to be in their prospective paths, followed their passage day and night on a board, notified Convoy and Routing of every U-boat located or suspected in their paths, and helped to steer them out of areas infested by U-boats.

The nerve-wrecking mission in which the lives of thousands of Americans were at stake (and on whose success, up to a point, the outcome of the war depended) was accomplished with one-hundred per cent impunity. Typical was the crossing of the twenty transports and troopships of Convoy UT-2. Fully laden with men and material, it left New York on September 5, 1943, on its ten-day passage, just when Doenitz was coming out of his summer swoon and was sending hastily re-enforced U-boats back into the North Atlantic. The U-boats were balled together in a powerful wolfpack, the *Leuthen*, and carried two formidable new devices: the acoustic torpedo and *Aphrodite*, the anti-radar decoy. They had orders to move to their operational area in deepest secrecy—even refraining from using their radios to evade the Huff-duff—and to surprise Allied traffic on the great arc between New York-Halifax and the United Kingdom.

But the Admiralty and the Tenth Fleet had the *Leuthen* accurately plotted. UT-2 was routed safely to its destination by swinging it north to latitude 55° where Knowles assured C&R no U-boat lurked. Although Doenitz had twenty-two U-boats in the North Atlantic, not a single one as much as sighted the precious convoy. It goes without saying that the safety of these convoys east of the Chop Line was the result of similarly skilled routings by the Tenth Fleet's British opposite number.

We never lost a single troopship or transport going to Europe! So dependable were the plots Knowles had prepared for the sailings of the Queens that no U-boat ever got a crack at them!

The Milk Cow Operation

The protection accorded these convoys was a tremendous victory, to be sure, but it was of a *negative* nature: it saved our most important ships, but it did not sink any U-boats. Another spectacular feat of the Knowles organization, in close collaboration with the British as always, then enabled us to score a *positive* victory—the total liquidation of Doenitz's big supply submarines.

In 1941, Doenitz hit upon the idea of keeping his U-boats longer at sea and substantially increasing their radius of action by refuelling and replenishing them from U-boats especially constructed for the job. Type XIV was then designed and built, big and bulging U-boat tankers that had a cruising range of about 12,000 miles at a maximum of fifteen knots an hour on the surface, but had certain disadvantages: they were unarmed except for deck A.A. guns, and were clumsy and difficult to manueuver. The first of the "milk cows" was commissioned in April,

1942. During the next year, nine more were built and then, through the addition of the 1600-ton Type IX mine-layers, the milk cow herd was brought up to a fleet of nineteen boats.

These supply operations were carried out according to a basic pre-arranged plan that, however, still necessitated considerable radio traffic to work out the details of each individual rendezvous. The usual procedure was for a U-boat to signal the U-Boat Command for a milk cow, and then for the U-Boat Command to make the arrangements, giving date, time and place of the *Treffen.* These operations took place just before and after sundown at spots indicated by various grid references.

For a year, these arrangements worked astonishingly well and only one milk cow was lost. After a while, the operation became routine and the grid references became standard, referring mostly to spots north and west of the Azores. It was an ideal area for these operations, in the heart of the mid-Atlantic gap for which the Allies could not provide air cover. Efforts were made to persuade Dr. Salazar, the dictator of Portugal, to let us into the Azores, but when he refused we had to abandon the area more or less to the U-boats to do as they pleased.

Between April, 1942, and May, 1943, the milk cows refueled and re-victualled nearly four-hundred U-boats. A milk cow carried 720 tons of fuel of which it could dispense four to six hundred tons. It was enough to refuel twelve medium-sized or five large boats. Thanks to this arrangement, even medium-sized boats could operate as far away from home as the most distant parts of the Caribbean and the Cape of Good Hope.

Something had to be done about the milk cows—but how could they be singled out for special attention? It was difficult enough to locate just any U-boat at sea. It was virtually impossible to pick out the supply boats from among the scores of U-boats on operational cruises.

As soon as he became head of the Antisubmarine [Intelligence] Section in COMINCH, Commander Knowles became interested in the specific problem of the milk cows and began to work on a solution. Gradually a pattern emerged from these refueling operations as the U-Boat Command, lulled into complacency during their long victory streak, became reckless and slipshod. In a log kept of the U-Boat Command's transmissions Commander Knowles and Parsons discovered certain groups of apparently related signals. Those groups were then interpreted as the specific signals put on the air to arrange the supply operations.

From bearings on this traffic it became possible to establish the approximate locality of various refueling areas. Then, by pinning down the pattern, it became theoretically possible to obtain advance warning whenever a supply operation was in the making. It became evident to Knowles and others that the moment the gap around the Azores could be closed, the milk cows would be expelled from it and would probably be doomed.

When, then, the escort carrier groups moved into the breach, they had a special assignment—to liquidate the milk cows, four of which were continuously stationed in the gap. The carrier groups were supplied with the information they needed in a dossier Commander Knowles had prepared.

The escort carrier groups moved into the Azores area in May, 1943. By June 12—when the *U-118* was sunk by the *Bogue* group—only one of the four tankers on station was left. Then in an operation lasting a little over three months, the escort carrier groups sank eight milk cows; and, by August, Doenitz had only three of them left altogether. On August 5, the U-Boat Command's War Diary recorded that "there are no more reserve tankers available." Doenitz decreed that "only the most essential supply operations" be carried out henceforth, "and then only on an outward passage." As a result of the milk cows' liquidation, he had to give up operations in the Central Atlantic much sooner than he had planned.

There was much grumbling inside the U-Boat Arm about the manner in which headquarters managed the supply operations. But the arrangements did not show any improvement as the war drew on, perhaps because these rendezvous had to be arranged in a certain set manner and no changes could be effected in it. On October 4, 1943, the *Card* carrier group caught a concentration of four U-boats on the surface within a radius of 500 yards. On closer scrutiny the idyllic scene turned out to be an ambitious refueling operation: the milk cow *U-460* was keeping a pre-arranged date with the *U-264*, the *U-422* and the *U-455*. In the course of this chance encounter, the *Card* sank the milk cow and the *U-264*.

Eight days later, the *Card* came upon the *U-488*, another milk cow, and damaged it so badly that it had to return home. Next day, the *U-402* was sunk while trying to rendezvous with a milk cow. The *U-488* returned to the Atlantic in April, 1944, only to be sunk in full view of *U-66* which it was about to supply. Three months before, two thirsty U-boats—the *U-129* and the *U-516*—witnessed the destruction of their milk cow, the *U-544* of Kapitaenleutnant Willy Mattke, The skipper of *U-516* was a young but thoughtful Oberleutnant named Tillesen and he fell to brooding about Mattke's fate. When he logged in the original signal that had directed him to the rendezvous with *U-Mattke*, the grid reference of the spot where they were to meet sounded familiar. He looked it up on a chart he kept of all previous dates and discovered that several U-boats had been directed to exactly that same spot in the past and all of them were sunk by Allied aircraft that happened upon the U-boats in the psychological moment.

When the *U-Mattke* was thus prevented from being of any more service, U-Boat Command signalled Tillesen to rendezvous with *U-539* instead at another spot whose grid reference he did not even have to look up in his chart. He knew it by heart—it was *Grid Reference D*, a notorious U-Boat graveyard where Allied aircraft always managed to arrive just ahead of the U-boats to give them a hot reception. But Tillesen obeyed his orders and sailed to the spot despite his misgivings. Of the milk cow there was no sign. But cruising directly over his head was an American bomber. *U-516* barely escaped by diving away.

Tillesen was now convinced that the recurrent presence of the Allied planes was no accident. He was convinced that the cipher of the U-Boat Command had been broken and Allied intelligence was reading their signals at will. He was not impressed when U-Boat Command—and even Doenitz in person—tried to assuage the fears of the U-boat commanders like Tillesen by assuring them that "it was *absolutely impossible* for the enemy to decipher the signals." (In his post-war memoirs Doenitz was no longer as positive but wrote: "To this day [1958], as far as I know, we are not certain whether or not the enemy did succeed in breaking our ciphers during the war.")

In 1952, on a visit to Germany I exchanged notes with several former U-boat skippers. I found them unanimous in their belief that we had the key to their cipher. However, I could find no evidence that we located the U-boats by the simple shortcut of reading their mail.

The Anglo-American intelligence effort was simplified by an amazing single tool that played the decisive part in the Allied victory over the U-boat. It was the high frequency direction finder that covered the oceans like a giant ear, listening eagerly and relentlessly to the sounds the U-Boat Command was putting on the air.

Reduced to the simplest terms, the Allies won the U-boat war and Germany lost it because Doenitz talked too much. Walpole once said that he feared Sir William Pulteney's tongue more than another man's sword. We had a high regard for Doenitz's fearsome sword, but gained aid and comfort from his tongue.

This reflected a strange contradiction in the man. Doenitz put premium on secrecy and plagued the U-Boat Arm with recurrent investigations. He suspected an Allied spy behind every chestnut tree in the park of the *Sardinen-Schloesschen* and feared treason even in the circle of his close collaborators.

We exploited his mania and once succeeded in keeping a U-boat in port by playing on it. From an agent in France we learned that a certain U-Boat of the Tenth Flotilla at Lorient was about to sail for patrol, and even received its crew list. The day before it was to sail, we mentioned the boat in a carefully worded Norden broadcast and inferred that the information on which it was based resulted from the indiscretion of the boat's chief mate whose name we casually mentioned.

The Norden was monitored, of course, and it put the security officer of U-Boat Command on his toes. At midnight, when the boat was being readied for immient departure, a detachment of the *Abwehr's* secret field police boarded it and took the chief mate into custody. The crew was thrown into panic and the patrol was cancelled. For a while every man from that U-boat lived in a mist of suspicion.

Treacherous B-Bars

But Doenitz betrayed his own U-boats when he insisted that a permanent link in radio communications be maintained between headquarters and the vessels at sea. To be sure, wars cannot be conducted behind closed doors, but all belligerents take reasonable care to conceal their moves and dispositions from each other. Radio silence was a strict rule strictly enforced in all Allied navies, because it was realized that once a ship or a fleet went on the air, it gave up its cover. Locations can be ascertained by piling the transmissions, and information can be gained by breaking the ciphers.

Doenitz chose to violate this basic tenet when he put his whole campaign on the air by broadcasting every one of his operational moves, the most important as well as the most trifling. While some observers—including Commander (now Captain) Knowles—agree with him that he had no choice and had to take the calculated risk, others regard this sacrifice of radio silence as his major blunder. "His desire to keep tactical control of his boats was so strong," Morison wrote, "that, even after he knew that their radio conversations were being monitored by Allied HF/DF, he went right on doing it."

Doenitz himself said, "Before the war, when we had just started our training in wolfpack tactics, we had discussed the question whether the use of their radio by U-boats would not enable the enemy to locate their positions.... But it was obvious that radio could not be dispensed with entirely. The signals from the U-boats contained the information upon which was based the planning and control of those combined attacks which alone held the promise of really great success against the concentrated shipping of any enemy convoy."

He concluded: "Whether and to what extent the enemy reacted to radio transmissions was something which, try as we might, we were never able to ascertain with any certainty. In a number of cases drastic alterations in the course of a convoy led us to assume that he did. On the other hand, many cases occurred in which, in spite of U-boat activity in the area, enemy ships sailing independently, and convoys as well, were allowed to sail straight on into the same area in which only shortly before sinkings and even convoy battles had taken place."

In preparation for this war of words, Doenitz had his scientists work out complicated communication techniques and instrumentation. A special radio station, called *Goliath*, was built near Frankfurt-on-the-Oder, and a technique was developed that enabled the U-boat to transmit from below the surface, at a depth of five to fifteen feet.

Boats sailing through the North Sea to their operational areas in the Atlantic kept radio silence while navigating the British mine-fields, but as soon as they were clear of them, they were obliged to contact headquarters and check in. The system was spelled out in a special directive Doenitz issued to his commanders. It read:

"*In the actual operational area:* Radio to be used only for the transmission of tactically important information, or when ordered to do so by the U-boat Command, or when the position of the transmitter is in any case already known to the enemy.

"*En route to or from the patrol area:* As above. Signals of lesser importance may be sent, but only very occasionally; in this connection care must be taken that the transmission does not compromise the area for other U-boats either already in the area or on their way to it.

"*Technical:* Frequent changes of wavelengths, additional wavebands, and wireless discipline to add to the enemy's difficulties with direction finders."

Special cipher was then developed for these transmissions—the so-called "unbreakable cipher"—and a kind of microdotting was introduced with the "squirt" transmissions in which lengthy messages could be compressed into brief signals, some lasting only for a few seconds while telling quite a lot. This was done to expose the transmitters as briefly as possible and make direction finding difficult, if not impossible.

The British needed some time to organize a system of their own to "bug" Doenitz. It is possible that their initial inefficiency and gropings were instrumental in persuading Doenitz that he had nothing to fear. Early in the war, U-Boat Command watched very carefully, as he himself put it, for any indication that the Admiralty was making use of direction finders to locate U-boats from their transmissions. During the first months of the war, they had no particular cause for anxiety on this score, because British direction finding was far from precise and no well-organized effort was made as yet to spot the U-boats by those means. Thus Doenitz was justified when he wrote in the War Diary:

"As far as we have been able to check, errors in D-F are in proportion to the distance from the enemy coast, and at a distance of some 300 miles the average error is 60-80 miles. Often it is considerably greater. The best result of D-F that had come to our knowledge showed an error of 30 miles, and that was in close proximity to the coast of western France. The largest error was one of 320 miles at an approximate distance of 600 miles."

After such reassurances, and being convinced that the radio link was indispensable, U-Boat Command made no further comprehensive effort to explore the enemy's progress in direction finding. The U-Boat Arm developed into the most gabby military organization in all the history of war. The wolfpack technique did necessitate a lot of use of the radio: the patrol boat making the first sighting had to report it to headquarters, then U-Boat Command had to alert and gather together the other U-boats in the area and egg them on to the convoy. When the wolfpack was assembled, the Germans broke radio silence again to report themselves ready to begin the attack, and then stayed on the air, giving a blow by blow description of the ensuing bout. The battle over, they went on the air to call in their claims, because Doenitz could not wait upon the return of his boats to get the results.

Much nonsense and useless information was also put on the air, U-boats breaking radio silence on the slighest provocation, to report a toothache on board or congratulate a friend at headquarters on his birthday. U-boat transmissions were unmistakable. They invariably began with a set Morse symbol—the *B-Bar.*

At noon on June 30, 1942, Lieutenant Richard E. Schreder, USN, flying a Mariner on submarine patrol out of Bermuda, received a call from Commander W. A. Thorn, his squadron leader, alerting him to a U-boat about fifty miles way. "It's a sure thing, Dick!" Thorn said. "If you don't kill him, I'll kill you!"

Thorn told Schreder in no uncertain terms where he could find that U-boat. "The S.O.B. is at lat. 33° N. long. 67° 30′ W," he said, "a hundred and thirty miles west-south west of St. Georges. Now go and get it!"

Dick Schreder flew to the spot and sure enough, found the U-boat within ten miles of the position. It was the *U-158* of Korvetten-Kapitaen Erwin Rostin, just loafing on the surface, its crew sunbathing on deck. Before the boat could crash dive, Schreder was on top of it. He dropped two demolition bombs, then a couple of depth charges, and one of the latter fell on the superstructure. It detonated just as the *U-Rostin* was trying to dive. It went down allright, but it never came up. The *U-158* perished with all hands on board.

There was not a single Allied observer within hundreds of miles of the *U-Rostin* when its position was suddenly established. It was not actually seen by any unauthorized eye on its leisurely cruise. How was it possible, then, to ascertain its position with such amazing accuracy? The answer is the story of the Huffduff.

Huffduff

In the morning of June 12, in accordance with his standing instructions, Rosten called his home office on his short-wave radio just to report that he had nothing to report. His transmission was picked up in Germany by *Goliath*, but also by Allied stations in Bermuda, Hartlant Point, Kingston and Georgetown. The ranges they got were sent to the U.S. Naval Operating Base in Bermuda where HF/DF specialists, plotting the bearings, came up with a deadly fix. Their finding was sent to Rear Admiral A. D. Bernhard, USN, Commander Patrol Operations, who in turn passed it on to Thorn, whose Mariner with Schreder in the cockpit was closest to the U-boat. It was as simple as that. The entire operation, from the pick-up of the first bearing to the kill, lasted three hours.

Schreder was justly credited with the kill, but a number of others also had a hand in it. They were the anonymous— and "classified"—men of a secret fraternity working at a string of outposts from Jan Mayen, a narrow strip of barren tundra land in the Arctic Ocean, all the way to tropical Bahia in Brazil. This was the Allied network of Huffduff stations.

Huffduff was used as a teammate of radar and sound devices which, however, spotted the targets at a much shorter distance only. With Huffduff the sky was the limit and that made it the basic tool of anti-loop-finder that fishermen and other ships use to get cross-bearings on submarine intelligence. The technical principle was as simple as the radio beams. But instead of getting the bearings from known shore stations, the network maintained direction-finders at a number of coastal stations to get cross-bearings on subs that talked to other subs or reported to U-Boat Command. The device picked up any voice or code signal transmitted on the international shortwave communications channels, and within a split second visually showed the direction of the signal's source. When two or more Huffduff units ashore or afloat got such bearings, it was a simple mathematical exercise for a control center to determine where the lines of direction met on the earth's surface. This fix usually proved accurate within miles at long distance and could be sharpened by getting more or closer bearings.

Radio direction finders were in use before World War II, but they were slow and subject to a multitude of errors. The British began improving Huffduff immediately after the outbreak of the war, but even in 1941 the technology of this crucial detection method was rather crude. One of the first shipboard direction finders was installed on HMS *Hesperus* in the spring of 1941, but it proved poor and unreliable. Then the Canadians produced a device that recorded the bearings semi-automatically. The United States developed one that plotted the bearings geometrically. The finished Huffduff eventually overcame all the problems of correction and provided a device which automatically scanned the entire horizon twenty times a second. This speed completely crossed up the strategy of the U-Boat Command which persisted in the belief that the Allies only had old-fashioned types of manually turned detectors.

The Huffduff network began in the United Kingdom with the establishment of stations from the Shetlands to Land's End, and even that provided a good basis for D/F in a westerly direction. Then other stations were erected, on Iceland, Greenland and Newfoundland, until they covered the whole North Atlantic. The later American network tied in with the British. In the end, we had four major nets: the British, the one in Iceland, another in Africa, and one in Brazil.

The American part of the operation converged on a Huffduff nerve center at a carefully guarded spot in Maryland to which the nets sent in their findings by a special reporting procedure. From Maryland, the reports were flashed to a super-secret communications center on Nebraska Avenue in Washington, D.C.—melodramatically identified as "X"—where Commander Knight McMahon prepared the initial plot and sent it on to Commander Knowles. It was the first of a series of plots. When others—like the British plot, for example—also arrived, a master plot was prepared and sent to the fleet in top operational priority messages.

Using the most up-to-the-minute means of communications from pneumatic tubes to Telefax facsimile transmitters, the whole procedure required only fifteen to thirty minutes. Often a fix obtained hundreds of miles from Knowles' desk, and processed in several stages, reached CINCLANT within a single hour. The traffic was handled by watch officers unless certain doubts arose or bearings had some special significance. Then Knowles himself, or Parsons, handled the plot with the help of their Huffduff specialists.

Within this outer procedure was an inner procedure that not only sharpened the fixes but pinpointed the information they inherently contained. Huffduffing became an art in the hands of its British and American virtuosos. After a while the form and nature of recurrent signals became familiar to the Allied monitors and they could add such information as "U-boats report sighting of convoy" or "U-boats going into attack," without actually breaking the German code. Using an especially intricate method called "fingerprinting," which distinguished the touch on the Morse key of one operator from another, even the identity of given U-boats could be established. The peculiarities of a signal transmitted on a wet aerial indicated that the U-boat had just surfaced. It was possible to keep transmissions apart and then establish the number of U-boats in individual concentrations with a reasonable degree of accuracy. By tuning in on individual subs and analyzing their successive transmissions, it could be established how fast they were moving and in what direction, how long they operated submerged and, most important, the area where they were operating.

In order to take all doubt out of the system and make the fingerprinting yield better results, the so-called "Tina" was developed. Oscillographs spread out the tone of the transmissions and clearly indicated the differences between several different transmissions. This was especially important when several U-boats operated in close proximity and it was difficult to keep them apart by the fixes alone.

How accurate was the Huffduff and how close to the target did it hit? Readers of Professor Morison's history of the Atlantic battle may get the impression that it was not too accurate and that often it missed the target by an appallingly large margin. He pointed out time and again how far off Tenth Fleet plots, based on fixes, turned out to be and how exasperated the fleet sometimes became when it was sent on wild goose chases with erroneous bearings.

In actual fact, the Huffduff was amazingly accurate even when it was "a hundred miles off." In the beginning, before Dr. Harry Goldstein, a civilian scientist at the Naval Research Laboratory, succeeded in developing an improved American version of a British model, the accuracy of Huffduff left much to be desired, but then it did not yet matter too much. Prompt action to run down Huffduff bearings required an enormous and exceptionally mobile combat organization, very fast ships and especially planes. Up to May, 1943, we did not have any too many of them, and so the majority of the long-range Huffduff bearings went to waste. Later, however, when fast forces were available in adequate numbers and they were properly deployed in accordance with Tenth Fleet's master plot, the accuracy of Huffduff improved vastly. With planes capable of making enormously broad sweeps within given areas, a Huffduff plot within fifty miles of the target was enough to enable the patrol pilot to find the U-boat. In this sense, plots locating the target within 100 miles were accepted as accurate. Huffduff plots remained invaluable when Doenitz saw the light at last and ordered a radical curbing of U-boat transmissions; and even when the appearance of the snorkeling boats reduced transmissions to a minimum.

Of course, important as it was, Huffduff was but one of the means at Commander Knowles' disposal to procure necessary intelligence. While he himself did not go into the cloak-and-dagger phase of the intelligence activity, he had full access to the British data and to that assembled by the Special Activities Branch of the Office of Naval Intelligence which dealt with *live* U-boat men—the growing number of prisoners of war.

The Secret of the Zaunkoenig

Op-16-Z of Commander Riheldaffer served as Knowles' liaison, so to speak, to the U-boat men. Its intelligence reports for Tenth Fleet, procured through the skilled, scientific interrogation of prisoners, produced information, both in quality and quantity, that no agent or army of agents could have procured even from inside the *Sardinen-Schloesschen* in Lorient or the Hotel am Steinplatz in Berlin.

The close and smooth cooperation of Knowles' Atlantic Section and the Special Activities Branch of ONI yielded many dividends, but none was more valuable than the first documented intelligence report that exploded one of Doenitz's greatest secrets of the whole war and his potentially most dangerous new weapon—the acoustic torpedo.

In the second half of 1942, Doenitz was troubled by the continuing inadequacy of this torpedoes that, he believed, had cut his victories in half. On June 24, 1942, when those inadequate torpedoes were raising havoc with our shipping, Doenitz wrote in a report: "After two and a half years of failures, experiments, set-backs and improvements, and in spite of our most strenuous endeavors, the depth-keeping gear and the firing device of our torpedoes today are not as efficient as were those in 1918 . . . . The explosive and destructive effectiveness of the torpedo— when used with contact pistol—are inadequate, as has been proved by the inumerable cases in which several torpedoes have been required to sink an ordinary freighter." He figured out that between January and June, 1942, his U-boats needed 816 torpedo hits to sink 404 ships.

His concern about the old torpedoes was overshadowed by his interest in a new one, one of the fiendish *Wunderwaffen* (wonder weapons) Germany began to produce in growing varieties. The new torpedo steered directly at the sound of an escort's screws. Equipped with it, his U-boats could engage a destroyer bows on and hit it. They would score even if aimed inaccurately or fired from an unfavorable position.

The first *Zaunkoenigs*—as the wonder torpedo was called—were delivered in August, 1943, and Doenitz hoarded them for a grand opening. He assembled twenty-one boats in a *Rudel* called *Leuthen*, loaded them with the *Zaunkoenigs* and directed them to form "a north-south patrol line seventeen miles apart, starting at a point about 500 miles east of Cape Farewell, in order to straddle the great circle route between Halifax and the United Kingdom."

"The Fuehrer is watching every phase of your struggle," he radioed to the group. "Attack, follow up, sink!"

The group sortied on September 9, and on September 20, Convoy ON-202 of forty-one ships with a screen of two destroyers, a frigate and three corvettes, ran right smack into them. Then another westbound convoy, ON-18, comprised of twenty-five ships and nine escorts, also had the misfortune to bump into the *Leuthen*.

It was 5:56 in the afternoon of the twentieth when the *Zaunkoenig* had its baptism of fire. Kapitaenleutnant Horst Rendtel in *U-641* yelled out the order: "*Rohr Eins . . . Achtung! . . . Torr-peedo . . . Los!*" Lured by the sound of HMCS *St. Croix's* propeller, the *Zaunkoenig* hit the Canandian destroyer, but Rendtel needed a second "wren" to sink her.

Then at 8:30 P.M., the British corvette *Polyanthus* was zaunkoeniged with such telling force that she disintegrated completely. The battle continued unabated, now under Doenitz's personal direction by radio. At 9:55 P.M. on September 22, the *U-666* of Oberleutnant Willberg fired a *Zaunkoenig* into the *Itchen*. It exploded the corvette's magazine and sank her in a technicolor drama of red and blue flames. From the crews of these three victims of the *Zaunkoenig*, only three men survived.

The battle ended on September 24, when the convoys received ample air cover from America and Doenitz thought it expedient to withdraw the *Rudel*. He could hardly wait for the report of his U-boats and when they arrived, Doenitz was jubilant. The *Zaunkoenig* had proved itself in action. A new chapter had just been opened in the Atlantic battle. A *Sondermeldung* straight from U-Boat Command headquarters announced that in the four-day engagement, the *Rudel* had lost but two of its members, but "destroyed" twelve of the fifteen escorts with the new torpedo and sank "nine merchantmen" with the old convenionals. Doenitz was back in fool's paradise! In actual fact., the two convoys lost but six freighters, and three escort vessels: the *St. Croix*, the *Polyanthus* and the *Itchen*.

This was the grandiose beginning of the highly touted *Zaunkoenig*, and it was also the beginning of its end. Even in the next convoy battle, it proved a dud—not because there was anything wrong with it— but because we had its secret.

How did we know it?

On July 13, northwest of Cape Verdes, a Wildcat Avenger from the escort carrier *Core* sighted the *U-487* of Oberleutnant Konstantin Metz, a new 1600-ton supply boat, lingering on the surface, its crew engaged in pulling a wayward bale of cotton on board for want of anything better with which they could have amused themselves. Although they quickly recovered their composure and even succeeded in shooting down the Wildcat, their fate was sealed. A team of three planes now led by Lieutenant Commander Charles W. Brewer, USN, the squadron commander, dropped four bombs on them and the U-boat went down rather unceremoniously.

The *Core* group recovered thirty-three survivors and their shock interrogation revealed that one of them was a chief torpedo mate who had been recently transfered to the *U-487* from the Torpedo Experimental Establishment at Kiel. By the time the survivors arrived at Fort Hunt, Op-16-Z's super-secret interrogation center near Washington, the torpedo mate had a tag on him. Prisoners of war with any specialized knowledge were singled out and subjected to interrogation-in-depth by specialists; and now, with rumors about a new wonder torpedo floating about, this particular C.P.O. was worth his weight in gold.

While he readily conceded that he had served a tour of duty at Kiel, he refused to reveal anything beyond that. His interrogator was a young lieutenant (j.g.), "Z's" torpedo specialist. Although he was a school teacher in civilan life, he knew as much about the ordinary German "fish" as the torpedo mate, if not more, but did not yet have the specifications of the *Zaunkoenig*, a secret every Allied Intelligence agency was breaking its neck to get. The j.g. had plenty of savvy and also knew his Germans. When he could not get anywhere with the chief mate, he switched to casual conversation, subtly teasing the strapping U-boat man.

"Well," he said, "I really don't care if you won't say anything at all. First of all, there is little if anything we don't know about the U-Waffe; and second of all, Doenitz has nothing anyway he could use to turn the tide which, as you undoubtedly know, is running heavily against you in the *Atlantikschlacht.*"

As he continued in this vein, he could see how the German was getting red in his face, hot under the collar, and restive at the edge of his chair.

"What are you talking about?!" the chief mate blurted out at last when he could no longer take it. "We have something that will sink every one of your *verfluchte* destroyers!"

"Oh, yes," the young American shot back a bit contemptuously, flaunting his omniscience. "I know what you've in mind. I bet you're thinking of the *Zaunkoenig!*" Then, as he watched the German paling at the mentioning of the word, he added: "It's a *Wunderwaffe* allright—it'll be a *wunder* if it works."

This was entirely too much for the cornered mate. Provoked beyond endurance, he blurted out the details of the acoustic torpedo to prove to that *verfluchte Amerikaner* that it would work, too! He showed such detailed knowledge of the new weapon that he was promptly transferred to the Tenth Fleet where he was taken in tow by scientists from its Antisubmarine Warfare Operations Research Group. Prodded by them, the man agreed to sit down at a draftboard and draw a sketch of the torpedo from memory.

The information was then rushed to Dr. Robert M. Elliott and Dr. Edwin A. Uehling, at the National Defense Research Council. They produced the FXR or "Foxer" gear. It was a simple device, consisting of a pair of noise-makers towed some distance astern which would attract the acoustic device of the torpedo and lead it astray. It was cumbersome at first and the fleet hated to use it. The scientists were put back to work and produced a simpler version, called CAT, which used only one noise-maker.

"One of the great achievements of scientists in the war," wrote James Phinney Baxter, 3rd, in his report on the Office of Scientific Research and Development, "lay in the anticipation of enemy moves and the devising of countermeasures against them." In the case of *Zaunkoenig*, it was the Special Activities Branch of ONI that supplied the data which enabled the scientists to devise their countermeasures.

"Intelligence" is a many-splendoured thing. In one sense, it is our capacity to understand and manage ideas. In another sense, it is functional information the probability and plausibility, the meaning and importance of which is duly established and evaluated, and which is then disseminated to people who need it most and can make the best possible use of it. The "intelligence" which Commanders Knowles and Riheldaffer handled so intelligently was, of course, in the latter category. While it proved invaluable for the success of the Tenth Fleet, and the anti-U-boat campaign in general, it aided the effort only up to a certain point. Beyond that, other endeavors were needed to clinch victory in the Battle of the Atlantic.

The Battle of Wits and Devices

Early in October, 1943, the Huffduff network picked up a number of U-boat transmissions from a broad area in the North Atlantic. When the various intercepts were correlated in Tenth Fleet, the pattern emerging from the collation of all pertinent data indicated that a *Rudel* was in the making dangerously close to Iceland, apparently in the paths of two convoys, the westbound ON-204 and the eastbound SC-143. The plot was sent to the Iceland command, and American and British planes were dispatched immediately to track down the U-boats the Tenth Fleet suspected in the area.

The conclusion deduced from the intercepts turned out to be correct. The U-boats were there! They belonged to a group named *Rossbach* (after Frederick the Great's famous come-back battle). They were being assembled against those two convoys to whose departure a few days before, from Halifax and Liverpool respectively, the B-Service of German cryptoanalists had alerted the U-Boat command. The B-Service then supplied further aid to *Rossbach* in the form of accurate tactical information, culled from other intercepts the B-men continued to decrypt.

Both sides thus had ample intelligence to guide them. But while data at the disposal of the Germans was specific and precise, enabling them to make their dispositions with a sure hand, the information the Allies had about *Rossbach* was generic and conjectural at best. It needed a lot of sharpening before it could be used. The planes from Iceland had to patrol a vast ocean area to find the U-boats of the *Rudel*, in something like 10,000 square miles of water.

Nevertheless, in the afternoon of October 4, Commander Charles L. Westhofen, USN, of Bomber Squadron-128, found the very U-boat

Doenitz had delegated to locate the convoys and keep contact during the assembly of the group. It was the *U-335* of Kapitaenleutnant Hans Hunger. Westhofen came upon it some 230 miles southwest of Reykavik. Sixty-five miles westward of and but two hours after this sighting, a British Liberator spotted another member of *Rossbach,* the *U-279,* commanded by Kapitaenleunant Otto Finke. Then at dawn, 160 miles southwest of Iceland, a British Hudson spotted yet another member of the group, the *U-389* of Kapitaenleutnant Siegfried Heilmann.

The search that began in the afternoon of October 4 resulted in the destruction of these three U-boats by the morning after, and the threat to ON-204 was averted. By October 9, the heat was taken off the other convoy as well, when three additional members of *Rossbach* were found and sunk, leaving but two of the original group, the *U-378* and the *U-645,* to escape unharmed. Thus the group lost six boats in exchange for a single merchantman, the American *Yorkmar,* and the Polish destroyer *Orkan,* which Kapitaenleutnant Erich Maeder in *U-378* hit fatally in the after magazine with a single torpedo strike.

The intelligence which the Knowles organization had developed from those scattered Huffduff intercepts was undoubtedly the seed from which this astounding victory had grown. However, it was one thing to establish the presence of those boats in a general area and another to track them down, one by one, for the kill. In the search for U-boats in the vast ocean areas, Huffduff-inspired intelligence, the eagle eyes of lookouts, even the keener feelers of radar and sonar proved to be of only limited effectiveness. The finding of the U-boats with pinpoint accuracy could not be left to chance encounters. Something was needed to sharpen the search, a firmly fixed, simple and practical system to lead the hunters to their quarry.

Out of the recognition of the need a complex scientific enterprise developed in which electronic devices and other means were manipulated somewhat in the manner in which a hand of cards is used to its best advantage in a brisk poker game. Set search patterns were devised and the so-called *"planned search"* replaced haphazard groping known as *"general search."*

In "general search" the planes had to go out on patrol missions just to look around in the hope of finding stray U-boats. But following directions in "planned search," they could home-in on the U-boats intelligence suspected in given areas. The latter was the scientific distillation of all sorts of data. It was based on a study of the basic laws of sighting, for instance; on deductions from combat experiences; on the computation of both known factors and various imponderables; on guesses and hunches, on chance and probability calculations; and on laboratory experiments.

In order to devise a search plan for a plane like Commander Westhofen's Ventura, the range at which a submarine could be detected had to be established; from that finding and the plane's speed, the course had to be deduced that held out the best chance of leading to the U-boat. Such elaborate calculations could not be expected to be made by busy pilots in their cockpits, flying their missions. They had to be reduced to simple rules and tables from pages and pages of graphs and calculations.

Westhofen conducted such a "planned search" and found the *U-336*. He then used still another scientific trick—or "gambit," as it was called—to destroy it. When his Ventura burst out of the clouds, Kapitaenleutnant Hunger promptly dived. Westhofen then retired over the horizon, but only to induce the U-boat to surface again, now that it seemed the danger had passed. Hunger fell for the trick, as did many U-boat skippers both before and after him. He surfaced exactly as and where Westhofen expected, exposing himself to the depth charge attack the shrewdly returning Ventura held ready for exactly this eventuality.

Both the search plan that led Westhofen to *U-336* and the gambit that enabled him to bag the boat had been developed by scientists specializing in the problems of the U-boat war. The "inventor" of the planned search was Dr. George E. Kimball, a distinguished mathematician. The scholar who figured out the "continuous gambit tactics" for aircraft was Dr. Jacinto Steinhardt, a chemist. They belonged to a small group of scientific workers engaged in an intricate and unique effort to integrate science into the war machine as a quasi-operational arm of the war machine itself.

The Wizards' War

This was an important phase of what Churchill called the "Wizard War"—a secret war, as he put it, whose battles were lost or won unknown to the public. "No such warfare had ever been waged, by mortal men," he wrote. "The terms in which it could be recorded or talked about were unintelligible to ordinary folk. Yet if we had not mastered its profound meaning and used its mysteries even while we saw them only in the glimpse, all the efforts . . . would have been in vain."

The value and significance of this extraordinary venture was attested by Admiral King. In his wrap-up report of the war at sea, he paid unstinting tribute to a group of men who "formed an integral part of the Navy" but "remained civilians" throughout the war, and who enabled the United States Navy "to maintain the technical advantage over the navies of our enemies, which contributed so materially to the outcome of World War II."

Even before American participation in the war, the Navy had come to the conclusion that scientific aid for the development of weapons and devices met only part of the bill. "The complexity of modern warfare in both methods and means," King wrote, "demands exacting analysis of the measures and countermeasures introduced at every stage by ourselves and the enemy. Scientific research cannot only speed the invention and production of weapons, but also assist in insuring the correct use."

The initial impulse to form a group of qualified scientists, to apply the scientific method to the improvement of naval operating techniques and material came from Captain Wilder DuPuy Baker, USN, a suave and erudite Kansan, Annapolis 1914, whose broad vision and energy had triggered the ASW effort. In April 1942, with the cooperation of the Antisubmarine Division of the National Defense Research Committee, he enlisted the services of seven scientists to conduct what became known as "operations research" for Baker's Antisubmarine Warfare Unit in the Atlantic Fleet (see page 142). The group continued intact when Baker went to sea, on December 5, 1942, in command of the battleship *North Carolina*. In July, 1943, when it consisted of about forty members, it was incorporated into the staff of the new Tenth Fleet.

Called "Asworg"—short for Antisubmarine Warfare Operations Research Group—it became, as Admiral Low expressed it, one of the pillars on which the American ASW effort rested. From July 1943 to October 1944 (when the decline of the U-boat menace in the Atlantic and the intensification of the naval war in the Pacific necessitated its transfer to the Readiness Division of COMINCH), it played as significant and frequently as dominant a role in Low's think factory as Commander Knowles' Intelligence Section. It remained a small and tight organization throughout the war. At the close of it, it still had only seventy-three scientists. They were drawn from a wide variety of backgrounds. Only a few of them were experts in such pertinent specialties as radar, ordnance, or underwater sound. The group consisted of physicists, mathematicians, chemists, biologists, geologists; of actuaries recruited from six of the largest insurance companies; and even had a chess champion among its members. They were chosen as Dr. Steinhardt put it, "for their general scientific training" and their ability to adhere to the principle of "applying the scientific approach, analytical, statistical and technical, to naval operations."

Throughout the war, Asworg was directed by Professor Philip McCord Morse, a research physicist who specialized in the problems of sound. From 1940 to 1942, he was director of the Sound Project at the Massachusetts Institute of Technology for the Navy's Bureau of Ships. Dr. Morse was ideally qualified to skipper Asworg, by more than just topnotch scientific competence. He had the perfect personality a civilian needed to survive and succeed in the Navy where there was traditional suspicion of eggheads. Morse succeeded in "selling" Asworg even to the most hidebound brass, by adhering to the principle that "no scientist was to claim credit for anything, since he took no responsibility for the ultimate decision" and that the duty of the Asworg man was "simply to help the fighting Navy to improve its antisubmarine technique."

Operations Research in Action

Some members of the group worked at Washington, in close proximity to Tenth Fleet and intimate collaboration with Admiral Low whose intellectual qualities and high regard for the "scientific method" made smooth cooperation a foregone fact and kept morale in Asworg perennially high. Low's personal liaison to Asworg was Dr. Steinhardt, a graduate chemist from Columbia University. He was engaged in research in several universities, as well as the National Bureau of Standards, before becoming one of the original members of Captain Baker's Operations Research Group in 1942. In Asworg, he did research work in anti-submarine operations and planning, air search, naval air warfare, and anti-aircraft fire with the fleets both in the Atlantic and Pacific.

Others were attached, as the need arose, to the staffs of fleet and type commanders, or worked at operating bases in war theatres. Under orders from Admiral King himself, they were afforded opportunity to observe combat operations at first hand. To study the effectiveness of attacks on U-boats, one member of Asworg crossed the Atlantic with the first American destroyer escort group that accompanied a convoy to England. Another made a combat trip on a baby flattop to North Africa. Others served on destroyers and destroyer escorts to study depth charges and depth bombs, and helped in improving the weapons and in working out the most effective ways of dropping them.

Operations research fell into two main categories: (1) theoretical analysis of strategy and tactics, and of the various implements of war;

and (2) statistical analysis of operations. Naval operations of all kinds were analyzed by members of the group to determine the optimum potentialities of the equipment involved, the probable reaction of the personnel, and the nature of the tactics that promised to combine equipment and personnel in maximum efficiency. Action reports were studied in a quantitative manner in order to amplify or correct the theoretical analysis with what was actually happening on the fields of battle.

The knowledge that emerged from this continuous cross-check of theory with practice made it possible, as Admiral King put it, to work out improvements which sometimes increased the effectiveness of weapons by factors of three or five; to detect changes in the enemy's tactics in time to counter them before they became dangerous; and to calculate force requirements for future operations. This was a crucial facet of World War II which was the first war in history in which the interplay of new technical measures and opposing counter-measures attained enormous significance with direct influence on victory or defeat.

"In this see-saw of techniques," King observed, "the side which countered quickly, before the opponent had time to perfect the new tactics and weapons, had a decided advantage. Operations research, bringing scientists in to analyze the technical import of the fluctuations between measure and countermeasure, made it possible to speed up our reaction rate in several critical cases."

The classic example of this was Asworg's role in the see-saw battle of radar. Quite early in the anti-U-boat effort, the Allies introduced radar along broad tactical lines, but the Germans were usually quick to counter it with so-called search receivers that betrayed the encroachment. Radar works by sending out a signal from a transmitter, detecting the target through the reflection or echo of this signal. The signal must be powerful or else its echo dies away before getting back to its source. The Germans, therefore, had a very strong signal to work with and found it relatively simple to develop counter-devices which then warned the U-boats of the approach of the Allied planes using radar, even while they were still too far away to receive echoes.

In addition, the Germans also developed devices either to confuse or to neutralize our radar. One such device was the *Aphrodite*, a radar decoy balloon trailed in the wake of the U-boat, whose reflective reaction was similar to the conning tower of a submarine. Thus on August 8, 1943, at the height of the see-saw radar contest, the *U-566* of Kapitaenleutnant Hornkohl, cornered in an uneven action near the

Nantucket Shoals Lightship, escaped from what seemed his inevitable doom by using *Aphrodite*.

The situation confronted the Allies with serious dilemma. They had to decide whether to use radar at all and possibly betray the presence of their antisubmarine planes, or to abandon it altogether and so diminish their chances of locating the U-boats. In order to solve the problem, Admiral Low called in Professor Morse and Dr. Steinhardt and asked them to find an answer to the troublesome question.

Asworg tackled the problem by first making an analysis of the contacts between aircraft and U-boats, in order to establish with mathematical certainty how often the Germans did in fact succeed in detecting our approaching planes on their search receivers. Then, comparing these findings with what could be mathematically expected, they sought the measure of the change we would have had to make in our tactics and doctrines. The initial solution proposed was not too encouraging. Asworg recommended that we restrict the older type radar to "the conditions under which it [was] needed most, i.e., when visibility [was] poor or at night." In addition, several (largely unsatisfactory) methods were recommended to use radar so as to deceive the U-boats about the tactics of the planes, These recommendations represented half measures or, *in extremis,* meant the renunciation of radar.

It became imperative to device a radar which the most up-to-date German devices could not detect. Using the Asworg data, the laboratories in the United States and Britain developed the microwave air search radar (SCR-517 and 717, the ASG and others). It took the Germans a year even to find out about the mere existence of this device, and then only by a chance event—by capturing a gear almost intact from a British plane that crashed in the Netherlands near Rotterdam. Then they had to toil for months to develop something to counter the dreaded new radar they called the *Rotterdam Geraet.* After that, the Allied radar policy had to be subjected to another reconsideration, but by then the tide of the U-boat war had been stemmed, and no major crisis was expected from even the most widespread and efficient use of the *Naxos*, for example, one of the German anti-microwave radar search receivers.

"In all this battle of wits and devices," Dr. Steinhardt wrote in his report on the role of operations research in the Navy, "the ORG played a multiple role. First there was the analysis of the contacts between planes and U-boats mentioned above. Then by consulting with the laboratory scientists they learned the limitations of the various devices and so could advise on tactics to be used in flying. Finally the [Asworg] men at the Navy test stations helped in the development and testing of mock-ups of the German instruments."

Another vital phase of the U-boat war posed the problem of bringing convoys safely across the Atlantic. Asworg analyzed information produced by the numerous convoy battles which took place both prior and subsequent to our entry into the war, to establish the basic principles underlying this type of warfare. L. A. Halloway, an Asworg man working with British scientists in London discovered that "the total number of ships lost in each battle was about the same, however many were present in the convoy." From this Halloway concluded that convoys could be made larger without any increase in casualties. As a result of his discovery, the number of ships in each convoy was increased until they reached an average of over 100 by the late spring of 1944. This enabled the Allies to sail fewer convoys per month and lessen considerably their losses.

Dr. R. F. Rinehart of Asworg improved the effectiveness of air-umbrellas of the convoys by proving conclusively that they provided less potent protection directly overhead than in front and on flanks. We have seen how Drs. Elliott and Uehling organized the counter-measures which led to the development of the Foxer gears and stymied the *Zaunkoenig*, Doenitz's vaunted acoustic torpedo, as soon as it appeared. They accomplished this by measuring the noises of ships as well as the behavior of all possible or practicable counter-weapons. While these measurements were conducted at several test stations, Asworg men in Washington made a mathematical analysis of the torpedo's behavior, based on what they knew of sound detection under water, and on a close scrutiny of the torpedoings.

In the end, they were able to conclude exactly what the counter-measure should be and how it should be used. The actual development of the various Foxer gears became the job of the laboratories, but Asworg took a hand in the design problem as well.

MAD-Men off the Rock

Between June, 1943, and the spring of 1944, the U-boats were giving us considerable trouble in the Mediterranean. By the end of 1943, they sank some thirty Allied ships, at a time when sinkings in the Atlantic diminished almost to nil. Conventional measures to deal with this menace yielded unsatisfactory results, but then Asworg came to the rescue by devising a complex scheme and means which closed the Mediterranean to the U-boats and eventually terminated German operations in that sea.

These measures were developed by John R. Pellam, the Asworg

scientist stationed at Admiral Hewitt's headquarters at Casablanca. He proceeded from the premise that since the U-boats had to enter the Mediterranean through the Strait of Gibraltar, we had to deny the Strait to them to prevent them from reaching their stations. However, the boats had instructions to make the passage through the Strait fully submerged. So it was concluded at first that aircraft could not be of much help to take them out, if only because they could not spot them. Pellam then hit upon the idea that certain planes of Navy squadrons VP-63 and VB-127, which Hewitt had in his area, could do the job, especially if equipped with a certain secret weapon. He discussed his ideas with Hewitt and also with the British staff at Gibraltar, then made a trip through the Strait in a submerged British submarine to see how the U-boats had to do it.

Thus gaining a comprehensive overview of the whole situation, Pellam devised a scheme. First he picked the best place and time for flying the patrols. Then he arranged for the cooperation of British surface units. Finally he brought the mysterious device into play. It was the MAD (short for Magnetic Airborne Detector), a magnetic "divining rod" so sensitive that tests with the instrument once were confounded by the presence of a bit of steel needle broken off in the finger of a laboratory assistant.

Informally called the "aerial doodle bag," it was a magnetometer or measurer of minute quantities of magnetism. It was one of the war's most closely guarded secrets, although its basic principles are known to every high-school boy. It works by recording the magnetic lines of force passing near any piece of steel or iron, however large or small, because steel or iron has the property of concentrating those magnetic lines of force.

Work on MAD began early in 1941 by a group of scientists organized by Columbia University's Air Instruments Laboratory working with specialists at the Bell Telephone Laboratories and various Naval research installations. Pearl Harbor accelerated the work, but it was not until the end of 1942, that enough of the instruments became available to equip patrol planes and blimps on duty in the Atlantic.

Pellam found MAD ideal for the operation he had in mind because the small, round-nosed, bomb-like device, towed at the end of a long cable from an airplane in flight over water, proved infallible in detecting submerged submarines. In the case of such submerged subs, the large mass of their metal attracts and "concentrates" some of the earth's natural magnetism above the surface of the sea. When this happens, the magnetic "ear" of the detector suspended beneath the plane passes through this area of concentrated magnetism, a delicate needle swings upward on a scale, and the submarine's presence is betrayed. It is then left to other flights over the area to locate the submarine exactly and to attack it when found.

By early January, 1944, the Pellam plan was worked out in minute detail, and a trap was set by combined air and sea forces, both British and American, to catch any U-boat trying to sneak into the Mediterranean. On February 24, then, the MAD operator in a plane of Patrol Squadron-63 flying over the Strait, suddenly saw the needle swinging on the scale, unmistakable indication of a submerged U-boat below. It did not take long for units of an Anglo-American air-sea force the patrol plane had summoned to the spot to locate the submarine and sink it, even before its crew knew what hit them. It turned out to be the *U-761*, commanded by Oberleutnant Horst Geider. It perished just below the Rock, after it had successfully negotiated the Strait, presumably the most perilous part of its passage. On March 16, the Pellam plan led to the sinking of the *U-392*, skippered by Oberleutnant Henning Schuemann, even before it could reach the Strait; and then also of *U-731* of Oberleutnant Alexander Count Keller, inside the Mediterranean, when Keller must have thought he was over the hump.

Doenitz Had Nothing Like It

Tenth Fleet through Asworg thus made a major contribution to the decisive defeat of Doenitz in the Mediterranean, when all other measures failed to put an end to his operations in that sea. It was the Pellam plan utilizing the magnetic airborne detector that put the absolute seal on the Strait of Gibraltar. After Normandy, part of the U-boat fleet was bottled up in the Mediterranean and remained there to the bitter end, thanks to the unceasing vigilance of the MAD-men John Pellam of Asworg had mobilized in an almost single-handed effort to end the war in the Mediterranean long before the U-Boat Arm was prepared to concede defeat.

Admiral Low, a discreet and taciturn man by nature who enforced the strictest secrecy about the operations of Tenth Fleet, drew an especially dense curtain around Asworg, to assure our advantage in this interplay of measures and countermeasures. Assuming that everything we had to harm them the Germans also possessed to do damage to us, Low frequently asked Morse or Steinhardt: "Do you think Doenitz has an Asworg of his own?" Deducing their answer from several glaring mistakes Doenitz had made, they assured him that Asworg was unique and indigenous to Tenth Fleet. "Nothing in Doenitz's measures indicates," Steinhardt told Low, "that he ever makes a careful analysis of his operational results or that he employs a group of scientists such as we have in Asworg."

In actual fact, the U-Boat Command had a scientific research committee, so called, under Professor Kuepfmueller, a distinguished electronic engineer. It was set up in the wake of the introduction of our airborne microwave radar, when several U-boats on war patrols reported to Doenitz that their search receiver, the Metox (which the Germans had obtained from the French Navy by courtesy of Admiral Darlan), frequently failed to warn them of the approach of Allied aircraft.

Now Doenitz had to face the kind of dilemma we confronted when his increasingly sophisticated detecting and decoy devices virtually nullified the effectiveness of our old radar. Doenitz called in Kuepfmueller and told him bluntly that "the U-boat war would be lost unless an antidote were found to the enemy's radar." The Kuepfmueller organization, that went by the pompous name of *Wissenschaftlicher Fuehrungsstab der Kriegsmarine* (Scientific Leadership-Staff of the Navy), did produce a new search receiver with a greater variety of frequencies that enabled the U-boats to pick up more of our signals and give them an added feeling of security from surprise attacks.

However, it never became as useful to and closely integrated with the U-Boat Command as Asworg was with Tenth Fleet. If he ever fathomed the concept or realized the importance of what King called the interplay of measures and countermeasures, Doenitz certainly never indicated that he appreciated "operations research." Primarily a practical tactician, incapable of grasping the sweeping strategic-operational problems of the U-boat war, he could not bring King's and Low's interest to the scientific aspects of his specialty.

He relied on aides to deal with this important facet of the war—on Kapitaen-zur-See Thedsen, an old shipmate, his chief engineer, and on Kapitaenleutnant Meckel, his communications expert—but the relatively low rank of Thedsen and Meckel indicated *ipso facto* how subordinate they were and how little influence they wielded in the greater order of the U-Boat Command.

Even so, the technological vision and skill innate in Germans aided Doenitz, without an "Asworg" to help, in countering virtually every Allied weapon or equipment in due course and, indeed, in developing innovations in both tactics and techniques which were in turn to baffle us. However, there always was an inevitable time lag between the appearance of the Allies' offensive weapons and the development of the counter-weapons the U-Boat Command eventually succeeded in pitting against them. What could be called the rhythm cycle of weapon development and operations research made all the difference. Aside from a few major innovations, such as the snorkel for which we were but inadequately prepared, we were always slightly ahead in weapon developments and usually had a countermeasure ready for anything Doenitz had conjured up to throw against us. It was this visionary quality which never ceased to animate Asworg that endowed it with a measure of added importance to the anti-submarine effort. Like starry-eyed children who build castles in the sand or tinker up futuristic gadgets, the long-haired scientists, engineers and designers of Asworg lingered in a technological Utopia. However, theirs was a highly pragmatic pastime, for in that scientific twilight zone they sought to anticipate every possible and impossible, plausible and implausible innovation Doenitz would or could devise in the never-ceasing contest of technical evolution.

The value of Asworg to the war effort was attested by Admiral King when he decided to continue it "as part of the naval organization" after the war. Now called Operations Evaluation Group, the old Asworg thus survives "as part of the naval organization," its influence radiating far beyond the confines of the military establishment, as its stock in trade, "operations research," becomes a significant activity in the atomic age. "The techniques and principles of analysis developed by the group during its history have wide application to modern government and industry," wrote Dr. Steinhardt in the conclusion of his report, and one is inclined to add, "to modern life as a whole" as well. He added eloquently: "Briefly, these techniques are those of the competent scientist, applied to a large-scale human operation as a whole, with the aim of fitting the operation to its purpose, and of measuring the effectiveness with which the operation is being carried out."

The pragmatic value of this effort during World War II, as part of Tenth Fleet, was best formulated by Admiral King in his summing-up of naval research of development. He described the assistance the Navy received from science as indispensable. "Without this assistance," he wrote, "many of the weapons which have come into being as the result of intensive wartime research and development never would have been completed and introduced into the fleet."

☆

★

CHAPTER XVII

Global Guerilla War at Sea

On May 20, 1944, the Tenth Fleet was exactly one year old but Admiral Low does not recall that the sentimental significance of the day had occurred to him at all. Nobody in the phantom fleet thought of hoisting a fanciful broom on an imaginary mast, the traditional symbol of the clean sweep. But the twelve months Low and his small band of dedicated men and women had behind them produced some notable victories. The bare record of the various Doenitz offensives showed plainly the magnitude of the Allied accomplishment to which the Tenth Fleet had made as valuable a contribution with its own unorthodox means as any of the hunters and killers afloat.

"A Hell of a Lot to be Thankful For"

The protracted and bitter campaign of the wolfpacks against North Atlantic convoy routes—that flared up with a bang in February-March 1943, subsided in July and flared up again briefly in September—petered out, never to regain its former ferocity.

In the ocean area east of Brazil, the blitz which Admiral Ingram regarded as a personal affront, was checked with such finality that on November 25, in his regular situation conference at Recife, Ingram could indulge in a modest celebration. "Today is Thanksgiving," he told his staff when informed of the sinking of the *U-849* that very morning east of Ascension (the next to last U-boat to perish in his bailiwick). "I don't see any snow or football games, but we have a hell of a lot to be thankful for. In this global war there are lots of worse places to be than here."

This was patently the achievement of Ingram and his gallant Fourth

Fleet. But the tough admiral was the first to concede that the Tenth Fleet, with which his cooperation was avid and smooth, had a crucial share in the remarkable victory.

In the area between the Azores and Freetown, which Doenitz had chosen after the summer disaster of 1943, as a safe hunting ground for his U-boats, his presumtive blitz was aborted, then turned against him. From January 1942 to April 1943, thanks mostly to Dr. Salazar's refusal to let the Allies combat the Germans from bases on Portuguese soil, the U-boats could operate with virtual impunity in this part of the East Atlantic. Even in May, 1943, they still succeeded in sinking ten of our ships. Then their monopoly was terminated abruptly. The American escort carrier groups moved in and, in exemplary collaboration with the Tenth Fleet, seized control of those waters, never to relinquish it again in the war.

This was a remarkable record, to be sure, but the U-boat war was not yet over. If anything it had taken an ominous new turn that kept everybody in the Tenth Fleet far too busy to pay any attention to birthdays. "After the spectacular phase of the anti-U-boat campaign in the Summer of 1943," Admiral Low reflected as he looked back on things past, "we now had to face a novel kind of threat, what you could call a guerilla war, no longer only in the Atlantic Ocean areas, but virtually on all the seven seas."

During those days, even a brief glance at Commander Knowles' big plot showed graphically how the trend had changed in the U-boat war. Gone were the clusters of pins whose very density used to indicate the presence of the boisterous big wolfpacks. Now the map was full of single markers. Admiral Doenitz had his U-boats like so many Jumblies scattered far and few, from the Spanish Main all around the globe to waters close to Japan, from the Arctic Ocean all the way south to the Cape of Good Hope. The *U-154* of Oberleutnant Gerth Gemeiner was raiding fitfully in Panama waters; the *U-218*, with Kapitaenleutnant Rupprecht Stock in command, was trying to sow mines off Trinidad and Puerto Rico; the *U-530* was moving furtively around the Verdes to a rendezvous with a blockade-running Japanese sub, the *I-52*. Other U-boats patrolled as far apart as Flores and the Nantucket Lightship, Madagascar and Baer Island, left to their own resources in *ad hoc* operations that stretched human endurance to the limit.

The tangled tactics of this global guerilla war were as hard on the U-boats' crews as on those who had to fight them. "This unceasing struggle against the dispersed U-boats was a rather tedious chore," Admiral Low recalled. "It necessitated the dispersal of our own antisubmarine forces and demanded attention to innumerable minute details. The campaign against the U-boats became far more difficult and taxing than the sweeping measures of 1943."

Low had imbued the Tenth Fleet with a spirit of detached conservatism. Viewing the greater picture of the U-boat war with a sense of proportion, he had no illusions about the state of the enemy or the prospects of the U-boat campaign. He realized that while the fantastic Anglo-American "blitz" of the magic summer had knocked the U-boats off balance and left the U-Boat Arm limp and dazed, it did not destroy the formidable strength—both quantitative and qualitative—Doenitz had succeeded in building into this branch of the *Kriegsmarine*. The *espirit de corps* of the U-boat branch was as fierce as ever, and the morale of its officers and men was unimpaired. In sheer numerical terms, and despite its severe recent losses, the U-Boat Arm was actually stronger than ever. It consisted of hundreds of U-boats, the largest underseas fleet in history. New constructions still outnumbered losses. In the twelve months of the Tenth Fleet's existence, between June 1, 1943, and May 31, 1944, losses totalled 240 boats as against 278 new boats completed and ready for sea, with scores of others in reserve or refitting, or in various stages of completion.

Debacle at Bowmanville

Yet Doenitz had his troubles that the high morale of his "boys" and the numerical strength of the U-Boat Arm could neither obscure nor mitigate. Most of them were old headaches, long masked by spectacular successes, now coming sharply into focus to plague him. His smug faith in the U-boats' technical superiority and, indeed, invulnerability now found him unprepared for the new wonder weapons of the Allies. In the face of the mounting Allied air attacks on the German industrial base, it became increasingly difficult to meet the monthly quota of new constructions, at a time when replacements began to attain crucial importance. Last but not least, Doenitz found it even more difficult to recruit and train a new crop of officers for the exacting U-boat service as casualties bit ever deeper into his manpower reservoir.

His plight on this latter score became amply evident to us in ONI in the most melodramatic episode in the whole cloak-and-dagger history of the U-boat war. From the interrogation of prisoners and scattered agent reports, from Doenitz's own overt efforts to entice young men into the U-Boat Arm, we knew of course that he was experiencing some difficulties with his growing manpower shortage. Then a remarkable scoop scored by an American Intelligence analyst suddenly exposed the true magnitude of his problem, in the desperate nature of a measure to which he had to resort to solve it.

It was Doenitz's habit to keep in close personal touch with his officers in a system of paternalism he cultivated assiduously to maintain high morale and unquestioning loyalty in the U-Boat Arm. He continued this close relationship even with the fallen angels of his command, by conducting a brisk correspondence with his officers in our prisoner-of-war camps. It was the routine job of Lieutenant Victor Taylor, USNR, an alert and imaginative member of Op-16-Z, to keep an eye on this correspondence. In the course of his assignment, Vic Taylor thus read every single letter that passed between Doenitz in Germany and his *hors de combat* officers in the various P/W camps in the United States and Canada.

Most of the time, there was no pay dirt for Taylor in this formal correspondence of seemingly ephemeral pleasantries. For a long time, not even his native ingenuity and probing mind could attribute any special significance to the letters or deduce anything useful from them. But then in January 1944, he hit upon something that seemed to be inconsequential at face value but somehow intrigued Taylor. He found that in the dateline of his epistles Doenitz sometimes spelled out the month in so many letters, but sometimes he abbreviated it by using Roman numerals. Thus some of the letters in this month had "January" spelled out in full while others merely had "I" in their dateline. Assuming that this had some hidden significance, Lieutenant Taylor persuaded Commander Riheldaffer to arrange for a cryptographic examination of this correspondence. It did not take long for the United States Navy's seasoned cryptoanalysts to establish that the letters which bore Roman numerals contained a simple code in their contrived texts.

From the reading of Doenitz's code emerged the contours of a major plot the Grossadmiral himself was hatching in a desperate effort to recover some of his outstanding skippers. He was organizing a mass escape of U-boat officers from the Canadian P/W camp at Bowmanville on Lake Ontario. Doenitz had good reason to concentrate on Bowmanville. It held the greatest aces from the U-boats' proudest days, including the incomparable Kapitaenleutnant Otto Kretschmer, commanding officer of *U-99* that was sunk in March 1941.

Leader of the group was Kapitaenleutnant Werner Heidel, one of the old-timers at Bowmanville whose boat, the *U-55*, was sunk on January 30, 1940, four years before. Others in his group of veteran prisoners of war, who had spent years at Bowmanville and now yearned for the freedom the Doenitz plot had promised, included Kapitaenleutnant

Dietrich von der Ropp whose *U-12* had perished below the white cliffs of Dover on October 8, 1939; Kapitaenleutnant Horst Wellner, skipper of *U-16* that was sunk in the same place in the same month; and others of the first Doenitz-generation of highly qualified U-boat commanders like Korvettenkapitaen Juergen Deecke, Oberleutnant Peter Frahm, Korvettenkapitaen Johannes Franz, Kapitaenleutnant Werner Lott, Kapitaenleutnant Wilhelm Froehlich.

Most eager to go was Kapitaenleutnant Gerhard Glattes, dean of the officer-prisoners at Bowmanville. Glattes was literally seething to return to the command of a U-boat because he had a score to settle with the British. On September 14, 1939, west of the Hebrides on his first war patrol in *U-39*, he sighted the aircraft carrier *Ark Royal* and attacked her with three torpedoes. They exploded close to the carrier but their faulty magnetic pistols detonated them prematurely, a bitter disappointment for Glattes who thus saw the "sure thing" vanish from his grasp. That was not all. The explosions betrayed the *U-39* to the carrier's destroyer screen. They closed in promptly and bore down on it, Glattes becoming skipper of the *first* U-boat that had the dubious distinction of being sunk in World War II.

That was four years before. During those long years of enforced idleness that followed the moment of his stillborn triumph, Gerhard Glattes yearned for another go at the British. Now he seized upon the hope the escape plot held out and worked harder than most on the success of the venture.

The letters that continued to pass to and fro across the barriers of war revealed the scope of the daring and ambitious plan. In missive after missive, Doenitz outlined to his idle skippers how to organize their escape. He instructed them to clinch it by sneaking *en masse* to a certain secluded spot at the estuary of the St. Lawrence River where, he promised, a U-boat would be waiting to take them aboard and ship them back to Germany, for yet another round after all.

The quaint conspiracy progressed with astonishing efficiency, apparently without a hitch. It was effectively aided by Doenitz through the exploitation of yet other means of clandestine communications. He sent the captive officers Canadian currency, maps, cipher keys, neatly bound into the covers of gift books the prisoners received from home via the International Red Cross. Other escape material was concealed in double-bottomed cans of food, allegedly sent by solicitous relatives to relieve the monotony of the camp diet.

Doenitz's master plan called for the building of a 230-foot tunnel out of the camp. It required the U-boat skippers to proceed to Maisonette

Point in Chaleur Bay which their Grossadmiral had chosen for the rendezvous with the U-boat ferry. He picked it off the map because he thought it could be reached best by the escapees coming from Lake Ontario and the U-boat coming from the east. A quick glance at the map shows how bold and intractable the concept of the plan was. The Bowmanville camp was some 600 miles from Maisonette Point. The escapees were required to pass through Vermont and Maine on their way to the rendezvous, re-enter Canada somewhere between Edmundston and Rivière de Loup, then work their passage north to Chaleur Bay along the salmon-rich Restigouche River.

However, the forbidding arduousness of the proposition did not daunt these eager adventurers. From parts which arrived in those double-bottomed cans, and from odds and ends they found in the camp, they managed to build a two-way radio set for more direct and sophisticated communications with Doenitz. The set was in daily use. Only once did it dampen the enthusiasm of its clandestine listeners at Bowmanville, when it picked up the SOS of a German blockade runner in the process of being sunk off Tristian da Cunha in the South Atlantic.

In due course, the Germans built their tunnel and then, when this masterpiece collapsed, a second one. It was an impressive feat, considering that every palmful of earth had to be removed inconspicuously in order to keep the scheme a secret. After the war, one of the ringleaders of this remarkable venture boasted, "For almost a year, the work went on under the noses of the guards and despite repeated security checks by the camp staff." There is, however, an explanation for this which I am confident the erstwhile conspirators will now be interested to learn for the first time.

In actual fact, their plot was known in minute detail and in every one of its phases to our Intelligence authorities. Lieutenant Taylor's protean *coup* enabled them to "muscle in" on the whole operation. For reasons in which both security and sporting considerations played a part, Washington and Ottawa decided to let the Germans proceed with their game. The decoded letters were, therefore, forwarded to their addressees, as were the books containing money and maps, and the tins with other escape material. Receiving everything Doenitz had sent them and growing complacent in the light of apparent Anglo-Saxon stupidity, they moved confidently and industriously to the *denouement* of their plot. In the end, it was to deprive Doenitz, not merely of this badly needed crop of seasoned officers, but also of the U-boat he had sent to pick them up.

At last, everything seemed to be ready for the mass escape. Doenitz was advised by radio and he in turn signalled back to Bowmanville that each night for a week during the next new moon a U-boat would be waiting for Maisonette Point. Now the Canadian authorities put into operation the two-pronged counter-move they had devised in anticipation of the break-out: they made elaborate arrangements to scoop up every one of the escapees before they could reach Maisonette Point; and they held a small fleet of fast antisubmarine vessels ready in and around Chaleur Bay to entrap the U-boat as well.

On the eve of the break-out, a totally unexpected mishap then made part one of the Canadian counter-plot superfluous. The earth the prisoners had removed so laboriously when building the tunnels was stowed away, for want of a better and more accessible hiding place, in their own living quarters, inside a double ceiling. On what they thought would be their last day at the camp, they discovered to their dismay that the ceiling was about to cave in and had to be repaired post haste. The conspirators piled up furniture on the floor to reach the ceiling, but the improvised pyramid collapsed and the noise of the crash alerted the guards.

The cat was now out of the bag. The Canadians could no longer pretend that they knew nothing of the plot. The carefully laid plans of this surreptitious exit thus collapsed abruptly with the furniture, under the broken ceiling from which good Canadian earth kept cascading down on friend and foe.

In the ensuing confusion, a single German still managed to break out. He was Kapitaenleutnant Werner Heidel, and his escape was a bravura performance of courage and skill. He left Bowmanville by scaling an electricity pylon inside the camp, then hauling himself in a self-made boatswain's chair over the cables to another pole outside the camp. Dressed in Canadian uniform and carrying money and forged identity papers, Heidel made his way to Montreal where he bought a flashlight. He then continued the journey and reached his destination without a hitch, only to discover in the end that the whole area around Maisonette Point was covered with Canadian troops under canvas.

A sentry stopped him but Heidel in a remarkable show of *sang froid*, talked his way out of the trap with the help of his fake papers. As he was trying to work his way through the tents, another sentry stopped him, found his papers suspicious, and arrested him. In the meantime, the U-boat Doenitz had sent to the rendezvous had entered Chaleur Bay. It was sailing furtively toward the Point when four Canadian corvettes suddenly appeared and pounced upon it.

The fabulous plot that began almost two years before in Doenitz's feverish brain thousands of miles from Bowmanville thus ended in the blaze of the corvettes' guns with the capture of the only German who managed to escape and the sinking of a precious U-boat. After that, no mass escape was ever attempted at Bowmanville. It was only in 1948, *three years after VE Day,* that the last batch of these veteran prisoners-of-war reached Germany. In the meantime, Doenitz was compelled to procure the replacements he so badly needed by less romantic means, closer to home.

Fateful Misconceptions

Doenitz's most serious trouble at this stage accrued from major deficiencies in his own basic planning and his management of the U-boat war. If he had a grand strategic concept at all, to match tangibly his ideas about the presumably decisive role of the U-boat in World War II, it revolved around his "integral tonnage theory." Firmly believing that ultimate victory depended on his ability to sink more ships *per se* than the Allies could build, he went for tonnage in sheer quantity, disregarding the crucial factor of quality in the effort. According to his theory, a westbound freighter in ballast was as valuable a target for his U-boats as an eastbound troopship, for example, chock full of soldiers, or a Liberty ship heavily laden with war material consigned to Britain or to North Africa.

Moreover, he had no acute appreciation of the relative importance of the various operational areas. Instead of employing his U-boats when and where they could have inflicted the greatest damage, he assigned them to areas where he expected the best results in numbers at the lowest cost to himself. He thus built up his score without regard to the value of the sinkings to the overall German war effort.

Although he kept voluminous records of the ships his skippers reported as sunk, Doenitz never knew with any semblance of accuracy what his submarines were actually accomplishing. How different the situation was in the Allied camp! Both the Admiralty and Tenth Fleet had hardheaded, incorruptible and exasperatingly skeptical evaluation committees at work to check up on every single action report claiming the destruction of a U-boat. The committees had orders to give the benefit of every doubt to the U-boats and confirmed sinking claims only when they were accompanied by the most conclusive evidence.

The euphoric American claims of 1942, that averred the sinking of forty-odd U-boats by our forces when none was yet sunk, were purely for popular consumption. The United States Navy was never deceived by its own propaganda. As I myself could discover when I had my opportunity to examine the top secret sinking records, the score the Navy kept for its own information was rather on the conservative side. Thus in 1942, the combined Anglo-American forces actually destroyed eighty-five U-boats, but when the action reports were put through the wringer of the assessment boards, they confirmed the sinking of only seventy-five. In the four-month period in 1943 that preceded the establishment of the Tenth Fleet, the Anglo-American antisubmarine effort resulted in the actual sinking of fifty-five U-boats, but the evaluation committees of the Admiralty and COMINCH acknowledged the destruction of only forty-three.

When the job of evaluation also came under Admiral Low, even more stringent criteria of assessment were introduced, until the skippers of the American antisubmarine vessels and the hard-working pilots of our ASW planes complained with some bitterness: "What do they expect us to do? Unless we bring back the bloody periscope of the goddam U-boats, Washington won't believe us we had really sunk the bastards!"

While we thus underestimated our own successes, Doenitz invariably overrated the accomplishments of his U-boats. He never had anything even remotely resembling the Allied evaluation committees and rarely went to the trouble of checking out or toning down the claims of his exuberant commanders. We in Op-16-W thus had ample opportunity to point up this self-deception in the German camp, by composing a number of Norden broadcasts about spurious claims, especially whenever the U-Boat Command's scoreboard lit up with bulletins alleging the sinking of major Allied vessels.

In the fall of 1943, when she was part of Admiral Sir Bruce Fraser's task force in Arctic waters, the USS *Ranger* was thus repeatedly "sunk" by several U-boats, although the gallant American carrier was never as much as scratched by enemy action during her successul career in the Battle of the Atlantic. Undaunted even by the repetitiousness of the claims, Doenitz released several communiques claiming again and again the demise of the *Ranger*. Even at the end of the war, when we captured the archives of the U-Boat Command and could examine the record the Germans kept for their own enlightenment, we found the *Ranger* still listed among the Allied vessels sunk on Doenitz's tally sheet.

It was his blind reliance on the integral tonnage theory, and the inadequacy of his intelligence system (whose corroborated facts could have demolished his house of cards), that prevented Grossadmiral Doenitz from conducting the U-boat war most lucratively. In his opportunistic disregard of the strategic picture, he rarely if ever realized after 1943, in which areas an aggressive concentration of his U-boats would have harmed us most. In 1944, he thus shifted to what Admiral Low aptly described as the "global guerilla war at sea," dispersing the U-boats to secondary areas where he hoped for good results in numbers and expected the least resistance. He thereby missed an opportunity that, in all probability, would have resulted in another humiliation of the United States, with incalculable consequences. He could have mounted another offensive against the East Coast of the United States at a time when the Eastern Sea Frontier, this notorious Achilles heel of the American antisubmarine effort was, amazingly enough, still in no shape to deal effectively and conclusively with such a blitz.

"Paukenschlag" Redivivus

The fierce series of *Paukenschlags* had ended almost a year before the Tenth Fleet was born. Between July 1942 and April 1943, thousands of merchantment sailed up and down the coast between Cape Sable and the Straits of Florida, and not one of them fell victim to enemy action. This was not because American coastal defenses had so improved, but simply because Doenitz had withdrawn his U-boats from these waters.

No longer taking anything for granted in a struggle with a capricious and impressionistic foe, the United States Navy looked forward to the return of the U-boats to their erstwhile "Paradise." Yet Admiral King decided nevertheless to reduce the antisubmarine forces at the disposal of Admiral Andrews at Eastern Sea Frontier, just when Doenitz moved gropingly to confirm our expectations and subject our defenses to another test.

In March 1943, he began to send a number of raiders back to our East Coast and by May, he had six of them operating in waters close to the United States for which the Andrews Sea Frontier had primary responsibility. This handful of U-boats again proved sufficient to overtax the preparedness and ingenuity of the Eastern Sea Frontier and, indeed, to create a situation that was, as Morison ruefully put it, sadly reminiscent of the 1942 massacre.

Sinkings soared again while we managed to retaliate but feebly. The invasion of these nuisance raiders was followed by a mining offensive that began in June and lasted until October. An expeditionary force of only three U-boats succeeded in closing several East Coast ports for brief periods of time and, more importantly, in throwing our defenses back into the old confusion and bungling, this despite the fact that the

Tenth Fleet was already in action during the second phase of the invasion and was contributing substantially to a vast improvement of conditions virtually everywhere else.

This new intrusion began in mid-March, 1943. It was meant clearly as a sideshow or a minor diversion, because Doenitz had concentrated most of the 116 U-boats he had at sea in the North Atlantic convoy areas, in the South Atlantic, and in the Azores and Freetown areas, where they sank an aggregate of 134 Allied merchantmen in March, April and May. The first hint that a latter-day *"Paukenschshlag"* might be in the making came on April 2, when a U-boat, later identified as the *U-129*, was found moving northward from the Bermuda area, sinking a British freighter as it went. The *U-161* was sighted on April 12, about seventy-five miles south of Nantucket Shoals. On April 17, the *U-174* was seen off Halifax, apparently southward bound. In May, this spearhead was reinforced by the *U-66*, the *U-521* and the *U-190*, to constitute a loose group of but six boats trying to rekindle the fading memories of Doenitz's most remarkable victory.

The true significance of this improvised group—pitifully small by the standards of those days—was in the exceptionally high quality of the skippers Doenitz had picked for the operation. Four of the boats were commanded by the foremost aces of this Doenitz generation—Kapitaenleutnant Albrecht Achilles in *U-161*, Korvettenkapitaen Witt in *U-129*, Kapitaenleutnant Markworth in *U-66*, and Kapitaenleutnant Klaus Bargsten in *U-521*. Although they could not repeat the hat tricks of 1942, they supplied a persuasive demonstration that the U-Boat Arm was still a formidable adversary demanding the utmost from those who had to fight them. They operated boldly off Cape Hatteras, Cape Lookout, Cape Henry, in the Gulf Stream, inshore off Savannah, returning the U-boat war to sensitive waters where the achievements of their predecessors should have engendered greater caution and better preparedness on the part of the American defenders.

The presence of these boats was keenly felt, partly by their successes against our ships (including several tankers) and partly from their radio transmissions our Huffduff was intercepting as usual. Yet only two of the six boats could be disposed of. One was the *U-174* of Oberleutnant Wolfgang Grandefeld, which was sunk on April 27, southeast of Sable Island, by Lieutenant (j.g.) Thomas Kinaszczuk, USNR, flying a Vega Venture shortly after these new Navy bombers had been pressed into service; the other was Bargsten's *U-521* whose destruction by Lieutenant Flynn's plucky little *PC-565* was described above. Both sinkings resulted from individual enterprises, rather than from any concerted action staged higher up.

Witt and "Ajax" Achilles returned to their bases at Lorient, and the *U-174* was sunk, before the Tenth Fleet was born. However, the second wave of boats remained in American waters for some time after its establishment. It was ominous by itself that, in the light of past experiences, U-boats could operate again with such impunity at the very doorsteps of the United States. It was even more disturbing that they could do as they pleased, more or less, even after the establishment of Tenth Fleet whose influence had been made paramount in the Eastern Sea Frontier as well. In practice, however, cooperation between Admiral Andrews and the Low organization left much to be desired, mostly on account of the former's inability to make the most of the services Tenth Fleet was providing for him. The situation changed for the better only when Andrews retired in November 1943 and was succeeded by Admiral Leary, but team work remained inferior to Tenth Fleet's close collaboration with the other American forces engaged in fighting the U-boats.

The case of the *U-66* (the very boat Tenth Fleet would later expose fatally to the wrath of Commander Abel's *Buckley*) offers a dramatic demonstration of this deficient teamwork so perilously close to home. *U-66* departed Lorient at the end of April and its arrival in American waters coincided with the establishment of Tenth Fleet. However, it evaded its surveillance for weeks, penetrated to Savannah and made its presence there known by sending two torpedoes into a heavily laden tanker, the *Esso Gettysburg*. Vicious fire lighted by explosions in the tanker's engine room and after holds quickly enveloped the ship, the burning oil wrapping Ensign John S. Arnold, USNR, who commanded the Naval Armed Guard, in a sheet of flames. Arnold extinguished them by rolling on the deck, then—although badly burned—manned his bow gun and fired a round at the U-boat.

The *Esso Gettysburg* was supposed to be protected by a blimp. But its cumbersome escort experienced difficulties with a thunder squall to which these lighter-than-air ships were very sensitive, and had trouble with both its radio and radar. It had left the scene when it did not receive explicit orders from shore to stay with the tanker. Consequently, the presence of *U-66* off Savannah became known only on June 11—nine days after its arrival in its operational area off the American shore and twenty-four hours after the sinking of the tanker—and then only from a report from an Army B-25 whose crew had spotted survivors from the *Gettysburg* and directed the transport *George Washington* to them.

The signal from the B-25 sent the Eastern Sea Frontier into vigorous but disorganized action that produced no results, in spite of the fact that the *U-66* remained in the area where the tanker had gone down and used its radio several times to report to Doenitz. On July 2, but forty miles from the spot where it sank the *Gettysburg*, the U-boat returned to the fracas and torpedoed another tanker, the *Bloody Marsh*, that had also been abandoned by its supposed escort, another blimp caught in another thunderstorm. If proof was still needed to show how little defenses in this area improved in the summer of 1943 over their dismal state in the disastrous spring of 1942, it was provided conclusively by what followed in the wake of the *Marsh's* sinking. It took place ninety miles southeast of Charleston. An SOS from the *Marsh* was duly received. The *U-66* surfaced to report the sinking to Berlin. Nevertheless the U-boat remained undetected by a search group the Sea Frontier sent after it, consisting of a destroyer, a blimp and several Catalinas and Mitchells.

To add insult to injury, Markworth then attacked still another tanker, the *Cherry Valley*, in Mona Passage, before turning eastward to begin the long journey home. The *Cherry Valley* was saved only by the prompt action and intrepidity of its Armed Guard, commanded by Lieutenant (j.g.) A. C. Matthews, USNR.

The situation was still bad in August when the sextet of invaders was relieved by a trio of mine-laying U-boats to operate in the same general area in American waters. One of them was the *U-107*, a 740-tonner carrying a consignment of acoustic mines for Charleston Harbor. It sneaked up to the Carolina coast on the night of August 26-27, laid a dozen mines at the harbor entrance, then turned to attack the freighter *Albert Gallatin* off Savannah. Yet it was only after three P.M. on August 28, that Eastern Sea Frontier was ready to stage a spirited search for the boat; and the search began in earnest only in the morning of August 29, two destroyer escorts and nine small craft trying the whole day to locate it.

The Tenth Fleet joined the action somewhat peremptorily at 8:15 P.M. on August 31, reporting a Huffduff fix at 233 miles east of Cape Lookout which was then evaluated as the U-boat the Eastern Sea Frontier was so frantically seeking. By then, however, the *U-107* was hundreds of miles away, on its way home, "ignorant of the hullabaloo it had raised, but smugly conscious of having done a good mine-laying job." As a matter of fact, the adventure of this particular U-boat had its ironic side. If the Eastern Sea Frontier had failed to run it down and sink it, the intruder also failed to accomplish its mission.

It was aided by lighted gas buoys on its approach march to Charleston Harbor, yet it refrained from entering the main channel and sowed its mines so far outside that they could do no damage. The field was detected a month afterwards during a routine sweep and eliminated before it could cause any harm.

Two other mine-laying boats—the *U-566* and the *U-230*—which succeeded in penetrating to the East Coast inside the Virginia Capes, also failed to accomplish their missions, for no trace of the mines they had allegedly laid was ever found; yet they exposed the Eastern Sea Frontier at its weakest. The *U-566* in particular, ably commanded by Kapitaenleutnant Hans Hornkohl, unleashed a helter-skelter hunt lasting from August 2 to August 8, during which the boat was sighted a total of eight times and attacked five times with varying degrees of inaccuracy, by both surface craft and planes. In the course of the hunt, the *U-Hornkohl* sank the gunboat *Plymouth*, one of the hunters, but survived, virtually unscathed, all encroachments upon it.

In his frank critique of this action, Captain Stephen B. Robinson, USN, of the Eastern Sea Frontier staff, listed so "many mistakes made by so many people" that he could not fix specific blame on any particular command or individual. The "mistakes" included blunders of procedure and communications (which, as Morison remarked, were "usually bad in the Eastern Sea Frontier"), but also grave technical defects, such as "failures of bomb release gear, of bombs to explode, of guns to operate, and of radios to function." At one point in this engagement, a Martin Mariner sighted the *U-566* surfacing in the moonlight on August 7, and the pilot tried to home-in the destroyer *Laub* for an attack on the U-boat. But the plane's voice radio conked out and its flares refused to flare. When fuel shortage then forced the Mariner to leave, it was relieved by another PBM whose flares did function, but illuminated only the *Laub*.

All this occurred in the twentieth month of American participation in the Battle of the Atlantic, in the vicinity of the Nantucket Shoals Lightship, within two hundred miles of the East Coast. Fortunately, Grossadmiral Doenitz never realized how much confusion and waste he had created with these ill-conceived, haphazard, hit-and-run operations. If his objective was to pin down our antisubmarine forces, in the area closest to America's front yard, he succeeded brilliantly, with a tiny fleet of only thirteen boats all told, over a period of five months. He compelled the Navy to restore substantial forces to Admiral Andrews' command at the Eastern Sea Frontier, at a time when they were badly and urgently needed elsewhere. On May 1, Andrews' reduced surface forces consisted of 172 units, mostly small craft, without a single destroyer escort or destroyer. On July 1, his air strength was reduced to fifty-five B-25s, fifteen B-17s, ten B-18s, and only seventeen very long range Venturas. But on September 3, under the impact of this strange U-boat offensive, he again had sixteen squadrons of planes, four squadrons of blimps, two frigates, fifteen gunboats, a hundred Coast Guard cutters (of the 85-foot variety), and about 125 other vessels, a total of 242 surface craft and hundreds of planes.

Even so, the inherent defects of this Sea Frontier—perhaps the only organization of the United States Navy that remained unaffected by the coming of the Tenth Fleet—left the East Coast as vulnerable in the summer and early fall of 1943 as it was in the winter and spring of 1942. Had Doenitz decided to unleash one of his old-fashioned offensives at this time along the Eastern Sea Frontier, our forces would have been unable to stave off another disaster, as they proved hardly able to deal effectively even with the mere handful of U-boats he actually dispatched to those precarious waters.

The Penang Shuttle

However, this was the sole bleak spot in the entire antisubmarine picture. On the day of the Tenth Fleet's first anniversary, Commander Knowles could dispose of two of the off-beat areas which formed an integral part of Doenitz's guerilla war at sea. "April was again a good month for our side," he said in one of his morning briefings in May, 1944, "due chiefly to the fact that we have succeeded in terminating effective U-boat operations in the Mediterranean and in checking the Doenitz blitz in the Indian Ocean."

The Mediterranean throttle was a joint Anglo-American enterprise to which the Tenth Fleet had contributed John Pellam's ingenious MAD scheme, (see page 239). On this auspicious May morning, when Low arrived in Knowles' plot room for the situation conference, he found tangible evidence to bear out his Intelligence chief's optimistic remark. There was a brand new pin on the big map, at a spot due north of Cape Tènès in the Mediterranean, some fifty miles northwest of Algiers. It was placed there only an hour before, when a signal from the Casablanca headquarters of Vice Admiral H. Kent Hewitt, USN, reported the sinking of *U-960*. The ill-fated U-boat, skippered by Oberleutnant Guenther Heinrich, was caught in the neck of the bottle-shaped Western Mediterranean, at the far end of what the bitter-tongued quipsters of the U-Boat Arm had dubbed the "Gibraltar mousetrap."

Following by only two days the destruction of *U-616* of Kapitaenleutnant Siegfried Koitschka west of Algiers, it was the sixth kill of the month in which the forces of the United States had a hand, and the third kill within four days in the "mousetrap," as the methodical Allied measures reduced Kapitaen-zur-See Werner Hartmann's forlorn Mediterranean flotilla from eighteen boats in February to only eleven in this May. The *U-960* turned out to be the last U-boat to threaten our convoys in the western Mediterranean, for its fate persuaded Doenitz never to send another U-boat into that sea.

It was left to Doenitz to pen the best summary of this ill-starred expansion of the U-boat war to yet another extraneous area, undermining his power and strength in the Atlantic where they counted most. "Taking into consideration the opposition which confronted them," he wrote in his memoirs, "I am convinced that the U-boats in the Mediterranean achieved all that could possibly have been expected of them." However, he added: "Their average sinkings, nevertheless, compared with the successes in the Atlantic in 1943, were low, and their losses disproportionately high. Of the sixty-two boats which were sent to the Mediterranean from 1941 onwards, forty-eight were lost. In addition, since no concrete shelters were available at their bases, no fewer than eleven were destroyd by air attack while in port."

In actual fact, the Mediterranean was virtually eliminated from the war at sea half a year before VE Day. By the end of November, 1944, it became so peaceful that convoys could be dispersed at Point Europa and the ships allowed to proceed independently to their destinations. Between May 1943, the establishment of the Tenth Fleet, and August, 1944, American forces sank twenty U-boats within the Mediterranean and three in the Strait of Gibraltar. Although the area was beyond its immediate commitments, the Tenth Fleet contributed directly to the destruction of five of the U-boats, including the three that perished in the Gibraltar nutcracker through an application of the Pellam method.

The victory in the Indian Ocean, on the other hand, was a predominantly American accomplishment in which Low's phantom fleet played an invisible and discreet but invaluable part.

The idea of extending U-boat operations to the Indian Ocean originated with Admiral Wenneker, the German Naval Attache in Tokyo. Wenneker was, as Doenitz put it, "very active to organize an effective coordination of the German and Japanese war effort at sea"—in the face of what Doenitz omitted to mention: opposition to his scheme by both the German and Japanese Naval authorities. Already In December, 1942, Wenneker recommended that a U-boat base be established in one of the Japanese-held ports in the Indian Ocean and eventually persuaded the Japanese Naval High Command to let the Germans use Penang in Northwest Malaya on the Strait of Malacca.

At that time, Doenitz was enjoying a full tide of success so much closer home and ignored Wenneker's suggestion. He turned it down again in the spring of 1943, telling Wenneker bluntly: "As long as the opportunity to sink ships in the Atlantic exists, I am not prepared to operate in the Indian Ocean." When the summer massacre of 1943 made operations in the Atlantic inopportune, he decided to accept Wenneker's invitation and transfer a number of U-boats to Penang for operations in the Indian Ocean. The boats he chose for the venture were the 740-ton IXC type and the 1,600 ton U-boat cruisers, the IXD2 type especially designed for remote operations, capable of a maximum range of 30,000 miles at ten knots of surface speed.

The first U-boat sent to Penang was the *U-178* of Kapitaenleutnant Wilhelm Spahr. It belonged to a group of six boats Doenitz had named "Monsoon" (after the seasonal winds of the Indian Ocean) which, in May 1943, had rounded the Cape of Good Hope and operated around Madagascar, sinking 130,000 gross tons of shipping without causing undue concern in Allied naval circles. When in June the *U-Spahr* was due to return home, it received instructions by radio to proceed to Penang instead, to aid in the setting up of a U-boat base on the exotic island familiar to Joseph Conrad fans.

The operation that followed was to give the U-Boat Arm a sorely needed shot in the arm and enabled Doenitz, in the wake of his recent resounding defeat in the Atlantic, not only to keep his U-boats at war, but also to score a set of impressive pseudo-victories. Though groping to begin with and lame in conclusion, this campaign in the Indian Ocean was the most profitable during this period, surpassing all Atlantic areas in number of ships and amount of tonnage destroyed. While it supplied some compensation to Doenitz for his lack of success elsewhere, it had no influence whatsoever on the outcome of the war. Moreover, it proved enormously costly even by Doenitz's standards, for he lost almost eighty per cent of the U-boats he assigned to the Indian Ocean operations, or thirty-four out of forty-five boats.

In the end, only sixteen U-boats made Penang or other Malayan ports during the entire war, but even so, they proved adequate to mount still another Doenitz offensive of sporadic blitzes. It began in June, 1943, with the sinking of seven ships; mounted to fifteen ships in July; and totalled forty ships of over 200,000 gross tons by October when this first blitz of the Indian Ocean campaign ended. A second phase began in November, modestly enough with the sinking of only four merchantmen, but gained momentum and yielded a total of thirty-eight ships by March, 1944, when it ended as abruptly as it began, to flare up in July and August, sinking fourteen more ships. The entire

Indian Ocean escapade lasted fifteen months and bagged a grand total of 102 ships of a little over 600,000 gross tons.

After an initial shoulder-shrugging, the extension of the U-boat war to the Indian Ocean, just when it seemed that the backbone of the U-boat was broken, created grave concern both in London and Washington. As usual when they moved into yet another ocean area, the Germans had the Indian Ocean very much to themselves, to maraud as they pleased in the face of slight opposition. The Allied navies, grown as they were to formidable proportions, could not spare escorts for convoys in those vast and distant waters. Other means had to be found to deal with this new menace, and the Admiralty and COMINCH ordered that a study be made of the problem and measures be developed to solve it before it got out of hand.

The job of seeking this solution was assigned to Admiral Low's Tenth Fleet and once again, the Intelligence section headed by Commander Knowles stepped in to supply the basic information from which a plan could be developed. Knowles and his aides reconstructed with uncanny accuracy the blueprint Doenitz had drawn for his U-boats operating in the Indian Ocean. It revealed that no U-boat was permanently stationed in those remote and romantic waters but chosen boats sailed singly from the Biscay ports to their operational area, down the East Atlantic. They rounded the Cape then moved to their scattered stations in the ocean, doing their sinkings on their outward or homeward passages, putting into Penang only for rest, replenishments and repairs.

It was then left to Low and his aides to design a master plan from this reconstructed blueprint, to deal with these long-range marauders. Since no U-boat hunt could be organized for the Indian Ocean on the Atlantic pattern, Low decided to intercept the Penang-bound U-boats in the Atlantic and render them harmless long before they could reach their operational areas.

It took some time to make the most of this master plan and, for a while, a handful of U-boats managed to sneak through the noose. But even before a definitive end could be put to this venture, the Tenth Fleet succeeded in curbing it by "fingering," so to speak, one boat after another on the transit lanes from France to the Indian Ocean. Now in May, 1944, Knowles could list fourteen such U-boats already destroyed in transit. This meant the total destruction of the "Monsoon" group, for example, from which but a single boat, the *U-188* of Kapitaenleutnant Siegfried Luedden, managed to complete the long journey home, arriving at Bordeaux on June 19, 1944, only to perish a few weeks later as she tried to escape through the Bay of Biscay to its new berth in

Norway, when the Allied invasion of France made the Biscay bases untenable.

Of the forty-five boats which went out, only five boats ever returned home. The *U-181* was one of them and its fate, under its able skipper, Fregattenkapitaen Kurt Freiwald, somehow symbolized the futility of this whole useless operation. The big U-boat cruiser made its first round voyage from Bordeaux to Bordeaux in 198 days in 1943, sinking eight ships of 39,155 gross tons on its outward and homeward passages. It was, according to Wolfgang Frank, the longest U-boat patrol of the entire war. Freiwald was then ordered to take his boat back to the Indian Ocean for a second patrol in October, 1944, but by then the U-boats were living on borrowed time. On May 6, 1945, when Doenitz's melancholy order to cease operations was received at Penang, on the eve of VE Day, Freiwald handed *U-181* over to the Japanese. It continued fitfully at sea, until the surrender of Japan, when the hapless U-boat, foremost hero of this wasteful adventure, reached its last harbour. It was scuttled in alien waters at Singapore.

Last of these "Flying Dutchmen" to perish *in combat* was the *U-183*, disguised as Japanese, but operating with its German crew under Kapitainleutnant Fritz Schneewind in waters thousands of miles from the Reich. On April 23, 1945, it had the misfortune of bumping into the United States submarine *Besugo*, patrolling the Java Sea. The *Besugo* fired a spread of six torpedoes at a range of 1500 yards, sending this last of the Indian Ocean marauders to its final fathom in a matter of seconds, to close this dismal chapter of the U-boat war.

Although he remained blissfully ignorant of the Tenth Fleet's significant role in first restricting and then foiling his Oriental escapade, Doenitz has paid a handsome tribute to the Low organization when he wrote after the war: "By the end of the war we had unfortunately lost twenty-two [sic] of the U-boats sent to the Indian Ocean. Of these no fewer than sixteen were known to have been sunk by aircraft, [from the various American escort carrier groups in the Azores and Freetown areas] most of them while on passage through the Atlantic."

The war was taking yet another turn. Even as Commander Knowles, in the situation conference of May 20, 1944, was closing these inconclusive chapters of the U-boat war, the global guerilla war at sea was overshadowed by two major developments in the making.

One was the Normandy invasion, only a few days away.

The other was still another come-back effort on the part of the indefatigable Doenitz—his swan song, at that: the final snorkel blitz in the North Atlantic that was to return the U-boat war, in its final gasp, to the East Coast of the United States.

CHAPTER XVIII

The Goetterdaemmerung

On the morning of May 31, 1944, Konteradmiral Godt held a top-secret situation conference at U-boat headquarters at the Koralle, new headquarters of the U-Boat Command at Bernau near Berlin, to which it was moved from its hotel, in the shadow of the Allies' imminent return to the Continent. He began in his customary manner, skirting the issues before warming up to them, as he told the assembled brass that included all the flotilla commanders especially summoned from their bases to attend the meeting:

"*Meine Herren*, our efforts to tie down the forces of the enemy, as is abundantly proved by U-boat reconnaissance, by the reports of secret agents and the summaries issued by Naval Intelligence, have been successful so far. Far from decreasing, the numbers of enemy aircraft and escort vessels, U-boat killer groups and aircraft carriers have increased. We all realize, of course, that for us submariners the task of carrying on the fight solely for the purpose of tying down enemy forces is a particularly hard one.

"More than in the case of any other arm," Godt continued, "success has hitherto been won thanks to the team work of the crews as a whole, and this has imbued them with exceptional fighting spirit, determination and steadfastness in the face of the enemy's counter-measures."

Godt was having a hard time. He was talking in generalities that showed wear and tear, and his audience manifested some exasperation with the old cliches, by shifting and coughing through the lecture. Then at last, the little Konteradmiral switched to the topic of the day that was foremost on all minds. He began to enumerate the problems the invasion of the continent would pose for the U-boats and the arrangements Gross-admiral Doenitz had made for that eventuality.

Among the problems Godt now listed the shallow waters of the English Channel in which the U-boats would have to operate; the tremendous concentration of antisubmarine vessels he expected the Allies would have waiting for them; and the mortal threat from hundreds of land-based aircraft. It was Godt's unsavory chore to tell his audience that though there seemed to be no solution for those problems, the U-boats could not remain aloof from the invasion battle.

"The U-boat is the sole instrument of war which, with a handful of men aboard, can make a wholly disproportionate contribution to our success in that battle," he said, "by sinking, for instance just *one* ship laden with munitions, tanks or other war material, even if it was itself lost in the process. How many soldiers would have to be sacrificed, how great an endeavor made, to destroy on land so great a mass of enemy war material?"

Even at this late hour, Godt had to concede that the exact date and direction of the Allied effort were unknown to the German High Command and that, indeed, there still was substantial disagreement on this topic even inside the Fuehrer's own headquarters. Hitler, trusting his intuitions more than the reports of his *Abwehr*, persisted in the belief that the main Allied effort would be in Norway. Others including Doenitz, in possession of fairly accurate intelligence reports, were convinced that France would be the goal of the Allied invasion.

Godt reviewed the arrangements U-Boat Command had made for these split estimates that also split the U-boat armada in two separate forces. "As you know, *meine Herren*," Godt said in his polished delivery, "we have Group *Mitte* in Norway to oppose any invasion of that country or of Jutland. We have Group *Landwirt* at the Biscayan bases to repel a possible attack on France. We are ready for either eventuality or, indeed, for both of them. Group *Mitte* now has twenty-two U-boats and *Landwirt* had been built up to thirty-six boats. In addition, we have a squadron in the Atlantic to provide the *Luftwaffe* with accurate weather forecasts and the *Abwehr* with information about the Allied preparations."

He then paused before concluding his diagnosis with a prognosis. "We all agree, I am sure," he said, "that the U-boat campaign must be continued even in the face of heavy losses and, under the circumstances, we must accept even losses that are out of all proportion to the successes achieved. When the invasion comes, the U-boats must be there! We hoped that we would have snorkels on all the boats of *Landwirt* but, as of today, only those of the flotilla at Brest are equipped with it. That makes seven boats. For those without snorkel the invasion battle might mean the last operation—but there is no choice! We possess no other means with which to oppose or tie down the vast array of forces the enemy will throw against us—only the U-boat!"

On that same Wednesday of May 31, the Tenth Fleet also held its regular morning conference, also in the shadow of the imminent invasion. But here *Overlord* figured merely as a passing reference in Commander Knowles' briefing, for it was beyond Tenth Fleet's responsibilities. Its every phase was handled by General Eisenhower. Knowles knew that SHAEF was fully aware of both *Mitte* and *Landwirt* and had made all the necessary arrangements to deal with them at the proper time.

The Capture of U-505

Knowles was concerned with two different phenomena in Tenth Fleet's own back yard. He had a developing plot of that elusive squadron of five U-boats deployed between Newfoundland and the Azores, sending weather reports to *Goliath* and snooping on the Allies. But on this particular spring day in 1944, he was more preoccupied with what seemed to be a couple of wayward U-boats which appeared on, then vanished from the Tenth Fleet's plot with intriguing regularity. As the fixes sharpened, there remained but a single definite U-boat flitting in and out of the Tenth Fleet's noose, identified with increasing clarity from its recurrent transmissions by the characteristic touch of its wireless operator. It was a mystery boat, in spite of Knowles' growing familiarity with it. It seemed to be a certain German the Tenth Fleet had been tracking since March but never succeeded in pinning down.

It belonged to the impromptu groups Knowles had under surveillance for some time, a few of them bound for the Indian Ocean, others prowling along the west African coast. Several of these boats had been sighted outward bound through the Bay of Biscay and were then tracked by Huffduff whenever they used their wireless sets. As soon as their presence was definitely established in the area, the Tenth Fleet directed a succession of escort carrier groups to the Cape Verdes to pick out as many of them as could be intercepted at that crossroads of the U-boat war.

A number were subsequently sunk, including Henke's *U-515* on April 8, but two days after U-Boat Command had warned all boats in the area that an American carrier group was looking for them. Even so, on April 10, the *U-68* could be caught on the surface in broad moonlight. It was sunk as were others, in this precarious sub-theater of the Atlantic battle over which the Tenth Fleet kept unflagging surveillance, tipping off the carrier groups to one U-boat after another.

Now there was this particular U-boat very much at large and becoming ever more distinct on the Tenth Fleet's plot. Its story on the index cards of Commander Knowles' file of cross references began late in March when it was first sighted in the Bay as it departed from Brest on *Feindfahrt.* It was tracked from its periodic transmissions all the way down the Ivory Coast to Freetown, then to Cape Palms where it remained, the intercepts indicated, for some time apparently looking for victims. If it could not make its presence physically felt by actually sinking any Allied ships it was only because traffic had dwindled in those parts and prowl though it might, the mystery boat could not find a single target.

Knowles had its number! From the telltale evidence the Huffduff had produced, he deducted it must have been one of the older boats that could stay about ninety days at sea. So he figured that, unless it would refuel in the operational area (an unlikely prospect in the absence of any milk cows) it would have to begin its homeward journey toward the end of May.

Sure enough, on May 27, a transmission several Huffduff stations identified as coming from the mystery boat located it just off Bissagos Island of Portuguese Guinea, about 750 miles north of its last known position off Cape Palms. Then the electronic chase began. Next day it was located off Dakar sailing a straight northward course. On May 30, it was checked out just as it was turning eastward as if trying to get closer to the protection of the French West African Coast; and now, on this crucial May 31, it was found it had turned north again, creeping up long. 20° with a direct course on Cape Blanc.

Since the day before, however, the mystery boat was no longer alone. Its presence in the area and its projected course had been signalled to CINCLANT. Admiral Ingersoll immediately instructed Captain Dan Gallery's "Can Do" carrier group, then only about 300 miles south of the last fix, to run down the latest bearings.

The elusive German was the *U-505,* homeward bound, just as the Tenth Fleet had figured it, with Oberleutnant Harald Lange in command. It was a strange boat, to be sure, even if its mystery was getting thinner by the hour. A Type IX-C eleven-hundred-tonner, it was one of the venerable veterans of the U-boat war whose own ups and downs were almost symbolic of the fluctuating fortunes of the whole U-Boat Arm. Commissioned in the summer of 1941 at the Deutsche Werft in Hamburg, it went on its first war cruise on February 11, 1942, with Kapitaenleuant Axel Loewe, a competent and intrepid skipper of the second Doenitz generation, under whom it had chalked up more than 50,000 tons on three missions. Then all of a sudden its long prosperity changed until it became the hard-luck boat of the First Flotilla. It suffered from recurring mechanical troubles that once kept it five months at Lorient. On a *Feindfahrt* in November 1943, it was so hard pressed by its own technical difficulties and Allied attacks that its new skipper, Kapitaenleutant Zschech could take no more. At the height of the depth charge attack, Zschech committed suicide by firing a single bullet to his right temple from his Luger.

The stigma of that weird episode rested heavily on *U-505* and when it returned to the Atlantic battle on March 16, 1944, Lange tried his best to erase it. He patrolled diligently and aggressively even if unsuccessfully. Proceeding south and starting with Freetown, where it arrived on April 24, she reconnoitred every harbour along the Ivory Coast as far east as Grand Bassam. She looked in at Monrovia, Harpers Village, Port Bouet, and Grand Lahou, but found nothing.

Returning west she took station off Cape Palmas and spent the rest of its *Feindfahrt* patrolling back and forth across the route from Palmas to the Cape of Good Hope. All it saw there were three neutral steamers, some fishing vessels and one large British passenger liner. Lange gave chase but the liner was too fast and got away. In between he had several serious machinery breakdowns but he repaired them at sea. Although the Tenth Fleet had an eye on him, Lange managed to elude its electronic gropings with relative ease. He ran at periscope depth in daytime and on the surface between sunset and sunrise. He had to crash dive to get away from planes only nine times in a whole month. Three times his lookouts actually sighted aircraft and at least once, aircraft from Gallery's *Guadalcanal* had sighted him. Six times his Naxos gear gave warning before any hostile plane could be seen. While Lange had a real sense of the enemy's presence and made his arrangements accordingly, no bombs were ever dropped near him on this frustrating *Feindfahrt*.

On May 24, it turned around and embarked upon the long journey home but Captain Gallery with the *Guadalcanal* group had different plans for the *U-505*. By the strangest quirk of fate, the boat bound for Brest in France wound up in Chicago, Illinois.

Now on this May 31, *U-505* was off Marsa in French West Africa while the *Guadalcanal* group, that had just turned south then north, was still far out at sea, left more than a thousand miles behind. But it was moving up fast, following down fix after fix reaching Gallery from Knowles. Then on June 2, "Captain Dan" received first hand evidence from his own Combat Intelligence Center that the U-boat was actually nearby. His own HF/DF had picked up strong transmissions on the U-boat's frequency. There were erratic radar blips at night. Several of his search pilots reported they had heard the distant propeller noises of a U-boat on sono-buoys.

In the meantime, Lange became painfully aware that someone was breathing down his neck. From May 30 on, his Naxos search receiver gear kept warning him of aircraft, but it did not specify how far away they were. Following those warnings, he kept crash diving—once three times within a single four-hour period during the moonlit night—then surfaced and continued his course at high speed, until his Naxos picked up more and more radars that sent him crash-diving again and again, sapping his strength by rendering his batteries rather anaemic.

Lange recognized at last that this was not just a single wayward plane shadowing him from a landlocked airfield but that he was being followed by an aircraft carrier group. It was then that he decided to make an eighty-four mile jog due east. But just when Lange was making his detour towards the African coast, Gallery started up on his trail, catching up on June 3, when both stood south of Port Etienne on lat. 20°, only 150 to 200 miles apart.

That morning, Commander Earl Trosino, USNR, his chief engineer, went to Gallery to warn him that he had reached the end of the chase and would have to abandon his quarry. "Captain," Trosino said, "we've got to quit fooling here! I'm getting down near the safe limit of my fuel!" Gallery argued with Trosino all day about the fuel then, next day being Sunday, he prayed at mass along those same lines. It was a beautiful, clear day with a light breeze and medium sea, but Gallery was all clouded up because he feared he had lost the sub—when, at 11 a.m. sharp, the squawk box on his bridge told him the best news he was ever to hear:

"Frenchy to *Bluejay,"* it said, "I have *possible* sound contact."

Then exactly twelve minutes later:

"Frenchy to *Bluejay*—contact evaluated as sub! Am starting attack!"

Frenchy was the USS *Chatelain* with Lieutenant Commander Dudley S. Knox, USNR, in command, and *Bluejay* was the *Guadalcanal*. The message sent the volatile Gallery into a frenzy of action. "Left full rudder!" he yelled. "Engines ahead full speed!" Then he grabbed the TBS radio and shouted: *"Bluejay* to *Dagwood*—take two destroyers and assist *Frenchy!* I'll maneuver to keep clear."

Dagwood was Commander Frederick S. Hall, USN, the escort commander who had his pennant in USS *Pillsbury,* to whom Gallery was passing the ball. "It was his party from here on," the captain recalled. "An aircraft carrier right smack in the scene of a sound contact is like an old lady in the middle of a bar room brawl. She has no business there, can contribute little to the work at hand, and should get the hell out of there leaving elbow room for those who have a job to do."

Hall broke off with *Pillsbury* and *Jenks* to assist *Chatelain*. Two Wildcats circled overhead. Gallery had sent them up to lend a hand if needed, but warning the pilots: "Use no big stuff if the sub surfaces! Chase the crew overboard with 50 calibre fire!"

Chatelain was attacking with hedgehogs on sonar when the Wildcat pilots actually sighted the sub at last and signalled frantically to Knox: "You're going in the wrong direction, come back!" Then fired machine gun bullets into the water to indicate the position of the U-boat.

No matter how much his Naxos had warned him before, now in the moment of truth Lange seemed unaware of the fact that the enemy was at him. He was having his lunch on the *U-505* that was gliding smoothly under the unruffled sea like a big fish when *Chatelain* delivered a full depth-charge pattern. The attack holed the outer hull, dumping crockery and food as well as the sailors into the bilges. Convinced that the U-boat had been mortally hit, Lange blew his tanks and surfaced, barely 700 yards from the *Chatelain,* with the crew streaming through the hatches, their hands raised and jumping overboard. That was the signal for Commander Hall to start the most melodramatic part of this sea saga, by issuing the order:

"Cease firing! Away boarding parties!"

This was exactly how Gallery had planned it and how he hoped it would happen at least once when he came up against a U-boat thrown at his mercy. He had studied several actions in which U-boats had been sunk—like the sinking of Otto Kretschmer's *U-99* in March 1941—and came to the conclusion that several times there was a good chance to capture the boats before their crews had succeeded in scuttling them. Determined not to miss such an opportunity, he organized boarding parties within his task group and drilled them for just such an eventuality. But he never had a chance before to make any use of them. Now, however, there was his big moment, as he had told Admiral Ingersoll and Admiral Bellinger at their departure conference in Norfolk when he announced that he would capture the next U-boat that he encountered.

The boarding party on *Pillsbury* consisted of Lieutenant (j.g.) Albert L. David, USNR, two petty officers, Arthur W. Knispel and Stanley E. Wdowiak, and a chosen group of enlisted men. They shoved off in a whaleboat that had all the necessary salvage gear stowed and ready at hand. A few moments later, David led his party with a leap on board.

The lieutenant and the two petty officers scrambled below and found that the U-boat had been completely abandoned by its panic-stricken crew. David quickly bundled up all important-looking papers, charts and code books, and sent them away in the whaleboat. Then he set to work to disconnect demolition charges, close valves, and stop an eight-inch stream from a bilge strainer. Within half an hour the engines were secured. At 12:30 p.m.—but an hour and a half after Knox had first established contact with the U-boat—a salvage party from the carrier was on the *U-505* and then, the *Guadalcanal* took the U-boat in tow, a big American ensign now flying from its conning tower.

A snapshot taken of this scene was sent to Commander Knowles whose tip had triggered these remarkable events. Now he still had one more service to perform. The capture of *U-505* was the climactic single episode of the American antisubmarine effort in the Atlantic. But this was only the middle of 1944. The war was not over yet. Absolute secrecy became imperative to conceal the *coup* from the Germans, to enable us to make use of all the captured documents, and especially of the code books Lange in his haste had failed to destroy.

From then on, therefore, the name "*U-505*" was to vanish from history and a cover-name was to take its place. Knowles flew to Bermuda as member of the reception committee awaiting the arrival of the captured boat there, and as senior Intelligence officer on the spot, who had such a valiant part in the U-boat's capture, he was asked to think up a cover-name for *U-505*. An avid Jules Verne fan, he suggested that the boat be named "Nemo." It was by that romantic and clandestine designation that the hapless boat was carried in the records of the United States Navy until peace at last made it possible to disclose the details of this greatest single feat in the Atlantic battle.

As I said before, the ill-fated boat wound up in Chicago, Illinois. After the war, it was lugged to the Windy City and ensconced there life size, as the Atlantic battle's foremost souvenir, on a massive pedestal in front of the Chicago Museum of Science and Industry. Well cared for and pampered by the Museum staff and thousands of visitors, it now shines in better shape than it ever was in all its long career in the Battle of the Atlantic.

This great *coup* was the result of perfect teamwork between Tenth Fleet and Captain Gallery's enterprising escort carrier group. The Tenth Fleet spotted the boat, kept it under constant surveillance, and pinned it down for Gallery to kill it; and Gallery was, as Commander Young put it, the only naval man, American or British, who deliberately set out to capture a U-boat.

But the *U-505* was not the first submarine to be captured in World War II, and Gallery was not the only Allied officer in the Battle of the

Atlantic who thought of organizing a boarding party. In 1940, the Germans captured the British submarine *Seal* and the British captured the Italian *Galilei*. In 1941, Kapitaenleutnant Hans Joachim Rahmlow panicked during an attack on his *U-570* by a Hudson of the RAF and meekly surrendered his boat to surface forces of the Royal Navy the Hudson had summoned to collect it.

From early in the war, boarding parties were established in all the Royal Navy's antisubmarine ships and the boarding of submarines was part of the routine curriculum of exercises. But no effort was ever made to actually board a disabled U-boat, and nothing is known of deliberate preparations to capture one in the dashing Gallery manner. This was an oversight at best, and one the Tenth Fleet never got around to correct. However, there was good reason for not being too eager to capture U-boats. A surfaced German submarine in the vicinity of a convoy or vulnerable suface craft always represented real and present danger. The natural reaction of a prudent commander, concerned primarily with the safety of his own ship, was to kill the U-boat as quickly as possible, before it could make any desperate aggressive move in its last ditch.

However, there was in fact another excellent chance to capture a U-boat and that in the immediate wake of Gallery's *coup*. Exactly one week after the capture of *U-505*, the Tenth Fleet guided the *Croatan* carrier group of hunter-killers to a group of U-boats in the North Atlantic. On their way to the pinpointed target, the *Croatan* bumped into a big boat that was somehow overlooked in the excitement of those days. This was mid-June—the historic period in the immediate wake of the Normandy landings, the Allies fighting for a foothold in France and Doenitz's handful of do-or-die U-boats struggling desperately in the Baie de la Seine area to cut the Anglo-American lifeline across the Channel. A lone-wolf U-boat plodding down the Atlantic was too insignificant a target to warrant special attention.

The loner the *Croatan* group now encountered at a point midway between Flores and Flemish Cap was the *U-490*, a 1600-ton cruiser, outward bound for Penang with supplies for the Indian Ocean raiders. Captain John P. W. Vest, USN, commanding officer of the *Croatan* group, sent two destroyer escorts of his screen, the *Frost* and the *Huse*, to attack it. The action began at six o'clock in the morning on June 11, and at first it seemed it would be over quickly, with the initial attack. But Oberleutnant Wilhelm Gerlach, in command of *U-490*, took his big boat to the unprecedented (and probably grossly exaggerated) depth of 164 fathoms, hoping to sit out the attack.

But he could not shake off the *Croatan* group. Contact was maintained the whole day, until the crew of the *U-490* could not take it any longer. Conditions were truly unbearable inside the harassed boat at its abysmal depth. The air turned foul, and the crew began to panic as they listened helplessly to the recurrent explosions of depth charges, to the continuous pinging of sonar, and the buzzzing noise of the escorts' Foxer gear that penetrated to them. A dozen guinea pigs which their surgeon had on board for some experiments panicked even more. They started squealing so loud that Gerlach ordered them killed for fear their shrill clamor might be picked up by American sound gear.

Yet it was only at 9:47 P.M., almost sixteen hours after the initial attack, that Gerlach ordered his tanks blown and surfaced. The *U-490* broke water about 8,000 yards from the *Frost* and another destroyer escort of the *Croatan's* screen, the *Snowden*. Gerlach realized at once that his situation was hopeless and, coming out on deck just as the two escorts opened fire, he sent a blinker signal to the *Croatan*: "SOS. Please save us!"

If this was an invitation to board, Captain Vest chose to ignore it. Instead of pulling a Gallery, so to speak, he signaled to Commander Frank D. Giambattista, his screen commander: "Don't take any of that guff! Illuminate and let him have it!"

The probable opportunity to capture a second U-boat within a single week went up in the smoke of Giambattista's guns. At 10:53 P.M., more than an hour after the hopeful SOS, when it became amply evident to the U-boat's thoroughly demoralized crew that the *Croatan* was not interested in taking possession of *U-490*, the German engineer officer opened his Kingston valves and scuttled his boat.

Pimpernels of the Atlantic

The exciting interlude of the *U-505's* capture was now over, and the Tenth Fleet, in a buoyant mood, returned to the humdrum job of hunting wayward U-boats in the ocean areas assigned to the United States Navy west of the Chop. In a real sense it was fortunate that the melodrama of the *U-505* occurred at this time because some such spectacular victory was needed to buoy morale in the Low organization. For the Tenth Fleet, the war had taken a strange and somewhat exasperating turn. Emphasis had shifted to other operations compared with which the war against the U-boats seemed puny and *passé*. What Admiral King in a rare flush of rhetoric flourish had called "our inexorable movement across the Pacific" went into high gear. Two and a half years after Pearl Harbor, the forces of the United States stood 3,000 miles to the westward in the Pacific, on the offensive everywhere. What the U-boats used to do to Allied shipping in the Atlantic, American submarines were now doing to the Japanese.

The grand strategic design for Japan's defeat was emerging with growing clarity and force, yet it was still overshadowed by events in Europe where the decisive phase of the war had opened with a bang. In the U-boat war, too, emphasis now shifted from the open ocean areas to the congested waters of the English Channel. The majority of the U-boats Doenitz had at sea operated around the British Isles in what was tantamount to close combat in the thick of the densest Allied defenses. In a sense it was still another Doenitz blitz and it did yield substantial dividends—but at what price?! In June, July and August, 1944, when there still seemed to be a chance to check the invasion by cutting off its umbilical cord at sea, out of 131 U-boats at sea, eighty-two were killed. The average thirty per cent of U-boat losses thus soared to sixty-five per cent. It was a casualty rate which only that of the Kamikaze pilots bested in World War II.

Yet even though the backbone of the U-boat arm was now clearly broken, its morale and fighting spirit remained exceptionally high. As a matter of fact, there was but a single man in the whole *Kriegsmarine* who cracked under the hammerblows. It was the Grossadmiral himself! In August, he was at the Koralle, his headquarters in Bernau near Berlin, exposed like a latter-day Hamlet to nothing but bad news. He tried with a superhuman effort to absorb the body blows and return the punches. But his power of resistance was crumbling fast. It had approached the breaking point already in July when Konteradmiral Godt reported the loss of twenty-three U-boats out of thirty-four in the Atlantic. Then came this wretched August! The dam was now smashed and through the broken dyke, bad tidings streamed in like turbulent mudwater. At Toulon alone, American flyers caught and destroyed eleven of his U-boats, the miserable remnants of his Mediterranean flotilla. The escort carrier *Bogue* killed the *U-1229*, southwest of Cape Race, the secret mission submarine taking the spy Oskar Mantel to a landing in Maine (see pages 6-7). The Biscay bases became untenable. Of the beaten armada moving out of them towards Norway and an uncertain fate, four were killed in transit. But the worst news came from the Channel. By August 23, the casualty list had thirty-four inked-in crosses indicating the loss of that many U-boats.

Doenitz could take no more! "I myself could no longer match the moral fortitude [*Seelenstaerke*] displayed by the U-boat crews!" he wrote. On August 24, he summoned Godt and instructed him to recall all boats still operating in the invasion area. He professed himself relieved when five battered and bruised boats responded to the summons and made base—five out of fifty!

The Tenth Fleet followed developments in European waters avidly, of course, especially since now it also had a pot of trouble Doenitz had brewed in the backwash of the invasion battle. On that same May day when Knowles could close the chapter of the Indian Ocean, he had to start a new one in the Tenth Fleet's own back yard, so much closer home. Since the middle of the month, the Huffduff stations that ringed the Atlantic monitored a steady stream of transmissions from the mid-ocean area between Newfoundland and the Azores. Interpretation of these intercepts enabled the Tenth Fleet to draw the contours of what seemed to be a concerted operation by what appeared to be an orchestrated team of at least five U-boats.

From the nature of their transmissions, the Tenth Fleet deduced that they were sending in daily weather reports; and from their failure to engage in offensive operations, Knowles assumed that they formed a meteorological picket line on the great Atlantic arc. It is quite possible that these uncanny deductions were much facilitated by the Tenth Fleet's new ability to read the transmissions instead of merely intercepting them, thanks presumably to the possession of the code books and cipher keys from the U-505. At any rate, the deductions and assumptions were correct. The five boats were there and they were weather pickets. Each had a *Luftwaffe* meteorologist on board who supplied data for both short-range and long-range weather forecasts from the center of the ocean area where Western Europe's weather is "made."

Judging from the log the Tenth Fleet kept of their transmissions, they took up their stations late in May, clearly in anticipation of the imminent Allied invasion of Europe. The first to broadcast the weather, on May 25, was the *U-853*. It was followed by the *U-804*, the *U-858*, the *U-855*, and another that remains unidentified to this day.

Aside from the fact that no U-boat was ever welcome in any part of the Atlantic, these boats were doubly unwelcome at this time because their mission had a direct bearing on General Eisenhower's big job. Their work was supposed to aid the *Luftwaffe* in making flight arrangements for missions against the Allied expeditionary forces. It took Knowles some time to develop the plot of this operation and so it was only on June 3, but seventy-two hours before D Day, that Tenth Fleet could enlighten CINCLANT about them, their presumed stations, and mission.

Admiral Ingersoll picked the *Croatan* group of Captain Vest to break up the group, and the carrier departed on the mission on June 4. It was detained en route to the picket area by the sinking of *U-490* (see page 271) and reached its destination only on June 15, nine days after D Day. That same day, a top priority signal from Tenth Fleet reported three bearings on a U-boat. It turned out to be the *U-853*, commanded by Kapitaenleutnant Helmut Sommer, a skilled and cocky skipper who prided himself on his ability to elude his hunters. The *Croatan* group moved immediately to run down the bearings, but though it searched eagerly for seventy-two hours, it failed to locate the elusive Sommer.

A weather report Sommer put on the air on June 17 was picked up by a score of Huffduff stations and a sharp fix was obtained on the *U-853*, still in the same area where it was first spotted. This time Sommer's luck had a few holes punched into it. Running down this latest fix, two fighter planes from the *Croatan* found and strafed him, inflicting so many casualties that Sommer, who was himself wounded seriously, decided with a heavy heart to "commence return passage," as the U-Boat Command's War Diary put it, "on account of a large number of the crew being unfit for duty."

On June 24, its mission unaccomplished, the *Croatan* group retired from the hunt. It was replaced by the *Wake Island* group, commanded by Captain James R. Tague, USN, that also failed to dispose of the remaining pickets but suffered the loss of a destroyer escort in its sole encounter with the only picket boat it managed to stir up. It was the *U-804* which the destroyer escort *Douglas L. Howard* spotted in the process of breaking surface eight miles away, 480 miles east of Flemish Cape, on August 2. The U-boat submerged promptly and fired three torpedoes from periscope depth, hitting the *Fiske*, another destroyer escort of the *Wake Island's* screen, as it moved cautiously to aid the *Howard* in its sonar approach. The *Fiske* virtually broke into two and sank, and the *U-804* slipped out of the noose.

Undaunted and unbowed, the four remaining weather pickets then departed for home, leaving behind some apprehension at Tenth Fleet. Low was highly displeased with the dismal record of this hunt, in the light of the fairly comprehensive intelligence plot Knowles was able to supply. It was an inconclusive operation for both sides, at that. The irresistible momentum of the Allied invasion considerably reduced the value of the contribution these weather boats could make to the German effort to stem it. They showed, nevertheless, that U-boats in the Atlantic were still tough nuts to crack, and were still capable of inflicting painful damage, even on the run.

The qualified success of this mission induced the German High Command to return a second wave of weather picket boats to the same general area, to supply vitally needed meteorological data for the frenetic counter-thrust with which Hitler hoped to turn the table—for what was to become known as the Battle of the Bulge. Not unlike everybody else in the Allied camp, where a creeping complacency took hold, the Tenth Fleet was off its toes and failed either to anticipate or to size up this second weather venture. This was probably due to the fact that nothing seemed to stir in the ocean. After a brief flurry in September, naval warfare virtually ceased in the Western Atlantic. In November, only forty-one U-boats were operating in the entire ocean, the smallest number since 1941. A few boats still operated fitfully off the Eastern Sea Frontier, but none in the Caribbean and along the Central Atlantic Convoy Route. Huffduff was almost mute, for the first time in the war.

Thus deprived of its crucial hearing aid, the Tenth Fleet attributed no special significance to the occasional transmissions the high frequency-direction finder stations still monitored and forwarded from December 5 on, traced as they were to the vicinity of Rockall and to a point between the Faroes and Greenland. In actual fact, those transmissions originated with three weather-reporting U-boats—the *U-870*, the *U-1052* and the *U-1232*—which Doenitz had sent out on Hitler's personal orders on a vital weather mission. Totally undetected and operating with complete impunity, these boats supplied the data Hitler needed to unleash his Ardennes offensive. The information broadcast by them enabled the Fuehrer's meteorologists to predict the foul weather on the Western Front that grounded Allied planes and immobilized the ground troops. An invaluable contribution even under the circumstances, and despite the eventual failure of the thrust toward the Meuse, it was appreciated by Doenitz who radioed these boats on December 20, four days after the start of the offensive when its German tide was the highest: "Your weather reports in this last period carried decision for establishing the start of our major offensive in the West, begun December 16."

Nothing whatever was done to interfere with this operation, not even when the three U-boats, their mission accomplished, turned around and commenced their homeward journey. Emboldened by the impunity they enjoyed during the crucial part of the expedition, they looked around for victims to enliven their homeward passage. Thus on December 22, the *U-870* pounced upon a slow westbound convoy, torpedoed a landing ship out of it, then blasted the fantail of the destroyer escort *Fogg* (in which the convoy commander had his pennant) killing fourteen men. Later it sank a Liberty ship, a British freighter and a French patrol craft, virtually as an afterthought, for this was not the major assignment of its mission.

Only now did Tenth Fleet awaken to this new menace but found only the *U-1053* still reporting the weather. By the time a search party could reach the location where Huffduff fixes indicated its presence, the *U-1053* moved out of the danger zone and sailed for home. However, surveillance was sharpened in the wake of the fiasco, and Tenth Fleet then found *U-248*, with Oberleutnant Johann-Friedrich Loos in command which Doenitz had dispatched to relieve *U-1053*. Owing to some confusion in the evaluation of the Tenth Fleet fixes, a search party sent after the *U-Loos* returned empty handed. But with all the Huffduff station now tuned in on its weather transmissions, the elusive U-boat lived on borrowed time. It was not until January 16, and only after CINCLANT had sternly reprimanded the hunters for the low quality of their search, that Loos' boat was found and sunk—the first sinking in the new regime of Admiral Jonas Ingram who had relieved Ingersoll as CINCLANT exactly two months before.

Even the elimination of the *U-Loos* failed to put an end to these weather pickets. Where the *U-248* vanished "like a breath from a mirror" now appeared an especially troublesome U-boat, the *U-1230*. It had taken up meteorological duties after ferrying two German spies, the Sad Sack pair Gimpel and Colepaugh, to Maine. It was never found and survived the war.

It may sound somewhat anticlimactic, this exposition of futile hunts in a virtually empty ocean, indicating an apparent decline of the great Tenth Fleet before the U-boat war had run its course. Yet on the contrary, there was nothing anticlimactic about the effort for the Tenth Fleet was busier than ever, compelled to work harder as targets thinned in the ocean. It became a herculean effort, as the war was approaching its close, to locate the forlorn U-boats, wandering more or less aimlessly in the big ocean, subsisting on memories and illusions in a campaign of false pretense.

There was, to be sure, a major change inside the Tenth Fleet but I doubt if it had an adverse influence on its efficiency. Admiral Low had left, to take command of a cruiser division and to distinguish himself in due course in the Battle of Okinawa. His place was taken by Rear Admiral Allan R. McCann, Annapolis 1917, a submarine specialist like Low, coming to Tenth Fleet from command of the battleship *Iowa*. He found few oldtimers of the Low regime still in harness. The lure of the Pacific war was becoming far too strong for these able and gallant men to remain in the taxing but sedentary berths the Tenth Fleet provided.

But Knowles still held the helm in Intelligence, though even he was restive, hoping for a detail at sea. When Low was ready to leave, he invited "Kennie" to accompany him to the Pacific as his Intelligence officer and Knowles accepted the invitation avidly. But his old eye trouble that had forced his retirement a decade before, prevented him from going. It was fortunate for McCann who needed this invaluable aide; for Tenth Fleet that stood or fell with his contribution; and for the American antisubmarine effort that was just about to flare up again, in a last convulsion, with the arrival of the new snorkel boats in waters for which Tenth Fleet bore major responsibility.

CHAPTER XIX

The Last Harbour

~~~~~~~~~~~~~~~~~~~~~~~~~~~~~~~~~~~~~~~

> *. . . there is some sort of Cape Horn*
> *for all. Boys! beware of it . . .*
> *Greybeards! thank God it is passed . . .*
>
> HERMAN MELVILLE
> in White-Jacket

The *U-107* was a *Renommierboot*—an esteemed model boat close to the heart of the Grossadmiral and famed throughout the U-Boat Arm. A veteran of the *Atlantikschlacht*, it usually bloomed with cotton pennants, those coveted buntings of victory, whenever it returned from *Feindfahrt*, welcomed by reception committees as brass bands blared out the *Deutschlandlied*. Its high repute stemmed from its first skipper, none other than Kapitaenleutnant Hessler, celebrated equally as a torpedo virtuoso and as Doenitz's son-in-law. Under Hessler, a brilliant tactician, the *U-107* chalked up a phenomenal score (allegedly 87,000 tons); and then, under Oberleutnant Gelhaus, it had the honor of spearheading the second wave of the first *Paukenschlag* in 1942, raising havoc with our ships off the Capes of the Delaware.

Commisisoned in 1940, it was still in the thick of it in 1944. Now commanded by Leutnant Karl-Heinz Fritz, a young skipper Doenitz had scraped up from near to the bottom of his manpower barrel, it left Lorient early in May bound for waters off Nova Scotia.

In the career of *U-107*, this *Feindfahrt* was doubly meaningful. For one thing, it was destined to be its last war patrol, for the proud old lady and her young commanding officer had but a few more weeks to live. For another thing, it was a kind of maiden voyage nevertheless, because the boat sailed with a sensational new contrivance from which Doenitz, chastened as he was, still expected to regain the upper hand in the Battle of the Atlantic.

It was the snorkel, the quaint gadget that enabled the U-boats to breathe fresh air freely under the water. Old *U-107* had the special distinction of being the first snorkel-equipped U-boat to reach American shores.

Snorkel to the Rescue

The sudden appearance of the fabulous device returned excitement and uncertainty to the Atlantic battle. It galvanized the U-Boat Arm in the midst of its worst doldrums and filled it with new hope. It revitalized the Tenth Fleet that gradually realized it had a grave new challenge confronting it, just when it seemed it had solved all the old problems. The coming of the snorkel somehow symbolized the peculiar nature of the U-boat war that, in Doenitz's hands, kept renewing itself. The U-Boat Arm bounced back from all its setbacks, restoring again and again vigor and style to the unflagging campaign and prolonging the Battle of the Atlantic long after Doenitz had to admit, as he did on November 12, 1943: "The enemy holds every trump card."

As Commander Knowles expressed it, "Those who dismiss the U-boat war after July, 1943, don't know what they're talking about. It ended only on VE Day. Until then, it kept going like the dragon in the Nibelungen saga. You cut off a head and it grew two new ones. You smashed a tail and it sprouted another. If the war had lasted another year or two after 1945, the U-boat menace would have been revived, and probably in a graver form than during its darkest days. After 1943, Doenitz lost most of his battles and, in the end, he lost the war. But if the coming of the snorkel proved nothing else, it showed he never lost the initiative."

The snorkel grew from the old desire to make the submarine into a "true submersible." Ever since Alexander the Great descended into the sea "in a device which kept its occupants dry and admitted light," men sought to build a boat that could stay submerged indefinitely and use its maximum power for speed. Until quite recently, the submarine was essentially a surface craft so built as to be capable of operating below the water. It had to spend most of the time above it, however, submerging only for limited periods and staying below only as long as it could subsist on batteries and on canned air within its pressure hull.

In his grandiose illusion about the decisive potentialities of the U-boat, Doenitz felt keenly this limitation and from 1936 on, worked assiduously on the development of a "true submersible." Yet as late as 1944, he still had only boats whose "mobility," as he put it, "was restricted for all practical purposes to operations on the surface."

The snorkel was to change that. It was not a new idea. Alexander of Macedonia is credited with the first use of an underwater warrior breathing through a reed projecting upward. Simon Lake described the snorkel principle in 1900. The Royal Netherlands Navy used "snorkels" on two of its pre-World War II submarines which the Germans actually captured in 1940.

But according to Doenitz, the idea first popped up in the German Navy only late in 1942, and then in the suggestion of an outsider. At a conference in Paris in November of that year, that was attended by the big brass of the OKM's bureau of ships—Schuerer, Brocking and Waas—an engineer named Walter, who was working on improved underwater propulsion with a turbine running on high test hydrogen-peroxide—proposed that "the U-boats should be equipped with a ventilating apparatus by means of which, while the boats was submerged, air could be drawn through a tube from the surface for the Diesels and the exhaust gases expelled." Doenitz jumped eagerly at the chance, he said, because he immediately realized that the U-boat, equipped with an apparatus of this kind, would no longer be compelled to surface in order to recharge its batteries. "The demand for a 'one-hundred-per-cent underwater vessel' of high speed, or at least sufficiently high speed for its tactical employment, could thus be met with current types modified in this manner," he wrote. "Permission for immediate experimental construction was granted, and at home practical experiments were started with Professor Walter's air intake and explusion apparatus, which in modified and practical form, was later given the name of 'Schnorchel'."

In actual fact, Doenitz was not as eager as this to embrace the snorkel, if only because at that time he still expected to win the war without it. The idea was shelved for a while, but was dusted off in the summer of 1943, when the mounting attacks of radar-equipped Allied aircraft virtually banished the U-boats from the surface. Work on the snorkel began at forced speed and an operational model was put into mass production at the end of 1943.

The snorkel which was then added to the standard equipment of a number of U-boats was a 26-foot extensible dual intake-exhaust tube, combined as an air-intake and gas-outlet, that could be folded when not in use or telescoped up from the pressure hull while the U-boat was at periscope depth. When snorkeling, the only portion of the submarine exposed was the top of the tube, producing a "feather" on the water hardly bigger than that of a periscope head; the top of the tube was usually covered with a rubberized anti-radar material.

The venerable *U-107* was one of a first contingent of eight U-boats which, in the early spring of 1944, at a special plant in St. Nazaire, was fitted out with snorkel, to breathe, not merely fresh air to the submerged Diesels, but indeed new life into the U-boat war. After a shake-down cruise in the Baltic, the boat was to leave for the Western Atlantic in April, but teething troubles with the device detained it. It was thus only on May 10, that it could depart on a double mission—to sink as much as it could of the strategic cargoes then moving briskly for the build-up of *Overlord* and to pin down American antisubmarine forces thousands of miles from the English Channel. It was a dual mission doubly unaccomplished. In Leutnant Fritz's inexperienced hands, the *U-107* sank nothing; and it operated with such caution that it remained totally inconspicuous through its sojourn. Far from pinning down American-Canadian antisubmarine forces, it never as much as attracted their attention and, in fact, never appeared on a single Tenth Fleet plot.

The Snorkel Pioneers

The next batch of snorkel-equipped boats Doenitz sent into the Western Atlantic proved far more effective. They were the weather pickets I have just described. Their ability to escape detection despite the constant monitoring of their radio transmissions and the spirited searches of three aircraft carrier groups—the *Croatan, Wake Island* and *Bogue*—caused some concern in Tenth Fleet, although the exact nature of the new menace was not yet evident.

Tenth Fleet was misled in its appreciation of the snorkel by reports which tended to emphasize the deficiencies of the device. Prisoners from recently sunk U-boats who had some experience with the gadget on training cruises in the Baltic, and who were now subjected to intensive interrogation by Op-16-Z at Fort Hunt, professed to be rather unhappy about the gadget. They described with some feeling and eloquence how unpleasant if not unbearable life was in the snorkelers; how the wind was apt to make exhaust gases back up whenever the boat turned to leeward in a strong breeze; how the Diesels exhausted the oxygen below when waves caused the float-valves, designed to keep out slopping seawater, to close. Such derogatory information induced us in Op-16-W to compose a number of Norden broadcasts ridiculing the snorkel. Basing its attitude to the device on disparaging reports from Op-16-Z, Tenth Fleet became inclined to regard the snorkel as capable of doing more harm than good to the U-Boat Arm.

Apprehension mounted, however, when a single snorkeler, in the capable hands of Oberleutnant Hans Offermann, returned the U-boat war to the East Coast, in a persuasive demonstration of the new gadget's lethal effectiveness. Early in July, just when Leutnant Fritz was going home with an empty bag, Offermann's *U-518* departed from Lorient to subject the defenses of the Eastern Sea Frontier to another test. They proved to be as deficient as ever, only this time the possession of the snorkel by the *U-Offermann* served as an extenuating circumstance. Crossing the ocean mostly at periscope depth on snorkel, Offermann reached the Carolina coast early in September and promptly produced a Tenth Fleet fix that unleashed a spirited search by three different escort carrier groups. The search was called off prematurely, and Offermann proceeded promptly to torpedo the *George Ade*, the first American merchantman to run afoul of a snorkeler, a little over 100 miles off Wilmington, North Carolina. He then returned home unscathed, arriving at his new base in Norway on October 22.

Even on the very small scale of this initial test, it was already evident that a new menace had been added to the U-boat war and that the snorkelers would be very hard to catch. During this period, Doenitz had three U-boats so far west in the Atlantic, the two snorkelers and the *U-233*, a 1500-tonner sent to Halifax on a mining mission, that had no snorkel. Tenth Fleet was prompt to lead the *Card* escort carrier group to the *U-233* and the hapless boat was duly sunk in the afternoon of July 5. But both of the snorkelers eluded all hunters and went home.

By the time of the *U-Offermann's* departure, Tenth Fleet had a pretty good picture of the snorkel and came to regard it as a clear new threat that had neither been properly anticipated nor prepared for with appropriate countermeasures. There was little if anything in our anti-submarine tactics and doctrines pertinent to this menace. The escort carrier planes in particular were baffled by the new German tactics the snorkel inspired, especially when improved versions produced several snorkel virtuosos among the U-boat skippers.

In a very real sense, then, the snorkel thus succeeded in doing exactly what Doenitz hoped it would accomplish: it provided effective protection from the U-boats' most dangerous foes, the planes of the escort carrier groups. The protection was so effective, indeed, that from September, 1944, through March, 1945, the escort carrier groups managed to sink but a single U-boat, and a non-snorkeler at that, although they accounted for forty-six U-boats during the prior sixteen months.

This sole victim of the escort carriers was the *U-1062*, commanded by Oberleutnant Karl Albrecht, homeward bound from Penang when Tenth Fleet pinpointed it for the *Mission Bay*. It was disposed of on

September 30, by the destroyed escort *Fessenden* of the escort carrier's screen, within fifteen miles of the position indicated by Tenth Fleet's estimate. In that same action, another U-boat was also claimed by Captain John R. Ruhsenberger, USN, commanding officer of the group, as a "sure kill" but Tenth Fleet's hard-boiled assessors disagreed. After a close scrutiny of the action report, their verdict was, "No damage." And they were right, too. The U-boat in question was the *U-219* with Korvettenkapitaen Walter Burghagen in command. It not only escaped from this encounter in perfect health but managed to survive the war by sitting it out at Batavia. On VE Day, it surrendered to the Japanese.

Admiral Low Leaves the Tenth Fleet

The apperance of the snorkel coincided with other changes in the U-boat war that altered radically its whole complexion. They had nothing to do with techniques or tactics. They involved its top-ranking personalities—Admiral Low and Grossadmiral Doenitz—in manners as different as were the men themselves. Unknown to each other, although locked in what was tantamount to a personal contest, the two great war leaders now reached the parting of the ways. Low went to even greater personal glory. Doenitz marched off to total defeat and prison.

Even in September 1944, Low felt he had done his job at Tenth Fleet, and yearning for the action his contemporaries shared in the active theatres of war, he asked Admiral King to give him a command at sea. Preparatory work was in full swing for the Okinawa invasion in which the Navy was to assume a greater than usual role, going all out to support General Bruckner's Army forces on the island for weeks, as the plans envisaged, long after the landing operations. Cruiser Division 16 was slated to play a major part in this support operation, and King gave its command to Low, effective January 1, 1945.

It promised to be a welcome relief, no matter how one looked at it, the sound and fury of "real war" after twenty months of vitally important but sedentary duty in the Navy Department. Most of his colleagues at Tenth Fleet had gone into combat. Haines was with a squadron of submarines at a secret base in Australia, and was recently upped to command Task Force 72. Sample was back in the Pacific, flying again and collecting more Gold Stars for his Legion of Merit. Isbell was being groomed for command of the *Yorktown*, serving temporarily on the carrier *Franklin* (on which he was to perish on March 19, 1945, off Okinawa). Fitz was about to go, having just received command of the cruiser *Santa Fé*.

During those days and weeks, when the U-boats appeared to be licked, Low so yearned for a real ship under his feet that he even envied King for his little *Dauntless* at the Navy Yard. The 1460-ton former Dodge yacht was King's flagship from which he commuted daily to his office in the Navy Department. Its "operations" consisted of weekend runs down the Potomac during which the Commander-in-Chief held conferences on war strategy with Low and other members of his staff.

Now suddenly it seemed Low would not be able to leave after all. The Atlantic was astir again and the U-boat war showed ominous signs of revival. Reports about a possible buzz-bomb attack on the East Coast began to arrive at Tenth Fleet. They were followed by definite evidence that Doenitz was preparing another major blitz in American waters, now that he had the snorkel and it worked.

Virtually last of Low's functions in Tenth Fleet was to evaluate the significance of the snorkel to the U-boat war and figure out a remedy against it. He called in Morse and Steinhardt and asked them to analyze the situation in Asworg—(1) to develop a precis on the snorkel operations from which Tenth Fleet could evolve new tactics and doctrines; and (2) to suggest possible countermeasures the laboratories could make.

Low reviewed the future with King, on one of the *Dauntless'* "operational cruises" down the Potomac, and the *de iure* Commander Tenth Fleet, his dour Commander in Chief, reassured him: "There is nothing more you can do here, Low," King said. "Pack up and go!"

In November, then, Admiral McCann arrived in Washington to relieve him, and Low left Tenth Fleet as quietly and unceremoniously as he came, with the Distinguished Service Medal as his only tangible reward. His career as the *de facto* boss of his Navy's unspectacular but phenomenally successful antisubmarine effort was succintly summed up in the citation that accompanied his DSM. It spelled out—the "Well done" of a superhuman job whose magnitude and diversity staggered the imagination and would have felled a lesser man. It read:

"DISTINGUISHED SERVICE MEDAL:

"For exceptionally meritorious service to the Government of the United States in a duty of great responsibility as Chief of Staff. United States Tenth Fleet, from March 1943, to January 1945. Exercising command of the Tenth Fleet under the delegated authority of the Commander in Chief, United States Fleet, Rear Admiral Low conducted an aggressive campaign against submarines in the Atlantic. Maintaining effective liaison with the General Staff of the United States Army, the British Admiralty and Canadian Naval Headquarters to insure maximum efficiency in combined operations, he coordinated and directed the activities of Allied anti-submarine forces as they systematically tracked down and destroyed German under-sea marauders ranging the vast reaches of the Atlantic. Responsible for the protection of Allied shipping in the Eastern, Gulf and Caribbean Sea Frontiers, he exercised close control over all convoys under United States cognizance. Working tirelessly throughout the European phase of World War II, he correlated United States anti-submarine training and material development, consistantly supplied anti-submarine and training procedures to our forces afloat, and made available the latest intelligence data to the Commander in Chief, United States Fleet, and to other Fleet and Sea Frontier commanders. By his outstanding professional skill and judgment, Rear Admiral Low ably discharged the multiple responsibilities of his highly specialized command, thereby contributing substantially to the success of our Naval forces in the Battle of the Atlantic. The brilliant achievements of the Tenth Fleet reflect the highest credit upon Rear Admiral Low, his loyal staff, and the United States Naval Service."

The Tragedy of Doenitz

The loaded adjectives and unusual rhetoric blossoms of the citation go far to show how vast and difficult the job was and how well he performed it to King's absolute satisfaction. That was all the fanfare that accompanied his departure. Despite the magnitude of his responsibilities and the brilliance of his performance, Low was no glamor hero. Outside COMINCH, few ever heard of him.

Low's anonymity was in sharp contrast to the growing notoriety of Doenitz as the Grossadmiral was falling with increasing momentum from the lofty frying pan of his military assignment into the scorching fire of Nazi politics. If there still seemed to be a set pattern in his conduct of the war at sea, precision in his dispositions, and purpose in his operations plans, it was merely the reflection of his past performance like the light that lingers for a while after the sun had set. In actual fact, he was resorting to improvisations as the dice fell, to haphazard moves and ruthless measures, no longer thinking through his decisions or making his moves with painstaking deliberation. He no longer had the time.

The fact that the *Kriegsmarine* under him had no part whatever in the attempt on Hitler's life on July 20, 1944, and that Doenitz rushed headlong to Rastenburg after the attempt to assure the badly shaken Fuehrer of this Thousand Year Reich (that had barely a year to go) of his unshakable fealty, propelled him to great prominence as the most trustworthy among the highest commanders. He was drawn deeper into the bottomless morass of Nazism, his doubts overcome by his admiration of Hitler and gratitude for the trust and favors he received at the Fuherer's hands. Now admitted into the inner circle, he was allowed to attend the super-secret conferences at which Hitler openly discussed his plans to go down "in a holocaust of blood—not only the enemy's," as Shirer put it, "but that of his own people."

At one of these conferences Hitler proposed to denounce the Geneva Convention and "treat enemy prisoners without any consideration for their rights"—meaning to shoot them summarily—"to make the enemy realize that we are determined to fight for our existence with all the means at our disposal." Hitler then turned to Doenitz and asked him: "Herr Grossadmiral, please consider the pros and cons of this step and report to me as soon as possible."

Doenitz returned with his answer the next day. He told Hitler that, in his opinion, the disadvantages of such a step would outweigh the advantages. After all, he had an enormous personal stake in the question, because thousands of his own U-boat men were in Allied prison camps, subject to reprisals. He equivocated nevertheless, and told Hitler slyly what the Fuehrer wanted to hear: "It would be better in any case to keep up outside appearances and carry out the measures believed necessary without announcing them beforehand.

If in August, 1944, only his nerves gave way, now his soul disintegrated. The tragedy of Karl Doenitz was mounting to its climax. The former undisputed hero of the *Atlantikschlacht* began to cut a pathetic figure in the company of Hitler and his knaves, and we in Op-16-W now thought we could make him the butt of our jokes, especially when he continued to threaten us with future offensives. We chose his ephemeral threats for our theme, and wrote a pun-filled Norden script that was to become a popular topic of conversation in the *Kriegsmarine*, its message wrapped up in a catchy refrain.

The broadcast purported to be a historical review of four significant periods in Doenitz's career in the U-Boat Arm that began, we said, genially enough in 1939-40 when his top skippers were still allowed to address him with the familiar *Du* ("Thou"). That was, we said, the first period—the *Period of the Du-Sager* (Thou-Sayers).

Then he rose in prestige and rank, and his head swelled, until he tolerated only yes-men around him. That was the second period, we said—the *Period of Ja-Sager* (Yes-Sayers). Then came the great debacles—the *Period of Versager* (Sorry-Sayers). And now, we concluded, he predicts, as so often in the past, that the U-boat would stage a come-back

in the *Atlantikschlacht*. How do you call a period like this? Ah, yes—
it is the *Period of the Wahrsager* (Soothsayers), we jeered.

Du-Sager . . . Ja-Sager . . . Ver-Sager . . . Wahr-Sager

This was the recurrent refrain of this broadcast and very soon it was
echoed, we learned from the incoming new batch of prisoners of war,
throughout the German Navy.

Then a strange intelligence report that passed through my desk jolted
me out of this smug, comical mood. It originated inside Germany, in
October, 1944, with one of the best-informed contacts of a major Allied
intelligence agency. As a matter of fact, the informant—a very high
ranking Army officer—pretended to be a loyal cohort of Hitler's and
worked close to him, but used his exceptional vantage point to keep
the Allies posted of developments at Fuehrerhauptquartier.

Now in October, 1944 (!), he sent through a fantastic piece of intelligence that was, in the context of those days, hard to fathom and impossible to believe. It averred flatly that *Hitler would soon make his
exit in some dramatic fashion and that prior to his departure, most
probably by suicide, he would appoint Grossadmiral Doenitz to succeed
him as Chief of State.*

The report from Germany stated all this in so many words, as a foregone conclusion—months before the final drama in the Nazi Valhalla.

Even if it could not be accepted as a piece of useful intelligence, the
report suggested the propaganda theme of another Norden broadcast.
It was always our aim to disturb the cosy relationship Doenitz had with
his officers and men—one of the cornerstones of the U-Boat Arm's
coherence and strength—and to drive a wedge between them. We also
knew that Nazism had lost much of its former appeal to the U-boat men
and that many of them began to make Hitler and the Nazis responsible
for the holocaust into which the war was deteriorating.

After consultation with Commander Albrecht in Op-16-Z and obtaining the green light from Tenth Fleet via Commander Knowles, we wrote
a script, potentially the most important in Norden's career, based on
that strange intelligence report. Its appeal was inherent in the prediction
that Doenitz would succeed Hitler, thus linking him directly with the
Nazis. This meant, even to the most untutored U-boat man at the receiving end, that his Grossadmiral would no longer have the welfare of
the U-Boat Arm on his heart, would no longer preoccupy his mind with
the conduct of the U-boat war, but would leave the sinking ship like
all the other Nazi rats.

The intelligence report on which this Norden broadcast was based proved correct in every one of its predictions. Six months later, Hitler committed suicide and Doenitz became his anointed successor.

It was a moment of fantastic triumph in Op-16-W, even if the war itself had only but a few more days to go. But Tenth Fleet and our own Special Warfare Branch still had an important function to perform, a most delicate function at that. We knew that a strange operation going by the code-name *"Regenbogen"* was being prepared in the U-Boat Arm as an answer to the imminent unconditional surrender of the Third Reich. As soon as the code-word *"Regenbogen"* (Rainbow) would be flashed to the fleet, all units still afloat, both on and under the seas, would scuttle. We feared this. We were even more apprehensive that some of the more desperate U-boat commanders would continue the war as free-lancing raiders for a while, delaying the return of peace to the seven seas.

It was, therefore, Norden's new job to appeal to the U-Boat Arm with which it had this peculiar intimacy to obey the orders, to refrain from scuttling, and especially from the senseless adventure of continuing the war *"auf eigene Faust"* (on one's own). We thought that the re-broadcast of the old record in which the fantastic prediction was made would enhance his authority, so we called the Office of War Information at once and instructed them to put the record back on the turntable and beam it to the U-Boat Arm.

To our amazed surprise we were told by an OWI executive named Leonard Doob that the record was never played. When OWI originally received it, its brass regarded it so far fetched that they put a kill order on this particular Norden. Disappointing though this experience was for us, it did nothing to diminish Norden's standing in the eyes of the U-boat men. His appeal to disregard the "Rainbow" was not heeded and 215 U-boats were scuttled by their crews. But only two fanatical Nazi U-boat commanders disobeyed orders and refused to surrender their boats.

The U-Boat Arm that embarked upon the war with fifty-seven units, many of them mere canoes fit to operate only in the Baltic, grew and grew and grew like Topsy, until it had a grand total of 1,170 U-boats, 863 of which became operational. *Its losses totalled 781 boats!* At the end of the war, Doenitz still had the fantastic total of 336 U-boats, nearly seven times the number with which he started the war.

His tragedy is reflected even more darkly in the U-Boat Arm's human sacrifices. Over 39,000 officers and men served in U-boats in the German submarine fleet in World War II. All but 7,000 of them found an ocean grave.

It was the worst defeat of any branch of service in any war in history, for which Karl Doenitz bears the major responsibility. After the war, he faced Allied judges at Nuremberg who extracted from him a personal forfeit. I thought then and still believe today that it was a foolish act and a miscarriage of international law. For Doenitz did not sin against the Allies. His crime was against Germany and it would have been more appropriate for the German people to judge him.

"Moby Dick"

As if Admiral Low's tidy mind and pedantic presence had kept a certain orderliness and symmetry in the whole U-boat war, it seemed to become all confusion and anarchy after his departure. The Battle of the Atlantic was about to burst in its final issue, not like a balloon, but rather like a Roman candle.

If Commander Knowles was somewhat at a loss to brief Admiral McCann with his customary clarity and force, it was because everything in the U-boat war became blurred. The very location of the sinkings illustrated the metastasis at this terminal stage of the Atlantic battle. U-boats perished around the Azores, inside the Eastern Sea Frontier, off Land's End, southwest of Gibraltar, but also in Germany. The greatest devastation was caused, not by the Navies of the Allies, but by the U.S. Army Air Forces. On March 30, 1945, AAF bombers destroyed fifteen U-boats in raids on Wilhelmshaven, Bremen and Hamburg. A few days later, another AAF raid destroyed six more at Kiel, Germany's historic naval base.

As far as the U-boats were concerned, January, 1945, still found them operating briskly, with their old skill and verve, in the North Atlantic and within the Canadian Sea Frontier, sinking a total of ten Allied ships. But after that, only in the North Sea and the English channel did their persistent offensive amount to anything.

In this twilight it was difficult to see clearly even the contours of moves and events. And certain tidings floating to and fro now tended to compound the confusion. Agents reported from Norway the apparent assembly of a group of U-boats amidst preparations whose thoroughness and unusual secrecy hinted at something extra special in the making. Linked to this development, it seemed, was the dispatch of a trio of spies to the United States, for the first time since the summer of 1942, when the *U-202* and the *U-584* landed saboteurs in New York and Florida.

Feverish minds, stimulated by the havoc the V-bombs had wrought in England, now predicted Doenitz would stage a buzz-bomb attack on

American East Coast cities from U-boats equipped with missile launchers. Several intelligence reports arrived to support the *canard*, including a vague communication from an ambiguous character, a self-styled master spy who later became famed (to movie audiences rather than intelligence experts) as the "Counterfeit Traitor."

Although, of course, it was not as clear then as it is today, all this reflected the gradual decomposition of the *Atlantikschlacht* as a coherent and purposeful battle, and the spread of guerilla tactics even to the major ocean areas.

Despite all the confusion, perplexity and anarchy, Doenitz was to perform yet another service, not to his own country over which he was soon to rule in a brief binge of chaos, but—if its lessons are learned and heeded—to the United States. In his last feeble gesture of a blitz, he proved conclusively that this country remained vulnerable to intruders from under the sea, and that all the sweat and toil of the years had failed to devise and erect foolproof defenses against them. This proof was provided in the so-called Operation *Seewolf* of March–May, 1945, which I described at some length in the first chapter. It was reiterated in a far less spectacular but potentially more dangerous manner by a single U-boat that, it seemed, had nine lives.

It was the *U-853*, Kapitaenleutnant Sommer's elusive raider, familiar to us from that meterological operation in the late spring of 1944, when it evaded the search of two escort carrier groups in mid-Atlantic. Now it was back with a new commander, Oberleutnant Helmut Froemsdorf, outwitting all—the Tenth Fleet, the Eastern Sea Frontier, the formidable force of vessels patrolling off our shores—to perish at last in an uneven engagement as the last U-boat to die in World War II.

In following down the career of this boat, we have to go back a bit, to June 1944, to a point not too far from Flemish Cap. For a whole month, despite continuous search by two British MACs (catapult ships capable of sending off five aircraft each) and the entire *Croatan* group, the U-boat stayed there and was so difficult to locate that the American carrier's crew nicknamed it "Moby Dick." There was indeed pathos in the fate of this boat for which Melville's words were strangely appropriate: "Give it up, Sub-Subs! For by how much the more pains ye take to please the world, by so much the more shall ye forever go thankless!"

But "Moby Dick" refused to give up. In the spring of 1945, it was back in the Western Atlantic, as if seeking the "final harbour whence we unmoor no more." A type IX-C, 740-ton boat equipped with the snorkel, the *U-853* reached its operating area off southern New England late in April. Ably skippered by Froemsdorf, it was as elusive as ever, and the Tenth Fleet had no idea of its presence so close inshore.

It remained undetected on this well-travelled route between New York and Boston, until 5:40 P.M. on May 5, when just off Naragansett Bay, it torpedoed the small collier *Black Point*, Boston-bound with a load of soft coal. The *Black Point* settled quickly by the stern and was gone twenty-five minutes after the explosion. The Yugoslav freighter *Kamen* happened to be passing by and put an SOS on the air, to stir up a hornet's nest and bring a small armada of American warships dashing to the scene. First to arrive was the *Moberly*, a Coast Guard frigate, commanded by Lieutenant Commander L. B. Tollaksen, USCG. He assumed tactical command, pending the arrival of the Task Group commander, F. C. B. McCune, USN, who had his pennant in the destroyer *Ericson*. Others at the scene were the destroyer escorts *Amick* and *Atherton*. Now these four warships were to write a special saga for this concluding chapter of the U-boat war in the American area of the ocean.

There was nothing Froemsdorf could do to break out of the noose that became tighter by the moment, and he never as much as showed a hand while the four American warships peppered him with everything they had. The punitive action began at 7:20 P.M. on May 5, a hundred minutes after the torpedoing of *Black Point*. At 11:37 P.M. it was all over. A hedge-hog attack from *Atherton* killed the *U-853*, but the hunters kept up the hunt. Everybody sensed this was their last chance to work over a bottomed U-boat, to shoot off ammunition, and have a "little fun" all 'round. The group now led by Commander McCune, kept hammering at the dead boat until noon May 6, when Froemsdorf's cap was recovered from the flotsam and debris, together with his chart table. McCune called off the operation.

At that very moment, thousands of miles from the spot, surrender negotiations were in progress between General Eisenhower's emissaries and the German senior officers Doenitz had delegated for the pathetic job. And exactly nine hours and forty-one minutes after Task Group 60.7 had dropped the last depth charge on the limp body of *U-853*, General Alfred Jodl and Admiral Friedeburg, Doenitz's friend and personal representative at the somber ceremony, signed the unconditional surrender papers at Rheims, France. It was 2:41 A.M. May 7 in France. It was forty-one minutes past nine o'clock, still on May 6, in Narragansett Bay.

Like "Moby Dick," the *U-853* sank "without a ripple of renown."

Today it is in twenty fathoms of water a few miles south of Newport, a favorite target for skin divers in Rhode Island. During the years, teams of those divers made their way into the sunken submarine, brought up life rafts, clipped off the upper part of the periscope, and even removed human bones, including a complete skeleton.

On June 15, 1945, the Tenth Fleet was dissolved.

This phantom force of the United States Navy rated only a casual "Well done" from the Commander in Chief but in a brief eulogy, Admiral King expressed most succintly nevertheless, the job that was behind them all.

"The effective work of the Tenth Fleet," Admiral King wrote of the war's strangest Naval organization whose nominal Commander he was, "contributed outstandingly to the success of the United States naval operations in the Battle of the Atlantic."

Epilogue

THE IMPENITENT CYCLE

All these tidal gatherings, growth and decay
Shining and darkening are forever
Renewed; and the whole cycle impenitently
Revolves, and all the past is future:
Make it a difficult world . . . for practical people.

ROBINSON JEFFERS
in Practical People

EPILOGUE

The Impenitent Cycle

...'tis a poor relief we gain
To change the place, but keep the pain . . .

Isaac Watts (1674-1748)

World War II ended in a bizarre paradox. At the conclusion of its European phase, huge Allied armies were chopping and hacking their paths over vast rubble toward the foregone conclusion. In the Far East, a stupendous and costly but slow build-up was under way to push our invading forces to the doorsteps of Japan. But while the enormous preparations to defeat Japan in 1946—or maybe only later —were still in the making, two atomic bombs dropped at random finished her off within a week in August 1945. And while a vast effort was needed to enable the Allies to approach the waterfront of *Festung Europa*, the Germans were, at the very end of the war, but a few miles off the American coast and stayed there, without too much effort, at that.

The Fateful Triangle

During the last weeks of the war, in April-May 1945—when the U-Boat Arm was disintegrating at its seams and, presumably, American defenses in the Sea Frontiers were at their peak of efficiency—there were nevertheless as many as eight U-boats close to the East Coast, doing more or less as they pleased. This was no reflection on the alertness and efficiency of the Tenth Fleet. It demonstrated rather how difficult if not impossible it was (and, as we shall see, still is) to account for every submarine at large in the oceanic mass.

This was the exact order of battle of those U-boats in American waters on the eve of Germany's surrender:

297

U-805 and *U-858,* the two boats of *Seewolf* which broke through Admiral Ingram's formidable barriers, were at their appointed battle stations close to the United States shoreline.

U-881, the Johnnie-come-lately of *Seewolf,* stood on the 60th meridian and *U-853* operated inside Narragansett Bay off Newport.

U-234, U-873 and *U-1228* prowled off the coast of Maine and *U-530* was on active war patrol off Long Island.

None of these U-boats was detected either by the huge American antisubmarine forces deployed all along the coast or by the intricate apparatus of the Tenth Fleet. Two of them were sunk in the end, to be sure, but only after their skippers, restive and trigger-happy to the last, decided to show their hands in the face of overwhelming odds. Five others were brought in when they heeded orders and surfaced meekly to surrender. The one off Long Island was never as much as suspected of being there, although it made several senseless attacks on shipping around New York both before and after Germany's surrender.

The concluding chapter in the career of *U-530* is especially interesting. It was commanded by an Oberleutnant named Otto Wermuth, a brash, fanatical Nazi who took literally the slogan the morale officer of his flotilla had posted on the bulletin board of his base at Christiansand, Norway. "We will never capitulate!" it read. "Better death than slavery!" Wermuth sailed on his last *Feindfahrt* with his fighting spirit intact and his wrath at fever pitch. Crossing the ocean at snorkel depth, he reached American waters in early May, sneaked up to the entrances to New York harbor, and scattered his torpedoes at several startled ships. Then disregarding Doenitz's injunction and the Allied order to cease fire and surrender, the *U-530* shaped a course for the River Plate and arrived safely in Juan Peron's Argentina in July, two months after VE Day.

The bracketing of this preposterous little flotilla of wayward U-boats and the cataclysmic bomb dropped on Japan may seem arbitrary and incongruous. But there is a close connection between the two. Submarines today are nuclear powered and carry missiles with nuclear warheads. The United States has them on station. The U.S.S.R. has them in whatever state of preparedness the Kremlin deems it useful. The British have their *Dreadnought,* and other nations—including Germany—will have them in due course.

Submarines that could sneak up to the enemy's coast would now carry and could launch nuclear missiles in a strategic onslaught with the promise of victory at the outset. The implications of the triangle

—submarines, missiles and nuclear energy—are important, not only for a general nuclear war that might confront the United States and the Soviet Union, but also for any of the wars Pentagon estimates miniaturize—for "finite" or "limited" wars, or whatever the jargon calls them.

We have seen what the submarine could do with the old weapons of World War II. The Germans started with fifty-seven submarines, and an increasing building program which by early 1943 brought them to their peak war strength of 374 despite continuing losses. Their top performance was more than 700,000 tons of ships sunk in the month of June, 1942, when Doenitz's inventory totaled 290 submarines. Their war total of sinkings was 2,753 ships amounting to 14,557,000 tons. (For comparison with these figures, the present U.S. Merchant Marine totals just over three million tons.)

The Allied anti-U-boat effort of World War II involved the employment of some 950 Allied oceangoing antisubmarine warfare ships and 2,200 antisubmarine warfare aircraft. When the war ended, Germany still had 336 submarines, and deliveries of new construction were exceeding twenty U-boats per month. Thus the Allied antisubmarine victory resulted, not from total destruction of the German submarine force, but from destruction of submarines at a rate too high for the survival of the effectiveness of that force.

If these statistics are astounding, the capabilities of the new weapons system packed into the nuclear-powered missile-firing submarine staggers the imagination. Admiral Burke called it "the most powerful weapons system ever devised." The atomic submarine is not the half-amphibian that depended on the earth's atmosphere to breathe and could but creep submerged on the miserable power of its precarious batteries. It is the absolute submersible, Jules Verne's utopian design come true. American nuclear submarines can stay at sea for three years and could theoretically spend all that time under the water. Their maximum sub-surface speed is thirty knots. They can dive to depths of five-hundred feet or more.

Each carries sixteen "A-2" Polaris missiles whose range is 1,500 nautical miles and whose aggregate destructive power equals that of the total of all bombs dropped in World War II. The firepower of the missiles is supplemented by the mobility and operational flexibility of the submarines. The solid-fuel missiles can be launched from submerged submarines stationed virtually anywhere in the oceans of the world or under the Arctic icepack where they are supposed to be "undetectable." Because of their mobility and stealth, they are not subject to the military disadvantages of fixed bases. The long range of the missile enables the submarine to stay away from the sources of retaliation and reduces their exposure to shore-based antisubmarine measures. Since it is not dependent for its own survival on a hair-trigger response to the first indications of a hostile ballistic missile attack, the weapons system lends itself, as Defense Secretary Robert S. McNamara expressed it, "to a more calculated and deliberate response," reducing the danger of accidental nuclear wars.

The Polaris submarine closely approaches another utopian dream, the single weapon concept. In addition to its missile capability, this submarine has the latest sonar equipment, torpedo tubes, and fire control equipment which give it an antisubmarine warfare capability. Most important is the fact that this submarine is of unprecedented and unequaled stealth and secrecy.

There is no reason to doubt that the U.S.S.R. also has nuclear submarines capable of launching Polaris-type missiles. And there is no reason to indulge in the smug belief that those who are friends today, or profess to be friends, might not suffer a relapse and become enemies again at another juncture of history.

The Military Revolution

While the offensive power of the American Polaris submarine weapons system is stupendous and probably decisive, American defenses against hostile submarines are inadequate. I am willing to go so far as to say that they are in as bad a shape as they were at the time of the *Paukenschlag*. While there is much partisan talk about the so-called missile gap and the space gap, and all sorts of other gaps that may or may not exist, there is very little talk of the antisubmarine warfare gap that actually exists. It is real and urgent both in absolute and relative terms, in relation to the Soviet submarine threat in either limited non-nuclear or general nuclear war, in conventional or nuclear submarines (as long as they are capable of launching missiles), in the defense of individual ships or convoys or, indeed, of the United States.

I realize it is incumbent upon me to explain and substantiate this assertion. I will, therefore, examine the various factors that produced this situation and survey the threat in the topical context of Soviet intentions and capabilities; then I propose to review the state of American ASW in the ideals and realities of its concepts, implements, installations and organization.

For centuries, war moved in essentially the same groove along more or less identical patterns. The final test was, as Oliver Wendell Holmes expressed it, the battle in some form. Then all of a sudden war burst its confines in time and space, in concepts and implements. It happened so recently and so fast that we could hardly recognize the change in all its ramifications or had time to appreciate it.

"Today," wrote General Pokrovsky of the Soviet Union in 1956, "the development of military technology, together with the resultant changes and the increasingly complex structure of all armies and navies, proceeds so rapidly that we have not only progressed far beyond the period of World War II, but also beyond the conditions of the war in Korea." We saw how different World War II was from World War I. "Those military commanders," Pokrovsky wrote, "who failed to understand this difference suffered cruel defeat on the battlefield as well as on the theoretical 'front'. One can now predict that, under contemporary conditions, a formalistic use of the experience of past wars can—if the new essence and the new means of warfare are not analyzed—only lead to severe failures."

How rapid the acceleration of change was could be demonstrated on Hitler's example. He triumphed in the beginning because he intuitively recognized the difference between World War I and World War II; but he succumbed in the end because he had failed to comprehend the *radical* differences between the first and the second halves of World War II. What does this mean? It means that the art of war is in the throes of a violent revolution. It is determined mostly by the invention and introduction of new implements of war.

This is not a new development by any means. When primitive man extended the range of his arm with a heavy club and picked up a stone to lend added force to his blow, he started this revolution that was never to subside. The introduction of gunpowder in Europe in the fourteenth century not only revolutionized warfare completely but also played a significant part in the change of the patterns of living from medieval to modern. The machine gun created another such upheaval at the turn of this century, uprooting tactics, which were maintained precariously by the equilibrium of firepower and mobility. The equilibrium was restored to the battlefield temporarily with the invention of the tank, only to be upset again, and now on a broad, operational scale, with the coming of nuclear weapons. Their stupendous firepower threatens to banish mobility altogether, a threat that demands brand new strategic considerations and tactical approaches.

In this effort to reconcile mobility and firepower, the submarine now moves to the center of the stage, somewhat in the manner but on a vastly larger scale than the tank appeared in World War I. Its furtive passage assures the well-nigh only mobility left in war, in the face of the stifling and devastating firepower of the nuclear weapons. The historic significance of this development was eloquently expressed by Captain J. B. Osborn, USN, commanding officer of the American nuclear submarine *George Washington*, after she successfully fired the first two Polaris missiles on July 20, 1960, submerged to a depth of fifty feet off Cape Canaveral. "This is an achievement of the same historical magnitude," Osborn said, "as the firing of the first artillery cannon, the dropping of the first aerial bomb and the launching of the first ballistic missile." He left no doubt that they were designed specifically for the conflict with the Soviet Union, when he said: "The crossbow and the atomic bomb were both conceived as weapons against tyranny. Now they are joined by the Polaris submarine."

Where did these breathtaking developments find the Soviet Union in the quality and quantity of its submarines, in the evolution of its comparable weapons system, and in its military policies?

The Soviet Factor

"Every Russian feels himself a member of the empire that will be the world empire of the future. And that empire will be a great sea-empire, since the sea is now what the land once was in the matter of communications. At some future date the great struggle . . . that so many prophesy, may come off. The day is probably yet far distant ere this new Punic War comes about. . . Yet the war of the future, when it comes, is none the less likely to be absolutely decisive, for one mighty empire or the other will in all human probability split into fragments."

These words which have such a familiar ring today were not spoken by Nikita S. Khrushchev or Marshal Malinovsky, his Defense Minister. They are not of any recent vintage. They are the words of Fred T. Jane, the great English naval expert, written in 1899, eighteen years before the Bolsheviks seized power. They sounded as authentic in the context of those days as they seem to be acute today—yet what happened in the wake of Jane's prognostication?

The imperial naval ambitions which Czarist Russia nurtured were shattered at Tsushima where the Japanese dealt a savage blow to Admiral Rozhdestvenski's main battle fleet and to Russian seapower. It exposed the timidity of Russian naval leadership, the deficiencies of the fleet, the poor work of Naval Intelligence, and showed that the concept of offensive sea warfare was alien to Russian planning. "To the St. Petersburg authorities," wrote Admiral Ballard, "a fleet was merely an assembly of armed ships with men on board to work the guns and engines."

In World War I, the Russian Navy was concpicuous mainly by its absence from the war at sea. And in World War II? In 1937, Navy Commissar Smirnov told the Supreme Soviet: "Certain of our capitalist neighbors, who consider themselves great naval powers and harbor antiquated conceptions, think that the U.S.S.R. is Old Russia. They will find that they are greatly mistaken. The new fleet of the U.S.S.R. . . . will rout the enemy wherever and whenever it will be necessary in the interest of the defense of the Fatherland." Only two months before the outbreak of the war, Admiral Ivan S. Isakov promised, "In the event of war we will beat the enemy in his own waters." Yet when the showdown came, the Red Fleet proved incapable of defending its own waters and needed the all-out naval aid of the Allies to sustain the lifeline over which the crucial supplies from the West poured into the U.S.S.R.

The backbone of the fleet which was supposed to keep the promises of Comrade Smirnov and Admiral Isakov was the submarine. Already in 1936, the Red Fleet had ninety-six submarines, at a time when France had ninety-two and Germany only twenty-eight. But by 1937, the Soviet submarine fleet increased to 112 operational units, with thirty-seven building, when Japan had only sixty-eight. In the summer of 1941, when Germany attacked the Soviet Union, the Red Fleet had 245 submarines.

On March 5, 1943, the Kremlin claimed that in the twenty months of the war, the Red Fleet had sunk 771 German warships and merchant-men, and damaged 216 other vessels, but it was a loss of which the Germans were blissfully unaware. Russian submarines based on Kronstadt did break through the dense German minefields and penetrated into the Baltic, but they failed to hamper the considerable German traffic. In the spring of 1943, the Germans bottled them up completely by closing the Gulf of Finland with a steel net that reached all the way down to the bottom of the sea. From then on, until the fall of 1944, Russian submarine attacks on German shipping ceased and the imports of iron ore from Sweden, absolutely crucial to the German war economy, proceeded through the Baltic "in a constant and unmolested stream."

In other areas, there was a similar discrepancy between the Soviet claims and the actual accomplishments of the Soviet submarines. In June, 1944, Admiral Frolov claimed that "more than 1.5 million tons of enemy shipping and warships have been sent to the bottom of the Barents Sea;" and next month General Grigoriev asserted that "between July 22, 1941, and April 30, 1944, Soviet submarines had sunk four hundred and forty enemy vessels totalling more than two million tons of shipping." These were grossly exaggerated claims, to put it mildly. The Russians claimed that a submarine commanded by Captain Nikolai Lunin attacked and damaged the German battleship *Tirpitz,* on July 5, 1942, "at a time when, in an attempt to destroy a large British convoy bound for a Russian port, the *Tirpitz* was escorted by more than ten warships." No confirmation of such an attack was found in the German records and no damage to the *Tirpitz* or, for that matter, any other major German warship was ever inflicted by Soviet submarines. The only German warship whose loss might be attributed to action by the Red Fleet was the *U-144* of Kapitaenleutnant Gerd von Mittelstaedt. It sank on August 9, 1941, north of Dagoe at the entrance to the Gulf of Finland, but it is possible that it was the victim of one of the Germans' own mines. Not until the final phases of the war, when everything Germany could float in the Baltic was pressed into an immense Dunkirk-type operation to evacuate German nationals from regions falling rapidly to the Red Army, did the Red Fleet succeed in inflicting any appreciable damage on the *Kriegsmarine.*

Most remarkable in this monumental failure of a major fleet and its much-vaunted submarine service was the conspicuous absence of Soviet warships from the defense of the lifeline to Murmansk and Archangel. Between June 22, 1941, the day Hitler attacked the Soviet Union, and September 20, 1945, the day Allied aid to the U.S.S.R. was terminated, the Allies shipped 17.5 million long tons of cargoes to Russia. Of this, 2.7 million tons went from the United States to North Russia, on the legendary Murmansk Run, through waters infested by German U-boats and harassed by the planes of the *Luftwaffe.* But it was left entirely to the Royal Navy and the United States Navy to protect these shipments and, indeed, to keep the lifeline open. Soviet contribution amounted to virtually nil at sea, while ashore the inefficiency and hostility of Soviet authorities actually hampered Allied aid.

However, past failures could easily obscure present strength and lull one into dangerous complacency as far as future capabilities are concerned. In his evaluation of the Russians as naval opponents, Juergen Rohwer, a German historian of the first rank specializing in the war at sea, found much in the Red Fleet's performance in World War II that was dismal by any standards, but also elements of strength. "Owing to its policy of remaining aloof from the outside world," Dr. Rohwer wrote, "the Soviet Navy began the war with ships that were technically inferior to those of its opponents, and with crews whose training in the use of modern weapons left much to be desired." However, he added, the Russians proved themselves masters of speedy improvisation. "In the Baltic Sea as well as in the Northern Fleet," he wrote, "the technical and tactical competence of the submarine crews improved as the war progressed."

However dismal the Red Fleet's performance was in World War II, the lessons of modern naval warfare were not lost on Soviet leadership. Moreover, there are ample indications that the U.S.S.R. was faster than the United States in its recognition of the military revolution unleashed by nuclear energy and rocketry, keener in its visualization of future wars, and more imaginative and thorough in the adaptation of its military forces to the realities of the new art of war. According to General Bela Király, Hungarian officers who attended various Soviet maneuvers in the 1950's were deeply impressed by the bold departure of Soviet military leadership from the old concepts of war and their adjustment to the new concepts. In this new orientation, nuclear weapons, missile and space developments figured most prominently. That the naval aspects of this reorientation were not overlooked was evident in Marshal Zhukov's statement to the Party Congress in February, 1956, when he said: "In a future war the struggle at sea will be of even greater importance than it was in the last war."

In the very center of the Soviet Navy's post-war development was the fantastic expansion of the submarine fleet. "The Soviet submarine force is far larger than can be required to implement a purely defensive strategy," wrote Captain Macintyre. Taking his cue from Khrushchev who, in November, 1957, bluntly threatened a strategic employment of the huge Soviet submarine fleet in any future emergency, Dr. Rohwer wrote: "It is obvious that in war the Soviet Union would not confine itself to coastal waters, but would attack the ocean supply lines of the Western powers, which are the backbone of the NATO alliance, and also launch missiles at vital centres of industry."

The Soviet Submarine Threat

The post-war expansion of the Soviet Navy with the submarine fleet as its hard core coincided with the submarine's own evolution from a tactical weapon to a strategic weapons system. Russia was among the first powers to recognize the potentialities of the submarine, in line with traditional Russian preference for smaller warships best suited for coastal defense. When at the turn of this century such pioneers as the American Simon Lake and the German Friedrich Krupp were unable to find buyers for their submarines in their own countries, they succeeded in selling them to the Czarist Navy. From then on, the underwater craft never relaxed its hold on Russian naval imagination.

The buildup of the Soviet submarine fleet began in earnest during the first Five Year Plan in 1926-31, and progressed at such rapid rate that very soon Soviet submarine strength exceeded that of any other naval power. Already in 1938, the German Admiralty warned: "It is necessary to recognize the incontestable fact that the U.S.S.R. possesses at the present time the most powerful submarine fleet in the world." The situation has never changed. In 1962, spokesmen of the United States Navy echoed the German statement, adding that the estimated four hundred submarines of the Red Fleet (contrasted numerically by 117 American submarines) "constitute a great threat to sea communications between the United States and its allies in Europe and the Far East."

Despite their historic preoccupation with underseas vessels, it was not the Soviet Union that either pioneered or promoted the recent great revolution of the submarine. It was rather the United States Navy that produced the "absolute submersible." And while Germany and the U.S.S.R. blazed the trail in ballistic missile development, it was again the United States Navy that came up with the "ideal" missile for which the submarine serves as the perfect carrier.

However, the Soviet Navy enjoyed certain advantages in this evolution. After World War II, it received its full share of the rapidly developing scientific and technological resources of the Soviet Union, with the result that "it has been able to expand and at the same time modernize its ships and weapons in a remarkably short period."

The first stage in this development was featured by the adoption of the designs and manufacturing techniques of new types of equipment the Russians captured from the Germans. Among the devices they found in Germany were torpedoes with hydrogen peroxide propulsion, special types of assault boats, rocket weapons for use in submarines, oyster mines, midget submarines, and submersible fuel barges. They also found about seven operational prototypes of the Walter boats on which Gross-admiral Doenitz had pinned his hopes for a comeback in the Battle of the Atlantic, and a number of Type XXI and Type XXIII prefabricated U-boats whose high-capacity batteries gave them substantially increased underwater speed.

Aside from these inert treasures which fell intact into Russian hands, teams of German experts were taken to the Soviet Union to continue their work and train a new generation of Soviet submarine builders. While Britain (and later the United States) got Dr. Helmuth Walter, the erratic engineering genius behind the boats named for him, scientists and technicians associated with him were taken to the Soviet Union and were encouraged with liberal contracts and high salaries to continue work with the equipment on which they had been engaged when the Red Army so rudely interrupted them.

How far these German inventions and specialists did in fact influence Soviet submarine developments is difficult to assess. The degree of their importance diminished, of course, with the trend favoring the nuclear submarine wedded to the ballistic missile, a concept that never figured in Doenitz's most ambitious and hopeful plans.

The most significant new development in the Soviet Navy, that began in 1958, was a shift of emphasis from the quantitative build-up to a qualitative improvement. As older boats were gradually scrapped or retired, the Soviet submarine force was reduced in overall numbers, but its total power steadily increased. Already in 1961, the United States Navy told Congress that the Soviet Union was actively engaged in a nuclear submarine construction program: "The Soviets have an obvious requirement for nuclear submarines and have the capability to build them. It is probable that the Soviets have some nuclear submarines, although it is problematical whether any are yet full operational. A Soviet version of our Polaris firing submarine must be expected in the near future."

On July 21, 1962, the Soviet Union announced officially that it had nuclear submarines "in action" and that they had undergone successful exercises in the Barents Sea that included the "firing of ballistic missiles from submerged positions." Rear Admiral Aleksandr I. Petelin was identified as the commander of a "flotilla of atomic submarines," Captain Lev M. Zhiltsov as the commander of an "atomic submarine," and Engineer Captain Ruurik A. Timofeyev as the officer in charge of the submarine's "electro-mechanical combat section." With this a peak in qualitative improvement was reached, matching more or less the American development, and adding another factor to the Soviet submarine threat.

What are the simple statistics of this threat? According to Anglo-American intelligence estimates, the Soviet submarine force now consists of about four hundred submarines, about 250 of them believed to be modern, long-range, snorkeling units constructed during the massive post-war building program. The backbone of this fleet is the *W Class* submarine of which well over two hundred have been built since 1947. Patterned after the German Type XXI, the 1000-ton, 235-foot boat is supposed to be capable of a speed of thirteen knots submerged, with an endurance of 12,000 miles.

The largest type Soviet submarine is the *Z Class* boat of which the Red Fleet may have as few as eighteen or as many as fifty. Little is known about its endurance and armament, but it is estimated that its high-capacity batteries give it a speed of up to twenty knots surfaced and fifteen knots submerged. The third member in the family of post-war Soviet subs is the *Q Class* boat, resembling the standard German Type VIIC which was responsible for most of the Allied tonnage sunk in World War II.

The present distribution of this force is believed to be somewhat as follows, the bracketed figures referring to the comparable disposition of Soviet submarines in 1941:

Fleet	Medium range		Long range
Northern (Arctic)	none	[21]	110
Baltic Sea	50	[93]	40
Black Sea	5	[54]	70
Pacific (Far East)	50	[93]	60

This adds up to a current force of 385 operational submarines (as against 245 in June, 1941) whose distribution seems to bear out the widely held belief that they are destined for strategic employment in long-range operations. Aside from being fully capable of offensive action against the sea communications of the Western Allies, they can, as an estimate of the United States Navy recently put it, "operate directly off U.S. coasts from their bases in the U.S.S.R."

In 1941, most Soviet submarines were of medium range, but today about 280 of them are of long range, with endurance of up to 12,000 miles at something like fifteen knots of underwater speed. It is known that the Russians keep their long-range submarines as busy as possible, sending them, as part of their training, on extended cruises during which they are expected to evade detection. Already in 1955, a *W Class* submarine undertook an experimental voyage from the Soviet Union to the Antarctic to rendezvous with a Russian whaling fleet. Moreover, there is no reason to assume that Soviet submarines will be employed only in the defense of their own sea frontiers or against ships alone. "If fitted with nuclear missiles," wrote Admiral Horan, a keen British observer of Soviet naval developments, "submarines from the North Fleet could be most profitably employed against the United Kingdom and the eastern seaboard of the United States."

That Soviet sea power is, as Hanson W. Baldwin, military editor of *The New York Times*, summed it up, both a defensive shield for the Russian "Heartland" and "a strategic threat to the world's oceanic powers" is dramatized almost daily in the United States Navy's big ASW plotting room at Norfolk, Virginia, where black diamond-shaped markers indicate the "goblins" on a wall-to-wall map. They are Soviet submarines presumed to be at large in specific ocean areas. During one recent six-month period, the plotting room recorded 186 separate reports of what "may have been Soviet subs," apparently probing American submarine defense, testing the detection and tracking proficiency of the United States Navy's "goblin hunters."

An actual encounter occurred in the North Atlantic on a May afternoon in 1959, between the United States submarine *Grenadier* and a big long-range Soviet sub. The *Grenadier,* one of the "Guppies" (souped up with greater underwater propulsion power), was itself on a secret mission, creeping submerged into a certain area to test how far and how well she could pass undetected through the slim barrier of opponents on and above the North Atlantic.

Commanded by Lieutenant Commander Thomas F. Davis, USN, the *Grenadier* was supposed to be the only vessel in this area except for an American destroyer escort on picket station far over the horizon. Then all of a sudden, her sonarman found clear indications that she was not alone after all. He heard a faint noise in the hydrophone and diagnosed it as the unmistakable beat of a submarine's screws. Then sharpening the reception, he recognized the sound as the distinct signature of a Soviet underseas craft.

Here was a rare opportunity to obtain valuable data on a Soviet sub on operational patrol and Commander Davis decided to make the most of it. He maintained sonar contact with the stranger for several hours but nothing in the Russian's behavior seemed to indicate that he had any notion of being tracked. At one point of the subtle chase Davis brought the *Grenadier* closer to surface, radioed Norfolk of his contact and suggested that a plane of Patrol Squadron 5 be sent from Iceland to take pictures in the event the Soviet sub surfaced. Soon afterwards sounds of ballast being blown indicated that the Russian was about to show itself. It broke water just when a P2V burst into the area, a kingsized Soviet sub exposing itself to the Neptune's eager cameraman. Alerted by the roar of the plane, the Soviet crew went to work to cover an apparently classified section of the conning tower with canvas, but otherwise they seemed imperturbed. The sub—identified as one of the 2500-ton, 290-foot *Z Class* boats—continued slowly along on the surface for some time, then went below again and vanished. Davis had every reason to be satisfied with the "operation." He not only succeeded in tracking a Soviet sub and obtaining some data about its performance, but also handled his own sub in a highly efficient manner, so quietly in fact that the Russian never as much as suspected that the *Grenadier* was snooping on him from nearby.

Although such close contacts are rare, Soviet submarines are frequently tracked—and even harassed—on their ocean prowls. American fishermen trolling for king mackerel on The Hill, the part of the Florida coast near Cape Canaveral, often have ringside seats at such goblin hunts. They watch fat twin-engined "Dumbos" and fast slick patrol craft of the United States Navy search briskly in set square patterns for Russian submarines suspected in the transparent water. From time to time, a submerged object is identified as a "non-NATO submarine," the Navy's euphemism for a Russian. Each time a strange sub is thus found in waters close to the American shore, a mock action ensues with some of the sound and fury of a real engagement. The spot is marked with smoke bombs that send up red signals as high as a thousand feet; surplus ash-cans are dropped at a safe distance, not to do any real harm, but to prod the intruder to move out of shoal water into the open sea.

There is a lot of *quid pro quo* in this. By the same token, American submarines "case the joint" at the far ends of the oceans. Thus in October, 1961, the detonation of a 10-kiloton Soviet nuclear device in Arctic waters was "observed" by United States submarines on station as close as possible to the test area. There is a fair amount of hysteria in this particular cold war contest. The broad areas of ignorance and uncertainty, the furtive and sensitive nature of these operations produce nervous tension in both camps. It makes ASW personnel afloat jumpy and only too eager, as Commander Davis was, to stage impromptu war games with live quarries. They go through all the motions of the hunter-killer routine, short of actually killing the target.

The international waters of the oceans are free for all and the Russians have as much right as anybody else to prowl about in them. However, the presence of the big new Soviet submarines in distant ocean areas clearly indicates the changed Soviet trend with emphasis on the strategic-offensive. Photographs obtained of Soviet prowlers indicated that they were on extended cruises, obviously to test the boats and train their crews in the oceans of the world and not only in the Baltic and Barents Seas. The Japanese used to employ their submarines in this manner prior to Pearl Harbor and now the Russians go all the way to obtain data on missile activities off Canaveral in the Atlantic and the big Vandenberg base in the Pacific; to chart American coastal waters hoping to discover the thermal layers in which they could hide out in ambush; monitor electronic traffic; plot flight scrambles; and penetrate to the innermost secrets of the submarine defenses of the United States. While much of this probing seems to be haphazard, it proves nevertheless that the Soviet submarine ceased to be an instrument solely of defense. The grand strategic concept of the Russian undersea fleet is no longer continental and defensive, but rather global and offensive. There is every indication, moreover, that the current material efficiency of Soviet submarines is, as Admiral Horan put it, "well up to that shown by the German U-boats during the Second World War."

Let us now explore how the Soviet Union might use its considerable naval assets. Soviet grand strategy naturally assumes prudent preparation for any contingency and the use of all effective strengths. This was stressed in January, 1960, when Defense Minister Marshal Malinovsky said: "Since successful conduct of military actions in a modern war is possible only on the basis of combining the efforts of all types of the armed forces, we are retaining at a definite strength and in relevant, sound proportions all types of our armed forces." In accordance with this basic philosophy, the Soviet strategic concept is versatile and flexible. It calls for constant readiness of land, sea and air forces for a variety of contingencies. These range from the threat of the use of force all the way to a general war.

Soviet Naval Policies

"Although the Soviets are deterred from deliberate initiation of general war," an estimate of the U.S. Navy stated in 1961, "they nevertheless realize that the nature of their objective courts this risk. Regardless of how general war might possibly start, the Soviet Navy would be heavily involved. Undoubtedly, Soviet missile armed submarines would participate in the initial phase of nuclear war." The surface forces would then be primarily defensive. "The increasing pattern of Soviet use of the oceans during the cold war," the Navy paper stated with persuasive eloquence, "reaps immediate benefits in trade, penetration and prestige. It also means that the Soviets are developing a sure touch in the very medium they will have to use to isolate and destroy the free world maritime alliance in the event of general war. *They are training in cold war on one of the critical battlefields of limited and general war.*"

According to Raymond L. Garthoff, an eminent American student of Soviet strategy in the nuclear age, there are two roles specifically reserved for the long-range Soviet submarines. One is the neutralization of the enemy's naval and marine transport capabilities in an atomic age version of the *guerre de course*. The other is strategic striking power used against the enemy's miltary forces and installations, and his military industry.

The latter eventuality was dramatized by Admiral Horan who wrote: "The submarines from the Northern and Pacific Fleets could be sent out long before the outbreak of any future war, and then lie in wait off the coasts of the countries of the Western Alliance in pretty well all the oceans of the world. Then, at a word, they could deliver a nuclear attack or confine their attention to the shipping of their opponents."

Extremists of these strategic speculations believe that the Russians may regard their long-range submarines as an asset that would be fully expendable at the outset of the war. An indication of this is said to be the presence of a large number of but moderately trained submarines in the Red Fleet, presumably to commence hostilities with a strategic attack even though they are likely to perish in the process, much in the manner of a reckless gambler who will risk all he has on a quick gain.

In his brilliant review of the Soviet submarine threat, Captain Macintyre, the celebrated "U-boat killer" of World War II, called attention to the fact that in Bolshevik dialectics the concept of "war" is subject to various interpretations. "A war," he wrote, "which the Russian leaders may have persuaded themselves is defensive in nature may seem to the free world purely offensive in character and aim. It is therefore somewhat academic," he concluded, "to speak in terms of defensive or offensive strategy, for the hard fact remains that *the Soviet submarine force will be used in attack from the outset of any war.*"

The Sneak Attack in the Atomic Age

It may be a sign of the moral deterioration of our times or perhaps, on the contrary, of the abandonment of hypocrisy, that nobody expects the next war to begin with a formal declaration of war. In other words, the sneak attack is taken for granted. It is accepted all around as the only practicable commencement of hostilities in the atomic age.

Even so, of course, nobody in responsible position on either side will concede in so many words that plans for such a sneak attack are anywhere in the hatching or that, indeed, a nuclear war is likely to occur. Speaking of the threat of global war in the spring of 1962, Defense Secretary Robert S. McNamara voiced the opinion that while limited wars were distinctly possible, the outbreak of a general nuclear war seemed remote. The same idea was reiterated by successive Navy Secretaries and Chiefs of Naval Operations, Admiral Burke putting it most succinctly when he said:

"We have reached a stage now where both sides can destroy each other or at least wreak heavy damage on each other. That does not mean Russia is going to stop her aggression or her desire to dominate. She is going to try other means. That is why there might be a limited war. Because we have this capability of destroying one another now, a general nuclear war probably will not happen, and limited war is much more likely to occur just as it has in the past."

This led to an interesting exchange on Capitol Hill in the course of which Representative George H. Mahon of Texas asked Burke: "You would not be bold enough to say that there could or would be a limited war between the United States and the Soviet Union?"

"I would not say it is highly probable," the admiral answered, "but neither would I rule out the possibility."

"Do you think either side, when two great nations are locked in mortal conflict, would surrender without using everything at its disposal?"

With this question, to which Burke volunteered only an equivocal answer, the conversation reached its crux. It was the question of a direct conflict on whatever scale between the two great powers, and not war by proxies like Korea or Laos or Hungary. Maxim Litvinov once said that peace was indivisible. The same, of course, goes for war. Should the situation deteriorate to the point where the United States and the Soviet Union become involved in direct confrontation in a limited war, it is certain that sooner or later it would develop into general nuclear war with all its trimmings.

In the same conversation Burke said that "the theory [!] is that the United States will not initiate a general nuclear war." By the same token or rationalization, the "theory" is that the Soviet Union might or will. As a matter of fact, the Pentagon is divided down the middle on this issue. There are those who do not expect the Soviet Union to resort to this last resource, and those who believe the U.S.S.R is deliberately moving towards that goal.

According to this latter school, the Soviet Union will, at one point of the drawn-out cold war controversy, jump to the showdown at lightning speed, with a strategic sneak attack upon the United States. That there is some kind of an "estimate" along these lines was indicated by Admiral Burke when he said: "We will probably be damaged in case of a nuclear attack. In order for the country to survive, the theory holds that as many of the leaders of the country should be safe so they can continue to fight the war after the damage does occur. That is the reason for the command and control setup, I think, primarily so that the control system will enable the leaders of the Government to be in a position where they can survive and some government will exist."

Those analysts who expect the showdown to begin with the Soviet sneak attack assume that the Soviet leaders are also aware of the "command and control setup" and have a plan—indeed, a "Master Plan"—to prevent it from functioning. And according to them, the submarine plays the dominant and decisive part in that "Master Plan."

As far as I could reconstruct it from conversations with members of this school, the "Master Plan" calls for a series of attacks in rapid succession. It envisages a first wave of attacks by intercontinental ballistic missiles fired from secret launching sites behind the Iron Curtain. This, however—although of strategic importance—is planned merely as a major diversionary move.

The knock-out blow is reserved for a second wave of missile-borne attacks, to be launched from a fleet of Soviet submarines deployed at their stations well in advance off the East and West Coasts of America.

This hypothetical "Master Plan" probably emerged from Soviet studies of the Japanese sneak attack on Pearl Harbor and an analysis-in-depth of its failure. Japan's inability to follow its attack on Pearl Harbor with devastating strikes against the focal points of the continental United States, the Soviet experts are believed to have found, had foredoomed the Yamamoto Plan at its inception.

It was of course conceded by the Soviet experts that the implements of war and their carriers available to Japan in 1941 did not make her capable of launching a genuine strategic strike with the prospect of victory at the very outset. The situation changed radically, first, with the evolution of nuclear weapons; second, with Soviet progress in intermediate and long-range weapon development; and third, with the coming of the atomic or non-atomic missile launching submarine.

A careful study of the American defense concepts revolving around deterrence and retaliation, virtually recommended the "Master Plan" to its Soviet authors. It became abundantly clear to them that "something" was needed to follow up the first strike from mobile launching sites which not even the most massive American retaliation could find and reach; which would thus remain fully operational to further destroy the substantially reduced and badly disorganized defenses of the United States within its most vulnerable continental confines.

That "something" was found in the long-range submarine. The super-strategic mission of the *coup de grâce* was assigned to the Soviet Navy and specifically to the Soviet submarine fleet. Soviet submarines allegedly assigned to the mission are said to be conducting exercises at this very moment in the Atlantic and the Pacific, to test the feasibility of the "Master Plan," to ascertain the most auspicious oceanic stations for the attack, and to train officers and men for the showdown.

Whether it is the malicious pipedream of "warmongers" or the brilliant deduction of farsighted analysts, the plausibility of such a plan cannot be denied. True or false, the overwhelming fact is that even though Soviet leadership might not have the intention, it possesses the means to carry out the plan. "The Russian submarine threat is of tremendous size and scope," Macintyre wrote, warning that "daring and far-sighted steps will be needed to counter it." And Juergen Rohwer concluded his survey of the Russians as naval opponents by saying:

"Technical and tactical developments have turned the modern submarine into the most formidable of all weapons of attack, and this fact, added to our past experiences in the Atlantic and the Pacific, should incite us to create the means of countering the danger."

The Military Revolution and the U.S. Navy

The United States is of course in the forefront of the great military revolution and nowhere is this revolution more acute and sweeping than in the United States Navy. Despite radical reorganizations in its structure and revisions of its concepts, the United States Army remains by necessity the basically most conventional branch of the armed forces. The Air Force developed in a welter of confusion and propaganda at a time when the real directions of the transition were not yet evident. Thus it blossomed out as a hybrid force split between the atmosphere and outer space, between planes and missiles, between strategic ideals and tactical realities.

The Navy alone, I submit, recognized the fantastic change in the structure of war and moved to adapt itself to it. Of course, the evolution was not as prompt and straightforward as that and the initiative for it did not spring voluntarily within the Navy. As a matter of fact, the post-war development of the United States Navy began with an outrageous and pathetic conflict in which the frustration of certain senior officers produced a bitterly aggressive spirit that obscured the real needs and detoured that development.

This blue period in the Navy's post-war history reached its crisis in the notorious "Revolt of the Admirals" in 1949, during which a group of naval officers tried to thwart the Air Force's B-36 program in a move that bordered on subversion. One of the "conspirators" was Captain Arleigh Burke, USN. He plotted much of the Navy's insiduous campaign against the Air Force from a secretly improvised bureau deep underground in the Navy Department.

The return to sanity in the Navy is now personified nevertheless in Burke's own evolution as a military scientist of the first rank and a grand strategist, and in his emergence as the energetic leader of the constructive revolution that remade the United States Navy. This revolution began in the immediate wake of the great controversy. At the height of the crisis, President Truman dismissed Admiral Louis E. Denfeld, USN, the Chief of Naval Operations who tolerated the cabal, and replaced him by Admiral Forrest W. Sherman, USN, a quiet student of military history and geopolitics, a man of erudition and infinite tact, who believed in unification. How delicate the situation was and how deeply the controversy divided the nation was dramatized when Sherman had to be smuggled into Washington, arriving under an assumed name in civilian clothes.

He went to work at once to banish acrimony and reconstruct the Navy. However, his departure in 1950 put a temporary halt to the innovations he had initiated. The Chiefs of Naval Operations who followed him, Admirals William M. Fechteler and Robert B. Carney, USN, either did not possess the intellectual acumen to promote the overdue revolution or, if they possessed it, lacked the drive to continue it. Then came Burke in 1955, promoted over ninety-two other admirals.

He was widely known as an aggressive destroyer officer, nicknamed "31-knot" Burke by the Marines because their latrines along the beaches of Tulagi were flooded during the war by the wake from the fast-churning propellers of Burke's destroyers. From his past record and more recent association with the Radford cabal, Burke appeared to be the man most unlikely to succeed in revamping the Navy and adapting it to the needs of the new war. But Burke brought to his big new job, not merely drive and determination, professional competence and administrative skill, but also a broad philosophy. His common sense helped him to recognize the basic issues of international relations as dominated by the conflict with the U.S.S.R. and pinpoint the crucial role the United States Navy was destined to play in it.

There were no frills to Burke, no intellectual fireworks in his concept of the naval revolution. "I was born on a farm," he once said, "and my people were hungry at times. For a long time I went a long way to school on a horse. I never graduated from high school. But I had an opportunity. I had an opportunity to work like hell."

He was a fast-thinking, fast-talking, fast-moving CNO to whom tradition was no fetish and progress was no anathema. Often he was in such a hurry that he expounded his views in unfinished sentences, his thinking outdistancing his expositions, his actions getting ahead of his theories. In any history of the United States Navy, Arleigh Burke will be recorded as one of the great Chiefs of Naval Operations, because it was under him that the United States Navy emerged from its doldrums and was totally reborn, virtually from scratch.

He also had a sense of proportion—or maybe an instinct of proportion —that enabled him to perceive the new conflict beyond the confines of his own profession. Speaking of the balance of power, of the need to maintain the peace while sustaining the freedom of the West, Burke once said bluntly: "Military force alone will not do it. You must have more than military force. We built up this tremendous military power but it will not answer all the questions." He went on to say: "Willingness to use force is part of the solution, but there is more than that; it is a respect for the political stability which we demonstrate."

After the hectic publicity days of the Radford era, and the hibernation of the Fechteler and Carney regimes, the Navy under Burke shifted to low gear in its public relations and became inordinately shy to discuss the creative steps it was taking. Thus the people of the United States now hardly realize that their Navy had ceased to exist as the glamorous force Hollywood used to be so fond of depicting in brassy musicals with Dick Powell in the starring role; that it moved far away even from the stellar accomplishments of World War II; and that it became a great and superbly functional military organization adapted to virtually any of the exigencies the international situation of this period of revolutionary transition might produce.

The change can be illustrated on a few facts and figures. The United States ended World War II with the mightiest navy that ever put to sea, overtaking British sea power both in quantity and quality. On VE Day, it had over five-thousand ships with 4.1 million officers and men. Its bases girdled the globe. Its strength was in battleships and big cruisers, in aircraft carriers and planes, in hardware whose obsolescence became evident already during the war.

Submarine Warfare and the U.S. Navy

Today the Navy has fewer than nine-hundred ships. There is not a single battleship left in it. It employs only about 800,000 officers and men. The active fleet consists of attack carriers, antisubmarine carriers, destroyer types, amphibious lift for assault elements, submarines and ballistic missile submarines. "We have a strong Navy but a lean Navy," Burke said, "We are stretched taut." It was this new Navy that, after a painful period of convulsions and rivalries, gave the United States the two greatest elements of its current strength: the nuclear-powered submarine and the Polaris missile.

This is the Navy that must perform the most difficult dual task any military organization ever faced in history. On the one hand, it must develop and sustain the offensive power this country must have at sea to assure its survival in any contingency. On the other hand, it must organize and support a defensive program to prevent the enemy from ever mounting a strategic attack on the United States or from interfering with the sea communications of this country.

How does the United States Navy meet this dual responsibility?

The historic attitude of the United States Navy to the submarine was by no means unequivocal. The submarine as a practical implement of war was invented by Americans—by John P. Holland and Simon Lake— yet the United States was not the first country to recognize its enormous potentialities. Russia was. The first submarine of the United States Navy, a product of Holland's Electric Boat Company, was commissioned in 1900, with a lieutenant named Harry H. Caldwell in command. By then, however, it was the prejudice of the tradition-bound Navy rather than the technological problems of the novel craft Holland and Lake had to buck and overcome.

This negative attitude was stimulated by Admiral Mahan who was, as Bernard Brodie pointed out, a re-interpreter of old strategic concepts rather than a creator of new ones. Mahan ignored the submarine, Brodie wrote, "which was already a highly efficient instrument at the time of his death in December, 1914. In fact his dictum that 'the *guerre de course* (commence raiding) can never be by itself alone decisive of great issues'— a view he derived mainly from his study of the War of 1812—contributed, because of his great prestige, to the general under-estimation on the eve of World War I of what the submarine could do."

Between the two world wars, the submarine service strove in vain to gain recognition in the United States Navy. It was up against formidable odds; British propaganda was especially effective. As Arch Whitehouse put it, "It was difficult to erase the former air of contempt and disgust that was revived whenever the subject of the submarine was broached." It was more than just contempt and disgust. It was also apprehension cloaked as skepticism. Naval man feared that emphasis on the submarine would expose the surface fleet as outdated, doubly vulnerable as it became to the new three-dimensional attack, on the surface, from the air, as well as from under the sea. A vigorously positive attitude to the submarine would have inferred an essentially negative attitude to the surface ships. Tradition, jealousies, pride, and the sincere love of the historic fleet combined to mitigate against such a positive attiude.

Unlike the various other new weapons—and especially unlike the air-plane—the submarine somehow never succeeded in producing a spec-tacular advocate in the United States. No Billy Mitchell appeared any-where to ram headlong against traditions, conventions and prejudices. In the United States Navy of the 1930's when recurrent troubles with submarines tended to advertise the apparent vulnerability of this pre-carious weapon, Admiral Mahan continued to prevail. It was in this climate that the United States was called upon to face the challenge of Doenitz in the Atlantic and to challenge Japanese sea power from under the sea in the Pacific. After grave initial difficulties, it rose superbly to meet both challenges and perform this most difficult task of naval warfare: conduct antisubmarine warfare in one ocean and submarine warfare in the other.

Today this strange dualism is sharper than ever. There is now a peculiar professional schizophrenia in any Navy's current attitude to the submarine situation because the same navy that promotes the modern underseas craft as an offensive weapon must by necessity also promote the best means of destroying it. I am sure the leaders of the Soviet Navy suffer from this schism as much as do the leaders of the United States Navy, even if only the latter have the opportunity and freedom to air their woes publicly.

Each year around cherry blossom time, the top brass of the United States Navy must make their hegira to Capitol Hill to explain and justify their budget. Up go the assault admirals to sing the praise of the nuclear-powered Polaris submarine. They are followed by the defense admirals who croon in similarly rapturous terms about antisubmarine warfare and explain with charts and slides and models how simple it is to sink even a nuclear sub. In one of these recent hearings, Representative Ford of Michigan blurted out: "I've just been scanning the basic U.S. antisubmarine warfare strategy summary and believe me, if·I had to assume the Soviet Union had the same ASW capability we have, I'd be fearful of leaving an American port." Although this seems to be rather confusing—the same Navy talking out of both sides of its mouth— it is not necessarily so. At any rate it is a schizophrenia we must learn to live with and plan for.

The new super-submarine with its ballistic missiles is everything it is cracked up to be. The two currently leading naval powers of the world, the United States and the U.S.S.R., need it and have it, deploy it and will use it when and if the need arises. At the same time, both powers as well as the other navies of the world, develop ASW as quickly and as well as possible, in order to render those super-subs ineffective in the hands of their adversaries This is what Admiral King in World War II called the interplay of measure and countermeasure. "The competition between submarines and antisubmarine warfare is going to continue," Burke said.

As a result the foremost military truism of today is that the power which has the advantage in this interplay is the power that is likely to win. The question is, which power has this advantage? Admiral Burke sought to answer this question when, directly referring to the dual and contradictory American effort, he said:

"As we make advances in one area, we have to make advances in the other. For example, in our Polaris submarines, we are taking advantage of all the ASW lore that we have in order to train personnel and increase their capability against every ASW. We are training one group against the other."

I will say, however, that while the offensive power of the United States Navy's submarine effort is second to none and is bound to improve still further, so vastly and rapidly, indeed, that neither friend nor foe will be able to catch up with it and overtake it, the defensive power packed into its antisubmarine warfare effort remains inadequate and maybe even woefully so. This is conceded amidst the boasts and extravagant claims, by men at sea whose thankless job it is to handle ASW, in practice rather than theory. On November 12, 1961, Vice Admiral John S. Thach, USN, who commanded the West's ASW network in the Pacific, said in so many words that "this country had not 'faced up' to one of the major problems of nuclear age defense" because the "present methods of protecting the United States against submarine attack had been 'knocked out of the ball park'."

Admiral Thach made it crystal clear that "the United States was not now equipped to guarantee the detection and tracking of Soviet nuclear submarines armed with short-range missiles." Other American naval officers specializing in antisubmarine warfare said that "the marriage of the nuclear submarine to the missile meant that the Navy was trying to find 'today's quarry with yesterday's equipment'." Just prior to his retirement, Admiral Burke stated in so many words that he considered the American ASW preparedness inadequate, and the problem "unsolvable." His successor as CNO, Admiral George W. Anderson, USN, said on March 6, 1962:

"In World War I and World War II, we—along with our allies—had the task of protecting our shipping at sea. You know as well as I do the tremendous losses we suffered in both wars, and you know how we overcame the problem with the concentrated efforts of American science and industry, Yankee ingenuity, and the United States Navy. We licked the submarine problem, and we won both wars, but the U-boats were a continuous threat which was not easy to meet.

"Today we have that same threat, and we have a new tentacle grown into the same old sea serpent. I am speaking of the threat to our cities and military installations imposed by the missile-firing submarine. . . . There is no reason to believe that the Soviets will not eventually produce a submarine with capabilities similar to our Polaris. And we must make preparations to combat that ship, that threat. This is a great task; it is an urgent task. We must be able to detect and kill Polaris-type submarines which might be deployed against us to launch a surprise attack." However, Admiral Anderson concluded by saying:

"We see no major breakthrough on the horizon for antisubmarine warfare, no panacea to solve our problem."

Behind this signal failure of the United States Navy amidst its otherwise glorious revolution is that same peculiar attitude that was at the bottom of its inability to prepare for the U-boat in World War II. It is the empiric man's ingrained inability to visualize the future and the reluctance of the conservative man to break radically with traditions and conventions before circumstances actually force him to make the break.

This is neither a novel situation nor is it characteristic solely of the United States Navy. The military mind usually lags behind military realities. The confrontation with the changes of the military evolution frequently develops certain frustrations that then produce either an aggressive adherence to the old or an unduly boisterous advocacy of the new. The latter is then taken for fanaticism and arrogance, resulting in the dismissal of those new ideas as crackpot schemes.

Dialogue on Capitol Hill

The old saying that generals usually prepare for the next war with the concepts and weapons of the last one gains poignancy in the current popularity of tactical notions that hark back to even earlier wars—to the Peninsular War of 1804-12, for example, whose guerilla sideshow seems to have a glowing appeal today. Musings about "brushfire wars" and "graduated deterrence" in an age when strategy is trump and the weapons are "absolute" reflect the reluctance or inability of even the most orderly and scholarly military mind to come to grips with the military realities of the atomic age of ballistic missiles.

In the summer of 1944, in the immediate wake of the German bombardment of London with the mysterious new V-weapons, I hit upon the idea of putting those missiles on our submarines as soon as we could get hold of them after the defeat of Germany and using them for a devastating ship-to-shore bombardment of Japan. It was none of my business in Naval Intelligence to occupy myself with such schemes. But it so happened that one of the greatest American politico-military scholars, Dr. Bernard Brodie, was serving in our branch at Op-16-W as our naval adviser, and he encouraged me to develop the idea as far as I could, within the limitations of my thoroughly inadequate technical qualifications. We then jointly drafted a memorandum and, ignoring channels, sent it up directly to Admiral King. The memo drew an immediate answer of no, signed by someone on King's staff. There was a brief technical explanation appended to it, spelling out why the wedding of missiles and submarines would be impractical if not impossible, and that finished my brief excursion into the naval revolution.

I realize of course how nebulous it was for me, a total layman in all naval technical matters, even to entertain an idea like this. I mention it only to illustrate on an example of which I can speak from first-hand experience how ideas do pop up, how they are frequently rejected out of hand, and how they ultimately blossom into revolutionary realities. A brainstorm is by no means sufficient by itself to start a revolution, especially when it originates with people whose enthusiasm is not matched by their competence. To paraphrase Samuel Butler, ideas are like living organisms—they have a normal rate of growth which cannot be forced, certainly not beyond the entrenched military mind's point of resistance to new ideas. But human history is in essence a history of ideas, H. G. Wells remarked in a chapter of his *Outline of History* in which he also wrote: "The professional military mind is by necessity an inferior and unimaginative mind; no man of high intellectual quality would willingly imprison his gifts in such a calling."

With its development of the nuclear submarine and the Polaris missile, the United States Navy showed that there are exceptions to Wells' rule. Yet even in those two great accomplishments, certain individuals rather than the Navy as a whole were at the sources of progress. The military establishment of the United States was not too good in visualizing the trends of the great military revolution or in anticipating them. The two major developments that contributed so greatly to the bursting of the old confines and concepts of war were the ballistic missile and the nuclear submarine. Yet as recently as 1953-54, the Pentagon, while working on both, seemed to be blind to the imminence of their appearance and to the ramifications of their existence. In 1953, the concept of deterrence and retaliation was embodied in the B-70 Mach 3 aircraft, designed to replace the B-52. Why? Because, as Defense Secretary McNamara conceded it, "the important place the intercontinental ballistic missile would have in our strategic arsenal could not be fully foreseen." As far as the missiles were concerned, emphasis was on the first generation, liquid-fuel Atlas and Titan. Why? Because, again according to Secretary McNamara, the rapid development of the second generation solid-fuel Polaris and Minuteman missiles was not foreseen.

It was this same inability to recognize even the contours of the future— the situation soon to be created by the marriage of the submarine and the ballistic missile; and to draw the proper conclusions from the obvious change in the balance of power created by Soviet emphasis on long-range submarines that began in 1947 with the build-up of the Red Fleet, that retarded the development of the American ASW effort.

Fortunately for the United States, a "bunch of so-called laymen" muscled in on the scene and literally forced the reluctant Navy to embrace the cause of antisubmarine warfare. This initiative came from Congress, and more specifically from two groups. In one group were Senator Henry M. Jackson of Washington and Senator Stuart Symington of Missouri; in the other were the Congressmen who make up the subcommittee of the House Committee of Appropriations which passes on the budget of the Department of Defense—especially Mr. Mahon of Texas, the subcommittee chairman, Daniel J. Flood of Pennsylvania, Melvin R. Laird of Wisconsin, Gerald R. Ford, Jr. of Michigan and Glenard P. Lipscomb of California. Without their all-out intervention, I venture to say, and Admiral Burke's willingness to go along with them, American ASW would nowhere be even at its present stage of evolution.

The dialogue on Capitol Hill began in 1949, when for a fleeting period it seemed antisubmarine warfare would gain the attention it so urgently deserved. Admiral Francis S. Low, the man who was so instrumental in "licking the submarine problem" in World War II, was ordered to the Navy Department on temporary duty to review the ASW situation and develop measures to deal with it. But history was not to repeat itself. Low's survey commanded the respect properly due the findings of the United States Navy's greatest antisubmarine expert, but his recommendations were filed and forgotten. However, they ignited the interest of Congressman Mahon and from then on, this brilliant and influential Texan never ceased to "plug" the subject, foisting it on the Navy in the end.

"We have only been talking about ASW for four or five years, really," Congressman Flood recalled with his characteristic pungency. "Just a few years ago I had a whole room of Navy people up here. You couldn't get a decent conversation about ASW. You would talk about all kinds of things. When you went into ASW, I used to sit over here and I couldn't get anybody interested, secretaries, admirals, or anybody."

The seed which Admiral Low planted in 1949, and Congressman Mahon and his subcommittee so carefully nursed did produce some results in the Navy. Yet even in 1960, it still left so much to be desired that the Mahon subcommittee found it necessary to issue a special report on the topic. *"The Navy has failed to push undersea warfare programs with sufficient vigor,"* the report read in part. "Except for the indefatigable effort and obstinacy of one man [Vice Admiral Hyman G. Rickover, USN] we probaby would not now have the nuclear powered submarine which in itself, in the attack version, is one of the best antisubmarine weapons. The nuclear powered submarine has proven to be one of the major accomplishments of this generation.

"The marriage of the atomic submarine with the Polaris fleet ballistic missile promises to give us one of the greatest deterrent weapon systems yet devised. Both of these accomplishments have been notably successful because management at a crucial stage was divorced from the stagnation of the usual bureaucratic organizations and procedures.

"Studies made of our antisubmarine efforts indicate that both organizational and inspirational action along similar lines is required. The Navy says that it is giving antisubmarine warfare its highest priority rating, yet there is no indication of dramatic or dynamic leadership in this field."

Still a year later, in the spring of 1961, the dialogue continued. On April 14, Representative Phil Weaver of Nebraska thus said: "Admiral Burke, in your summary of the Communist bloc naval forces you stress the submarine threat, both to shipping and to American mainland cities. Do you think ASW progress has been satisfactory?"

"No, sir," answered the man who did more than any of his predecessors as CNO in the post-war period to invigorate ASW in the United States Navy. "We have made tremendous progress in the last eight or ten years, but it is not good enough."

"In what areas does ASW lag the worst?" Weaver asked.

"Largely in Research and Development," Burke said, "and in procurement of new equipment."

"I believe we will all agree," Representative Mahon then said, "the Soviet submarine threat is one of the greatest threats we face?"

"Yes, sir," Admiral Burke said.

"Do we also agree," Mahon continued, "the attack submarine is one of the more effective antisubmarine weapons?"

"Yes, sir," Burke said.

"It is pretty hard to understand," Mahon went on, "why in the light of this fact we do not press forward with more vigor in this program. I think this is a program the American people would support. Is it likewise true the Soviet submarine, which would be the target of our attack submarine, will probably have considerable capability to launch missiles upon the continental United States?"

"The Soviet's now have in operation a number of submarines believed to be capable of launching ballistic missiles," Burke said. "They will improve the missiles. They will improve their submarines, and they will probably build more of them. Most of their submarines at the moment are attack-type submarines, a great majority."

"If we look forward to 1970," Mahon continued the dialogue, "and what we will have and what they will have, I do not think we have much margin of safety in our program."

"That is correct, sir," the admiral conceded.

"I realize we cannot spend all the national resources on the Navy," Mahon said, "but I do think this program is not as ambitious as it ought to be. I realize we often spend money on things of questionable value, but I believe these things are of unquestioned value and necessity. I would like to move rather rapidly on them. I do not think we are doing enough."

The argument was clinched by a distant voice, as Admiral Thach chimed in from his outpost on Ford Island in the Pacific: For some time, he said, the Navy has been trying to keep up with the technological changes in antisubmarine warfare by scrimping or borrowing from other branches of the service. "We just can't gon on," he concluded, "robbing Peter to pay Paul."

ASW: The Pattern of Survival

This historic dialogue on Capital Hill produced some remarkable developments in the ASW arsenal of the United States, but left the glaring inadequacies virtually intact. It created scattered weapons of great promise but left the antisubmarine effort in a state of disarray reminiscent of early 1942. As a matter of fact, the ASW of today recalls those bygone days in more respects than one, chiefly because, as Admiral Lloyd M. Mustin, one of the United States Navy's foremost ASW specialists, put it, "The established U.S. antisubmarine strategy is derived from the victorious lessons of World War II." While this to Admiral Mustin represented a distinct asset, it is in fact a liability whose adverse influence is felt seriously throughout the ASW effort.

As a point of fact, and despite Navy claims to the contrary, the ASW preparedness of the Untied States did not progress too far beyond its state at the conclusion of World War II. In at least one crucial respect it is in worse shape than it was at the end of World War II—it does not have anything even remotely resembling the Tenth Fleet. This is a great pity because the complexity of today's ASW is staggering and it clamors for some centralization under command whose authority would be as absolute as was Admiral King's.

The basic strategy of modern ASW has several components—detection and location, classification and identification, the hunt and the kill. The resources this strategy requires include aircraft carriers, various destroyer types, antisubmarine subs, long-range land-based antisubmarine patrol aircraft, ship-based fixed-wing aircraft, helicopters, and a string of ancillary vehicles. They must have highly specialized equipment and weapons and must be closely coordinated with a hair-trigger intelligence system.

Nothing would be gained, I submit, from delving too deeply into technical details and describing the weapons systems of ASW that is far too sensitive a subject anyway for public discussion in too specific terms. Most of the weapons in use today are more or less familiar from World War II, and some even from World War I—sonar, radar, the sono-buoy, MAD, depth charges, homing torpedoes, mines. They are, of course, better in most cases than their World War II ancestors—they have to be in order to counter the threat of enemy submarines which have vastly increased speed, depth, endurance, and weapon capabilities.

Most of the Navy's current research and development effort in ASW is directed toward improvement in eight major areas: (1) to increase our intelligence-gathering capabilities; (2) to increase the detection ranges of ASW surface ships, submarines, and aircraft by improvements in ship sonars and by the development of new non-acoustic detection devices for aircraft; (3) to develop new classification devices for all vehicles; (4) to develop mobile and fixed ocean surveillance systems, both active and passive, for coverage in all areas in which ballistic missile submarines could operate against the United States; (5) to develop new ASW weapon systems to give quick reaction kill capabilities at ranges up to those of existing detection equipments; (6) to develop anti-submarine mines, both air and ship laid, and to develop means to locate, identify and neutralize mines that might be planted by enemy sub-marines; (7) to develop hydrofoil craft and hydroskimmers for possible use in antisubmarine warfare; and (8) to reduce the detectability of our submarines and surface ships through various noise-reduction programs.

The lower-power high-frequency sonar of surface ships was replaced in 1960 by high-power low-frequency sonar with variable depth trans-ducers. This put the sonar transducers physically below the thermal or boundary layers of the oceans where the paths of sound waves is radically refracted from their normal paths. A special kind of "refined, simplified and ruggedized" sonar (that is also "big, complex and ex-pensive") was developed for submarines to increase their detection range and capacity. Among the kill weapons, the Navy now has sophisticated lightweight homing torpedoes that can "search" a much greater area than the best of *Zaunkoenig* could in World War II. To meet the demands created by sonar's longer range, several quick-action rocket-propelled stand-off weapons have been developed, including the Asroc and the Subroc.

Among the "vehicles," only the Navy's hydrofoil program is really new. But no such craft is available for active service and the very fate of the program hinges on the eventual evaluation of these craft. Efforts are made to increase the speed and range, and improve the equipment of ASW aircraft. Where formerly two TBM carrier types were needed to do the job, now a single S-2F3 is supposed to be sufficient. There is considerable added emphasis on helicopters. Some of the newer sonars —so-called sound domes—are lowered into the water from helicopters to widen their range and free the sound gear from the disturbing influence of surface ships noises. The DASH (for "destroyer anti-submarine helicopter") is a very small helicopter that operates from destroyer type ships at the outside range of their sonar. It is a deliberate attack system in which the drop (of ASW homing torpedoes) can be controlled remotely.

Depth charges and torpedoes—still our principal ASW weapons— now pack vastly increased destructive power (including nuclear) for surer kills. Some advance was made in efforts to reduce the noise produced by the pumps and other machinery of attack submarines which create a distinct signature. Last but not least, significant progress was made in communications equipment that is especially important for prompt and safe contact with the Polaris type submarines on stations.

The billions of dollars the Navy spent since 1952 on ASW development have produced some progress, to be sure, but nothing spectacular occurred to justify the optimism frequently voiced by the Navy's ASW specialists. Listening to them as they claim "100 per cent reliability," you would think ASW ceased to be a problem. But most of the time, they are referring to research and almost invariably to research accomplishments. The American ASW effort is thus made to look "awfully good" and is supposed to give the ASW forces afloat or in the air "a much greater capability." The trouble is that not enough of the research accomplishments is translated into operational weapons, and only relatively few of the latter are in the hands of combat units.

While the United States is thus made to appear safe behind a fantastic shield of ASW weapons, actually it is wide open and vulnerable because most of those weapons are still in the research and development stage. Nobody professes to know when they will become available for operational use and whether they will work or not. The situation of such trial-and-error method was highlighted in the case of the OPS-44 radar on which the Navy spent millions of dollars then ditched the finished product when it was in mass production because it proved outdated by the time it became ready for use. An outstanding example of the discrepancy between the promise held out by a highly-tauted device and its actual value to the up-to-the-minute defenses of the United States is the Navy's most ambitious ASW effort, the so-called large area ocean surveillance research program. It is designed to close the "bolt holes," great gaps left in the ASW patrol line. It is a grave problem clamoring for urgent solution because today even whole oceans, like the South Atlantic, draw a virtual blank on the ASW situation maps.

Trident is the most powerful, longest range surface ship sonar ever developed, but it is available only in a few experimental models. The first of them was installed in a ship in the spring of 1961, and a second in the fall. But it will be some time before it will take its place in the ASW arsenal of the United States Navy to close the gap of the bolt holes.

The Navy's major effort in ocean surveillance is the Artemis project, originally proposed by Dr. Frederick V. Hunt, the world famous Harvard physicist, after whom it is named (Artemis being the name of the Greek goddess of the hunt). Dr. Hunt propounded the theory that water as well as air could conduct radar waves. The theory was turned over to some thirty scientific groups with Columbia University's Hudson Laboratory as the chief contractor. It is a fascinating project whose basic secret was borrowed from the dolphin.

Scientists in California and Florida discovered that the dolphin navigated at night by "radar" and also found his food by it. It was constantly sending out pulses through the sea and was receiving echoes which it was constantly evaluating. This "dolphin radar" was found to be operating on a wave length higher than sound but lower than standard band radio. The application of the dolphin's very low frequency then produced the Artemis.

However, the bare chronology of this program illustrates how long it takes to develop even such a crucial project, or even how long it takes just to find out whether it would make a system. The program began in earnest in November, 1958, with the measurements of sound, and continued in March, 1959, with the analysis of pertinent data obtained from TNT shots. The sound source trials were repeated in July, 1959; and in January, 1960, work began on the conversion of a tanker, the USNS *Mission Capistrano*, designated as the first Artemis vehicle.

The installation of the receiver modules was completed in October, 1960, and the tanker's conversion was finished in April, 1961, when the extremely high-powered transducer was first lowered through her bottom into the water. Experiments continued through 1961, in a most cautious manner because the Artemis needed electric power enough to light and heat a city of 50,000, and nobody knew what would happen when all this power was put in the water.

Even in 1961, although Artemis had picked up "everything that moved beneath the surface of the sea for 500 miles," it was only an exploratory development, as Admiral Hayward called it, and not a system. "We do not know enough about it," he said, "and all this program was meant to do was to test the feasibility of detection of submarines at hundreds of miles by use of sonar. We want to know what, also, is the limit of the receiver gain that you get in this sort of thing. This is strictly exploratory development. It is in the research business and it has been evaluated by the President's Scientific Advisory Committee and by the Naval Research Advisory Committee, and the Undersea Warfare Committee of the National Academy of Sciences, and my technical people have looked at this." He then added: "There is not sufficient technical information today for anyone to say that we should make a system out of this."

Then, however, the project went into high gear, was adopted as a system after all, a Texas Tower-type structure was constructed off Bermuda to serve as a relay point between several Arthemis ships. Then conversion of other ships began to accomodate additional transducers which are, in fact, underwater radar sets, each five stories high and weighing hundreds of tons. The importance of this project is comparable to that of the Polaris. In the interplay of measures and countermeasures it may tip the balance in favor of the United States.

However, it is only a step toward better ocean surveillance and not a tangible weapon the combat elements of the United States Navy can use, right now, to hunt and kill hostile submarines The forces afloat—the so-called action agents of the vast ASW activity—are full of complaints on this score. Their accredited spokesmen are flag officers like Admiral Thach, but junior officers can also be heard in their exasperation with the patent inadequacies of practical ASW. A young two striper thus decided to vent his anger in an article in which he described his experience during an ASW exercise. He had excellent sonar aboard and had no difficulty in finding a target, but he had nothing else and was thoroughly frustrated when he was thus prevented from making a kill. His revelation antagonized the Pentagon and the young man needed Congressional protection to save his neck he was so boldly sticking out.

Other officers buttonhole Congressmen whenever they show up on shipboard to attend ASW exercises. What some of those Congressmen found was described graphically by several. Representative Lipscomb said: "Mr. Laird and I were on an ASW task force, which was participating in some war games. We saw how a supposed enemy submarine got through and placed some missiles on our bases."

Representative Laird added: "The *Norfolk* spent one day when I was aboard, trying to classify an unknown submarine they thought they had and finally they gave up after about a whole day and decided it was not a submarine"

"Indeed not," Representative Flood chimed in. "I sat with a two-striper for two hours in the *Roosevelt* in the dark room. We picked up everything including asthma. But no submarine. We had a bad time."

The detection problem is the alpha and omega of the antisubmarine warfare effort, but as of now, it is nowhere near solution This was conceded by Admiral Burke in his usual frank and salty manner. "We have increased the range of our surface ship sonars four or five times. We have developed a number of techniques for locating submarines from passive listening gear. We have developed new sonobuoys which are much better than the old ones. We have developed weapons of much greater kill capacity at greater ranges.

"With all this," he added, "our progress is still not satisfactory because the oceans are big and the water is dense, and there is a limit on how far any technique that is now known can detect an object under water. We are doing a lot of research. We have improved our weapons. One of the big difficulties right now is that we have developed equipment which gives ships a much greater capability but which we are not putting in ships at a rapid enough rate."

If it is true what the Navy claims (and I have not the slightest doubt that it is true) that the submarine now represents the primary threat to the United States, an effective antisubmarine effort, in its various ramifications, represents the basic pattern of our survival. However, there are serious holes and gaps in the pattern, and the primeval difficulties with which the oceans confront us are but a part of the overall problem. Others are of the man-made variety, caused by the omissions and commissions of those whose job it would be to plug the holes, close the gaps, and solve the problem.

The responsibility for the current inadequacy is widespread. In a very real sense, the United States Navy is the victim rather than the villain in this development. Economic limitations on its budget rule out a proper emphasis on the ASW effort, for "billions would be needed," as Admiral Thach put it, "to put the United States in a position to protect itself against attack from submarine-launched missiles." Also, the current size of the United States Navy is by far inadequate to meet its antisubmarine warfare commitments. To mention but a single glaring fact, there are not enough ships in the fleets to provide adequate protection for our maritime traffic even in a limited war, or as Admiral Mustin expressed it: "In today's force levels the merchant marine would suffer grievous losses because the Navy does not have enough ships to provide escorts for merchant ships." This was the most crucial gap Admiral King found in the Navy of 1942. Today it is again one of the most severe shortcomings of the United States' ASW preparedness.

Moreover, there exists within the National Security Council and the Defense Department the same kind of indecision that retarded the United States in meeting the challenge of the U-boats in 1942 and early 1943. Sterile theoretical toying with the various kinds of wars, that is largely a semantic exercise, precludes purposeful preparation for what is most likely to occur. The Navy is not specifically told by the political leadership for what kind of war it has to prepare and, therefore, it has to scatter its resources by preparing for all kinds of wars. There is not even an established national policy about the use of atomic weapons in any forms of wars to guide the Navy or, for that matter, also the Army and the Air Force.

Within the Navy, decentralization of the antisubmarine warfare effort is, in the opinion of its Congressional critics, the most serious bottleneck. This is difficult to understand, especially in the light of the Navy's experience in World War II. The Tenth Fleet was created by Admiral King to remedy a situation that was very similar to the conditions which exist today. In 1943, too, the Navy's effort was seriously weakened by the dispersal of its forces and resources; today, this dispersal is even more widespread than it was two decades ago. I tried to draw up a sort of table of organization of the ASW effort in the United States and it may be useful to reprint it here, to illustrate how fragmented the ASW organization really is.

The fountainheads of the effort are, of course, the President, the National Security Council and the Bureau of the Budget. Then comes the Secretary of Defense who has ASW scattered in three major organizations, the Director of Defense Research and Engineering, the Advanced Research Projects Agency, and the Research and Development Advisory Committee.

Within the Navy, and at its highest civilian level, the Secretary has an ASW Committee and the Operations Evaluating Group. Under him, the effort is divided up between three major headings, the Military

Command, the so-called Business Administration, and Research and Development.

The Military Command, headed by the Chief of Naval Operations who has an Antisubmarine Warfare Readiness Executive, consists of the fleets with their ASW officers, and of agencies responsible for training and for the operational evaluation of the activities. In the Business Administration, the Bureau of Ships, the Bureau of Naval Weapons and the Bureau of Personnel has cognizance of various ASW endeavors. The current center of gravity of the effort is in Research and Development, and it is there where fragmentation appears to be the greatest. There is an Assistant Secretary of the Navy for Research and Development, a Deputy Chief of Naval Operations in charge of Development, then come the Office of Naval Research, the ASW Systems Analysis Group, the Underseas Warfare Research and Development Planning Council, the Naval Research Advisory Committee, and a string of Naval Laboratories, including the Naval Research Laboratory in Washington, D. C.; the Naval Underwater Sound Reference Center in Orlando, Florida; the Naval Ordnance Laboratory in Corona, California; the Naval Underwater Ordnance Unit in Key West, Florida; the Naval Underwater Ordnance Station in Newport, Rhode Island; and the Naval Underwater Sound Laboratory in New London, Conn.

Outsiders whose influence radiates to the Navy include the Atomic Energy Commission, the Undersea Warfare Committee of the National Academy of Sciences, and the Antisubmarine Warfare Advisory Committee of the National Security Industrial Association.

While nominally all the organizations, agencies and bureaus are coordinated at the top, in actual fact no such coordination and supervision exists. The individual segments operate more or less independently with an autonomy which they may not possess but which they actually arrogate to themselves.

The single management idea for antisubmarine warfare never ceases to haunt the Navy, especially because its brilliant and energetic Congressional "watchdogs" never let it forget the crying need for it. In 1960, in a strongly worded report, Congress told the Navy: "The development work in this area is not being divorced from control of the semiautonomous bureaus in the Navy Department. Until a single manager similar to that provided for the Polaris ballistic missile system, with delegated responsibility, and the full backing of top officials, is established, it is doubtful that antisubmarine warfare will attain the goals so urgently required.

"The Committee recommends that such action be taken immediately."

The recommendation was never acted upon. The Navy's argument against it was expressed at some length in a document called "Single Manager for ASW Research and Development" (which, of course, is but part of the complex activity although it constituted the kernel of the Tenth Fleet). It is important because it expressed the basic philosophy of the Navy as a whole on this crucial topic.

"The Navy's program in ASW research and development is not oriented toward a single weapon or weapon system," it read in part. "It involves rather the entire complex of our naval forces. It involves the effective utilization of passive and active techniques, of broad area surveillance and local area search operations, of surface, subsurface, and airborne vehicles, of every field of naval weapon and equipment technology, and indeed the ocean environment itself."

The rest of the document was a tissue of subterfuges and double-talk, most typical for which was this passage: "The Navy has considered with great care . . . the Committee's recommendation for a single manager for ASW R. & D. While such an organization could be established, it is considered less desirable than the current one in that it would impose a compartmentation of research, and would require extensive overlapping and duplication of research effort which also applies to many other fields of naval warfare in addition to ASW. Since the current organization appears to have been outstandingly successful as measured by its record of accomplishments, the proposed revision has not been adopted."

Even Admiral Burke who, more than any other man in or out of the Navy, was responsible for the invigoration of the badly neglected ASW effort, set himself up in opposition to the recommendation, denying in effect the historic record established by the Tenth Fleet under startlingly similar conditions.

He conceded that the management of the ASW program—the whole program, that is, and not merely its research and development aspect— is one of the most important areas in the whole Navy Department. However, he added: "The difficulty with antisubmarine warfare is that it extends through the entire Navy. Many ships have an antisubmarine capability. Research and development in antisubmarine warfare extends to every discipline in science. It deals with oceanography, it deals with electronics, it deals with every science. ASW operations are included in every operation that the fleet conducts. A large number of the ships of the fleet are not only interested in ASW but actually conduct ASW operations and have ASW equipment in them. Even the mine forces have underwater object locators."

That it is exactly this dispersion of the activity that literally clamors for centralized control and command in the face of the Soviet submarine threat did not seem to occur to Admiral Burke. The history of the Tenth Fleet—created as it was to terminate such a fragmentation by concentrating the management of the anti-U-boat war in a single agency while leaving the task of execution in other hands—has failed to make any impression on him. Even when the phenomenal success of the management system under Admiral Raborn that produced the Polaris was called to his attention, he rejected it out of hand as a pertinent argument.

Apparently the United States Navy, in its empiricism and pragmatism, needs an experience comparable to that of 1942-43 along the East Coast, to wake up to the importance of an organization that could, and most probably would, endow the American antisubmarine effort with the efficiency and purposefulness vitally needed. While two decades ago there was time to wait for the impact of experience, the changed conditions of nuclear war with ballistic missiles leave no margin for hesitation or error.

Despite all boastful protestations and contrived optimism, the fact remains and should be evident to all that the antisubmarine warfare effort of the United States Navy is woefully inadequate. It may even be so deficient that it actually courts disaster! The Navy has no ships for convoy duty even in a limited war! Its strategic detection apparatus is so defective that it could not locate even a wayward ship at large in the Atlantic, the Portuguese *Santa Maria*, when she fell into insurgent hands and vanished from surveillance by silencing her radio. It leaves gaping holes in the oceans through which a malicious power could easily penetrate to the United States, to stations from which even short-range missiles could be launched against this country's most essential and sensitive installations.

Yet there is no effort at the top to close the gap and remedy this situation. It is not true that the Navy cannot act decisively on crucial matters or that it has no men who could do today what Admiral Low did in World War II. It had a Rickover to promote and produce the nuclear submarine. It had a Raborn to make the Polaris missile a reality, against odds and obstacles that also seemed insurmountable. The Navy's own record in the development of the Polaris missile is the conclusive proof that it can act promptly and energetically when the proper pressure is applied. In 1956, the Polaris missile was not yet on the drawing boards. But only five years later, this powerful weapon, teamed with the nuclear submarine, was successfully proved and in service. In 1958, the navigation satellite Transit was barely conceived.

Yet three years later it was in orbit, successfully demonstrating the technical concept it embodies. These are typical advances which, as Burke himself put it, demonstrate the pace of technical developments in naval equipment, naval weapons systems, and naval science, as well as the speed and determination with which the United States Navy can move in the great military revolution.

The super-power of the submarine comes at the end of a long evolution. But the revolutionary implication of the submarine was recognized early in the game by at least one great naval prophet. In 1804, Robert Fulton placed the blueprints of his "electric torpedo" before William Pitt. The project mortified Admiral Sir John Jervis who immediately recognized in Fulton's "toy" a grievous threat to British sea power.

"Don't look at it!" the great First Sea Lord pleaded with Pitt. "Don't touch it! If we take it up, other nations will, and that will be the strongest blow against our supremacy on the sea that can be imagined!"

When Pitt permitted Fulton to demonstrate his invention and it succeeded in splitting the Danish brig *Dorothea* in two, Jervis exclaimed: "Pitt is the biggest fool that ever lived! He has given encouragement to a form of warfare which is not desired by those who command the sea and which may well deprive us of our supremacy."

The submarine can no longer be banished from the oceans of the world. But it is not too late to gain for the free world that margin of lead in the interplay of measures and countermeasures which Admiral King and his associates in the Tenth Fleet recognized as the margin needed to win.

☆

REFERENCE AND INDEX PAGES

ACKNOWLEDGMENTS

It is my pleasant duty to express my deep sense of gratitude to Admiral Francis S. Low, USN (Ret), Captain Kenneth A. Knowles, USN (Ret), and Mr. John E. Parsons, who allowed me to draw upon their memories. Mr. Ralph G. Albrecht, the legendary "Commander Norden" of World War II, has aided me at every turn with generosity matched by his wisdom and knowledge. I am indebted to Mr. Samuel W. Crosby, chief of staff of the House Subcommittee on Defense Appropriations, for his sagacious advise. Several distinguished members of Congress also took time out to enlighten me, especially Representatives Clarence Cannon of Missouri, George H. Mahon of Texas, Daniel J. Flood of Pennsylvania, and Senator Henry M. Jackson of Washington. I hasten to add, however, that all interpretations and conclusions are entirely my own and were not even remotely suggested or influenced by them.

In the Navy Department the Naval History Division (Rear Admiral Ernest M. Eller, USN, Ret), the Office of Naval Intelligence and the Office of Information (Lieutenant Commander F. A. Prehn, USN) were helpful with my follow-up research. Special mention must be made of the assistance received at the Navy Department Library from Mr. W. B. Greenwood, Head Librarian, Mrs. Margaret Edsall, Reference Librarian (whose late husband was closely associated with Tenth Fleet) and my old friend and colleague, Mr. Fred Meigs, Librarian. I was aided with promptness and unflagging service by Mrs. Josephine James, Head, Biographies Branch, and her exceptional staff of young ladies.

Nothing in this book represents their views and opinions or those of the Department of the Navy. No information included in the narrative is of a classified nature.

My own familiarity with the subject stems from my association with the American antisubmarine warfare effort in World War II when I was in charge of research and planning at Op-16-W, the Special Warfare Branch of the Office of Naval Intelligence. In that capacity I had access to the total documentation of the Battle of the Atlantic. Even prior to Pearl Harbor, at the request of the late James Forrestal, then Assistant Secretary of the Navy, I occupied myself with matters involving the *Kriegsmarine* and produced several monographs for the United States Navy, on morale, prisoner interrogation, and the *Arbeitsdienst*.

After the war, I cooperated in the writing of the history of the Special Warfare Branch, then had the job of examining and evaluating the mass of captured German naval documents. In no war of history have the innermost secrets of the enemy been bared so fully, and if our knowledge of the U-Boat Arm was astoundingly broad and accurate already during the war, it became complete and perfect after the war.

I am deeply grateful to the late James Forrestal, Fleet Admiral Ernest J. King, Rear Admiral Ellis M. Zacharias and Captain Joseph L. Riheldaffer, as well as to Rear Admiral Harold C. Train and Rear Admiral Cecil H. Coggins, who gave me this opportunity to serve and stood by me in all the ups and downs of my employment. In the same sense of appreciation I mention my associates in Op-16-W, Mr. William Cullinan, Mr. Jacques Futrelle, Jr., Commander John Paul Dickson, Prof. John Paul Reed, Mr. Dennis McEvoy, Dr. Stefan T. Possony, and especially Dr. Bernard Brodie, the eminent student of strategy.

In addition, I thank the office of the Naval Attache of the German Federal Republic and the office of the German Naval Representative to NATO in Washington, D.C., and the German Information Office in New York City; Mr. S. Joseph Warnon of the Electric Boat Division, General Dynamics Corporation of Groton, Conn.; the editors of *The Pilot*, journal of the National Maritime Union of America; the editors of *Space/Aeronautics;* and my friend, Mr. Edward J. Michelson, Washington editor of *Forbes*, for help generously given.

I express my gratitude to my Publisher, Mr. Ivan Obolensky, who commissioned and financed this book; and to Mrs. Ruth Aley of Maxwell Aley Associates: the aid and comfort they gave me far exceeded the call of duty. My friends Jay Nelson Tuck and Sidney Shelley as well as my neighbor in Connecticut, Mrs. Elizabeth Dresser of the *Lakeville Journal* proved invaluable with editorial advice and assistance. Miss Bettie L. Snyder and Mrs. Anna Walters have my vote of thanks for their help in the preparation of an unusually bulky manuscript. My son, John Michael Farago, was most helpful in the preparation of the Index. Miss Ruth Bornschlegel, art director and production manager of Ivan Obolensky, Inc., a fine young artist; Mr. Lindsay H. Metzger and P. Edward Schumacher of Hadfield Press suffered valiantly with me and helped generously all through the various phases of production.

Mr. John G. Ledes, general manager of Ivan Obolensky, Inc., shared with me the ecstasy and agony connected with the writing of the book. It was from his original idea that this project developed and then it was largely due to his close association with it that it could be completed. His dynamic efficiency and enthusiasm, mellowed by kindness and generosity, aided me throughout and kept me going through crises and doubts. To a friend of classic proportions, I say with all the emphasis at my command: "Thank you so much, John!"

BIBLIOGRAPHY*

No book, official or otherwise, was ever written about the Tenth Fleet. Even references to it in the various histories of the war at sea are few and brief. As a result, much of the material on the Tenth Fleet had to be assembled stone by stone in personal conversations, from documents, and from the broader records of the Battle of the Atlantic.

As far as secondary sources are concerned, my greatest debt of gratitude is owed to Professor Emeritus Samuel Eliot Morison of Harvard University, the incomparable admiral-historian of the United States Navy in World War II. His formidable account of the Battle of the Atlantic was my inspiration and guide, as well as my standard reference.

Although it is a fictional account of the Atlantic battle, *The Cruel Sea* by Nicholas Monsarrat must be mentioned here. A novel of enormous power and astounding accuracy, written with detailed knowledge of the sea, it is truly one of the finest books about the war afloat.

The following bibliography lists the works which I found useful in the writing of this book. To their authors I express my heartfelt gratitude.

Administrative History of the Atlantic Fleet, in Naval History Division, vols. I-XI, the basic official history of the various organizations of the United States Navy involved in the Battle of the Atlantic.

*Allen, E. S., "Sea Battle, 1958," an article from the New Bedford (Mass.) *Standard-Times,* in Congr. Rec., March 9, 1959, p. A1950.

Ames, Lt. Comdr. C. E., *"The inauguration and carrying out of convoy operations and its effect,"* memorandum prepared in Cominch Convoy and Routing, December, 1942, also his History of Convoy and Routing.

*Anderson, Adm. G. W., *Address to the New York Chapter of the Naval Order,* March 6, 1962.

*Anderson, Adm. G. W., Testimony before House Defense Appropriations Subcommittee, in *Hearings,* 1962.

Assmann, Adm. K., *Deutsche Schicksalsjahre,* Wiesbaden, 1950, history of World War II by an eminent German naval historian.

Assmann, Adm. K., *"Report on the German Naval War Effort,"* prepared for the Allied authorities in 1945-46.

Assmann, Adm. K., and Adm. Walter Gladisch, *"Report to the Office of the British Commander in Chief Germany,"* another study prepared in the immediate wake of World War II.

ASW: Anti-Submarine Warfare, Chief of Naval Operations, Navy Department, 1959, "a report on the increasingly important role of the United States Navy in Anti-Submarine Warfare."

*Baldwin, H. W., "Strategic background, 1958," in Saunders, *q.v.,* pp. 105-120, an essay on Soviet sea power.

*Baldwin, H. W., "U.S. seeks shield in undersea war," *New York Times,* November 5, 1961, report on a Navy commission to survey ASW.

Ballantine, D. S., *U.S. Naval Logistics in the Second World War,* Princeton, 1947.

---

* Items with asterisks refer to source references used in the preparation of the Epilogue.

*Barbey, Adm. D. E., "Our weakest spot," in *Saturday Evening Post*, Dec. 22, 1956, pp. 35, 73-74, about the deficiencies of ASW in the U.S.

Baxter, J. P., III, *Scientists Against Time*, Boston, 1946, the official history of the Office of Scientific Research and Development (OSRD), incl. "The seesaw of submarine warfare," and "Naval warfare on and above the surface."

Bekker, C. D., *Kampf und Untergang der Kriegsmarine*, Hannover, 1953, with a story of the sinking of *Laconia* and a chapter about the new U-boats of 1945. An American edition, *Defeat at Sea*, appeared in 1955.

*Blair, C., *The Atomic Submarine and Admiral Rickover*, New York, 1954. A partisan review of the development of the nuclear submarine.

Brennecke, J., *The Hunters and the Hunted*, London, 1958, a popular history cf the U-boat war from the German viewpoint.

Brodie, B., *Seapower in the Machine Age*, 2nd ed., Princeton, 1943, one of the classics of American naval literature.

Brodie, B., "New tactics in naval warfare," *Foreign Affairs*, Jan. 1946, pp. 210-223.

Brodie, B., *A Guide to Naval Strategy*, 4th ed., Princeton, 1958.

*Brodie, B., *Strategy in the Atomic Age*, Princeton, 1960, the most lucid and level-headed exposition of the military revolution.

*Burke, Adm. A., *Address before the National Press Club*, Jan. 6, 1958, in *Congr. Rec.*, Jan. 8, 1958, pp. A68-A69, one of the most significant utterances of the former Chief of Naval Operations.

*Burke, Adm. A., "Looking ahead," in *Now Hear This*, Jan.-Feb., 1958, pp. 4-8.

*Burke, Adm. A., Testimony before the Senate Armed Services Posture Hearing, January 26, 1959, *Congr. Transcript*.

*Burke, Adm. A., Testimonies before the House Subcommittee on Defense appropriations, in *Hearings*, 1958, 1959, 1960, 1961.

Busch, H., *So war der U-Bootkrieg*, Bielefeld, 1952, an account of the U-boat war by a former German naval officer. The English translation by L.P.R. Wilson contains valuable annotations. It has useful appendices on German U-boat types, ships sunk by U-boats, and the monthly number of U-boats at sea.

Bush, Dr. V., *Modern Arms and Free Men*, New York, 1949, the wartime director of the OSRD about science and scientists in national defense.

*Carrison, D. J., "The Soviet drive for sea power," in *United States Naval Institute Proceedings*, Oct. 1959, pp. 67-71.

Carse, R., *Lifeline*, New York, 1943.

Chalmers, W. S., *Max Horton and the Western Approaches*, London, 1954. An outstanding record of the British ASW effort in World War II by a former director of the Royal Navy's Staff College.

Chamberlin, W., "The tradition of the offensive in the United States Navy," *USNIP*, Oct. 1941, pp. 1375-1384.

Chatterton, E. K., *Q-Ships and their Story*, London, 1922.

Churchill, W. S., *The Second World War*, 6 vols., Boston, 1948-1950, the major document of World War II, with many references to the Atlantic battle.

Clarke, W. B., *When the U-Boats Came to America*, Boston, 1929, U-boat operations off the American coast in World War I.

Coale, G., *North Atlantic Patrol*, New York, 1942, an artistic account of the United States Navy's early participation in the Atlantic battle by a lieutenant commander of the U.S. Naval Reserve.

Craven, W. W., and Cate, J. L., *The Army Air Forces in World War II*, 2 vols., Chicago, 1949, indispensable for the Army-Navy controversy on antisubmarine warfare and the Air Force's participation in ASW.

Crowther, J. G., and Whiddington, R., *Science at War*, London, 1946, a semi-official British history on the "wizards' war."

Cunningham, Sir A. B. (Viscount Cunningham of Hyndhope), *A Sailor's Odyssey*, London, 1951. The autobiography of one of the towering British naval figures, important for its frank description of Adm. Cunningham's mission in Washington and his relations with Adm. King.

*Denfeld, Adm. L. E., "Why I was fired," in *Collier's*, March 25, 1950. pp. 32-33 plus.

*Department of the Navy, Washington, 1960, information on its organization and functions.

Dictionary of American Naval Fighting Ships, Washington, 1959, first in a multi-volume series, presenting an alphabetical arrangement of the ships of the United States Navy.

Doenitz, K., *Die Fahrten der "Breslau" im Schwarzen Meer*, Berlin, 1917, (reprinted in *Die Kreuzerfahrten der Goeben und Breslau*, with T. Krauss, Berlin, 1933). An early literary effort of the Grossadmiral, interesting for a description of his salad days in the Navy prior to his transfer to the U-Boat Arm in World War I.

Doenitz, K., *Die U-Boatwaffe*, Berlin, 1939. A slender technical volume revealing few if any of the future Grossadmiral's revolutionary tactical ideas.

Doenitz, K., *Zehn Jahre und zwanzig Tage*, Bonn, 1958. The memoirs of the outstanding figure of the U-boat war. Although slanted to vindicate Doenitz's conduct of the campaign, it is indispensable. The English translation (London, 1959, and New York, n.d.) is inferior to the German original because it omitted the Admiral's voluminous source references and frequently blurred the true meaning of his statements.

Dreyer, Sir F. C., *The Sea Heritage*, London, 1955. This book by a member of the Admiralty's Assessment Committee in World War II is especially valuable for its evaluation of the U-boat war and its statistical data.

Drummond, J. D., *H.M. U-Boat*, London, 1958, the story of Kapitaenleutnant Rahmlow's *U-570* which surrendered to the British and became HMS *Graph*, a "guinea-pig boat" that provided information about the capabilities of German submarines.

Eastern Sea Frontier War Diary, in the Naval History Division, covers the entire 1941-1945 period of World War II.

*Eller, Adm. E. M., "Will we need a Navy to win?" *USNIP*, March 1950, pp. 1160-1169, by the director of the Naval History Division.

*Eller, Adm. E. M., "Implications of Soviet sea power," in Saunders, *q.v.*, pp. 299-327.

Elliott, J. R., Jr., "Threat from the sea," *Barron's*, April 6, 1959, pp. 3, 15-21, industrial mobilization for ASW.

"Evolution of the escort carrier," *ONI Weekly*, April, 1945, pp. 1309-1317, 1397-1406.

Farago, L., *Axis Grand Strategy*, New York, 1942, from original German sources with several items on naval strategy and tactics.

Farago, L., *Morale and its Maintenance in the German Navy*, Office of Naval Intelligence, 1943.

Farago, L., "Grossadmiral Karl Doenitz. A Characterological Study," a wartime monograph prepared in ONI, 1943-1945.

Farago, L., "The Soviet Navy," in *Corps Diplomatique*, 1946.

Farmbacher, Gen. W., and Matthiae, Adm. W., *Lorient 1940-45*, Weissenberg, the major source on the establishment, development and defense of the chief German U-boat base in occupied France.

First Draft Narrative History of Cominch HQ, in the Naval History Division, prepared in 1945.

Forrestal, J., *The Forrestal Diaries*, edited by Walter Millis and E. S. Duffield, New York, 1951, excerpts from the day-by-day record kept by the wartime Secretary of the Navy and first Secretary of Defense.

Frank, W., *Die Woelfe und der Admiral, der Roman der U-Boote*, Hamburg, 1953, the complete story of the U-boat war as seen by the German war correspondent attached to the U-Boat Command. The English translation by Lieutenant Commander R.O.B. Long, RNVR, (New York, 1955) is more useful than the German original because it corrects Frank's inaccuracies.

°Frank, P., "The secret sea battle that goes on right now," *Saga,* March 1962, pp. 13-15, 95-96.

°Frolov, Adm. A., "The Red Navy at war," in *Lloyd's List and Shipping Gazette,* June 26, 1944.

°*Frontiers of Oceanic Research,* Hearings before the House Committee on Science and Astronautics, April 28-29, 1960.

Furer, Adm. J. A., "Naval research and development in World War II," in *J.Am.Soc.Nav.Eng.,* February, 1950, pp. 21-53, by the wartime Coordinator of Research and Development in the Navy Department, and the Navy member of the wartime National Defense Research Committee, King's old friend and classmate.

Furer, Adm. J. A., *Administration of the Navy Department in World War II,* Washington, 1959, the basic source.

Gallery, Adm. D. V., *Clear the Decks!,* New York, 1956. The breezily written story of "Captain Dan" of the "Can Do" (USS *Guadalcanal*) escort carrier group, describing the sinking of Henke's *U-515* and the capture of *U-505.* The British edition (*We Captured a U-Boat,* London, 1957) has an interesting introduction by Commander Edward Young, RNV(S)R.

German Submarine Activities on the Atlantic Coast of the United States and Canada, Washington, 1920, No. 1 in a series of monographs prepared after World War I by the Navy Department Historical Section. No comparable historical review of World War II exists.

°Garthoff, R. L., *Soviet Strategy in the Nuclear Age,* New York, 1958.

German Submarine Industry, Washington, 1946, by the United States Strategic Bombing Survey.

Gibson, R.H., and Prendergast, M., *The German Submarine War,* one of the best books about the U-boat phase of World War I.

Giese, F. E., *Die deutsche Marine 1920-1945, Aufbau and Untergang,* Frankfurt a/M., 1956, the evolution of the German Navy between the two World Wars and during World War II.

Gilbert, F., *Hitler Directs His War,* New York, 1950, an American historian's critical presentation of the *Fuehrer Conferences* (q.v.).

Goerlitz, W., *Der Zweite Weltkrieg,* 1939-45, 2 vols., Stuttgart, 1951. The famous journalist-historian of the German General Staff here presents a brilliantly written history of World War II.

Groener, E., *Die Schiffe der Deutschen Kriegsmarine und Luftwaffe,* Munich, 1954, an excellent reference work on the German Navy.

Hardegen, R., *Auf Gefechtsstationen!* The flamboyant skipper of *U-123* gives his version of the U-boat war in American waters in 1942-1943.

Hashegan, E., *U-Boats Westward,* New York, 1948.

Herlin, H., *Verdammter Atlantik,* Hamburg, 1959. A dramatized narrative of the highlights of the U-boat war by a German journalist. It contains much material not otherwise available.

Hinsley, F. H., *Hitler's Strategy,* London, 1951. A scholarly study of the major ideas which inspired the Fuehrer's conduct of the war.

History of Convoy and Routing, a compendium in the Naval Administrative Series, 1945, in Naval History Division.

History of the Antisubmarine Measures Division of the Tenth Fleet, unnumbered draft in Administrative History of the Atlantic Fleet, 1945.

History of the Fleet Sonar School, Key West, 1945.

Hitler's Secret Conversations, New York, 1953, with an introductory essay by Prof. H. R. Trevor-Roper, ("The Mind of Adolf Hitler"), English translation of the *Bormann-Vermerke.*

Hope, S., *Tanker Fleet*, London, 1948.

*Horan, Adm. H. E., "The navy of the Soviet Union," in *Brassey's Naval Annual,* 1960, pp. 124-132.

Introduction to Sonar, Washington, 1961, one of the Navy Training Courses.

*Isakov, Adm. I. S., *The Red Fleet in the Second World War*, London, 1946, by the political chief of the Red Fleet.

*Jackson, Sen. H. M., "We must catch up," address to the Washington Bankers Association in Spokane, Wash., Oct. 10, 1957.

*Jackson, Sen. H. M., "Statement on Polaris-atomic submarine program," January 6, 1958.

*Jackson, Sen. H. M., "How shall we forge a strategy for survival," address to the National War College, April 16, 1959.

Jane's Fighting Ships, 1939, *et passim.*

Johnson, A. W., *A Brief History of the Organization of the Navy Department,* Washington, 1940.

Karig, W., (ed.), *Battle Report: The Battle of the Atlantic*, New York, 1945, first in a five volume series presenting the dramatized history of World War II at sea.

Kelley, Dr. D. M., *22 Cells in Nuremberg*, New York, 1947, with a chapter on Doenitz by the American psychiatrist to the Nuremberg jail.

Kennedy, T. R., Jr., "The Magnetic Air-borne Detector," *New York Times*, June 2, 1946, reprinted in *USNIP*, July 1946, pp. 989-991.

King, Adm., E. J., "Naval research and development during World War II," in *The United States Navy at War*, Washington, 1946, the third report to the Secretary of the Navy, printed in *USNIP*, January 1946, pp. 170-175.

King, Adm. E. J., "Atlantic operations," *ibid.*, pp. 158-159.

King, E. J., with Walter Muir Whitehill, *A Naval Record*, New York, 1952. The monumental biography of the Commander in Chief U.S. Fleet and Chief of Naval Operations, 1941-1945. Though written in the third person, it presents King's records, views and actions.

Kirkby, J. M., "Some mechanical features in anti-submarine weapons," *Inst. Mech. Eng.*, London, 1948.

Korth, F., *Address of the Secretary of the Navy* at the commissioning of the US(N)S *Sam Houston* at Newport News, Va., March 6, 1962.

Kriegstagebuch der Seekriegsleitung, Sept. 1939-May 1945, the war diaries of the German Naval Staff.

Kriegstagebuch des Befehlshabers der U-Boote, war diaries of the BdU, Commander, U-Boats (Doenitz).

Land, Adm. E. S., *Winning the War with Ships, Land, Sea and Air, Mostly Land*, New York, 1958, autobiography of the War Shipping Administrator.

Langer, W. L., and Gleason, S. E., *The Undeclared War, 1940-41*," New York, 1953, for the Council on Foreign Relations. This book by two distinguished Harvard historians is indispensable for American naval activities in the Atlantic before the German declaration of war, with an interesting account of the *Greer* incident.

Leacock, S., and Roberts, L., *Canada's War at Sea*, Ottawa, 1946.

Lewis, D. D., *The Fight for the Sea. The Past, Present, and Future of Submarine Warfare in the Atlantic*, New York, 1961. Although Commander Lewis' narrative account of submarine warfare in the Atlantic contains only a single passing reference to the Tenth Fleet, it is fully rewarding for its comprehensive treatment of the subject.

Lohmann, W., and Hildebrand, H. H., *Die deutsche Kriegsmarine, 1939-1945,* Bad Nauheim, no date.

Lott, A. S., *Most Dangerous Sea,* Annapolis, 1959, by a lieutenant commander of the United States Navy, wiht details of German minelaying operations within sight of American shores in 1942.

Luedde-Neurath, W., *Regierung Doenitz. Die letzten Tage des Dritten Reiches,* Goettingen, 1951. Doenitz's last days in power by a member of his staff.

Lusar, R., *Die deutschen Waffen und Geheimwaffen des zweiten Weltkrieges und ihre Weiterentwicklung,* Munchen, 1959, German weapon developments in World War II.

*Lyman, J., "The oceans as the operating environment of the Navy," paper in *Office of Naval Research Symposium,* San Diego, Cal., March 1959.

Macintyre, Capt. D., *U-Boat Killer,* New York, 1956, the personal narrative of the legendary commanding officer of HMS *Hesperus,* written in a brisk literary style.

*Macintyre, Capt. D., "The Soviet submarine threat," in Saunders, *q.v.,* pp. 168-186.

Macintyre, D., *The Battle of the Atlantic,* London, 1961.

Martienssen, A. K., *Hitler and His Admirals,* New York, 1946. Excerpts from German documents.

Mason, B. F., *The Composition and Role of the Navy,* Harvard Defense Policy Serial, No. 78, December 1956.

Matlof, M., and Snell, E. M., *Strategic Planning for Coalition Warfare,* Washington, 1953, evolution of American strategy before and during the first year of American participation in World War II.

*Matveyev, Capt. E., "Naval battles in the Baltic," in *Strategy and Tactics of the Soviet-German War,* London, 1942.

*Meister, J., *Der Seekrieg in den osteuropaeischen Gewaessern,* Muenchen, 1958. Also see his, "The Soviet merchant ships and fishing fleets," in Saunders, *q.v.,* pp. 216-242.

Merchantmen at War, London, 1945, prepared for the Ministry of War Transport by the Ministry of Information.

"Mighty new Navy of the U.S.A.," with photographs by John Dominis, *Life,* June 22, 1962, pp. 52-72B.

*Mitchell, M., *The Maritime History of Russia 848-1948,* London, 1949, a massive study that is inclined to give the Soviet Navy the benefit of the doubt.

Morgan, Lt. E. M., "The patrol plane controversy," *USNIP,* July 1943.

Morison, S. E., *History of United States Naval Operations in World War II,* vol. I, *The Battle of the Atlantic September 1939-May 1954* (with an introduction "The United States Navy Between two World Wars," by Commodore Dudley W. Knox, USN), Boston, 1947, (thirteenth printing, March 1961); vol. X, *The Atlantic Battle Won May 1943-May 1945,* Boston, 1956, (fourth printing, October 1959). The foremost American work on the subject.

Morison, S. E., *Strategy and Compromise,* Boston, 1958.

*Moskin, J. R., "The shocking hole in our defense. The war we are not ready to fight," *Look,* May 26, 1959, pp. 27-45.

*Moskin, J. R., "Polaris," *Look,* Aug. 29, 1961, pp. 17-31.

"Narrative of Anti-Blockade Runner Operations South Atlantic 1 Dec. 1943 to 8 Jan. 1944," prepared by the Anti-Submarine Warfare Operations Research Group of Tenth Fleet.

Navy Department, Office of Naval Research, *A Decade of Basic and Applied Science in the Navy,* Washington, 1958, a symposium covering 1947-1957.

Navy Department, Office of Public Relations, *Communiques and Pertinent Press Releases,* 1941-1945, 2 vols., Washington, 1943, 1945.

"Navy tardy in driving off U-boats," *USNIP,* August 1947.

Navy Wings, Washington, 1955, the mission, history and organization of the Navy's air arm.

Nazi Conspiracy and Aggression, 10 vols., Washington, 1946. The collection of documents introduced as evidence at the Nuremberg trial of Grossadmiral Doenitz. Many of the documents deal with the U-boat war but unfortunately their translation leaves much to be desired. Also see *Trial of the Major War Criminals before the International Military Tribunal*, 42 vols., Nuremberg, 1946.

Newbolt, Sir H., *Submarine and Anti-submarine*, London, 1919, by the British historian who completed Sir Julian Corbett's monumental *Naval Operations: Official History of the War*. Sir Henry's slim volume is valuable for an appreciation of the British attitude to the U-boat after the war.

°Noel-Baker, P., *The Arms Race*, London, 1958.

Office of Naval Intelligence, *Interrogation of Survivors from German Blockade Runners*, 1941-1945.

Office of Naval Intelligence, *Post Mortems on Enemy Submarines*, Serials 1-16, ONI 250-G, 1942-1945.

Office of Naval Intelligence, *Fuehrer Conferences on Matters Dealing with the German Navy*, 1939-1945, 7 vols., Washington, 1946-1947. Also in *Brassey's Naval Annual 1948*, with an introduction by Rear Admiral H. G. Thursfield, RN.

Officer, C. B., *Introduction to the Theory of Sound Transmission with Application to the Ocean*, New York, 1958.

°*Organizing for National Security.* "Science Organization and the President," by the Subcommittee on National Policy Machinery, Washington, 1961.

Pawle, G., *The Secret War 1939-45*, New York, 1957, with a foreword by Nevil Shute (Lieutenant Commander Nevil Shute Norway). The story of the "Wheezers and Dodgers," the British equivalent of ASWORG.

Peace and War, United States Foreign Policy 1931-1941, Washington, 1943, Published by the State Department.

Pellam, J. R., *Analysis of A/S Warfare in Moroccan Sea Frontier, 1942-1943*, an ASWORG monograph.

°Pokrovsky, Maj. Gen. G. I., *Science and Technology in Contemporary War*, translated and annotated by R. L. Garthoff, New York, 1959.

°*Polaris Management*, Special Projects Office, Department of the Navy, February 1961, Washington, 1961.

Popple, C. S., *The Standard Oil Company in World War II*, New York, 1952.

°Probus, J. H., "An introductory survey of some of the considerations that influence the U.S. Naval shipbuilding program," *Committee on Undersea Warfare*, National Academy of Science-National Research Council, Jan. 1960.

Puleston, Capt. W. D., *The Influence of Sea Power in World War II*, New Haven, 1948, a study by a former director of ONI.

Radar Electronic Fundamentals, Washington, 1947, a Navy Department manual.

Raeder, E., *Mein Leben*, 2 vols., Tuebingen, 1956. Doenitz's predecessor supplements the Doenitz memoirs, with much useful information on German naval strategy.

Rechlis, E., *They Came to Kill*, New York, 1961, a profusely documented and vividly written account of the eight German saboteurs ferried to the United States in two U-boats in 1942. For the autobiography of one of the saboteurs, see *Eight Spies Against America*, by George J. Dasch, New York, 1959.

Review of Activity, 1 April 1942 to 31 August 1944, prepared after the war by Anti-Submarine Operations Research Group.

Richards D., and Saunders, H. St. G., *Royal Air Force 1939-1945*, 3 vols., London, 1954, with material on the Coastal Command controversy, and criticism of Admiral King.

Riesenberg, F., Jr., *Sea War,* New York, 1956, the profusely documented story of the U.S. Merchant Marine in World War II.

Robertson, T., *Walker, R.N. The Story of Captain Frederick John Walker,* London, 1950, about the British virtuoso of A/S warfare.

*Rohwer, J., *Sea Power Today.* A Symposium, Oldenburg, 1957.

*Rohwer, J., "The Russians as Naval opponents in two World Wars," in Saunders, *q.v.,* pp. 44-74.

Roscoe, T., *United States Destroyer Operations in World War II,* Annapolis, 1953. Prepared in collaboration with Rear Admiral Thomas L. Wattles, USN (Ret), a "magnificient monument" to the DD's and DE's, "these small ships with the lethal punch" to whom "no job was too small, no task too great." Many aspects of the Battle of the Atlantic which go unrecorded in official operational histories are treated with a high sense of drama.

Roskill, S. W., *The War at Sea,* vol. I, *The Defensive,* London, 1954, vol. II. *The Period of Balance,* London, 1958; II. *The Offensive,* London, 1960. Captain Roskill's massive history of the maritime war appeared in the official *United Kingdom Military Series,* edited by J. R. M. Butler. It is, next to Morison's books, the indispensable record of the Battle of the Atlantic.

Roskill, S. W., *Escort. The Battle of the Atlantic.* London, 1955.

Rosenthal, A. M., "U.S. admiral sees a submarine lag," in *New York Times,* November 15, 1961.

Rowland, B., and Boyd, W. B., *United States Navy Bureau of Ordnance in World War II,* Washington, 1946.

Ruge, F., "German Supreme Command in World War II," an eassay prepared for Allied authorities in 1946 by the German admiral.

Ruge, F., *Der Seekrieg 1939-1945,* Stuttgart, 1954, a translation of which was published by the U.S. Naval Institute (Annapolis, 1955), was hailed as the "best general account of the naval war from the German side."

*Saunders, Comdr. M. G., *The Soviet Navy,* New York, 1958.

*Schofield, Adm. B. B., "Russian naval policy," in *Brassey's Naval Annual* 1960, London, pp. 25-31.

Schull, J., *The Far Distant Ships,* Ottawa, 1950, the operational volume of the Canadian Navy's official history in World War II.

Shalett, S., *New York Times Magazine,* February 13, 1944, p. 11.

Sherwood, R. E., *Roosevelt and Hopkins,* New York, 1948, the indispensable record of the political-diplomatic background of World War II.

Ships of the Esso Fleet in World War II, New York, 1946, privately published by Standard Oil of New Jersey.

Sims, Adm. W. S., *The Victory at Sea,* New York, 1920, by the Commander U.S. Naval Forces in European waters, World War I.

*Spilhaus, A., "Turn to the sea," NAS, *Committee on Oceanography,* 1959.

*Springhall, D., "Tonnage sunk by Russian submarines in the Baltic," in *Russia Today,* July 1943.

Steinhardt, Dr. J., "The role of Operations Research in the Navy," in *USNIP,* May 1946, pp. 649ff. Also see, Navy Department *Release,* April 6, 1946.

Sternhell, C. M., and Thorndike, A. M., *Antisubmarine Warfare in World War II,* (Operations Evaluation Group Report No. 51), Washington, 1946.

Stick, D., *Graveyard of the Atlantic,* Chapel Hill, 1952.

Stimson, H. L., and Bundy, McG., *On Active Service in Peace and War,* New York, 1948, important for Army-Navy clash over ASW and Stimson's attitude to King and the Navy.

Submarine Recognition Manual, Washington, 1959, "designed to minimize the submarine's threat to our national security program by helping military and civilian observers to recognize accurately and report all submarines sighted to the proper government authorities."

Sulzberger, A. A., *The Joint Chiefs of Staff,* 1941-1954, Washington, 1954, concise, indispensable.

Summary Report [of the Anti-Submarine Warfare Operations Research Group] *to the Office of Field Service,* OSRD, December 1, 1945.

Taylor, T., *Fire on the Beaches,* New York, 1958. A former journalist, merchant seaman and Naval officer's exciting account of the struggle between the American merchant marine and the U-boats.

Terrell, E., *Admiralty Brief.* London, 1958. Off-beat weapons that contributed to victory in the Atlantic battle.

The Battle of the Atlantic, London, 1946, the British official account.

●"The goblin killers," *Time,* Sept. 1, 1958, pp. 9-14, the ASW organization of the U.S. Navy.

●*The New Navy — Mobile Power for Peace,* Annapolis, 1957, a compendium of the United States Naval Institute.

The Submarine, NAVPERS 16160-B, Washington, 1960. An easily written official manual prepared by the Submarine Base, New London, Conn., describing the submarine, its construction, systems and principle, for use in basic courses at the Submarine School. It contains a brief history of this particular ship.

Thomas, L., *Raiders of the Deep,* New York, 1921. Based on interviews with German U-boat aces of World War I. It is regrettable that Lowell Thomas did not compile a similar report after World War II.

Thomas, P. D., *Use of Artificial Satellites for Navigation and Oceanographic Surveys,* Washington, 1960. Technical Bulletin No. 12 of the U.S. Coast and Geodetic Survey.

Tollaksen, Ens. D. M., "Last chapter for U-853," *USNIP,* Dec., 1960., pp. 83-89.

Toulmin, H. A., *Diary of Democracy. The Senate War Investigating Committee,* with an intro. by Sen. Harley M. Kilgore, New York, 1947. Detailed account of the Truman Committee.

Tucker, G. N., *The Naval Service of Canada,* 2 vols., Ottawa, 1952, the official history.

United States Naval Aviation, 1910-1960, Washington, 1960.

United States Naval Chronology, World War II, Washington, 1955, based on official records. It includes a concise account of all significant events, ship sinkings and "damagings," principal officials and military commanders.

●"Watching for sea goblins," *Time,* Jan. 2, 1961, pp. 25-26, current ASW in the South Atlantic.

Weichold, Adm. E., "*German naval defense against the Allied invasion of Normandy,*" post mortem written for ONI by a German admiral.

Wemyss, D. E. G., *Walker's Groups in the Western Approaches,* Liverpool, 1948, first-hand narrative, exceptionally useful.

Wenk, E., Jr., *Ocean Sciences and National Security,* Washington, 1960, report of the Committee on Science and Aeronautics, U.S. House of Repr., by the Senior Specialist in Science, Legislative Reference Library.

Wenneker, Adm. P. W., *interrogation of,* by 441st Detachment, U.S. Army Counter Intelligence Corps, at Karuizawa, March-May, 1946.

Westcott, A., (ed.), *American Sea Power Since 1775,* Philadelphia, 1952.

Whipple, A. B. C., "The education of Willie," *Life,* Jan. 22, 1945, pp. 11-12. About W. S. Colepough, the ill-fated German spy.

Whitehead, D., *The FBI Story,* New York, 1956, the FBI's version of Gimpel and Colepough, on pp. 205ff.

Whitehouse, A., *Subs and Submariners,* New York, 1961, from Alexander the Great's underwater experiments to the nuclear submarine.

Wiedemeyer, G., *Waffe unter Wasser*, Berlin, 1941, a popular history of the submarine with emphasis on the German *Unterseeboot*.

Willoughby, M. F., *The United States Coast Guard in World War II*, Annapolis, 1957. (Also, the official Coast Guard histories of World War II, especially vols. I, XIV, XVII.)

Statistical data, such as the number of U-boats at sea, U-boat losses, shipping casualties, etc., based on several computations, including *German, Japanese and Italian Losses World War II* (colloquially called "The Yellow Book"), compiled in 1946 from the records of the Admiralty and CNO Assessment of Damage Committees; *Naval Losses of All Nations 3 September 1939 to 15 August 1945*, published by ONI; and the charts of the Fleet Operations Statistical Analysis Office of the Navy Department. If the figures in the text are sometimes discrepant, it is because there was no definitive auditing of the U-boat war. As a result, all such figures listed should be regarded as approximate.

Officers of the *Kriegsmarine* are referred to with their ranks in the original German. The American equivalents are:

Leutnant zur See	Ensign
Oberleutnant zur See	Lieutenant junior grade
Kapitaenleutnant	Lieutenant
Korvettenkapitaen	Lieutenant Commander
Fregattenkapitaen	Commander
Kapitaen zur See	Captain
Kommodor	Commodore
Konteradmiral	Rear Admiral
Vizeadmiral	Vice Admiral
Admiral	Admiral
Generaladmiral	no equivalent
Grossadmiral	Fleet Admiral

GLOSSARY AND ABBREVIATIONS

Alberich. Anti-sonar rubber coatings on U-boats.

Aphrodite. German radar decoy balloon.

Asdevlant. Antisubmarine Development Detachment Atlantic Fleet.

Asdic. British sonar.

ASV. "Air to Surface Vessel," airborne microwave search radar.

ASW. Anti-submarine warfare.

Asworg. Anti-Submarine Warfare Operations Research Group.

Bachstelze. One-man observation kite.

BdU. Refehlshaber der U-Boote, Commanding Admiral, U-Boats.

Bold. Cartridge fired from stern of submerged U-boat producing bubbles that reflected the waves of Asdic.

CAT. British "foxer" with one noise-maker.

Chop Line. Change of Operational Control, line of inter-Allied demarcation in Atlantic, starting at lat. 65 N, long 10 W, southwest to lat. 57 N, long. 26 W, then along long. 26 W to lat. 43 N,; westward along that parallel to long. 40 W, then south along that meridian to lat. 20 N, then east to long. 26 W, south along that meridian.

Cinclant. Commander in Chief Atlantic Fleet.

Cominch. Commander in Chief, United States Fleet.

CNO. Chief of Naval Operations.

CTG. Commander Task Group.

DD. Destroyer.

DE. Destroyer Escort.

Falke. T-4 acoustic homing torpedo.

FdU. Fuehrer der U-Boote, regional Commandant U-Boats.

Feindfahrt. War patrol of U-boats.

Foxer. Gear to mislead acoustic torpedo.

FuMb. Funkmessbeobachtungsgeraet, radar interception set.

Gnat. British for German naval acoustic torpedo.

Hagenuk. German device that replaced *Metox, q.v.*

Hedgehog. Device for throwing depth charges in patterns.

HF/DF. High-frequency direction-finder, called *Huffduff.*

Koralle. German naval headquarters north-east of Berlin (in 1944).

MAD. Magnetic airborne detector.

Metox. Radar search receiver Germans obtained from French.

Momp. Mid-ocean Meeting Point of Allied convoys.

OKM. Oberkommando der Kriegsmarine, German Naval High Command.

ONI. U.S. Office of Naval Intelligence.

O.T.C. Officer in Tactical Command.

P/W. Prisoner of war.

Seekriegsleitung. German Naval Staff.

Seetakt. German radar instrument.

TBS. "Talk between ships," voice radio.

Thetis. Radar decoy spar buoy.

T-5, T-11. *Zaunkoenig* I and II, acoustic homing torpedoes, improved models of *Falke.*

Zaunkoenig. Acoustic torpedo designed against convoy escort vessels, colloquially called *Zerstoererknacker,* destroyer knacker.

NOTES

CHAPTER I

Admiral Ingram's first flagship in the South Atlantic was the USS *Memphis* but when the cruiser was needed for patrol duty, he shifted his flag to the *Patoka*, a combination destroyer-tender-oiler-supply ship, and then to the *Melville*. The *Big Pebble* became his flagship on May 25, 1943, when Ingram changed her name to *Perseverance*. Finally on November 15, 1944, when he relieved Admiral Ingersoll as CINCLANT, he inherited the USS *Vixen* (PG 53), a 4,016-ton gunboat built in 1929 by the Germania Yards at Kiel, Germany.

For Ingram's sortie into the headlines, see *The New York Times*, Jan. 9, 1945, 1:5-6, 6:1; Jan. 10, editorial; May 17, 1:2-3; May 18, 18:3. The joint Army-Navy statement on the possibility of a buzz-bomb attack on the East Coast was issued on November 7, 1944.

For Gimpel's account of the adventure, see his *Spion fuer Deutschland*, Munich, 1956.

CHAPTER II

The brief biographical sketch mentioned in this chapter was obtained from Doenitz on Nov. 8, 1945, by Naval Judge Advocate Dr. Kranzbuehler, his chief of defense at Nuremberg. It read: "1891, born in Berlin; 1910, joins Navy as *Seekadett;* 1913, Leutnant zur See; 1912-16, cruiser *Breslau;* 1915, Oberleutnant zur See; 1916, transferred to U-Boat Arm; 1918, taken prisoner of war; 1919, returned to *Reichsmarine;* 1928, Korvettenkapitaen; 1928-30, commands destroyer flotilla; 1930-34, staff officer, North Sea Station (Wilhelmshaven); 1934, C.O. *Emden,* Fregattenkapitaen; 1935, C.O. Weddigen U-Boat Flotilla, Kapitaen zur See; 1936, Fuehrer der U-Boote; 1939, commodore; 1939, Konteradmiral, BdU; 1940, Vizeadmiral; 1942, Admiral; 1943, Grossadmiral; 1945, chief of state."

Doenitz's only famous ancestor was Paul Doenitz (1891) author of a well-known book on Papal history. Doenitz's son was killed in the sinking of *U-945*, on May 19, 1943, in the North Atlantik. The boat, sunk by a Liberator, perished with all hands.

For references to Doenitz at the Nuremberg trial of the major war criminals, see *Nazi Conspiracy and Aggression*, vol. II, 839, 842-843, 847, 857-858; IV, 45; V, 552, 911; VI, 815, 825; VII, 57, 100, 124, 136-145, 170; VIII, 657, 707.

Prior to his appointment to succeed Raeder in January 1943, Doenitz met Hitler only nine times on formal occasions; but then, between February 8, 1943, and April 10, 1945, they met a total of 119 times (cf. *Fuehrer Conferences*, etc.).

On September 3, 1939, Doenitz radioed his U-boats at sea "Secret Standing Order No. 154," reading: "We must be harsh in this war! The enemy began it to destroy us, so nothing else matters!"

CHAPTER III

Although Doenitz is invariably given credit for the invention of the *Rudeltaktik* (cf. his memoirs, pp. 22-28), other U-boat officers of World War I, notably Bauer, Rose and Otto Schultze, entertained the idea already in 1917. They were rebuffed by the higher command. According to Doenitz, "the First World War did not furnish a single occasion upon which even two U-boats operated in unison."

The first orders for what became the *Rudeltaktik* were drawn up in 1935; in 1939, the doctrine was included in the *Handbuch fuer U-Bootkommandanten,* the basic manual of the U-Boat Command. On the other hand, Doenitz made no reference to it in his book, *Die U-Bootwaffe,* although he discussed other doctrines, including U-boat surface attacks at night.

For the Admiralty's ignorance of the *Rudeltaktik,* see Roskill, I, pp. 354-355, where he says: "The development was, from the British point of view, full of the most serious implications since the enemy had adopted a form of attack which we had not foreseen and against which neither tactical nor technical countermeasures had been prepared." Also, Ruge, p. 98.

The English translation of Doenitz's description of his innate aptitude for tactical command does not reflect the true esoterics of the German original. He used the word *"einfuehlen"* which translates into "empathize," a technical term of psychoanalysis which means the "imaginative identification of oneself with another person or with a group."

A German criticism of Doenitz's tactical command is in Herlin, *op. cit.,* pp. 86-89. For Goering's refusal to aid the U-Boat Arm, see Ruge, *op. cit.,* pp. 126-128, and the *War Diary of the BdU,* Dec. 14, 1940, Jan. 7, 1941, and 1941-42, *passim.*

Headquarters of the U-Boat Command were at Sengwarden, Wilhelmshaven, to begin with. Doenitz moved to Paris (18 Boulevard Suchet) in the summer of 1940, then to Kerneval, at the mouth of the inner harbor at Lorient opposite Port Louis, into the villa of a sardine tycoon (hence the nickname *Sardinenschloesschen,* "little Sardine Castle"). U-Boat Command HQ was later moved to Angers, then to the Hotel am Steinplatz in Berlin, to Camp Koralle, and finally to Flensburg on the German-Danish border where it was at the time of the surrender.

CHAPTER IV

Roosevelt, F. D., "Freedom of the Seas," in *Vital Speeches,* Oct. 1, 1941, pp. 738-741.

For the German version of the "Undeclared War," see Assmann, *op. cit.,* and especially Ruge, pp. 128, 170-171. The U.S. was justly apprehensive when Doenitz, panicked by the loss of his three top aces in March 1941, shifted the U-boats to the area around Iceland and points west. Roosevelt regarded this shift and the appearance of the battleship *Bismarck* in those same waters as an encroachment and gave orders to intervene.

Incidentally, though Doenitz had 19 U-boats in the North Atlantic, none was sent to aid the *Bismarck* until it was too late. The BdU War Dairy has this entry on May 24, 1941: "In considering whether anything could now be done with these U-boats to support the *Bismarck,* I came to the conclusion that I must first wait until the intentions of the Admiral Commanding the Fleet became known." At 9:42 P.M. on May 26, Doenitz signalled his U-boats to go to the assistance of the *Bismarck* "but there were only two U-boats, *U-556* and *U-74,* in the vicinity; and the former had no torpedoes, while the latter was out of action."

CHAPTER V

The best description of the United States in the wake of Pearl Harbor is in John Toland's *But Not in Shame: The Six Months After Pearl Harbor* (New York, 1961). The day-to-day record of those tragic days emerges dramatically from the war diary of Admiral Andrews, quoted in Taylor, *op. cit.,* pp. 20, *et passim.*

CHAPTER VI

The title of this chapter was suggested by a remark of Fleet Admiral King, in *A Naval Record,* p. 464n. The scarcity of ships best suited for ASW is described on the basis of King, *op. cit.*, pp. 446-448. Morison, in X, pp. 32-33, disputes King's contention, citing records in the Bureau of Ships to show that President Roosevelt, "far from being an obstructionist in the DE [destroyer escort] program . . . was one of its earliest advocates."

The best description of the hedgehog's evolution may be found in Pawle, *op cit.*, pp. 123-140. Brief histories of the depth charge were printed in *U.S. Fleet Antisubmarine Bulletin*, July 1943, pp. 35-36; April 1944, pp. 40-42.

The "battle of the bulletins" section of this chapter is based on the author's special study of Navy Department statements and releases, as they appeared in press association (AP and UP) stories, in *The New York Times*, summarized in *Facts on File*, vols. 1942 and 1943.

For contemporary coverage of this period, see Adm. W. V. Pratt, "Tide is turning against the U-boat," *Newsweek*, Nov. 17, 1941, p. 28; "Submarine is still a grave menace," *ibid.*, Dec. 21, 1942, p. 24; "Why U-boat losses can now be revealed," *ibid.*, Aug. 30, 1943, p. 24; "Tide turns against the U-boat but it is still a grave menace," *ibid.*, June 14, 1943, pp. 19-21; "U-boat offensive, Doenitz musters submarines," *ibid.*, March 29, 1943, pp. 21-22; "What makes the German U-boat so formidable a foe," *ibid.*, Nov. 9, 1942, p. 25; E. S. Land, "Battle of the wolfpacks," *New York Times Magazine*, Feb. 21, 1943, p. 8; F. Pratt, "U-boats are coming," *Saturday Evening Post*, Dec. 6, 1941, p. 29; F. Pratt, "Caribbean Command," *Harper's*, Feb. 1944, pp. 232-241; P. Wylie and L. Schwab, "Battle of Florida," *Saturday Evening Post*, March 11, 1944, pp. 14-15.

Morison's verdict on the issue of responsibility appears in his vol. I, pp. 198-201. On p. 303 he quotes an officer of the Eastern Sea Frontier: "We are just like a housewife flapping her apron to chase the chickens out of the kitchen," driving the U-boats from one American coastal area to another. In the Navy there was at least one attempt to shift the blame to the merchant marine skippers. "At least fifty per cent of merchant ships sank in the Atlantic," said Adm. Manley Hale Simmons, USN, Commandant of the 5th Naval District at Norfolk, Va., "would have escaped unharmed if their captains had obeyed naval orders."

CHAPTER VII

The story of the Q-ships is told here from declassified portions of the *Eastern Sea Frontier War Diary*, October 1943, prepared by Lt. E. E. Morison, USNR; and scattered references in the *War Diary of the BdU*. For the British experience with these mystery ships, see Sir Henry Newbolt, *Naval Operations*, London, 1920, IV, pp. 334-37, 357-359; V, pp. 106-112; also see, Whitehouse, *op. cit.*, pp. 78-89.

CHAPTER VIII

References to Adm. King were developed in the author's conversations with members of his staff. Commander Whitehill's warmly written "A Note on the Making of this Book" (King, *op. cit.*, pp. 647-657) was helpful.

King himself illustrated his authoritarian streak when he described how he continued to argue in the Joint Chiefs although left *contra mundum*. "That did not affect him in the least . . . It was pointed out to him that everyone else was in agreement against him, but he did not consider that relevant when a matter of principle was involved." (King, *op. cit.*, p. 441.)

For his flagships in Washington, D.C., see "History of USS *Vixen* (PG 63)" and "History of USS *Dauntless* (PG 61)" in Ship's History Section, Naval History Division.

Although badly needed, the British fishing trawlers did not prove an unmitigated success. Of northern origin, their "defrosting" in the subtropical climate of the Gulf and Caribbean Sea Frontiers resulted in an attack on their American crews' olfactory sense that was harder to endure than the U-boat attacks.

That King was justified in his demand that the U-boat pens in France be subjected to energetic bombardment seems to be attested by Doenitz (in *op. cit.*, p. 409). He wrote: "It was a great mistake on the part of the British not to have attacked these pens from the air while they were under construction behind water-tight caissons and were particularly vulnerable." However, according to Comdr. Long, "no U-boat was ever destroyed by the bombing of the French bases, although a considerable force was from time to time allocated to this task, and some heavy losses were sustained among the bombers, and among the French population in the target area."

Adm. King met the anti-British charges head on (*op. cit.*, p. 442) when he quoted Field Marshall Dill's remark to Churchill and wrote: "At no time did King seriously question the accepted strategy of defeating first Germany and then Japan. He saw, however, that Japan was not likely to wait to be defeated at a time and place convenient to the Allies, and so was constantly concerned with accelerating the decision leading toward the defeat of Germany so that he might get on with 'his' war before the day was too far spent."

Allied ship causualties in U.S. defensive mine fields in the West Atlantic totaled 20 vessels of which 13 were sunk and 7 damaged. By contrast, German mines sank only six and damaged five ships in American waters. Cf., Lott, *op. cit.*, pp. 227-228.

CHAPTER IX

King's historic memo to Gen. Marshall is printed in full in his *op. cit.*, pp. 456-459. For Stimson's contention, see his *op. cit.*, pp. 66, 367-371, 386, 508-518.

CHAPTER X

For the Naval Armed Guards, see *Naval Armed Guards Reports* to Vice Chief of Naval Operations, in Armed Guard files; citations in Armed Guard Office, Cominch; and ONI *Summaries of Interrogations of Survivors*.

For personal narratives, see Lt. J. F. Childs, USNR, *Navy Gun Crew*, New York, 1943; Lt. R. B. Berry, USNR, *Gunners Get Glory*, as told to Lloyd Wendt, Indianapolis, 1943.

Data on the "Hooligan Navy" from the files of U.S. Coast Guard; also *Cruising Club of Amercia News*, 1942. Milt Machlin's book was published by Paperback Library, 1962. Other "amateurs and auxiliaries" of this period included the Civil Air Patrol (*cf.* OWI press release, June 25, 1943 and CAP files at New York headquarters). The CAP flew 86,685 missions of 244,000 hours, reported on 173 U-boats and 91 vessels in distress. The rescue of 365 survivors is directly attributable to CAP.

For the vicissitudes of the Merchant Marine during this period, see *The Pilot*, March 6, July 10, Nov. 27, Dec. 4, 1942; Feb. 19, Sept. 17, 1943; and *passim*.

CHAPTER XI

See, "The Special Warfare Branch of ONI. The History of Psychological Warfare in the United States Navy in World War II," prepared by the author in 1945-1946, in collaboration with Dr. Stefan T. Possony, under the direction of Lt. Comdr. John Paul Reed, USNR.

CHAPTER XII

On Admiral Bristol and his staff at Argentia, see *Administrative History of the Atlantic Fleet*, vol. II.

About Donald Duck Navy, see S. Shalett, "Our school of death-to-U-boats." *New*

York Times Magazine, February 13, 1944, p. 11; L. Roberts, "Little ships that saved the day," *Saturday Evening Post*, Feb. 12, 1944, pp. 28-29 plus. The origins of ASWORG, cf. Sternhel and Thorndike, *op. cit.*

Captain (later Vice Admiral) Wilder DuPuy Baker, USN, was born in Topeka, Kansas, on July 22, 1890. He attended Eastern High School in Bay City, Michigan, before his appointment to the U.S. Naval Academy, from Michigan in 1910. A submariner in World War I and after, an Assistant Naval Attache in London in 1935-1936, he commanded several Destroyer Divisions on the eve of World War II. After his pioneering work on ASW from March 1942 to November 1942, he assumed command of the USS *North Carolina* in the Pacific. One of the Navy's most decorated senior officers (Navy Cross, Silver Star, Legion of Merit with Combat "V," Bronze Star with Combat "V," etc.), he was Commandant Eleventh Naval District, Commander Naval Base, San Diego, Cal., and Commander Southern California Sector, Western Sea Frontier at the time of his retirement on August 1, 1952. (*Cf.* Navy Biographies Section, 01-02.)

Captain Thomas Lawrence Lewis, USN, was born in Amite City, Louisiana, January 10, 1898, attended Amite High School and Louisiana State University, and on July 21, 1917, entered the U.S. Naval Academy. The citation of his Legion of Merit awarded for his work as Captain Baker's successor in command of the Atlantic Fleet ASW Unit (March 1942 to May 1943) read in part: "Pioneering in research and development of effective anti-submarine measures, Captain Lewis rendered invaluable service in devising vital anti-submarine tactics and equipment for both air and surface craft and in providing for the training and indoctrination of anti-submarine units in the effective use of new weapons and techniques . . . [contributing] to our success in combating the enemy submarine menace in the Atlantic Area." At the time of his retirement in 1951, he was Chief of Staff and Aide Commandant Eighth Naval District, New Orleans, La. (*Cf.*, Navy Biographies Branch, June 17, 1958.)

Gallery's treatment of Henke contrasted sharply with widespread British coddling of German officer-prisoners. They rolled out the red carpet for Kapitaenleutnant Baron von Tiesenhausen who, in *U-331*, sank the battleship *Barham* on Nov. 25, 1941, and was sunk in turn a year later off Algiers. Kretschmer spent his first night as P/W on the HMS *Hesperus* playing bridge with the engineer officer of the destroyer and the master and first officer of a merchantman his *U-99* had sunk the day before, (cf. Macintyre, *op. cit.*, p. 49). Captain Riheldaffer tolerated no such pampering. The regime at Fort Hunt was stern and firm.

The highest-ranking U-boat officer to pass through Fort Hunt was Kapitaen zur See Juergen Wattenberg. He was on the *Graf Spee* in the River Plate, escaped back to Germany, transferred to the U-Boat Arm, received command of a U-boat and was sunk in it on his maiden voyage.

Herlin disputes Gallery's version of Henke's "seduction." In *op. cit.*, p. 228, Herlin claims Henke had shared his cell on USS *Guadalcanal* with fellow officers Gunther Altenburger, Hans Schultz, and the surgeon of *U-515*, Dr. Jorg Jensen. "All three officers are still alive today," he wrote in 1959. "They state unanimously that Henke never talked to them about the note he had to sign. There is an even more important reason to question Gallery's claim," Herlin continued. "Gallery says he had succeeded in persuading the crew of *U-515* to talk freely to their interrogators by showing them the note Henke had signed. In actual fact, none of the officers and nobody in the crew of *U-515* has ever seen Henke's note. And none had signed a similar statement."

CHAPTER XIII

For Captain (later Rear Admiral) E. M. Zacharias, see his *Secret Missions*, New York, 1947. It contains excellent material on Op-16-W and O-16-Z, two branches of ONI he vigorously supported while Deputy Director of Naval Intelligence.

For Anglo-American cooperation, see Kittredge, Capt. T. B., U.S.-British Naval Cooperation, 1940-1945. 2 vols., Washington, 1947-48, with notes and appendices. The sum total of printed material on Tenth Fleet consists of Navy Department communique dated Nov. 19, 1943; King, *op. cit.*, pp. 462-463; King, *War Reports*, III, in *USNIP*, p. 158; and Morison, X, pp. 21-26. Dr. Steinhardt's article in *USNIP* strangely omits to mention that Asworg was an integral part of Tenth Fleet.

CHAPTER XIV

Admiral Low was born in Albany, New York, on August 15, 1894, son of the late Commander William Franklin Low, USN, and Mrs. Anna Stuart Low. He attended Newton, Mass., High School and U.S. Naval Academy, graduating from the latter with the Class of 1915. In 1926, he completed the junior course at the Naval War College, Newport, R.I.

His first assignments after graduation were in the battleship *Connecticut* and cruiser *Montana*. In the early part of his career, he was designated a submariner, and subsequently commanded the submarines D-3, L-1, S-12, and served on the staffs of Commander Submarine Division Five and Commander Control Force subsequent to World War I. His continuous sea duty from 1915 to 1925 was briefly interrupted in 1918 for a six months' assignment with the Tactical Group Submarine Chasers, New London, Conn.

In 1926 he was an instructor in the Department of Seamanship at the Naval Academy, and following three years' service in the battleship *New Mexico*, became Officer in Charge of the Recruiters' Training School, Naval Training Station, Hampton Roads, Va. He later had staff duty with Submarine Squadron Five, and from 1932 to 1935 commanded the destroyer *Paul Jones*, on the Asiatic Station.

Returning to the U.S., he had two tours of duty in the Navy Dept., first in the Bureau of Navigation and later in the Office of the CNO. These were interspersed with service afloat as Commander Submarine Div. Thirteen between 1937 and 1939.

Prior to the U.S. entrance into World War II, Low, as a Commander and Captain, was operations officer on the staff of Admiral King, Commander-in-Chief, U.S. Atlantic Fleet. Admiral Low continued as operations officer of King until September 1942, when he went to sea in command of the cruiser *Wichita*. He became Chief of Staff, Tenth Fleet, in May 1943. In January 1945 he took command of Cruiser Division Sixteen that supported the Okinawa invasion and participated in strikes against Kyushu, Southern Honshu and the Nansei Shoto Islands.

Following the surrender of the Japanese in August 1945, he was in charge of surrender and neutralization of all Japanese Naval installations in South Korea and reported as Commander Destroyers Pacific Fleet, serving until March 1947, when, upon advancement to Vice Admiral, he was given command of the Service Force, U.S. Pacific Fleet. In Nov. 1949 he returned to the Navy Dept. to conduct a special survey of the Navy's anti-submarine program, and in February 1950 was designated Deputy Chief of Naval Operations (Logistics). He continued in that capacity until May 1953, when he became Commander Western Sea Frontier and Commander Pacific Reserve Fleet. He retired effective July 1, 1956, when he was advanced to Admiral on the basis of combat awards.

Captain Sample was born in Buffalo, N.Y., March 9, 1898, the son of Brig. Gen. W. R. Sample and Mrs. Betty Saunders Sample. He was appointed to the Naval Academy in 1915 by Pres. Woodrow Wilson. He died tragically on Oct. 3, 1945, on a familiarization flight in Japan. He was with Tenth Fleet from May 17, 1943, to April 8, 1944.

Captain Isbell was an Iowan, born in 1899, Annapolis '20. In September 1940, as commanding officer of VP-54, he surveyed and selected U.S. bases in Newfoundland. Prior to his assignment to Tenth Fleet, he was C.O. of the Naval Air Station at Sitka, and C.O. of CTG 21.14, the *Card* escort carrier group.

Captain (later Rear Admiral) Fitz was born in Somerville, Mass., on February 17, 1898, and was appointed to the Naval Academy in 1916. He retired on June 30, 1949. Captain (later Rear Admiral) Haines was born Nov. 5, 1894, son of Brig. Gen. Henry Cargill Haines, USMC, and Mrs. Emma Burgers Haines. He attended Berkeley (Cal.) High School and McKinley Tech, Washington, D.C., before entering the Naval Academy in 1914. He retired on June 1, 1949.

Rear Admiral Metcalf was born in Berkeley, Cal., February 28, 1881, attended Berkeley High School and the University of California before his appointment to the Naval Academy in 1889. Following his recall to active duty in 1940, he was promoted Rear Admiral on the Retired List, March 21, 1942, and was relieved of all active duty on Dec. 11, 1945. For his "exceptionally meritorious conduct" at the head of Convoy & Routing, he was awarded the Legion of Merit.

CHAPTER XV

For the escort carriers, aside from *ONI Weekly*, April 1945, see their own war histories, the *Bogue* War Diary, the mimeographed USS *Card* History of June 13, 1945, and Captain Isbell's "Report of A/S Operations," also his "Three Months' Experience as CTG 21.14," dated Nov. 15, 1943. Also see, J. Bishop, "U-boat meets its master. How planes from a new auxiliary carrier sought and destroyed convoy raiders," Sat. Ev. Post, Sept. 18, 1943, pp. 9-11; *ibid.*, Sept. 25, 1943, pp. 16-17.

Also, D. Middleton, "Killer groups versus wolfpacks," *New York Times Magazine*, Oct. 31, 1943, p. 15ff; "Welcome escorts," *Time*, July 26, 1943, p. 65.

The best description of the ASW weapons is in Pawle, *op. cit.*, pp. 113-190, and Rowland, Boyd, *op. cit.* Both Frank and Busch have interesting accounts of the German panic caused by ASV.

CHAPTER XVI

The sinking of *U-66* was described in words of appropriate melodrama in *U.S. Fleet Antisubmarine Bulletin*, June 1944. In actual fact, the Germans were not planning to "capture" the *Buckley*. They merely tried to escape to her from their own burning U-boat. Nobody on the *Buckley* understood German and the anguished cries of the U-boat's crew were voices in the wilderness.

For Huffduff, see Navy Department press releases, Jan. 2 and 12, 1946; also Macintyre, *op. cit.*, pp. 73-80; *USNIP*, February 1946, pp. 307-308; Morison, I, pp. 226-228.

Doenitz's "milk cows," in *USNIP*, October 1953. His trouble with torpedoes, German Naval High Command Memorandum MPA 2864/40, June 11, 1940, and Memorandum No. 83-a-42, February 9, 1942.

Churchill's reference to the *Zaunkoenig* in Charles Eade (ed.), *War Speeches*, New York, 1953, III, p. 7. The *Zaunkoenigs* were of the 30-knot electric type with a range of over 5000 yards.

CHAPTER XVII

Background material in Dreyer, *op. cit.*, especially on the work that went into the "assessment" of the U-boat war.

CHAPTER XVIII

For the significance of the capture of *U-Rahmlow*, see Ruge, p. 173. Gallery's best description of the capture of *U-505* is in his action report of June 19, 1944, his interview recorded in Navy Department, on May 25, 1945. Captured with the

U-505 were three acoustic torpedoes. A viciously anti-Roosevelt book found in Oberleutnant Lange's cabin was sent President Roosevelt and is now in the Hyde Park library.

CHAPTER XIX

Herlin's is virtually the only German voice critical of Doenitz and his conduct of the U-boat war: "They who gave the orders now claim to have a clear conscience (*mit reiner Weste dastehen*) and beat their chests saying, 'We always tried our best!' "

Admiral McCann, a native of Massachusetts, was born in 1896. Naval Academy '17, he served in *Kansas* in World War I. Between 1920-1943 held various submarine commands; 1935-1938, in cruisers *Indianapolis* and *Chicago*. After serving as Chief of Staff Tenth Fleet from January to June 1945, he became CTF in *Philadelphia* and Commander Submarine Force Pacific Fleet in 1945. He retired in 1950.

Admiral von Friedeburg, a competent and stern naval officer, was the "unknown soldier" of the U-boat, eclipsed in Doenitz's shadow. After a brief spell in command of a U-boat in 1937, Doenitz appointed him chief of Organization Section at BdU. He was later made Doenitz's deputy and ended the war as Admiral Commanding U-Boats, but had little if any influence on operational matters. He committed suicide after the war.

The figures of German losses are from a speech Konteradmiral Godt made at the Hamburg war memorial on May 16, 1954.

Another U-boat that defied the surrender order was *U-977* of Kapitaenleutnant Heinz Schaeffer, an arrogant young Nazi (see his *U-Boat 977*, with an introduction by Nicholas Monsarrat, New York, 1952). It escaped to Argentina. The voyage took three-and-a-half months "with the crew sometimes disciplined, sometimes on the edge of mutiny." At one time it spent sixty-six consecutive days under water.

There were altogether five "kills" on the last day of the U-boat war. The U.S. destroyer *Farquhar* sank *U-881* of the *Seewolf* flotilla, RAF Squadron 86 destroyed two U-boats in the Kattegat, and RAF Squadron 210 another one near Norway.

Doenitz closed the U-boat war with a statement to Konteradmiral Godt. Said he: "*Ich will jetzt nichts mehr vom Heldentod hoeren!*" (Now I don't want to hear any more about heroes' death!")

EPILOGUE

For source references, see Bibliography items with (°) asterisks.

For Admiral Burke's statements, see *Hearings* before the Subcommittee of the Committee on Appropriations, House of Representatives, 87th Congress, 1st Session, Washington, 1961, pp. 283-392.

INDEX OF NAMES

INDEX OF VESSELS